A DARKER SHADE

John-Henri Holmberg is the Edgar Award-nominated co-author of *The Tattooed Girl*, about the Millennium novels and their author, Stieg Larsson, who was a personal friend. He is a full-time writer, translator, and editor, living with his family on the southern coast of Sweden.

A DARKER SHADE

17 Swedish Stories of Murder, Mystery & Suspense

EDITED AND TRANSLATED
BY JOHN-HENRI HOLMBERG

A Mysterious Press Book
for Head of Zeus

First published in the United States in 2013 by Mysterious Press,
an imprint of Grove/Atlantic, Inc.

This edition first published in the UK in 2013 by Head of Zeus Ltd.

Translation copyright © 2013 John-Henri Holmberg
Introduction copyright © 2013 John-Henri Holmberg
Pages 359–361 serve as a continuation of the copyright page.

ISBN (HB) 9781781858172
ISBN (TPB) 9781781858189
ISBN (eBook) 9781781858165

9 7 5 3 1 2 4 6 8

A CIP catalogue record for this book is available from the British Library.

Head of Zeus Ltd
Clerkenwell House
45–47 Clerkenwell Green
London EC1R 0HT

WWW.HEADOFZEUS.COM

CONTENTS

INTRODUCTION

John-Henri Holmberg

This book is, in its small way, a landmark. It is the first overview anthology of Swedish crime fiction published in English, and consequently—given today's global culture—the first one accessible to readers around the world.

It presents seventeen stories by twenty Swedish writers. Several are original to this book. None has ever before appeared in an English translation. They cover a wide range of styles and themes: you will find examples of fairly traditional detection, of police procedure, regional tales, stories carried by social or political concerns, as well as stories written primarily to entertain. One story is historical, set in a fairly recent past of which few of today's readers even in Sweden are aware; another is set in the future.

The choice of authors is similarly diverse. You will find a story by the writing team Maj Sjöwall and Per Wahlöö, whose ten novels, originally published from 1965 through 1975, brought international attention to Swedish crime fiction and totally transformed the way in which that form of literature was written and perceived in the authors' home country. You will find another by Stieg Larsson, whose three Millennium novels have made him the most translated and read Swedish author of all time. You will find stories by many of the most highly regarded and award-winning Swedish crime authors of today—all told, the authors represented in this book have won twelve of the twenty best crime novel of the year awards (called the Golden Crowbar, and consisting of a miniature gilded crowbar) presented since 1994 by the Swedish Crime Fiction Academy (also translated as the Swedish Academy of Detection), as well as five of the eight annual Glass Key Awards for Best Nordic Crime Novel ever given to Swedish authors. But you will also find a surprise or two—the first professionally published story by Eva Gabrielsson, Stieg Larsson's life companion and otherwise an architect and nonfiction writer, and a story by Sara Stridsberg, currently perhaps Sweden's foremost literary author—but not one ordinarily associated with crime fiction.

In all, my aim has been to present as wide-ranging and eclectic selection of stories and authors as possible in the hope of giving a fair reflection of the diversity, vitality, and concerns of current Swedish crime writing. One item of note: a few of these stories contain references to customs, places, or other peculiarities known to most Swedes but probably unknown to most non-Swedes. In my introductory notes to the stories, I have tried to provide the brief explanations I think may help non-Swedish readers to fully appreciate each story.

That this book is possible is, of course, due to the enormous interest in Swedish crime fiction shown by international—and not least American and British—readers during the last five years or, more precisely, since the first of Stieg Larsson's novels, published in English in early 2008, became a publishing phenomenon. During the forty years between the first Sjöwall and Wahlöö novel and the first by Stieg Larsson, a number of Swedish crime authors were translated, but most of them only in other continental European countries. To English-language readers, only a very few authors—primarily Henning Mankell, whose work has been translated into English since 1997—were available. But of course Sweden had crime writers before Sjöwall and Wahlöö, as well as between them and the present. For those readers interested in the development of crime fiction writing in Sweden and its current and possible future state, I offer the rest of this introduction as a fairly brief historical and critical overview, with a few personal attempts to explain the specific directions in which Swedish crime writing has developed.

Crime fiction is a wide literary field, encompassing numerous, very different kinds of stories. You have the classical stories of rational deduction written by Edgar Allan Poe and fifty years later by Sir Arthur Conan Doyle, still later by Agatha Christie, Dorothy L. Sayers, Ellery Queen, and so many others. You have the hard-boiled private-eye stories of Dashiell Hammett, Raymond Chandler, Mickey Spillane, Ross Macdonald, Walter Mosley, Sara Paretsky, and Dennis Lehane. You have the psychological thrillers by such writers as Daphne du Maurier, Patricia Highsmith, and Ruth Rendell. An equally well-established category is the spy thriller, possibly created by W. Somerset Maugham, later with Ian Fleming and John le Carré as its most famous writers, but in Sweden with so far only one major practitioner, Jan Guillou, whose thirteen novels about Swedish secret agent Carl Hamilton have been immensely popular since 1986 but have so far had virtually no competition. For this reason, Jan Guillou and spy thrillers are excluded from the following discussion. You have most of noir literature, although my conviction is that noir is in fact defined emotionally, not by plot elements; even so, most major noir writers, from Cornell Woolrich through David Goodis and Jim Thompson to Roxane Gay, do include crimes in their bleak stories of alienation and hopelessness. You have the many depictions of police at work, where the earliest notable writers were John Creasey and the unsurpassed Ed McBain; the serial killer thrillers, from Robert Bloch's *Psycho* to Barry Malzberg and Bill Pronzini's *The Running of Beasts* to Thomas Harris' *The Silence of the Lambs* and innumerable later works. And we haven't even mentioned courtroom stories, financial thrillers, political thrillers . . .

Most, if not all, of these various subgenres within the field of crime fiction initially appeared in either Great Britain or the United States. The detective story, the hard-boiled private eye story, the police procedural, and most of the other dominant kinds of crime fiction are initially Anglo-Saxon developments. But just like science fiction, another of the important literary traditions first established in the nineteenth century, crime fiction also quickly became popular in other countries and is today read and written throughout the world.

In fact, not only today but for quite a while.

Sweden is a case in point. Forty years ago, American and British crime readers suddenly became aware of the existence of Swedish crime writing when the ten police procedural novels featuring Detective Inspector Martin Beck and written by Maj Sjöwall and Per Wahlöö were translated and became bestsellers. They are still in print, and Henning Mankell achieved considerable recognition in English translations, so perhaps it is unreasonable to say that Sweden was again quickly forgotten and remained so until only six years ago, when in 2008 the first novel in Stieg Larsson's Millennium trilogy was translated as *The Girl with the Dragon Tattoo* and became the next worldwide Swedish crime fiction bestseller. This time, however, the appeal of Stieg Larsson's talent and sales led to an increasing number of other Swedish crime authors being introduced in English translations, something that did not happen in the wake of Sjöwall and Wahlöö's success.

What virtually no one will remember is that if Stieg Larsson followed forty years after Sjöwall and Wahlöö, they had also followed forty years after the first internationally successful Swedish crime writer: the pseudonymous Frank Heller, who enjoyed considerable popularity not only throughout Europe but also in the United States during the 1920s.

But, even if Frank Heller was the first Swedish writer of crime fiction to achieve success in translation, he was far from the first Swedish crime author, and indeed stories of crime and detection have been a flourishing part of Swedish literature since at least the beginning of the twentieth century. But most of this tradition is entirely unknown to non-Swedish readers.

Most Swedish experts place the birth of Swedish crime fiction in 1893, when a novel called *Stockholms-detektiven* (*The Stockholm Detective*) was published. The author's name was Fredrik Lindholm, but he chose to publish his novel under the pen name Prins Pierre and, during the next decades, several other early Swedish crime writers also wrote pseudonymously. Individually, they may have had different reasons for this, but, collectively, a major reason was almost certainly that they shied away from being associated with what most critics and intellectuals at the time considered vulgar trash. We will get back to this a bit later.

Although *The Stockholm Detective* was hardly a bestseller—indeed, the novel was almost entirely forgotten for many decades until it was finally republished to coincide with its centenary—several other early crime authors were enormously popular. In 1908, a vicar named Oscar Wågman, writing as Sture Stig, published the first of two collections of parodic Sherlock Holmes stories; both clever and funny, his work remains the earliest still-readable Swedish crime fiction. One of his readers, according to his own statement, was the young Gunnar Serner (1886–1947), a brilliant scholar who entered Lund University at the age of sixteen and received his doctorate (on a dissertation written in English and entitled *On the Language of Swinburne*) at twenty-four. However, due to his family's relative poverty, Serner was forced to finance his studies by short-term loans, and in the end found himself with no other alternative than to forge a number of bank letters of acceptance; in September 1912, he fled Sweden. Trying to make his fortune at the Monte Carlo Casino, he instead lost everything and decided to try his hand at fiction. Surprisingly, he succeeded and quickly began selling stories under a variety of pen names—in Serner's case an absolute necessity, since he was wanted by the Swedish police.

In 1914 Serner's first book was published, establishing the name Frank Heller—from then on his only pseudonym. Until his death, "Heller" published a total of forty-three novels, story collections, and travelogues; he also edited anthologies of crime fiction as well as fantasy and science fiction, and he wrote poetry. Several further short story collections were issued at a later time. Heller became not only a bestseller in Sweden, but also Sweden's internationally most successful entertainment writer of his time. His inventive, humorous, and exciting stories of swindlers, gentlemen adventurers, and criminals were bestsellers throughout Europe and the basis for five feature movies; in the United States, eight of his novels were published by Crowell during the 1920s. With a single exception, the work of Frank Heller is the best Swedish crime fiction written during the first half of the twentieth century and is still both readable and interesting.

That exception is a short novel called *Doktor Glas* (1905; translated as *Doctor Glas*) by Hjalmar Söderberg, generally acknowledged as one of the major Swedish twentieth-century authors. *Doktor Glas*, however, was not viewed as crime fiction; it is a psychological novel of a young doctor who decides to commit murder, and it is still both chilling and convincing in its careful and empathetic portrayal of a good man convincing himself to do evil.

Other early authors include Harald Johnsson, writing as Robinson Wilkins, whose master detective, Swede Fred Hellington, was employed by Scotland Yard and so solved cases in England. Samuel August Duse, writing as S. A. Duse, who published thirteen novels about lawyer and genius detective Leo Carring, silly, racist, and snobbish entertainments, though with sometimes innovative plots (in a novel called *Doktor Smirnos dagbok*, *The Diary of Dr. Smirnos*, Duse already in 1917 lets the murderer record a police investigation in his diary without revealing, until the end, his own role. This contrivance became world famous when repeated by Agatha Christie in her 1926 novel *The Murder of Roger Ackroyd*). Julius Regis, often signing himself Jul. Regis and born Petersson, was immensely popular for his ten crime novels, most featuring journalist and detective Maurice Wallion.

These were the major Swedish crime writers until the 1930s. Most detectives had un-Swedish names; so did most major criminals. The crime story was perceived as a non-Swedish literary field, and so native authors chose to make their stories more international by importing both their protagonists and their adversaries. "Frank Heller" was the exception, writing primarily about Swedish heroes—but on the other hand, virtually all of his stories are set outside of Sweden: his method was simply the opposite, since he chose to export instead of import his detectives.

The reason for this is obvious. Foreign crime writers were voluminously translated and quickly became popular. The Sherlock Holmes stories began appearing in Sweden as early as 1891; they were followed by translations of work by Maurice Leblanc, G. K. Chesterton, R. Austin Freeman, Agatha Christie, Dorothy L. Sayers, Freeman Wills Crofts, and the other major British and American writers. During the 1930s, early crime-fiction pulp magazines also began appearing in Sweden. These were quite different from the American pulps of the same period, and in fact more similar to the German popular-fiction magazines: generally of small size, stapled, and usually presenting a single long story rather than many short works. Most were translations; when written by Swedes, they were mostly disguised as translations by being set in England or the United States and published under English-sounding pen names. The pulp crime magazines lingered in Sweden until the beginning of the 1960s, but had for a decade largely been replaced as a primary source of crime entertainment reading by low-priced original paperback novels and translations.

Meanwhile, the first Swedish crime writer to firmly place his stories in Sweden and also create thoroughly Swedish detectives with unmistakably Swedish names was Stieg Trenter. Most of his novels were told by photographer Harry Friberg, but the problem solver is primarily Detective Inspector Vesper Johnson, a friend of Friberg's. Trenter is generally considered one of the finest literary chroniclers of the growing Stockholm during the postwar years. He published twenty-six books from 1943 through 1967, the last few cowritten with his wife, Ulla Trenter, who after his death published a further twenty-three crime novels until 1991, many still featuring her husband's protagonists but with markedly weaker plots and little of his trademark depiction of Stockholm settings.

Stieg Trenter can be said to have been the author who made crime fiction accepted by Swedish critics. He had followers during the 1940s and 1950s, most notably Maria Lang, a pen name for Dagmar Lange (1914–1991), though as her novels always featured not only romantic but often erotic subplots, they were often dismissed as "women's romances" with detective intrusions. Nevertheless, Lang's

7

first novel remains interesting; *Mördaren ljuger inte ensam* (*Not Only the Murderer Lies*, 1949) was extremely daring in sympathetically depicting a murderer who turns out to be a lesbian killing the woman who scorns her passionate love. The shocked reactions to this book may well have contributed to the fact that Lang minimized her discussion of serious issues in her following forty-two adult novels; she had her social standing and position as a high school dean to worry about. Even so, the scorn heaped by male critics on her output seems out of proportion: the fact that the leading female characters in her novels (though the primary detective is always male) actually concern themselves with commenting on men's looks, potential as partners, and sex appeal—things male protagonists in novels from the same period written by men constantly do about women—seems to be one of the primary so-called failings of "Maria Lang."

The first Swede to write only about professional policemen was Vic Suneson, a pen name for Sune Lundquist, who published more than thirty novels and story collections from 1948 through 1975. Many of his novels are experimental, with shifting points of view, told in a nonlinear fashion, or combine depictions of criminal investigations with psychological portrayals. After Suneson, the last of the major Swedish crime writers before the 1960s published his first novel in 1954. H(ans)-K(rister) Rönblom wrote about historian and teacher Paul Kennet, who reveals killers not primarily to serve justice but to make certain that the historical record is set straight. Rönblom was in a sense the first recognizably modern Swedish crime writer, since his novels are also insidiously critical of the small-town life they portray: below the idyllic day-to-day life is seething corruption, religious intolerance, sexism, racism, narrow-mindedness, and self-righteousness, all brought to life by the meticulous, rigorously honest Kennet. Rönblom, a journalist, began writing fiction late and died early (1901–1965); still, he managed to publish ten novels.

Crime fiction became popular in Sweden first in translation. With the exception of the very talented Frank Heller, the relatively few Swedish crime authors writing before the 1940s were highly derivative and were considered unworthy of critical notice; Heller himself, though often praised for his prose, erudition, and inventiveness, was also often accused of "seducing the young" by glamorizing his amoral swindler heroes. Gradually, however, translated stories of clever detectives, primarily those of Christie and Sayers, later those of Ellery Queen, John Dickson Carr, and Georges Simenon, gained acceptance and were openly read as entertainment by the middle class. This paved the way for Swedish authors to write in the same style: Trenter, Lang, Suneson, and Rönblom dominated Swedish crime fiction for twenty years with their novels of murder within the upper middle class. With the partial exception of Rönblom, despite their storytelling and literary qualities, their novels were as conservative, unchallenging, and devoid of social criticism and daring themes as those of Agatha Christie. These were the writers published in hardcover by reputable Swedish publishers; one latecomer must also be mentioned, the hugely talented Kerstin Ekman, whose first six novels (1959–1963) were pure stories of detection, but who later mainly wrote contemporary literary fiction, though she often includes crime elements in her work and published two later novels which can reasonably be categorized as crime fiction. In 1978 she had the distinction of being the only author of initially popular fiction, and only the third woman in its then 192 years of existence, to be inducted as a life member of the Swedish Academy.

Simultaneously, an undercurrent of what Swedish critics and intellectuals referred to as "dirt literature" (yes, honestly) also began appearing in the period between the wars. At first this form of entertainment fiction was published in adventure weeklies and in small-size pulps, then starting around 1950 in original pocket-book lines sold only through newsstands and tobacconists, never in bookstores —and for that reason, absurdly, not considered to be books at all. By the mid-1950s several hundred such paperbacks had appeared, and with them the hard-boiled crime fiction of the 1930s and later had arrived in Sweden. Peter Cheyney, Mickey Spillane, and James Hadley Chase were bestsellers during the first years of the 1950s—but never mentioned in reviews or overviews, since they were published outside of the established and respectable book trade, as were the few but existing Swedish authors trying to imitate them. Swedish encyclopedias still claim that "pocket books first appeared in Sweden in 1956," since that was the year when one of the major publishers first began issuing pocket-size books to be sold in bookstores.

Consequently, an extreme double standard existed: blue-collar workers, teenagers, and presumably more than a few white-collar readers (though one can suspect without admitting it) consumed hard-boiled crime, but the only crime stories officially published in the country were of the traditional armchair detective variety. In fact, such crime novels are still written and published in Sweden, and have had leading practitioners continually: Jan Ekström, whose first novel was published in 1961, may be the most meticulous of all Swedish puzzle crime writers; his closest competitor in later years is probably Gösta Unefäldt (debut in 1979), though his detective is in fact also a policeman; a current practitioner is Kristina Appelqvist, who published her first novel in 2009.

The first authors to dramatically break with the Swedish upper-class drawing room crime tradition were also the first Swedish crime writers in forty years to become successful outside of the country: Maj Sjöwall and Per Wahlöö, who published the first novel in their cowritten, ten-volume police procedural series, The Story of a Crime, in 1965. This novel, *Roseanna*, was by no means an immediate success in Sweden: critics found it too gritty, too depressing, too dark, too brutal. However, gradually the Sjöwall and Wahlöö series began to be hailed as a unique literary experiment and became a bestselling phenomenon. They achieved this success largely due to the political message of their novels. Where earlier Swedish crime writers had been politically conservative or liberal, Sjöwall and Wahlöö were both left-wing activists and consciously planned their ten novels to become more overtly political. The motives behind the crimes gradually become connected to the social background of the victims and of the criminals; the later books in the series directly address issues like fascist tendencies within the police, the betrayal of the working class by the purportedly socialist government, the emptiness of the capitalist-bourgeois lifestyle.

Swedish political life since the mid-1930s was dominated by the Social Democrat party, to which all government heads from 1932 until 1976 belonged. Beginning in the 1930s, the party gradually transformed Swedish society into a centrally planned welfare state, though at a much slower speed than its rhetoric usually promised. A consequence of this was that many Swedish intellectuals, as well as a growing number of young people, began to view the Social Democrat party as derelict in its dedication to socialist ideals. Thus, during the 1960s, social criticism in Sweden tended to come from the radical left, and the Sjöwall and Wahlöö novels changed the way in which many leading intellectuals viewed crime fiction: what had once been dismissed as a pointless bourgeois pastime could be turned into a force for political analysis, education, and change. Suddenly reading, and even writing, crime stories became respectable among left-wing Swedes; interestingly enough, this coincided with the coming of age of generations of young readers who had grown up not on their parents' Agatha Christie-inspired novels, but on the hard-boiled crime novels published in the disreputable "kiosk books" lines, and this combination of circumstances quickly transformed Swedish crime fiction as a whole.

Of course, the success of Sjöwall and Wahlöö, and the following tide of crime novels written from a politically radical perspective, did not extinguish the more traditional or purportedly apolitical kinds of crime fiction. They had their readers, and continued to be published; indeed, one of the most popular writers of the 1968 through mid-1980s period was the pseudonymous Bo Balderson who, in a total of eleven novels, poked fun at Swedish government circles from a clearly conservative point of view. Other new writers, considerably more accomplished than Balderson, proved that the more traditional kind of detective novel could still be written brilliantly; among the foremost of these were psychiatrist Ulf Durling, with his first novel in 1971 and his sixteenth, and so far latest, in 2008, and the very prolific Jean Bolinder, whose first crime novel was published in 1967. Even so, around the time when the tenth and last of the Sjöwall and Wahlöö novels was published in 1975, most of the new authors were writing about police collectives, and most were combining their crime stories with an underlying political agenda. Some of the most notable authors of this generation were Uno Palmström, K. Arne

11

Blom, Olof Svedelid, and most particularly Leif G. W. Persson, a professor of criminology who published three novels in 1978–1982, then returned with a fourth in 2002, and has since written a further six crime novels; their intricate plots, often based in actual Swedish crimes (his trilogy *Between Summer's Longing and Winter's Cold*, 2002, *Another Time, Another Life*, 2003, and *Falling Freely, as in a Dream*, 2007, dealing with the unsolved 1986 murder of Swedish prime minister Olof Palme, is an impressive case in point), their careful atmosphere and obvious literary merits have made him one of the foremost Swedish crime writers; he is one of only two three-time recipients of the Swedish Crime Fiction Academy's Best Novel of the Year Award, the other being Håkan Nesser.

Persson, indisputably not only one of the best but also one of the most influential Swedish crime writers, also helped set the tone of social criticism in Swedish crime fiction. His background—as a criminologist with the national board of police, as an influential government adviser, as an expert adviser to the Swedish minister for justice—gives a unique weight to his novels, which are often extremely critical of Sweden's rampant police inefficiency, of the legal system, and of the political and bureaucratic establishment, whose primary aim seems to be to perpetuate and extend its own power and privileges.

Parallel to Persson, similarly critical views of Swedish society also played a central part in the novels of Kennet Ahl, pen name for journalist Christer Dahl and later writer and actor Lasse Strömstedt, who had spent eight years in prison. They wrote seven novels from 1974–1991, adding inside knowledge of the prison system, police brutality, the narcotics trade, and the precarious existence of addicts. Also important was the already mentioned Uno Palmström, originally a journalist, later a publisher, whose nine novels (1976–1990) also expressed fundamental doubts about Swedish society, which Palmström viewed as largely a corporate state where the unholy alliance of politicians and financiers repressed the population in order to further its own interests. Lawyer and naturalist Staffan Westerlund wrote a series of novels where a common theme was the inhumanity of both big business and big government; he wrote about the meddling and callous outrages perpetrated by Swedish authorities and the indifference towards individuals shown by medical, chemical, and energy corporations in their quest for profits.

By the late 1980s and early 1990s, this trend of social criticism was not only firmly established but further enhanced in the work of important new authors. Journalist Gunnar Ohrlander published a first thriller in 1990, chosen Best First Novel of the Year by the Crime Fiction Academy, and Henning Mankell published his first crime novel in 1991, chosen Best Novel of the Year by the Academy; these two were the first Swedish authors to seriously treat the subject of Swedish racism and anti-immigrant feelings in literary form, and they did so in crime novels.

When Stieg Larsson's novels were translated in 2008 and on, many critics seemed surprised at their negative depiction of a Swedish welfare state swollen to a monstrosity willing to sacrifice the rights, liberty, and lives of its citizens in order to preserve its privileges and power. This, to readers in the United States and Britain, seemed a dramatic reversal of the earlier, rosy picture painted of modern Sweden as a wealthy, liberal welfare society, characterized by openness, tolerance, and compassion. In fact, the bleak view of Swedish society set out in the Millennium trilogy was a direct continuation of the social criticism of the Sjöwall and Wahlöö novels, and thus established as central to Swedish crime writing since almost forty years.

We have already touched on the reasons why so many—though, as we shall also note, not by any means all—of the Swedish crime writers came to express strongly leftist political views. In brief, Maj Sjöwall's and Per Wahlöö's novels had broken entirely with the earlier tradition in Swedish crime fiction: they chose a much more realistic approach both to crime and to crime solving, they wrote from an underdog perspective, they were often critical of both the efficiency and motives of the police and of the close ties between the legal system and the political establishment, and they examined the social and economic factors contributing to crime. This made their novels not only acceptable but required reading for intellectuals sympathetic to their views, which created a whole new readership for original Swedish crime fiction. At the same time, their novels were published when the Swedish political landscape was being radicalized. The 1968 youth revolt throughout much of the western world also had a considerable impact in Sweden, where opposition to the Vietnam War became a unifying symbol to a number of radical groups: the Marxist-Leninists, the Maoists, and the few but intellectually significant Trotskyites. By taking control of the anti–Vietnam War movement, the Maoists and in some cases the Trotskyites managed to influence a generation of Swedish high school and college students. Very consciously, these groups also encouraged their members to choose professions which would give them the opportunity of influencing others; many became entertainers, actors, teachers, social workers, and certainly not least writers or journalists—for a number of years, the Stockholm College of Journalism was popularly called the "College of Communism." That a number of them also chose to follow in the footsteps of Sjöwall and Wahlöö by expressing their views and concerns via crime novels is hardly surprising, and indeed many of the major Swedish crime writers of the last decades have a background in the radical groups of the late 1960s and 1970s. Stieg Larsson was a Trotskyite; Henning Mankell is a Maoist, as was Gunnar Ohrlander; these three have spoken openly of their affiliations, which is why they are named while others are not.

Let me add, for clarity, that my point here is not to denounce these writers, but to give an intelligible background to the specific direction in which Swedish crime writing has developed: already in their teens or early twenties, the writers maturing in the 1960s and 1970s learned to view society from a principled standpoint, in a dialectical manner, and to attribute both social problems and individual actions to political and economic factors. I have no doubt that very similar forms of social criticism would have appeared if a number of leading Swedish writers had been guided by equally strong liberal or libertarian views, but such views are seldom part of the consensus-driven Swedish political discourse. On the other hand, there are certainly examples of politically conservative writers using crime fiction to criticize Swedish society.

★ ★ ★

By the mid-1990s, a new generation of leading writers had established itself, with Mankell, Håkan Nesser, who began writing crime in 1993, and Åke Edwardson, with a first crime novel in 1995, as its most important authors. Both Nesser and Edwardson to some extent broke with the social realist tradition. Nesser placed his highly literary novels in a fictitious city, Maardam, in an unnamed country which is a composite of Sweden, Germany, Poland and the Netherlands, with his emphasis largely on the psychology of his main characters, not least his police protagonist Van Veeteren. Most of Edwardson's novels feature his Gothenburg Detective Inspector Erik Winter, but Edwardson as well has chosen to deal primarily with existential and psychological issues, also in a highly literary fashion. Mankell, Nesser, and Edwardson brought the Swedish crime novel to a level of literary accomplishment that made it not only accepted as potentially serious fiction, as indeed it already was since the 1960s, but viewed as a potentially important part of contemporary Swedish literature.

What was largely lacking, however, were female authors. With the exception of psychiatrist Åse Nilsonne, virtually all of the foremost Swedish crime writers were men. The turning point came towards the end of the nineties, when Inger Frimansson, Liza Marklund, Helene Tursten, and Aino Trosell all published their first novels in 1997 and 1998. They also brought a much needed renewal to the forms of Swedish crime writing. Frimansson from the start concentrated on psychological thrillers with few recurring characters; Marklund wrote about a journalist investigator, Annika Bengtzon, and Aino Trosell featured crime-solving female "anti-heroes" in her largely proletarian realist novels. Of the four, only Helene Tursten, a registered nurse and dentist, writes about a police officer, Detective First Irene Huss at the Gothenburg police.

Despite this, the police procedural is alive and well in Sweden. Among those still writing in that tradition, the most important newer writer may well be Arne Dahl (penname of Jan Arnald), who introduced his fictitious "A Group," specialized in internationally related violent crimes, in 1999 and, after eleven books, in 2011 began writing about Opcop, a fictitious secret operational unit within the

European police organization. Other impressive police procedural writers include Anna Jansson, who introduced her police protagonist Maria Wern in 2000; Mons Kallentoft, writing about the brilliant but damaged and heavy-drinking Detective Inspector Malin Fors since 2007; Carin Gerhardsen, who began writing about the police in Hammarby, a part of southern Stockholm, in 2008; and Kristina Ohlsson, with protagonists Fredrika Berman and Alex Recht, introduced in 2009.

Nowadays, however, many of the most highly regarded Swedish crime novels fall outside the police procedural field. Camilla Läckberg published her first novel about writer Erica Falck and her police boyfriend Patrik Hedström in 2003, and quickly became one of the most popular authors in Sweden. Her novels, as do those of many of her later followers, emphasize the personal lives and relationships of her main characters while the crime story, though central to the plots of her novels, is not always the most important element in them. This kind of "crossover" between relationship novels and crime fiction has become a standard part of Swedish crime writing, in a sense harking back to the structure used in Maria Lang's 1950s novels, but written in a decidedly more realistic fashion. Others successfully writing in this vein include Mari Jungstedt and Viveca Sten; it also has attracted male writers like Jonas Moström.

Among those writing about lawyers, Åsa Larsson may be foremost. Her first Rebecka Martinsson novel was published in 2003 and was considered that year's finest first novel; two of her later four books have won the Crime Fiction Academy award for Best Novel of the Year. In her novels, regional traditions and religious and psychological conflicts play major parts; she is among the most accomplished, as well as original, current Swedish crime authors. A recent lawyer writing about a lawyer and using her novels to criticize or question aspects of the Swedish justice system is Malin Persson Giolito, daughter of the previously mentioned Leif G. W. Persson, who published her first crime novel in 2012. Among the finest of current crime authors are also Anders Roslund and Börge Hellström, writing together since 2004. Roslund is a journalist and previous TV crime reporter; Hellström a former criminal, now engaged in helping criminals readjust to society. Their novels are closely tied to the Swedish tradition of using crime fiction to discuss and criticize social problems, and have a traditional police protagonist, but rise above most similar work through their literary skill, their wide range of themes, and their level of ambition—all of their six novels vary greatly in plot, form, mood, and style.

In 2005, the first of Stieg Larsson's novels was published in Sweden, and by the time the second appeared in 2006, their success was already enormous. By the turn of the century, crime fiction in Sweden had been a thriving field, with a growing number of new writers adding diversity to what for almost thirty years had been a form strongly dominated by male authors writing about largely male police collectives. After the Stieg Larsson novels, the annual number of original Swedish crime novels has increased to an unprecedented number, currently around 120. A negative aspect of this is that since the total number of crime fiction titles remains largely unchanged, a diminishing number of foreign crime novels are translated into Swedish, making Swedish readers miss out on important new writers and trends, as well as depriving Swedish crime fiction writers not conversant in other languages the inspiration of new literary and thematic developments. On the other hand, by now it also seems obvious that the Stieg Larsson novels themselves led to lasting changes in Swedish crime writing.

Since the early part of the twentieth century, Swedish literature as a whole was dominated by the notion that, to be taken seriously, a literary work should be realistic, deal primarily with either psychological or social issues, and show restraint in its portrayals of characters and events. This view of literature spread also to include "good" entertainment literature, while works not conforming to it were more or less automatically considered inferior by reason of their insufficient realism. Perhaps one result of this is the fact that science fiction never managed to get a lasting foothold in Sweden; by not dealing explicitly with the here and now, it was viewed as primarily "escape" fiction, which was by definition neither good art nor worthwhile literature. When applied to crime fiction, the result of this view

17

was that the field as a whole can be characterized by its restraint and by its lack of imaginative freedom: in a field where social concerns and down-to-earth realism are primary virtues, there is no room for villains like Hannibal Lecter, heroes like Jack Reacher, or plots like those of Mickey Spillane.

Perhaps it took a writer like Stieg Larsson, whose favorite reading was American and British science fiction and crime fiction, and who paid no particular heed to the traditions upheld in the Swedish literary establishment, to write a work so completely *un*-Swedish—in its main characters, its action, its graphic sex and violence, and its sheer joy of imaginative storytelling—as the Millennium trilogy. The critical and popular triumph of the novels meant that later writers were suddenly freed from many of the previous taboos, which in fact hark back to the early-twentieth-century modernist rejection of the linear plot structure, heroism, moralism, and romanticism of earlier literature, which the modernists considered outdated and unsuited to cosmopolitan and urban civilization.

Consequently, in the last few years, Swedish crime fiction has suddenly been enriched by innovative authors writing in totally new ways. Karin Alfredsson and Katarina Wennstam, publishing their first novels in 2006 and 2007, write on the subjects of men's subjugation of women and homophobia, and are perhaps the two current writers whose main concerns are closest to the underlying theme of Stieg Larsson's novels; Alfredsson, using her physician protagonist Ellen Elg as a unifying link in her first five novels, has examined the horrifying situation of women in five different countries; Wennstam, in her highly accomplished crime novels, has dealt with trafficking, police brutality towards their domestic partners, sexual harassment in the movie business, and homophobia in sports. Lawyer Jens Lapidus, writing since 2006, is stylistically and thematically inspired by James Ellroy in his depictions of gang violence and corruption in the Stockholm suburbs, and has brought a unique voice to Swedish crime fiction. Johan Theorin, whose first novel was published in 2007, is a highly literary writer often combining crime plots with both regionalism and elements of fantasy, mythology, and horror. Dag Öhrlund, making his debut in the same year, writes violent crime thrillers much in the American hard-boiled tradition, and has created the first genius serial killer in Swedish crime fiction. Starting in 2009, the writing team Alexandra and Alexander Ahndoril, under their joint pen name Lars Kepler, write fast, imaginative, and moody action novels featuring both heroes and villains larger than life. Security expert Anders de la Motte's crime novels, starting with [*geim*] in 2010, are characterized by intricate, mazelike plotting and by a nerdy, half-criminal, and computer-savvy slacker protagonist who is anything but typically Swedish. Håkan Axlander Sundquist and Jerker Eriksson, under their joint pen name Erik Axl Sund and debuting in 2010, have so far published only one huge, three-volume novel; an intricate, hypnotically enthralling story of obsession, vengeance, psychoanalysis, and redemption which is an unmistakably central work in current Swedish crime fiction. Even later, Christoffer Carlsson is a highly unconventional, noir-inspired author whose three novels so far show huge promise, while writer team Rolf and Cilla Börjlind published their first crime novel in 2012: dark, atmospheric, and with one of the most original protagonist couples since that of Stieg Larsson; the Börjlinds, in creating their two detectives, are both playing with, parodying, and rising above the conventions of the form.

Given the proliferation of new writers; its sudden freedom from earlier restraints on themes, style, and elements; and its great popularity among readers, Swedish crime fiction today is at both an enormously exciting and a chaotic stage of its ongoing development.

Ancient controversies have resurfaced—how much graphic description of violence, murder, or sex should be "acceptable" in fiction; how much literary experimentation should be "condoned" in a crime novel; how much adherence to the field's traditions of rational deduction should you "demand" of a crime novel; can supernatural events or plot elements be part of a crime novel? This makes for often heated and fascinating discussions, not least in the awards committees of the Swedish Crime Fiction Academy.

But despite the controversies, and despite the fact—not previously stated, but nevertheless fundamental—that the majority of crime novels in Sweden (as in all countries) remain both fairly undistinguished and are written in one or other of the already established traditions of the field, the future of Swedish crime fiction seems bright. And considering its sudden global appeal, there is also reason to believe that it will continue to attract talented, innovative, and original writers who will widen and enrich it even further.

After that optimistic thought, I won't keep you any longer. In the following pages, you will meet many of the writers who have shaped the Swedish crime fiction field as it exists today and a few who I believe will help shape it tomorrow. I hope you will enjoy getting to know them, and reading the stories they have to tell.

John-Henri Holmberg
Viken, July 2013

REUNION

Tove Alsterdal

Before publishing her first novel in 2009, Tove Alsterdal worked mainly as a journalist and playwright. As with most writers, her experiences are many and varied. She was born in Malmö but has lived mainly in Stockholm; nevertheless, she also has roots in the far north of Sweden, in Tornedalen, an area close to the Swedish border with Finland and largely north of the Arctic Circle. This was where her mother grew up, and Tove Alsterdal returns there for summers. It is the setting of her latest novel, I tystnaden begravd *(Buried in Silence),* runner-up for the 2012 Best Novel of the Year Award given by the Swedish Crime Fiction Academy. She walked horses at the Stockholm outdoor museum Skansen and worked as an aide in the closed wards at Beckomberga mental hospital. Later, she was a radio and TV news reporter, and she wrote scripts for TV dramas and a feature film, stories for computer games, stage plays, and an opera libretto. A close friend of crime author Liza Marklund, she has edited all except the first of Marklund's crime novels.*

Tove Alsterdal's writing is psychologically acute and full of the settings she knows and loves to re-create on the page. There is often a strong streak of the mystical, seemingly inexplicable, in her work—but one of her great strengths is that she leaves the choice of how to interpret such elements to her readers, as in this story of a late reunion of teenage friends.

SHE STEPS OUT OF HER CAR AND SLOWLY WALKS DOWN TOWARDS THE lake. It draws her. The paved walkway disappears between a couple of birches and becomes a path. A dizzying feeling of time rushing off, back to then.

Its black waters.

It is the same lake, the same time of summer as it was then. Just before midsummer, before the heat has permeated the ground and the greenery is still tender and young. The water as dark and tempting as in the nightmares she has had ever since. Not always, to be fair. There have been weeks, even years, when she has managed to sleep calmly, as when Lisette was just a baby.

"Ohmygaawd, it's been so long! Marina! Piiiaaaa!!"

"Agge!"

Two other cars have driven up and parked next to hers. The women yell loud enough to make the famous birdlife flutter up from lake pastures and reeds, take cover deeper into the woods.

She forces a smile and turns to meet them.

"Jojjo, is it really you?" Marina takes the last few steps at a run and hugs her. Watches her face, pushes back a strand of hair. "Shit, you look just the same. You haven't changed a bit." She turns

23

to the others, who are unloading baskets and bags full of food from their cars. "Have you seen who's here already? Johanna!"

They laugh and shout and soon she is wrapped in everyone's arms, they hug and agree that all are just as they were.

And it's fabulous to meet again! After thirty years! And you don't look a day over twenty-five! Well, neither do you! They laugh at absolutely everything. And as they tumble into the tiny scout's cottage she thinks, how great that I decided to come after all. That I didn't give in to that feeling of just wanting to hide. There is a warmth between them she had forgotten. They have known each other since such an early age that those thirty years are shed in just a moment. Or so it feels at that particular moment when they are jokingly chattering about who slept in the upper beds that time.

Johanna watches them and wonders which one of them actually came up with the idea of a reunion. She has just assumed that Marina did. Her parents had some kind of connection to the scout organization that owns the cottages. Marina, her hair almost black, though by now she surely must dye it—there are only slight touches of gray that paradoxically make her look younger. Almost more beautiful than she remembers her.

"Didn't you bring a sleeping bag, Jojjo?" Agge asks when the others are throwing their overnight things on the bunk beds.

"No, I'm not sure if I can . . ." She feels all of their eyes. It was a long time since anyone called her Jojjo. "I have to get up early and . . ."

"What are you saying, aren't you going to stay the night? Wasn't that the whole thing?" Agge's deep voice, always sounding as if something was self-evident. She has put on at least sixty pounds and it's still impossible to disagree with her. "I've got blankets in my car," she says, "it'll be all right."

Johanna nods and smiles. Why did she agree to this? Her first reaction on seeing the invitation was a ringing NO. And yet. Just that someone invited her, remembered her. Pia already has the coffee-maker going. Just as back then she slides in without saying much but still ends up at the center, the prettiest of them all. Tiny, attractive wrinkles around her eyes when she laughs.

"What the hell," Agge says, "let's have some champagne."
And the cork bounces against the ceiling.

The fire is burning, a genuine campfire. Their faces glow. The mid-summer dusk is blue and transparent. They pull their sleeping bags around themselves. She knows that she is drinking too fast and too much.

Marina's idea: that they toast each other, all round. They have toasted Marina's new executive position at the staffing company and Pia's new lover who has proposed, third time lucky! They have toasted that Marina has run the women's six-mile race and that Agge has retrained as a gardener; at last she is living her dream! Here's to our dreams! Marina has been married for eighteen years and still loves her husband—*skål!*—and Pia has gotten new tits after her pregnancies—*skål* to them!—and to all their kids who are all doing so well in school—*skål! skål! skål!*—and particularly to Agge's eldest who has been picked for the junior national swim team.

"And what about you, Jojjo, out with it!"

She knows it was a mistake to come here. Her life is nothing you hold up for inspection at reunions. She manages a toast to her daughter, Lisette, getting a job after graduating high school, then slips away, saying that she has to take a trip into the forest.

Nowadays there are toilets behind the cabins, but she does it the way they did back then. Squats down behind a spruce.

A little urine squirts on one of her shoes. Between branches she sees the fire die down to embers and the silhouettes of the middle-aged women around it.

What else could she toast? That she's divorced and has been unable to find someone new? That her apartment is mute now that Lisette has moved out? She can't even do Internet dating, since it makes her feel like the last passenger on the late-night bus going home from town, where everyone is desperately grabbing whatever is offered. And she knows that thousands of people are finding love on those sites, so of course it's all her fault. Like missing the last night bus and being left standing outside in the cold. A toast to that! She sleeps badly, because there will be more cutbacks and nobody knows who will be laid off. And here's to the body going downhill while time runs out, *skål!*

As she is pulling her pants up she hears a sound. Branches creaking. Somewhere down by the lake. She breathes silently and stands immobile, her hand on her zipper. Seems to see a shadow between the spruces, a shift in the weak light.

A voice. And everything within her is suddenly cold as ice.

"Have you saved me anything to eat?"

Someone is standing where the spruce forest ends and the shoreline begins. Thin and short. Her hair a flowing blonde tangle. Her green sweater.

"What is it?" Lillis says, laughing. Her face is unnaturally pale. As it was already back when they were playing with death. "Didn't you think I'd show up?"

I'm dreaming, Johanna thinks, I'm more drunk than I think. It can't be the same sweater!

"Don't you want to talk to me?" The figure steps closer to her, head a little askance. "And I always thought we were friends."

Johanna steps back. "I'm going back to the others," she says, half running through the forest, a branch scratching her face.

She doesn't turn round until she is sitting by the fire again. Then she stares at the forest, so long that the others also have to turn around.

"But what the hell . . ." Marina stands. "Lilian! I didn't even know . . . who managed to get hold of Lillis? Why haven't you said anything?"

Johanna doesn't even realize that the question is put to her. She sees the woman come closer. A smile animating her face. Now all the others are standing. Johanna feels that she has to stand as well.

Lillis' body is cool and thin in her arms. A quick hug. A darkness sweeping in from the lake and night has fallen.

"God, how great to see you."

"Where did you go? Didn't you disappear even before we started our senior year?"

Distantly she hears them toast Lillis, as if inside a glass jar. Now, for the first time, she actually sees the others. They aren't at all as unchanged as they fancied; they have aged. Their skin has lost its grip and is hanging loosely from their chins; the years have dug furrows even in Marina's once-perfect face. You can tell that they all dye their hair. Only Lillis is still young, entirely smooth and as dangerously and strangely beautiful as she was then. That tiny little squint.

"My God, you haven't aged a day!" Agge yells. "*Skål* to that!"

Johanna sees their mouths move and laugh. Lillis' face is so white that it shines, despite the embers having gone out and everything is cold.

Can't they see that it's wrong?

Lillis, who for a short while was her closest friend. The unreachable whom she incomprehensibly reached, the great happiness of being seen and being allowed in. Lillis, who was an adventurer and a center, one of those around whom the moon and the earth and the boys revolved, while Johanna was a vapid planet at the rim of the solar system. Vaguely she had understood that Lillis needed her, or someone, anyone, by her side. Johanna had never entered the competition, just followed. The first cigarette, the first high on beer and aspirin, the play in the hut where Johanna mostly waited outside while Lillis was making out inside, but anyway. Afterward she was allowed to share her secrets.

Johanna feels the scream grow inside of her, it wants to burst and escape, but she can't, it isn't possible. The silence is too huge. It has lasted for thirty years.

Wants to tell the others: But can't you see, don't you get it?

She pinches her arm, hard, and it hurts. It's no nightmare, it's happening. She has to project it when she looks into Lillis' paleblue and slightly squinting eyes. Project her words, silently, across the dead fire that is now all ashes.

You don't exist. You're dead.

And then she can't stay there any longer, because she is sucked into the pale blur and it makes her shiver. She has to rise and walk down to the lake.

There is a story about the Upper Lake. Have you ever heard it?

It is Lillis' voice, but is it then or now? They have walked along the water's edge, away from the others, because Lillis is tired of the endless competition between Marina and Pia. Johanna is thinking that Lillis is also competing, but she never says it out loud. They are sixteen years old and will sleep in the cabin all the weekend and tomorrow—Marina has asked some boys—they'll have a party.

Come on, let's swim. Aw, come on, now! We'll have to see if it's true what they say about the Upper Lake. That somewhere out there, there's a bottomless spot. Where those who have drowned live. They say that if you go down deep enough you can be caught in their trailing hair. Down there are those who died willingly, the suicides, and they're all women, unhappy and full of despair. Men shoot themselves, but women drown themselves, that's how it's always been. It's their hair you can feel under your feet, if only you dare swim out there.

Lillis throws her clothes into the high beach grass and starts wading out in the lake. Johanna has to do the same. Everything they share becomes meaningful and the more dangerous it feels, the more alive they become. Lillis has taught her that. They often play with death, strangle themselves with scarves until they pass out. It's become an addiction to them, an obsession, they have to do it every day. Johanna is panicky as she pulls the noose tight, yet she pulls it until all air is gone, her temples start throbbing and it feels as if her eyes were forced out of her skull. She sees pinpoints of light and outside sounds disappear and then everything goes black. There's no danger as long as you don't make a knot in your scarf, Lillis has promised her, since it loosens when you pass out. Before you die.

There is a moment in every person's life when you decide whether to walk with the living or with the dead. That time is now, before we go rigid. After, it is too late.

She can see that Lillis has started swimming out there and is pulling away. They are closing in on the middle of the lake. The cool water caressing her skin, so present and naked. She thinks that some boy may be standing somewhere on the beach, watching them, and it feels exciting, and then just a little bit shameful as she thinks about Lillis naked under the water maybe thirty feet ahead of her, her strokes powerful even though she is so thin and so cute, but it's not like that. Nothing sexual, that is, between them, or that's what she constantly tells herself even though it sometimes feels that way when Lillis snuggles into her arms on the couch or wherever. Like a puppy, sort of. But that's how Lillis is, without any boundaries against what is dangerous.

And they're alone under the sky, in the night, and they don't give a rat's ass for anyone else.

We have to know something about death to be able to choose, right? Otherwise, we'll just be victims.

She doesn't perceive it when it happens. Just sees that the surface of the water is suddenly smooth. You're kidding, Johanna thinks, and swims to the spot where Lillis' blonde head was just visible, swims around in circles, where the hell are you? She dives under to look, but it's dark and impenetrable. All she sees is water and you can't see water and she loses her sense of direction, of what is up or down, and she panics. That's when she feels it. Something moving down by her feet, slithering around her legs. Fear overwhelms her and she has to get up right now, up to the surface. She kicks and hits something below, there really is something down there, and in her head she sees all the images of the dead, of eels slithering out of eye sockets, and that thing that is tangled around her feet is still there, pulling at her, and she kicks wildly and brandishes her arms, up, up, and she has no air left, must get away from there. She doesn't breathe until she is at the shore. Doesn't think until she has stood up. The lake is glittering and black. She shakes so hard that it takes forever to get her clothes back on. Next to her are Lillis' clothes, spread out on the grass.

Time just passed, or perhaps it stopped. Finally she had to rise and walk back.

"Have you been out swimming? Where's Lillis?"

Johanna doesn't know where the lie came from. She had meant to tell them what happened, that Lillis swam out and disappeared. But then she would have to lie about the rest. About her being out there herself. About the dead in the water and her own panic, how do you tell someone something like that? About the sensation under her foot when it hit something soft and at the same time hard, and what she hadn't even dared to think through: that it was Lillis' face. Lillis, who just intended to scare her, that it had all been part of a plan, the stories about the dead and their silly hair. Lillis, who always trained to be able to swim farther underwater than anyone else in the public baths.

"She just split, I don't know. Maybe she got upset about something."

In the morning she had gone back to that place and picked up Lillis' clothes, buried them. Cried and dug. It was too late for the truth. It was the summer when everything changed. In the fall they all disappeared in different directions, knots being untied. Marina would attend high school in town, the others started different courses. Johanna quit after a single semester, then graduated from a folk high school up north in Ångermanland. Lillis' father was a heavy drinker and there never was any serious investigation. The police had appeared once to put their questions, and Johanna had described how Lillis was dressed when she disappeared: the sea-green angora sweater (stolen from H&M). They believed she had run away from home. She probably had reasons to.

The tree growing more or less alone at the edge of a grove. Johanna believes she recognizes the place and starts digging on the lake side of the trunk. Is it possible that fabric and angora wool are still there after thirty years in the ground, or do they decay? Sneakers? She digs, and there is nothing. Is it the wrong spot? Perhaps the wrong stretch of beach, new trees grown up, she has no idea of how much a forest can change over thirty years. Lillis is standing at the edge of the woods, looking at her. Johanna doesn't dare turn, but she can feel her presence as something cold in her neck.

We had a deal. A deal about secrets and betrayal, have you forgotten that, Johanna?

She has dirt under her nails, reaching far up to her elbows.

That's why she walks down to the water and kicks off her shoes, she tells herself. When she bends down to wash off the dirt she sees herself in a brief reflex, her adult self. She has never stopped being sixteen—it's just new ages added, like layers in a cake. Then the moon disappears behind a cloud and she is gone. No, not gone, there she is: pretty far out in the water already, where it's deep. She swims, still fully dressed, towards the middle of the lake, because she must. Closes her eyes and swims on, tries to find the power within her body, but there is only the awkwardness of her wet clothes and the fat that has lined her stomach; she can feel her own weight. At the middle of the lake she stops, treads water, looks around. It was here, just here. And she dives down, as deep as she can, looks and sees nothing, fumbles around and gets a grip. Something trailingly soft, and she seems to hear it whisper and sing. *There is a moment . . . to walk with the living or with the dead . . .* Now it is all around her, entangling her in its threads until she is caught and dragged down into the whispering darkness where no light will be and no dread to wake up to, just a quiet song, is that how death really is? She lets herself sink. Let me go, she wants to scream, I don't want to die. *Do you call that life*, it whispers, *that thing you believe yourself to be living?* Now she has no air left, and she sees dots of light all around. Is it Lillis' face she can see down below? Or someone else's?

No, she sees herself, and she is young again, and will do anything to be allowed to belong. No, she wants to scream, NO, I DON'T WANT TO ANY LONGER, but she has no air and there are no sounds in the water. She kicks, grabs the hair entangling her legs, tears it loose and rises towards the surface, and there is air, cold and clear.

Deep into her lungs she pulls life and power and a sense of reality. What the hell is she doing out here in the lake? She swims as well as she can manage, breathless and exhausted, towards land. Untangles her fingers from something in her hand.

Lisette, she thinks. *She needs me, even if she doesn't want to admit it.*

"Are you out of your mind—have you been swimming fully dressed?"

Pia is removing her makeup. Rubbing her face with expensive creams. Agge is snoring in her upper bed. Johanna looks around in the small scout cottage. No sea-green sweater.

"I was thinking about Lillis," she says, guardedly. "I thought I saw her out there."

"You must have drunk a lot. I didn't think anyone had any contact with her since she got out of here. And come to think of it, I never understood why you hung out with her. Want some tea?"

Johanna finds her scarf and dries her hair with it, it's still dripping. They sit down, each with her mug of tea. She has taken her wet clothes off and borrowed dry ones from the others. Seaweed, she thinks, the only thing out there is seaweed or some other kind of water plant. She is grateful her head is no longer spinning.

"What do you mean, why I hung out with Lillis?"

"You were cool, you were smart," Pia says. "You never needed to pretend or act. I was always so impressed by you. And then you let yourself be used by her."

Johanna stares at them, one at a time. A quick sensation of being visible, as if she suddenly was more clearly delineated. Was that really how they perceived her?

She gets one of Agge's blankets and wraps it around herself.

"You know, before, when we were sitting around the fire—" she starts. "I didn't think I had anything to contribute . . . I mean, my life is . . . it's okay, but I guess no more than that."

"Isn't that enough?"

"*Skål,*" Marina says, raising her teacup.

That's when the tears come, burning and overflowing. She rubs them away, sniveling, but they keep flowing. Suddenly she can't

32

remember what's so wrong about her life. And she thinks that all of it was just nightly imaginings, nightmares; she knows drinking too much makes her feel unwell.

Pia puts her arm around her and the crying abates. While light is growing outside, Marina starts talking about her uncertainties: that feeling that they'll discover what a failure she is as an executive, and Pia tells them that deep down she really isn't sure of loving this new guy. Finally they fall asleep, each in her own bed.

The next morning they say good-bye, outside the cabin.

"Thanks for setting this up," Johanna says, hugging Marina. The ghosts of the past night certainly seem childish in the morning light, the sun already high.

"What are you talking about? You were the one inviting us."

Marina exchanges glances with the others.

"We were pretty uncertain all of us, but then we thought, what the hell, get away from hubbies and kids for a weekend, why not?"

A few strands of mist have remained since night and are dissolving on the lake. Marina holds up her cell.

"It says here for anyone to see that you created this page. Is anything wrong with you?"

Johanna grabs the phone from her hand.

She recognizes the Facebook page. "Return to Upper Lake." At the top it clearly says that the group was created by Johanna.

She feels a taste of lake water in her mouth. A stinging sensation in her cheeks, a swaying unreality.

She hadn't even logged in to Facebook in half a year. Doesn't know why she's on it at all, but on the other hand she doesn't want to be left out. When the message arrived in her mailbox, nobody had contacted her in more than six months.

When she returns the cell phone her hand feels numb.

"We've got to do this again," Agge says. "Same time next year?"

"Sure."

She remains standing there for a while after the others have left. Remembers a strand of hair entangled in her hand. The lake has turned a pale blue. The air is so still that the images of the trees on the water seem as real as the forest around her.

"There really is another story about the Upper Lake," she says, slowly, into the air. "Have you ever heard it? I think it's about those trying to live, despite all."

Just as she steps into her car she feels a sudden chill on her neck. A wind creeping across her cheek, a quick caress. And the leaves are immobile.

Born in Malmö in 1960, Tove Alsterdal is a journalist and playwright. For many years, she lived in Umeå and Luleå in the far north of Sweden, but is now based in Stockholm. She has written for the theater and radio. She has also written opera librettos, and, with Helena Bergström, the script for the feature film So Different (Så olika). *She published her first crime novel,* Kvinnorna på stranden (The Women on the Beach) *in 2009, and her second,* I tystnaden begravd (Buried in Silence), *in 2012; they have established her as one of the major Swedish crime writers, a master of mood and subtle characterization.*

HE LIKED HIS HAIR

ROLF AND CILLA BÖRJLIND

No other living Swedish crime writers—regardless of how many bestsell-
ers they have written—have reached an audience as huge as have the
writing team of Rolf and Cilla Börjlind, who have been immensely pro-
ductive in the field, both separately and, for more than a dozen years,
mainly together, though they published their first crime novel, Springfloden
(Spring Tide), *only recently, in 2012. The Börjlinds are by far Sweden's*
most prolific screenwriters, with close to fifty full-length movies—virtually
all of them about crime, and most of them made for TV—to their credit.
They have written twenty-six Martin Beck movies, based on the charac-
ters created by Maj Sjöwall and Per Wahlöö; one movie based on Henning
Mankell's Kurt Wallander character; and five adaptations of Arne Dahl's
novels. Additionally, they have created original TV crime dramas, such as
Danslärarens återkomst (Return of the Dancing Master) *in 2004, the*
eight-part Graven (The Grave) *also in 2004, and the six-part* Morden
(The Murders) *in 2009, reaching an audience of many millions, both in*
Sweden and abroad.

Before his enormously successful screenwriting career, Rolf Bör-
jlind was known as Sweden's perhaps funniest and certainly most bitingly
satirical humorist. And lately, as noted, he and Cilla also have turned their

hands to crime novels. Their highly regarded first novel showed a hardly surprising mastery of the form, both playing with it and utilizing it to perfection; it was sold to more than twenty countries. Their second novel, Den tredje rösten (The Third Voice), *followed in 2013.*

They had never before written a short story, so it is a great pleasure to present their first one here.

HE STILL HAD TIME TO PACE THE ROOM, THAT SIMPLE AND MEASURED surface that was his home. A word he never used. To him it was a surface, not a space. He had put in a couch and a table, and had a wooden balsa model of the Dakota on his windowsill. There was no carpet on the floor and the narrow mirror by the kitchen door was hung too low. He hadn't put it there himself. When he wanted to see how his mouth looked he had to bend down; all he could see was dead meat. He had no relationship with his face, his eyes met the gaze of a stranger and he wondered why the nose was crooked.

He liked his hair.

It was the one thing he admitted as his. Brown, and slightly curly, it reminded him of his mother, the woman who had no hands. Her hair had been brown and curly, and her laugh—when she was finally told—was his only memory of her voice. But it made time pass.

That, and his pacing.

He was a night person, his biological clock set to night. That was when he came awake: when darkness fell, when he could escape being seen and could avoid seeing, when he could be indifferent to his surroundings, cut out, when he could walk from one neighborhood to another without knowing where he had gone.

Often, at night, he walked from one point to another and back along a different route. And always with the same purpose. It made time pass and it made him tired. And made it possible to fall asleep before light caught up with him.

That was important.

He had to fall asleep before it became light and sleep until it grew dark again. Sometimes he failed, woke out of a strange howl and stared out at the light, unable to go back to sleep.

Those times were when he missed it.

That which could lower him back into darkness. Which they had taken from him and which he had to get back.

In one way or another.

He began pacing the room, from wall to wall and back. For how long he didn't know. He had no watch; usually he felt from his body when he was done, when he could go to sleep. Tonight it took a long time. He sat down on the edge of his bed, felt his body. He ought to be tired by now, more tired than he was.

It bothered him.

He went to his window to look out. Nothing moved; all was as usual. In the corner of his eyes he was aware of the charred hands on his window ledge, two of them. They lay there every time he had to go. Not every time, it struck him, just the times he had to lower himself into darkness.

Then they lay there, as a reminder.

He opened his window, carefully, watching the hands. It was quiet outside. On some nights he could hear a blackbird not far away, a blackbird singing in the middle of the night. He never saw it but he knew what it looked like. Its beak was the same orange-yellow color his mother had had when she was told.

And they had the same black eyes.

He closed his window and went to the shelf above the mirror. The small blue-and-white box stood where he had put it four nights ago. He stuffed it in the pocket of his long, dark gray coat and left the room.

He had to.

★ ★ ★

38

Outside a soft rain was falling.

He liked rain, he liked something to happen while he moved between the buildings. Not pelting rain, but a monotonous, quiet drizzle. Tonight the rain was perfect. He knew the address where he was going and was in no hurry. He kept to empty streets; if he met anyone he crossed to the other side.

He never looked back.

When he came to the right part of town he stopped, not far from a green container. He stood quietly, for a long time, hidden in the darkness of a broken streetlight. He thought about a sentence he'd read (where, he couldn't remember) about a man standing on a bridge casting switched-off light across the water. Switched-off light, he liked that, as if your pocket was full of darkness and you could spread it when it became too bright.

Perhaps that was what he could do?

Switch off?

After all, he had the box in his pocket.

He turned to the container near him, having seen a movement, a woman alone pulling herself up to drop an unmarked plastic bag into the container. He watched her tired body and wondered what was in the bag. Perhaps a black wig and a tube of lip gloss? He watched her disappear in the darkness and remained standing. There were nights when he followed people walking alone, often on the opposite side of the street, followed until they disappeared into a doorway or a bar. He conceived of it as having company.

Tonight he wanted to be alone.

He twisted around.

The dogs were whistling down by the bus stop.

Sometimes he imagined that, that the dogs were whistling, late at night when shadows were his only company. The dogs nobody knew about, long, crooked, narrow bodies suddenly just there, out of nowhere, crossing a darkened street to disappear, then suddenly breathe right next to him and disappear again.

He heard them whistling to each other, the dogs, and he knew what it was all about.

Him.

It was connected to the third puppy, the drowned one. The one he pushed into the bucket many years ago and that fought for its life under the sole of his boot. A life it had just been given and that would be taken away from it, because it was the third and was deformed, lacking a fully developed spine. Sometimes he thought about it, being deformed. The animal was deformed and would have died anyway. He just did what the dog owners ought to have done; he took care of it. But the way the animal struggled under his boot left its trace in him. He had thought it would be quick.

It wasn't.

And while the animal fought and twisted under the sole of his boot there was time for him to start thinking. That wasn't a good thing. Suddenly he was thinking about what he was doing and about what moved under his foot. What had been only a quick decision to rid the world of pointless suffering turned into something else. The deformed animal refused to give up and forced him to make an entirely different decision.

He had to kill a puppy.

He might have lifted his foot and said that it didn't work, the pup didn't die, then give it back to its owners. But he didn't. That was what he considered now, in the soft rain. Himself as hostage to a situation he had created and that forced him to kill. Or confess that he was unable to do it.

He killed the pup.

That's why the dogs whistled to each other those special nights when he walked in the company of shadows and knew that he was a hostage again. And had to kill.

Or confess.

He waited until the lights went out in the stairwell and all sounds ceased. Then he pulled on his rubber gloves. In darkness he climbed one floor up and rang the bell by the door of the one he had chosen. It took the old woman a while to open.

"Yes," she said. "What's it about?"

"I'm looking for Ester."

"Yes, that's me?"

"I'm sorry."

Later, when he sat on the kitchen chair watching the thin, white cotton thread hanging from her mouth, he wondered about that. About why he had said, "I'm sorry." It was nothing he had planned, it just came to him spontaneously at the doorway. As if he apologized for what would happen.

It confused him.

The duct tape was the first thing he pulled out in the foyer. Putting it over the thin woman's mouth made quick work. When he lifted her into the kitchen he noticed how slight she was. Almost like a scarecrow he'd built once, just as fragile and wiry.

If he were to build a new scarecrow now he would name it Ester.

With a few blue cable ties he fastened her thin feet and arms to a kitchen chair. In the cupboard above the stove he found a glass. He filled it with water from the faucet next to the stove. He saw the woman's eyes follow his every movement and wondered what she was thinking about. Who he was? Probably, or perhaps more about what he intended to do. He put the glass down on the table in the middle of the kitchen and took out the blue-and-white box. A second before he would open it he hesitated and looked up at the old cobbler's lamp hanging from the ceiling. The light from the filament was soft. He watched the lamp. It was the kind of light he could stand, artificial light you could turn off at will.

He opened the box and pulled out a tampon. He put the thin plastic wrapping in his pocket; he disliked untidiness. With his left hand he pulled the tape from the woman's mouth. She opened it wide to scream, he had no idea for whom. He pushed the tampon down her air pipe to drown her yelling. Now she was silent. He grabbed her jaws with one hand and poured half a glass of water into her mouth before closing it.

Now he was done.

He pulled up another kitchen chair and sat down, almost directly opposite the old woman. He knew that the tampon was swelling inside her throat now, and there was nothing for him to do but to wait. He glanced down at the chair he was sitting on, an unpainted wooden chair. He liked wooden chairs, simple, functional furniture without any frills. His mother had five chairs around their kitchen table, all wooden and all unpainted. For a while they were four in the family, but never five. He never wondered about the fifth chair.

Then.

Now he did. For whom was it intended? He looked at the bound woman in front of him. Her knees were shaking, she no longer could breathe, her eyes bulged a bit. Was the fifth chair intended for visitors? But they never had any visitors. He supposed it was one of his mother's secrets, an extra chair for something unexpected. He smiled slightly. Now the woman's head sank down to her chest, she had stopped shaking. He bent forward and saw the thin white cotton thread hanging down from the corner of her mouth. It would soon be still. He wondered what was flashing through her mind right now. Where was she going?

We know so little about those things, he thought.

Soon he would leave.

He was on his way back, on foot, to his carefully measured surface. The streets were empty, his steps followed the edge of the gutter; he never needed to raise his eyes. At this time there were no movements in this part of town. A couple of hours ago homeless people had shambled past, carrying sacks full of empty cans; drunken teenagers had hunted for cabs or drugs; lonely hookers had tried enticing customers by lowering prices—everything had been drawing to an end. He had seen it a thousand times and another thousand.

Now it was all empty.

Now there were only gulls picking at the pools of vomit and the echo of distant sirens. Nobody saw him. Or perhaps at a distance? Perhaps a sleepless elderly man stood in a costly window a block away looking down at him? Perhaps the man wore a dark green smoking jacket and held a black cheroot in his hand? Perhaps he was listening to the Vienna Boys' Choir? The man who had come to his mother one night and tied a purple bow around her neck had done so. She didn't know that he was sick; she listened to "O Tannenbaum" and let the man stitch a veil of rapture to cover her eyes.

Then the man waved at the young boy.

He raised his head to glance up at the well-to-do building fronts. Perhaps he might glimpse the man?

The faucet water was freezing. He always washed his hands when he got back, held them under the running water until they grew numb, disappeared, until he could bite them without feeling anything. It made him calm. The day before he put a picture up on the wall above his bed. It was the only picture in the room. It pictured a young boy pushing a strange metal funnel under the skirt of a kneeling woman. Both wore medieval clothes. In the background two liveried men were sharing a melon. The picture was in color. He liked falling asleep to the picture and waking up to it. The only thing he lacked in the picture was sound. It looked as if the two men in the background were talking to each other; he would like to know what they said. Was it about the melon? Or about the strange funnel?

Now he lay in bed watching the picture. He was lowered in darkness and knew that he would be able to fall asleep. All he had to do was to ponder the question to which he always fell asleep; why didn't anyone ask for help? He often wondered about that. He could stand in a park, perhaps hidden by a maple, and watch faces walk by, silent, expressionless, as if nothing had happened.

It was very strange.

People ought to be more careful. Once he had stretched out a hand to a young boy walking past. He had wanted the boy to feel the pain in time. The boy had run away.

Since then he had never tried contacting anyone.

Now he was on the verge of slipping away. His eyes let go of the picture on the wall; he hoped he was slipping in the right direction, not towards the interface. He hoped to be here still when he woke up.

He is dreaming.

In his dream he is walking as if he really existed, walks across low, warm heather, through a sparse fir wood, towards dunes of sand; he wants to reach the sea. He has heard that it's supposed to be calm today. He is

43

just a young boy and has never seen total calm, never seen the sea all shiny and smooth. He never gets there. A large, dark bus pulls up in front of him, blocking his way. The door to the bus opens and the shape behind the wheel waves to him. He doesn't want to enter the bus, but there is nobody close he could call out to. He opens his hand. Only moments ago he caught a ladybug; he blows at the red-and-black insect until the ladybug flies away. He doesn't want it to come along into the bus. When the door closes behind him he runs to the seat at the very back of the bus, hoping that he'll be able to hide. The bus lifts from the ground and soars above the fir wood; he glances out and sees a small house far below. In a hammock behind the house a woman is lying; she waves to him. He presses a hand against the window. When the bus stops it is dark outside, green neon light pulses in through the windows. He sees darkened houses on both sides, houses of stone. It has taken him to a city. The figure behind the wheel turns around towards the back seat and brings out a microphone. He can hear the figure start singing.

He knows the song.

He was still there when he woke up.

He lay in bed for a very long time, trying to decide how he felt. Sometimes he didn't know if he was still inside his dreams; sometimes that's what he believed, that he was still in another world. That he was someone else.

But not this time.

He raised his hands and pushed them through his brown, curly hair. Even his hair was still there.

That made him feel calm.

Two nights in a row he stayed in his room. He didn't open the window, didn't touch any of the pills on his table, fell asleep without pacing his surface. He didn't know what this meant. Perhaps he wouldn't have to go out any more? In that way? That would be a relief. He didn't like the fact that it had dragged on the way it had.

That wasn't how he had first meant it to be.

At first it had just been a woman. Anyone of the right age.

And just one.

But it wasn't enough. He had thought that one would be enough, a single one, to lower him into darkness once and for all.

It wasn't that simple.

The light caught up with him again.

Now he didn't know when it would stop. That worried him; he already felt a tinge of weariness. The first time there had been a streak of excitement. Not because of what he would do, or did, but because of the chance of reaching the darkness. The second time the excitement had gone, it was more like a preliminary to what he really wanted; to what enveloped him when he saw the white cotton thread grow still in the corners of their mouths and it was done with.

Then he wished for the darkness never to end.

But it did.

He went over and opened the window. It was still night outside and the window ledge was empty, no charred hands, no singing blackbird.

There was no reason to go outside.

He sat down by his wooden model and thought about people in other places. I'll never meet them, he thought. Sometimes he gave them names, taken from plants or animals. On his wall he drew kings with saucer heads and completely ordinary people with long, extended noses, noses like slim roots, three feet long. You could see that they were prying into things they shouldn't. It was dangerous. Already in the sandbox there were children prying, small, round children with noses already long. He learned to recognize their kind.

He went up to his long coat and pulled out a slim brown leather glove from one of its pockets. It had probably belonged to a woman. He had found it on his way to Ester. It happened fairly often that he found lost gloves on his nightly walks. If they were made of leather he brought them back with him and boiled them in a steel pot, for a long time, until they had shrunk. He hung them on a clothesline stretched across the kitchen. Almost a hundred shrunken gloves hung there now, fastened by small wooden clips. He viewed it as a row of pennants.

He let the glove fall into an empty pot.

In good time he would boil it.

45

He glanced at the door to his apartment. Sooner or later there would be a knock on it, he knew that, if he still remained in who he was. It was a wooden door and there was no doorbell; someone would knock on the timber. He tried to imagine the sound and the hand that made it. Whose hand was it? At best it would be himself knocking, at worst someone who wished him ill. Someone whose long nose had discovered him.

He wouldn't open at once. First he would remove the picture of the funnel from the wall and hide it under his pillow; then he would hold his hands under the freezing faucet water until they were numb.

There would be another knock.

Then he would say something through the door, explain that he couldn't open it since he had no hands. What would happen after that he didn't quite know; perhaps they would fetch someone who could pick the lock or perhaps they would just break down the door.

He would have to be prepared for the worst.

He went over and took his long coat from the hanger. Soon it would become light and he wasn't tired; soon the light would come. He felt that it came too fast. He had paced his room for many hours and still wasn't tired. He ought to be.

He ought to sleep.

He ought to be more careful.

He went out.

Gunvor Larsson was seventy-eight years old and lived alone. Her husband had died from an intracranial hemorrhage four years ago. She missed him, on one level, as a life partner should, but at the same time she was relieved. Their last years had been marked by the immense bitterness her husband felt about his life, a life he viewed as ruined by many different things. Those few times Gunvor had carefully tried to suggest that, after all, they had loved each other and stayed together for all of their lives, he had started to weep.

That was almost the worst of it.

But now he was gone and Gunvor was in good health, given her age. Her only problem appeared at night; she always woke up after only a couple of hours and found it difficult to relax again. She had tried almost everything, from medications with strange names to books on tape with just as strange tales. One of her grandchildren had tried to get her to start meditating and made her make up a mantra, a special word which after being repeated interminably would make her relax and be able to go back to sleep. She had chosen the word "ocean." On the first few nights she had mumbled "ocean" for ten or twenty minutes and then brewed a cup of tea to pass the time.

Tonight was the same again.

Shortly after two she woke and got out of bed, wrapped in her worn, pale blue dressing gown. She put some water for tea to boil and sat down by the kitchen table. During the last few nights she had taken out some of her old photo albums—she had quite a few—and looked through them, image by image, to pass the time. Pictures of children and grandchildren, of trips abroad and summer houses and pets and people whose names she had forgotten. Now she held the last of her albums on her knee, the one from last year. Another of her grandchildren had printed out a number of digital pictures on paper and gifted her the album.

She had reached a photo of her single great-grandchild when the doorbell rang.

"Tonight you will dance."

The phrase from the lovely song floated to the surface of his mind. "Tonight you will dance." People sang it on bright midsummer nights when he was tied inside the greenhouse. He heard them trying to sing in parts, heard their wobbly voices searching for each other. Everyone was in high spirits, many were children. Later they would come in to weep in front of him and feel bad. When they loosened the harness it was almost dawn; his mother had put sour milk out on the steps. He never knew if it was intended for him or for the hedgehog.

He had time to think all that before the door in front of him opened. An elderly woman peered at him through the crack.

"Yes?"

"Is it Gunvor?"

"Well? I don't want to buy anything."

"Neither do I."

He looked at the photo album on the kitchen table. It was spread open. He stretched his hands out and took it. The two open pages were crammed with pictures of children. He let his eyes move across the images until they stopped on a small boy down by the corner of the page. He looked at the boy for several minutes, his brown, curly hair, his tight mouth. Finally he held the album out to the woman bound opposite him and pointed at the little boy.

"Is that your grandchild?"

The woman's face was dark blue, her eyes wide, her head shaking violently. He couldn't make out if she said yes. He turned the album back towards him and opened the next spread. It too was full of pictures of children; children hugging adults and children holding flowers. All of them looked cheerful and happy; none of them were harnessed. His mouth narrowed to a bitter streak; he knew that in time those children would grow very long noses. He turned the pages back to the picture of the little boy down by the corner; that boy's eyes were searching for his, he thought, perhaps as if he wanted to appeal to him. He felt something wet rise under his eyelids.

Suddenly he shut the album and watched the woman in front of him. It seemed to take much too long. He was impatient. He wanted what he had come here to find. He was on the verge of rising before she had died but remained seated. Finally her body went limp. He watched her and waited for his reaction.

For the darkness.

It didn't come.

Nothing happened inside him.

He poked lightly at the white cotton thread at the corner of her mouth. It hung slack and immobile. Everything was as it should be, but even so it was all wrong.

He remained sitting in his chair for several minutes, close to despair.

He had a feeling.

Suddenly he rose and threw the photo album across the floor. His heart beat unnaturally hard.

He kicked his chair aside and rushed out from the kitchen.

In the stairwell he felt his throat constrict in a cramp.

He left the house without giving a thought to remaining unseen. It meant nothing any longer. He tore off his heavy coat and started to run. It was still dark and he chose the nearest way. He noticed that he met a few nightly walkers; a couple of cars had to swerve. He continued straight ahead. He knew what was happening and he wanted it to happen where there was no one else. He had to make it back to his crypt.

He began screaming long before he had reached the door to his building.

Now his heart had calmed down, the scream had gone silent, his body had slowed down. He stood leaning against one of the walls of his room. He knew it to be the calm before pain. He had experienced it before, how everything went still for a little while before it began in earnest.

As if there was compassion.

He looked around his room to remember it, the couch, the table, the wooden model; his eyes caught at the wooden door in the wall. Inside it was a wardrobe. He knew that there were clothes in the wardrobe that weren't his. He didn't know whose they were, but that didn't matter to him.

Particularly not now.

He started by taking the picture down from the wall, the one with the funnel and the melon. He folded it, carefully, and put it under his pillow.

If he returned he would know where to find it.

He went over and opened the window. The window ledge was empty. He brushed his hand over it. He would miss the charred hands, those that never touched him.

Suddenly he heard the singing, the blackbird, far away out in the darkness. He tried to see it without succeeding. He pursed his lips to whistle but refrained from doing it. He didn't want to disturb the past.

He stood at the window for a long time.

When he closed it he felt tiny, rolling movements across his cheeks. He went to the mirror, bent down and saw a face.

Is that how I look?

He regarded the face in the mirror. He recognized it. He recognized certain features, those particular cheekbones, those arched eyebrows, the mouth he had never seen before. He leaned against the mirror and let his mouth touch the mirror mouth. Then he brushed away the things trickling down his cheeks and felt that it was time.

He lay down on top of the bed.

His time had run out, for this turn, it was pointless to try to fight it.

The first few times he had done that, tried to remain in who he was.

It never worked. He screamed and cut his own body not to lose touch with it. In vain; whenever he began slipping in the wrong direction there was no return.

Nowadays he just slipped along.

He lay stretched out on his bed, his hands clutching the blanket tight; his whole body began shaking. He knew what would follow. He knew that there were a few seconds, sometimes ten or fifteen, when he was right in the middle of the interface, inside the zone, on his way from who he was to something he couldn't even imagine.

Or someone.

A few seconds that brought an unbearable physical pain.

The first time it happened he was unprepared. He slipped into the zone and didn't know what would come, not until he saw the executioner. A shadow with no face and with a long object in its hands. He stared at the shadow and never had time to react; the glowing scythe cut through the base of his skull, down through his body and through his groin.

There everything ended.

Now he was going there again, into the zone, slipping, just at the verge of letting go when he heard it.

Or them.

The knock, on his door.

The one he knew would come.

He stopped himself.

Would he walk to the door or slide away? If he slid away they would never find him as who he was now. What they would find he didn't know. Perhaps a dead blackbird on his pillow. Or two charred hands under his blanket. He ought to stand up.

He ought to rinse his hands in the freezing water and walk to the door.

But he didn't do what he ought to do.

When the knock sounded again he closed his eyes, hid his tongue at the back of his mouth cavity, let go and slipped away.

Into the zone.

Rolf Börjlind, born in 1943, and his wife, Cecilia Börjlind, born in 1961, cowrite film scripts and crime novels. On his own, Rolf Börjlind was Sweden's most notable satirist, famous for once having been sued by one of the country's prime ministers for a faked interview published in Aftonbladet, *Sweden's bestselling daily tabloid, where he also published other faked interviews with, among others, tennis player Björn Borg. The prime minister lost in court. Rolf Börjlind is also a poet, an actor, a film director, and the president of the Writers Guild of Sweden, the national organization for Swedish playwrights and screenwriters. In addition, he and his wife are Sweden's most experienced script writers, having written almost fifty full-length movie scripts, including twenty-six Martin Beck movies inspired by the Maj Sjöwall and Per Wahlöö novels, as well as several based on novels by Henning Mankell and Arne Dahl, and several original crime TV serials. Their first cowritten crime novel,* Springfloden (Spring Tide), *was published in 2012 and was one of that year's most impressive debuts. Their second,* Den tredje rösten (The Third Voice), *published in late 2013, is a novel perfectly utilizing and parodying the conventions of the Swedish crime genre.*

The Börjlinds live in Storängen, a neighborhood of single-family homes built at the beginning of the twentieth century and part of suburban Nacka, which is just north of Stockholm.

NEVER IN REAL LIFE

ÅKE EDWARDSON

Most of Åke Edwardson's books are novels in his popular and critically acclaimed series featuring Gothenburg Chief Inspector Erik Winter, very consciously conceived as a policeman different from those featured in other Swedish police novels. At the time when Åke Edwardson wrote his first Winter story, the typical Swedish fictional policeman was a combination of Martin Beck (in the novels by Maj Sjöwall and Per Wahlöö) and Kurt Wallander (in the novels by Henning Mankell): middle-aged, shabbily dressed, a bit overweight, depressed, with a difficult if any family life, and haunted by sleeplessness and a conviction that both life and society are going down the drain. In contrast, Erik Winter—in the early novels—is young, vital, optimistic, elegant, socially and romantically active, and optimistic.

Edwardson has also written several books outside of his Winter series. Apart from juvenile novels, his other work comprises a stand-alone crime novel, a psychological thriller, character studies set in the bleak landscapes of a depopulated Swedish countryside, and, not least, short stories.

Throughout his career, Åke Edwardson has been praised for his stylistic perfection as well as for his psychological insights and his strong sense of drama. This story is an excellent example of his low-key, powerful storytelling, where the reader is only gradually led into full understanding.

SHE LISTENED TO THE WEATHER FORECAST AND HE CONCENTRATED on driving. He was chasing the tracks of the sun. A brief flash was enough, or a shadow. He was prepared to turn any number of degrees. U-turns had become his specialty.

She read the map. She was actually good at it. They drove farther and farther away from civilization, but she never missed a turn.

"It's as if you grew up around here," he said.

She didn't reply, just kept her eyes on the map covering her knees.

"There's a tree-road junction in about half a mile," she said, raising her eyes.

"Uh-n."

"Go left there."

"Will that get us to the sun?" he said.

"It's supposed to be better in the western part of the county," she said. "The local station just said so."

"So a better chance to find the sun," he said.

He could see a crack opening in the slate-gray sky far to the northwest, as if someone had stuck an iron lever into the clouds.

Maybe it's God, he thought. Maybe we'll finally get some use out of him.

"There's the junction," she said.

When they drove through the town, the sky was incomprehensibly blue.

"So that's what it looks like when the sun is out," he said, pulling out his sunglasses. "Maybe there is a God after all."

"Do you believe he's thinking about us?" she said.

"Maybe he even *believes* in us," he said.

"That's verging on blasphemy," she said.

"I don't think he cares. He's got his hands full building up air pressure."

"How do you know it's a he?" she said quietly, but he heard.

"And don't talk too much about God to people around here," she added. "This is a religious community."

"Isn't that where you're supposed to talk about God?" he said.

"There are different ways of talking."

"Aren't you suddenly the expert. On both people and God."

He didn't reply.

"In any case, we'll stop here," he said. "When we've been chasing the sun this long we sure won't leave when we've found it."

He turned right in the center of town, at another tree-street junction. A small church stood on a hill. It was plastered white and a thousand years old. Most people around here belonged to some non-conformist religion, but even so they took good care of their ancient state churches. Though maybe that had nothing to do with religion.

A man in a peaked cap was mowing his way down the hill on a riding mower. The engine sound was soft, almost like the buzz of a bumblebee. The grass was thick and succulent; no sun had burned it. Perhaps they've waited for weeks to mow the grass here, he thought. A couple of days more and they would have had to use a scythe. Go get the guy with the scythe, he thought, smiling.

The man in the cap raised his eyes as the car passed, then looked back down, without any greeting.

"Maybe there's some small place where you can swim around here," she said.

"If there is, we'll make camp," he said.

They were alone by the lake. Or the pond, or whatever it was. The creek ran past here and the townspeople had dammed the stream, creating their own small lake. He saw the dike on the opposite side of it, only some three hundred feet away.

The swimming nook had a table with two benches and two changing rooms, one for men and one for women.

"I haven't seen any of those since I was a kid," he said, nodding at one of the two red sheds. He stood in the middle of the grass. The water glittered in the sunlight. Suddenly the air was very warm. It was like suddenly being in another country.

This is where I belong, he thought. I hope nobody else finds their way here.

Close to the swimming pond was the campground, or whatever it might be called. At any rate there was a small wooden bench for washing and doing dishes, with two water faucets, an outhouse built from the same kind of wood, room for car and tent. What more could anyone wish for?

She looked up from their luggage.

"We have to go shop somewhere. All that's left in the cooler is some bottled water."

"I know, I know," he replied. "But we'll put up the tent first."

The closest town was less than twelve miles away, if it could be called a town: a closed railway station, closed shops with empty display windows, an empty main street directly beneath the sun. *If a display window no longer displays anything you really can't call it a display window, can you?* he thought.

But there was a cooperative store and a state liquor store.

What more do you need on a vacation? he thought.

"I'll do the liquor store if you do the Co-op," he said.

"Can't we shop together?" she said. "We're not in any hurry."

He didn't answer.

"It's what you're supposed to do on vacations," she went on. "Take your time."

"Yeah, yeah," he said.

The inside of the store was cool, verging on chilly. As far as he could see they were alone in there, apart from the girl at the cash register whom he glimpsed at the far end. Not a single customer. He had seen nobody in the streets as they drove through the town. Perhaps everyone had escaped before the sun finally arrived. This district was more or less midway between the east and the west coasts of Sweden. In the end people had lost their patience and went off to chase the sun in the west or in the east. He had done the opposite and it had paid off. The sun was up there to stay. Once high pressure had settled over the interior of the country, nothing could budge it.

"The chops look great," she said.

In the endless dusk he enjoyed himself. The sun just didn't want to sink beyond the treetops, now that it was finally allowed to show itself. He had drunk a small glass of whiskey while preparing the marinade and the chops, then another small glass while he assembled the grill. Life was wonderful. Look at him: Dressed in only a pair of shorts in the eighty degrees heat of the evening, the wonderful scent of the forest and another wonderful scent from the water and a wonderful scent from the whiskey and soon a wonderful scent from the grill!

He lit the grill and sipped another small one.

"Are you sure you don't want one?" he asked and held up his glass. A sun ray hit the liquor and there was a flash of amber. A lovely color.

"No, the wine is enough for me," she said, nodding toward the bottle of wine that waited uncorked in the shade beyond the camping table where she was mixing a salad.

He had wanted to uncork two bottles directly, but she had felt that they could open them one at a time. And they both agreed not to buy box wine since they were on vacation, not even in this out-of-the-way spot. He had always thought that box wine lacked style. And you must always have style, no matter what. People who drank wine from a box might as well use a paper cup to drink it. And eat their food from paper plates with plastic cutlery. And generally go to hell, he thought, smiling, and emptied his glass. The whiskey was great. Everyone could go to hell. This is my vacation and my sun and my lake and my camping ground. At least there's something good about this fucking country. You can put your tent up wherever you like without some fucking farm yokel shooting your head off.

Maybe I ought to run up to the road crossing and take down the sign advertising the lake, he thought. This is our place. I do have my box spanner. Suddenly the idea struck him as brilliant, but he also realized that the whiskey was pushing it. Some damned hick might pass by on his hay cart and wonder what he was doing and that would be no good, just lose him a lot of time unnecessarily.

He held his hand over the grill to feel the heat.

"I'll put the chops on now," he said.

Later on he sat in what might be called darkness during some other season, but not now. The sun was just down, waiting beyond the horizon of firs. The water was still. He could see the outlines on the other side. It was like a jungle, a jungle three hundred feet away.

Suddenly he saw a light.

"What was that?"

He turned to her, pointing across the water's surface. She had said that she would go to bed, but she was still sitting there. Typical. Said one thing, did the opposite. He would have loved sitting here alone for one last hour. Enjoying the silence, the peace. Now it seemed as if she was watching him. Yes. Watching him. He had felt that continuously more often lately. As if she studied him.

But now she was staring across the lake, as if she was doing it just because he did.

There was the light again, like a flashlight.

It blinked. One-two-three short blinks.

"There it is again!"

"Where," she said.

"But don't you see it?"

"Was there something blinking?"

"You bet your ass there was!"

"Maybe I saw something," she said.

"Maybe? It was someone with a flashlight."

"But couldn't it be some reflection?"

"Reflection?" he said. "Where would that come from?"

She shrugged.

"The sun won't be up for a couple of hours." He tried to see something moving within the contours of jungle, but now everything was still. "There was someone over there."

"Maybe someone out for a walk."

"Mh-m."

"No, I'm off to bed now."

"You sure aren't worried," he said. "Back home you hardly dare sleep with the lights off."

"It's different here," she said.

In the morning all the vague contours were gone. Everything was sharp and brilliant under the sun. He went directly out into the water, amazed at how clear it was, and how cold. He threw himself forward and felt the cold envelop him and when he returned to the surface he had rid himself of his hangover even before he had noticed it.

This was vacation!

He saw her walk out of the tent, stretch, yawn, screw up her eyes and peer at the sun, peer at him.

"Aren't you going to jump in?" he said, splashing his hand down on the surface of the water.

"In a while," she said and walked off to the outhouse.

"Didn't they have a bakery in that hole-in-the-wall town?" he called to her.

She turned around.

"Yes, I think so."

"I'm fucking dying for some fresh rolls. And a Danish. I'll drive down and get us some for breakfast."

He began swimming towards shore.

"Are you sure you can drive, Bengt?"

"What do you mean?"

"The whiskey."

"Fuck, that was yesterday. And I'd bet a hundred thousand there isn't a cop within fifty miles."

"We don't have a hundred thousand," she said and turned her back again.

He turned left at the swim sign and left again at the three-way junction in town. The church plaster gleamed so brightly that his head started to ache despite his sunglasses.

Three hundred feet ahead of him a pickup was parked across the road.

A man in a baseball cap stood in front of the car. He raised a hand.

What the fuck.

He rolled down his window. The man leaned down.

"What's happening?"

"A large family of moose is crossing," the man replied.

He spoke in a vaguely recognizable dialect, an intonation he'd heard somewhere but couldn't place.

"I can't see any."

"It's a bit further on. We don't want people to get hurt."

"You're really on it."

"It's our job."

"I thought your job was to shoot the moose," he said and gave a short laugh.

"So it is," the man said, smiled and straightened. "But this time of year, it's all about the moose safaris."

"Yeah, sure, like on all those signs."

"Did you see them?"

"Hard to miss them."

He had seen the blue-and-white signs at two of the exits from the town: the words MOOSE SAFARI, a fat, pointing arrow and a picture of a moose.

"So have you ever seen a moose?" the man asked.

"Lots of times."

"Really?"

"In photos," he said, giving another short laugh. "But never in real life."

The man smiled again.

"Wouldn't be hard to fix."

"How do you mean?"

"We're going out tonight, at dusk. I can guarantee you'll see something you've never seen before." He smiled again. "In real life."

"Well, I don't know." He tried looking past the pickup, but saw no moose. If he had seen any, it would have been easier for him to decline this offer, or whatever it was.

"What are they really?" he asked. "These moose safaris?"

"We're a small group of people who know where the moose usually can be found in these woods. So we bring people out there and show them those places. It's as simple as that." The man bent down again. "And of course we bring some food along, and some beer and schnapps. We have a lean-to where we set up a barbeque late in the evening." The man smiled again under the beak of his cap. You couldn't make out his eyes. "Mostly we have a pretty nice time."

Lean-to, barbeque, woods. Wild animals. It really sounded like an adventure, a very modest one, but still. Beer and schnapps. His throat was already dry, as were his lips. He could see himself by the fire, a glass of colorless liquor in his hand. Guys all around. A world of men, damn it.

"We do a pentathlon, too. Most people like it a lot." The man smiled again. His teeth were dark. Perhaps just from the shade cast by his cap. "Usually it's pretty wild."

"What . . . what do you charge for it all?"

"Five hundred kronor. But as much meat you can eat and as much liquor as you can drink is included. Along with the moose."

"What time?"

"We set out at seven. We meet up on the church green," the man said, nodding in the direction he had come from. "Just before the intersection."

62

"Will there be a lot of people?"

"So far five, six if you join us. It's just enough—too many people worries the woods."

Worries the woods, he thought. Well put. As if the woods had a life of their own. Maybe they had. Perhaps the winking lights he had seen last night were the eyes of the forest.

"I'll be there," he said.

When he returned she was just getting out of the water.

"That felt good," she said.

"So I told you."

"Did you get the rolls?"

"You bet your ass!"

"So what's made you so happy all of a sudden?"

"Anything wrong with that?"

"No, no."

"How about being a tiny bit grateful that I drove off to get you fresh rolls, and Danish?"

"Well, it was your idea."

"So there's no reason for you to give a fuck, is that what you mean?"

"That's not what I said."

"Maybe I should just have stayed here instead?" He hefted the paper bag in his hand. It felt heavier now than when he had carried it out of the bakery. "Maybe we'd just as well not have these for breakfast?"

"Bengt, please don't be silly now."

"Silly? So now I'm silly?" He took a step towards her. "Are you calling me silly?"

He saw that she flinched. As if he was going to hit her. It had happened before, but he knew that she understood why he had to do it that time. Or those times. She had gone too far and he hadn't been able to stop his hand, or his arm. They'd talked about all that. She got it. But what he didn't get was that it seemed that she still didn't get it. She called him stupid. On their vacation. When he'd been shopping, really exerted himself. Just as he'd started to feel relaxed.

When he was going to see real, live moose. Would she call that silly too?

He hefted the paper bag in his hand. He threw it as far away as he could.

It was heavy enough to fly pretty far out over the lake.

He saw it float with the current.

He heard her give a sob but didn't turn. So it went when you didn't appreciate what someone did for you. If you didn't there would be no fresh-baked buns. There would be hell to pay instead.

She was silent at lunch and that was just as well. He only drank two beers with his food. Any other day he would have had a couple of schnapps as well, but it would be a long evening.

He had told her and she had nodded, almost as if she'd already known. At least that was the funny feeling he got. He had told her about the moose safari and she had nodded and looked away, at the lake and the opposite shore, towards the place where the lights had winked last night. As if someone was standing there. But it was just her way of taking in what he'd said. She knew that it wasn't her place to object. Christ, it was his vacation as well, wasn't it? Shouldn't he too be able to have some fun?

"Will you . . . spend the night?" she asked after a few moments.

"No, no. We'll break camp sometime after midnight."

He liked that expression. Break camp. There was something robust about it, between men. Breaking. Camp.

"Where is that . . . lean-to?"

"Out there," he said, pointing to the woods all around them. "That's all you need to know."

Again, she looked away.

He drank the last of his beer and stood up.

"Enough of this, I'll have a dip."

He went straight in and let his body sink through the water. It was much warmer now than it had been this morning. He took care not to swim out. He had heard somewhere that it could be dangerous to swim after eating; you could sink like a stone. He didn't want to become a stone. There were enough of them on the bottom of this lake, on the shore.

He saw her stand up and walk into their tent. After a minute or two she came back out and went off to the washing bench to get a plastic tub for the dirty dishes. If she had just taken it easy for a while he would have had a chance to offer to take care of the dishes. Now it was too late.

He lay on his back to float on the surface. It was easy, as if there was at least a little salt in the water. He smelled the fragrance of the forest and the beach and the water. This swimming spot was really something. The only strange thing was that they were the only people who'd come here. It was true that this was a deserted part of the country, but this was vacation time, and even the deserted places were filled with people from all over half of Europe. He had heard German spoken when he walked into the bakery. The Germans ought to have found their way here. The main road was a blacktop and the swim sign was easy to spot. There should have been more tents in the camping ground. Thankfully there weren't, but still. And some people from town ought to come here to swim. There must be kids on the farms. There were several farms nearby. And the fucking yokels themselves at least ought to come here to wash off the hay after a working day.

But nobody came.

Maybe it was too hot, he thought. Maybe the kids had all gone to some summer camp by the sea. But hardly. In any case it was more probable that a few kids from the city should have come here for the summer. Summer kids. A funny expression, as if those kids existed only during the summer, were kids only as long as the summer lasted.

She had been a summer kid. He couldn't remember when she had told him, or if somebody else had. Whoever that might have been. But surely she had spent a couple of summers in the country when she was a kid? Maybe somewhere similar to this, he thought. He couldn't remember where she had been. But she never became a farmer's wife. The only thing left since then was a strange remnant of some strange dialect, a single word or two now and then. Strange, like that baseball cap guy, the moose safari guy. Maybe all hicks sounded the same, maybe it was a universal thing.

He smiled, kept on floating.

At five to seven he parked his car below the church green. The sun was still very strong. He locked his car and walked up the hillside. At some point during the evening she would come here on foot to pick up the car. It wasn't more than two or three miles to the camping ground and the lake. She had suggested it herself. He'd like her to come up with more ideas as good.

The church looked almost fluorescent in the white sunlight. Everything here was white: the church façade, the grass and the graves against the light, the sky all above him. In an hour or so the blue evening light would lower from the sky. That was the best time of the day.

He stood in front of the iron gate. The graveyard inside was quite small, just some twenty graves bearing witness that few people lived here, or rather had lived here. Few had led their lives around here and so only few had died. He wondered briefly if he would be able to live here. The answer to that question was a simple no. Sure, it was okay when the sun was shining, but when it didn't? This was the uplands. In the middle of winter it must be around twenty below. Even the thought almost made him shiver. He looked at the graves again. Could he die here? Hardly. If you didn't live here you didn't die here, did you? He smiled. He heard the sound of a car motor behind him and turned. The pickup truck drove onto the gravel and the man with the baseball cap stuck his head out the driver's window.

"Jump in," he called.

He went down to the car and jumped in on the passenger seat.

"Where are the others?" he asked.

"Waiting out in the woods."

"I thought we were supposed to meet here."

"They were early. My partner drove them out."

He asked no more questions. They drove back the same way he had arrived. The wind blew warm through the open window. He saw grazing cows on the pasture to his right. Their udders were swollen. It would soon be milking time. The cowboys would come riding to drive the animals in. *Movin', movin', movin'.* Many years back he had watched some TV show, and the theme song had stuck. That show could have been set here. Nothing seemed to change here, except for the horses having been replaced by pickups. But there were still plenty of riding horses in the fields.

They drove past the turning to the lake. Or at least he thought they did.

There was no longer any sign there.

He turned back when they had passed.

Yes, no doubt it was their turning. He recognized a twinned spruce about a hundred feet down the road to the lake. He turned to the driver.

"The sign is gone."

The man in the baseball cap gave him a brief glance but didn't reply.

"The swim sign for the lake. I've put my tent up down there."

The man raised his glance to the rearview mirror.

"Sign?"

"Yeah, sign. Blue and white. An ordinary swim sign."

"Yeah. You're right," the driver said, his eyes still on the rearview mirror. "I think there used to be one of those."

"It's not there any longer."

"Well. Maybe they took it down to fix it or something."

"In the middle of vacations?"

"Well, how should I know?" The man threw him a brief glance. "Does it matter?"

"No, I guess it doesn't . . . I just think it's fucking strange."

The man gave no reply. He suddenly swung onto a forest road impossible to make out even a few seconds ago. There was no sign.

The road was no road, more like a broad track. Maybe a moose thoroughfare, he thought. Here they calmly walk along, without any apprehension, while the yokels sit waiting up in their moose towers, aiming their guns. He glanced at the driver. Better be careful.

He had a hick beside him. Wouldn't do any good if he suspected what he was thinking. He looked like a tough bastard.

They arrived at a three-way forest junction. The road split like a crooked poker and he suddenly remembered the late-night barbeque. The schnapps and the beer. He hadn't even had his afternoon whiskey and he was starting to feel it. His throat was dry. His tongue felt like something not quite belonging in his mouth. I'll never again waive my afternoon whiskey, he thought.

The pickup bumped up a slope. The forest thinned out and disappeared entirely at the top. The driver stopped and turned off the ignition.

"Here we are," he said and climbed out.

Up here it was like standing on the roof of the world, or at least of the county. You could see for miles. It was like the middle of an ocean, the tops of the spruce forming the horizon all around you. The sun had finally started to sink towards the western horizon. Your eyes could follow it all the way down until it turned yellow as a firebrand, then follow it as it rose again if you just stood there long enough.

But it was time to move.

"There are the others," said the man in the baseball cap.

A few people came strolling out of the edge of the forest below them. He counted four men. They were dressed in sturdy jeans and plaid shirts, rough boots and baseball caps, just like the man standing beside him. They all looked to be from around here. He himself didn't look like a local. He had a blue linen shirt tucked into a pair of chinos. And Top-Siders, by all means sturdy, but still. He didn't have a baseball cap.

The man in the baseball cap introduced him to the others, as if he were the only stranger. Perhaps he was, he thought. Perhaps five hundred kronor is a lot of money to these hicks, a hundred each. With that money they can drive down to the farmers' co-op and buy a few sacks of whatever the hell they need.

But nobody has asked me for any money yet, he thought.

"All right, let's take positions," the man with the baseball cap said. He thought of him as the man with the baseball cap even though they all had baseball caps. The expression was a bit strange: Let's take positions.

The man in the baseball cap walked ahead to a kind of watchtower that looked newly built. It almost seemed unnecessary to have such a thing up here, but perhaps it gave a still better view of the moose. Perhaps the idea was not to disturb them.

It was higher than it looked from the ground, but then that was always the case. He always got that feeling when he stood at the top of a diving platform, but it was a long time since he last stood at the top of a diving platform. Or any kind of tower. Suddenly he felt that it was a long time since he had done anything at all. Mostly he had existed, whatever that might be. He hadn't climbed any tower, as he did now. Nor lit any fires. He had drunk liquor, but then you could do that anywhere. He believed that he had lived in reality, but this was reality.

Up there he felt the wind.

He felt both large and small at the same time.

"Look down there," he heard one of the men say.

He looked.

Something moved below among the spruce. He could see the branches shake, rise, fall. He saw something brown, or black; it was difficult to see any colors now since the sun had begun sinking beneath the horizon and that meant that colors had begun sinking into the ground.

He saw the moose walk on to the three-way junction down there, or the three-track junction, and walk on east. The moose! His first moose! They looked like a family, even though from up here all the moose seemed to be about the same size. They appeared as if to order. For a moment he thought that they were trained to show themselves just when people had climbed the tower, but that was just too impossible to believe. Though you never knew. People in this backwoods might well communicate better with animals than with city dwellers like himself.

The moose walked on east, without hurrying. A couple of times they stopped to nibble the branches, as if to check on their freshness and taste. Their movements were jerky and a bit clumsy, but at the same time there was something magnificent about them. Kings of the forest, and queens. Suddenly he wished that his wife had been standing here beside him. He surprised himself with that thought. He thought that everything might have been different. They might have been a family, a real family.

Like the moose down there.

Now they were disappearing, walking back into the forest again. The moment was past. He had had his moment in reality and now it was gone, slowly walking east.

He looked around and saw that all the men were watching him. Watching his reactions. He was fairly certain of being the only one here paying, but that didn't matter. He had had his moment.

He had become someone else.

He wanted to tell her that, do it at once. But that wouldn't be possible. He wouldn't be able to find his way back, nor walk the whole way back, and the other men would have to give him his money's worth. To them it would be a matter of honor and if he demanded to be driven back already he would insult them.

The man in the baseball cap took the lead again and they climbed down the ladder.

Down there the man dragged a large wooden crate from under the tower and began taking something out. He couldn't see what it was since the man was standing with his back to him.

He moved closer and saw the silhouette targets the man had laid out on the ground, the hunting targets, the shooting targets. They depicted moose, close to life-size. The man in the baseball cap stood one of them up. It looked almost alive.

One of the other plaid shirts had walked back to the pickup truck and returned, arms full of rifles.

The man in the baseball cap shook the moose.

"Right, let's do some hunting."

"How . . . do you mean?" he asked.

"We put the targets up down at the edge of the woods," the man in the baseball cap replied, smiling. "Then we plug them!"

"I've . . . never shot," he said.

"High time, in that case."

70

The man in the baseball cap nodded to one of the plaid shirts, who handed him a gun. He supposed it was the kind called a moose-hunting rifle. He had heard that expression. He accepted the rifle, felt its weight. Suddenly he thought of the weight of the paper bag full of rolls and Danish he had thrown out over the lake. He regretted having done it. Suddenly he regretted that more than anything else he had ever done. Standing here, with the damned gun in his hand and the fucking hicks around him, it felt as if he had done something unforgivable in throwing the paper bag. He didn't know why he thought so at this particular moment, but it felt as if he had crossed a line in doing it. A final line. A final line in their relationship. He had crossed the final line.

A few times she had wanted to take another direction, away from him. Towards another line. But he hadn't allowed her to take even a single step. She had known what would happen if she tried to leave him.

"Let's put the targets up," said the man with the baseball cap.

He really didn't know what would happen if she tried to leave him. Perhaps she knew more than he did. Knew more about him. What he would do to her if she tried.

Christ, let me get away from here. I want to get away from here before it's too late. Soon it will be too late, he thought, wondering at the same time why he would think so.

He stood still while the men placed moose at different ranges down by the fucking edge of the woods. Some of them were visible and some weren't visible, as if he was supposed to just shoot into the forest. But he wouldn't shoot, for him the adventure was over. He wanted to get away from here, back to her. He was someone else now.

The men were standing around him, their guns in the crooks of their arms. They looked as if they'd been born with a gun in their arms. Which he supposed was more or less the case in regions like this.

They were looking at him as if they expected him to fire the first shot. Whoever fires the first shot, he thought, almost smirking. But nobody had even shown him what to do. They hadn't even given him any bullets, or whatever the fuck they were called.

"I think one of the targets has fallen down," the man in the baseball cap said, nodding at him. "Could you walk down and raise it back up?"

"I?" he replied.

The man in the baseball cap nodded again.

He carefully put his gun down on the ground, as if it had been loaded, and started walking down to the edge of the forest.

He couldn't see any moose-shaped target lying flat on the ground. If there had been one it was gone by now, just like the sign pointing to the lake.

"A bit to your left," he heard the voice of the man in the baseball cap somewhere behind. "On the other side of the juniper shrub." And suddenly he recognized the dialect.

It was the same melody she sometimes spoke in.

This was where she had been a summer child.

Right here.

She knew these men.

They had also been children here, though not just in the summers.

She had read the map.

It felt like a hundred summers since.

She had guided them here.

In real life, there was no camping ground.

Now he saw the target on the other side of the juniper. It was upright. The moose leered at him from the corner of its eye, or maybe it leered at something behind him. He turned. He saw the plaid shirts, the baseball caps, the boots. The guns. Now they were raised. They pointed at him. You're fucking supposed to aim at the moose, he thought before understanding. Truly understanding. He heard a sharp, metallic sound from the guns, a sound he couldn't identify. But he knew what it was. There are certain things you recognize the first time you encounter them, he thought.

Beyond the men the sky was flame colored. He saw the tower as a silhouette outlined by fire. He saw the figure standing at its top. He wanted to wave. He wanted to cry out. He wanted to explain all. He wanted to run up the ladder. He wanted to fly. The evening breeze suddenly took hold of her skirt and blew it out like a black banner.

Born in the small town of Eksjö in 1953, Åke Edwardson initially worked as a journalist, then as a teacher at the Gothenburg School of Journalism before publishing his first novel in 1995. That book, Till allt som varit dött (To All That Has Been Dead), *won the Best First Novel Award from the Swedish Crime Fiction Academy; it was also the first novel in his series about Chief Inspector Erik Winter, who has since appeared in eleven novels. For two of the later Winter novels,* Dans med en ängel (Death of Angels) *and* Himlen är en plats på jorden (Frozen Tracks), *Edwardson received the 1997 and 2001 Best Novel of the Year Awards from the Swedish Crime Fiction Academy. The Winter novels have been adapted for film in Sweden and are being published in numerous countries, including the United States.*

IN OUR DARKENED HOUSE

INGER FRIMANSSON

Inger Frimansson's novels have no recurring protagonists, although characters, places, and events in one book may appear or influence what happens in others. In that sense, she is gradually creating what she calls Frimanssonland—a fictitious world in which her characters interact and influence one another and events. Similarly, although many of her novels are viewed as psychological thrillers while others are primarily psychological portraits, the line dividing the two is fluid and uncertain—in all of her novels are streaks of inner darkness, of the damage we do to each other, and of its consequences for our lives.

Readers of this story should know that December 13 is Lucia Day and important to most Swedes, particularly children and teens. The tradition was initially a combination of ancient midwinter rituals and imports from Germany during the eighteenth century, but was in its modern form introduced in the late 1920s via newspaper contests for a town Lucia. The main event is a Lucia procession very early in the morning, consisting of a Lucia, dressed in white with a scarlet ribbon around her waist and with candles in her hair, and her followers—girls dressed in white, usually with tinsel in their hair and boys dressed variously as "star boys," in white with cone hats decorated with golden stars, as Santa's helpers, or

75

as gingerbread men; together they sing a few traditional songs and wish a Merry Christmas. Lucias are often elected by popular vote in towns, business offices, schools, day care centers, and other places where people gather; regional Lucias will visit hospitals, old people's homes, churches, shopping malls, and the hotel rooms of visiting Nobel laureates to sing and often serve coffee, mulled wine, gingerbread, and specially made saffron buns, also traditionally associated with Lucia mornings. In most homes, the children will do something similar.

The name Lucia, of course, is taken from the Sicilian Saint Lucia, killed in the early 300s. But there is nothing religious about the Swedish tradition, nor is December 13 a holiday. On the whole, the Lucia tradition is viewed as a pre-Christmas celebration and is beloved not least by teenagers, who take the opportunity to stay awake all night, drinking and celebrating, and ending their revelries by dressing up to wake their parents and teachers.

DOCTOR ROSBERG WAS AN OLD MAN, SO OLD THAT HE REALLY SHOULDN'T be practicing medicine any longer, Inga-Lisa had told her.

"But who cares," she had laughed, loudly enough for the makeup on her face almost to crack. "That's why I see him. He gives me anything I want to get, just a short lecture and then he pulls out his prescription book."

Inga-Lisa was her newest acquaintance. She had met her out in Hovsjö. A woman of around fifty, fresh and loud. But with a heart of gold. They had met coming home from the mall, same suburban bus, same apartment house entrance.

"What the hell, do you live here, too?"

She cussed constantly. And she knew people everywhere. Jannike did neither. One evening, while they were sitting in Inga-Lisa's cosy kitchen playing the two-player version of whist, she told her about Doctor Rosberg.

"I've seen him for years. He prescribes for me. Whatever I need. He knows I can hardly fucking sleep. It's my arthritis and my fibromyalgia. Stuff you get when you're an old hag. He's one of the few doctors who'll go to bat for a woman. Last time he gave me pills that would kill an ox . . . if you're not careful."

She kept thinking about that. Kill an ox. Nothing was clear to her as yet, no plans or anything of that kind. But perhaps that was how they began taking shape.

Now she was standing outside the door of his office and had to press the bell hard and long, so long that she was at the verge of giving up. But finally she heard stumping from inside and the door opened. A lined, wrinkled male face appeared.

"Miss Linder? Is it you?"

"Yes," she mumbled.

"Welcome, Miss Linder. Please step inside."

His hands were long and so thin that they looked as if the veins lay on top of his skin. She didn't like the idea of having to feel those hands on her body. But she would have to. She had to play along.

"How do you do," she said and put on an expression of suffering while she made her breaths heavier and strained.

"Please sit down and wait. I will call you in a moment." He made a gesture towards a group of chairs and disappeared down the hallway.

His office was part of a huge apartment in the Östermalm part of town. Heavy, plush furniture, stained cushions. Inga-Lisa had said that as far as she knew, he lived alone in the apartment. She had never heard of any Mrs. Rosberg, nor had she ever seen any nurse. On the couch was a small stuffed dog, its fur made from crocheted silk strings. Its nose was almost entirely worn away, only loose remnants of black, torn yarn. She imagined a child hugging it, holding it up to ward off the smell of ether and the metallic clattering and the tiny screams now and then penetrating from the examination room.

She put her fake fur coat on a hanger and unwound the long, striped scarf that had covered her head and warmed her ears. Cold had arrived already in late November along with several inches of snow that for once hadn't melted but remained as on a Christmas card. She supposed they were talking about that snow right now at work as they sat around the coffee table. The highlight of the day, when they were all gathered in the tiny canteen. Two candles would be lit, for next Sunday was the second in Advent. She supposed Sylvia as usual would have gotten hold of some bog moss for the Advent wreath and bought candles. She would have been down in the cellar to get all the electric candles and the red tablecloth with Santas that usually covered the table for all of December and part of January until someone, mostly Evy, brought it home and washed it. Surely they had also bought gingerbread biscuits and a saffron ring. She could still hear the crackle from the small sugar granules when you crushed them under your feet in the canteen. However carefully you tried to cut the saffron ring and put the pieces on plates, there were always crumbs on the floor. Sometimes someone put up an angry sign by the sink. YOUR MOM DOESN'T WORK HERE. CLEAN UP YOUR MESS! It usually helped for a while.

Jannike sank down in one of the armchairs and reached for a magazine. They were popular women's or family weeklies, *Allers* and *Husmodern*, but at least fifteen years old and thumbed to shreds. She looked at the photos of celebrities with outmoded clothes and hairstyles. Mullets and shoulder pads. It looked weird. After a short while she heard the door of the examination room open. The old man cleared his throat.

"Your turn, Miss Linder."

As if his waiting room had been full of patients!

He had slid down in the chair behind his gigantic, worn desk. Papers and documents piled high almost hid him from view. He had to lean forward to be able to look at her. To his left, on a smaller table, stood a skeleton made of plastic or bone. Its naked teeth grinned at her. She shook herself.

"Well, Miss Linder, so tell me why you're here."

"Well . . . a friend recommended you, Inga-Lisa." She was suddenly unable to remember Inga-Lisa's last name, and it disturbed her.

The man lifted a bunch of papers out of a suspension file lying on his table. She got a glimpse of notes written in a shaky, sprawling hand. She started to cry. She didn't know why, the tears just came, like a strong swell of despair. Embarrassed, she covered her mouth with her hand.

His eyes turned towards her. The skin beneath them was slack and baggy, as if his eyeballs might fall out at any moment. She fumbled for a handkerchief.

"I'm in such awful pain," she whispered.

He regarded her sadly.

"Where does it hurt?"

"Here and . . . here. All over."

"Hmm." Again he thumbed his papers. "Have you seen a doctor previously?"

"No-o."

"And why not?"

"I just thought . . . That it's part of it, sort of."

"Part of it?"

"Yes, my mother has it and my aunts and my grandmother as well. They've told me it's part of it, it's just something women get. Something with fibro . . . There's no point, they've told me, doctors just don't care. But then I met Inga-Lisa. We're neighbors. She told me about you, Dr. Rosberg, how kind and considerate you are. That you hate to see people suffer."

He put his papers down and looked out the window. His nostrils twitched slightly.

"I have to examine you, as I'm sure you understand."

"Of course."

"I can't just go writing prescriptions left and right without knowing what I'm doing."

"No, of course not."

"I'm an old man. I'll very soon close down my office."

"Oh," she mumbled. "I'm sorry to hear that."

He snapped his bony fingers.

"Yes. It's sad. But sooner or later everything in life comes to an end."

He asked her to undress down to her underwear and lie down on the examination table. The paper covering was wrinkled and torn.

80

She saw that it was the last piece of the roll. She was freezing, but she undressed as he had told her and lay down. He had turned his back to her while she got ready, stood fingering the skeleton. Tapped its arms, which rattled.

"Are you ready, Miss Linder?" he asked after a short while. She was lying on her back and felt goose pimples on her stomach.

"Yes."

"Then I'll be with you."

She turned her eyes up to the high ceiling. Far above a lamp dangled on its cord. She saw wafting thread and spiderwebs. The doctor was leaning over her. He had a stethoscope, pressed it hard to her chest and listened.

"Mm," he muttered. He touched her body with his cold, smooth hands, he pressed, squeezed, pinched. He was so close that she saw the coarse hairs growing from both his ears and his nostrils. He smelled vaguely of acetone. She felt a floating dizziness.

"Yes," he said. "Being in constant pain is no holiday. It can dull your entire existence."

She nodded slowly. Her tears began flowing again, down her cheeks and into her hairline. He patted her head. His sad cheeks were sagging.

"Just stay calm, now, please be calm. We'll fix this, don't you worry."

While she dressed he went back to his desk. She felt suddenly uncertain. What if he had seen through her.

But he hadn't.

"I'll give you a prescription for something called Dextromordiphene. But I must also inform you of the risks."

"So?"

"The truth is, this medication is really too strong to use as a first treatment. But you have a family history of the same illness, going back for generations as I understand it. And so I plan to give you a radical cure."

Jannike held her breath.

"However, I must ask you to be as careful and as circumspect as this medication warrants."

She didn't really understand what he was saying, but she nodded.

There was a watchfulness in his misty eyes as he handed her his prescription.

"Do you have a driver's license, Miss Linder?" he asked.

She shook her head.

"I ask because you are not to drive while taking this medication. Doing so is illegal."

"I understand."

He stared at her, seemed to look straight through her.

"And how about alcohol?"

"I'm sorry?"

"Imbibing even a mouthful of an alcoholic beverage when you have taken one of these pills can cause suspension of breathing. Or, in fact, not *can*, but *will*. Do you understand what I'm telling you, Miss Linder? I'm talking about an acute, life-threatening condition. At first the patient will notice nothing. But after around thirty minutes . . . And by then, it is often too late. It is almost as wily as the mushroom poisons. But faster. Much faster."

He fell silent and turned his gaze toward the window.

Jannike swallowed.

"I understand. I would never dream of . . . Well, I'm honestly not very fond of strong drink, you see."

His lips curled very slightly.

"Very sensible of you. And one thing further. Do you have any children, Miss Linder?"

"No," she whispered.

"Nor any you are in close contact with? The children of siblings, or of neighbors, for instance?"

"Why do you ask?" she managed.

"Lock away your medicine. Never let any child come near it. The fact is, it tastes far from unpleasant."

She took the commuter train to Södertälje. When Arthur left her she had also lost her home. Well, or his, if you had to pick nits. His condo in the Tantolunden area of Stockholm. A two-room apartment with a breathtaking view. He had more or less just thrown her out. Jannike had gone back to her mother and lived with her for a few days, but they had rubbed each other the wrong way. Her mother had managed to get her the secondhand lease on the single-bedroom apartment in Södertälje.

"How old are you now, Jannike? Thirty-six, isn't it? Won't you ever grow old enough to stand on your own two feet?"

Jannike knew that deep down her mother was relieved that she and Arthur had split up. He was a Muslim, and not only that; he was black as well. Her mother had never been comfortable with anything that was different.

She looked out on the snow-covered suburb and remembered the first time they had met, her mother and Arthur. The sudden aggressiveness. "Do you want to put a burka on her as well?" Arthur had remained silent; he was a quiet man. He carried most things within, but at the end he had been unable to take any more. He had put his coffee cup down on the table so hard that its little handle had broken. Grandma Betty's cups, the ones with the ivy. She had had to run downstairs after him, all the way out on the yard. Beg and beg.

"Don't be mad, she can be so clumsy sometimes, my mom. She didn't mean it."

Though deep down she knew that what she said wasn't true. Her mother had meant every word she'd said. And as far as she herself was concerned, she had no other alternative than to choose. Arthur or her mother.

She picked Arthur. He was kind to her and took care of her, comforted her when she was sad. He was good in bed as well. She had never been as satisfied with anyone else as she was with Arthur. And when she lost her job, or at least during the first period after it happened, he was there for her. Bought delicacies on his way home from work. Spoiled her. Got in touch with the union and asked them if Swedish law really allowed someone to sack a conscientious employee without any cause at all.

There were negotiations. And then of course the reasons why she had been laid off crept out. Fucking Gunhild and her lies. She and Arthur on one side of the table, Gunhild on the opposite and between them, at the short end, the trade union representative. Gun-hild the hag had taken off her ugly, old-fashioned glasses. Her hands shook, you couldn't miss it. You might wonder who actually had liquor problems.

"Your girlfriend has been intoxicated practically every day during the last several months. We have been patient with her, very patient. But . . . we simply can't take it any longer."

Jannike heard Arthur draw a breath.

"I'm sorry, but I don't believe you to be quite full of truth." He spoke Swedish well for being an immigrant, but sometimes he made mistakes. Right now she wished that he'd be silent and not meddle in this.

"Indeed? And what do her colleagues have to say about it?" The union representative was jiggling a bottle opener. He seemed tired and aloof.

Gunhild, the hag who had been her boss, opened her brief-case and pulled out a rolled paper.

"This," she said. Slowly, and without taking her eyes off Jannike, she slid the rubber band from the rolled paper. The paper was full of signatures. Ten of them. All of her fellow workers. Even Marja, whom she had liked so much. Who had been her confidante.

The train was entering the commuter station in Södertälje. Jannike stood up and stepped out. She rummaged in her knapsack and thought about the prescription she had had filled at the Scheele pharmacy, two boxes of fifty capsules each. Her chest grew hot and she felt her heart flutter. Everything would be fine. Soon there would be an end to her suffering.

Her apartment was on the ground floor and, because people could so easily look in her windows, she always had the curtains drawn. Sometimes kids were running about outside, banging her windows or sometimes throwing dirt and mud. Telling them off was pointless. The best you could do was to turn a blind eye to them. Four or five kids were standing outside the door to the building. They didn't move as she approached. One of them stuck his tongue out. She thought of the capsules, of their taste which was "far from

84

unpleasant." She pushed herself past the children and opened the door. She felt a little dizzy.

Inside her apartment, she had to lie down at once. Hear heart was thudding, sweat ran from her pores. She closed her eyes, moaning. After a while she got up and walked into the kitchen. Poured a glass of silver rum and emptied it. At last the world steadied around her. But the images returned, the images from the meeting with the trade union.

Sustained abuse of alcohol at her place of work. Nothing had helped. Neither reprimands, warnings or confidential discussions with her hag boss. Arthur grew more and more quiet as the meeting progressed. His silence spread like cold and it scared her. In the evening, when they had returned home, he had to go to work. He was a ticket salesman at the Old Town subway station, one of the hardest places to work on the line. That's where the skinheads hang out, on the helipad nearby. Sometimes they felt like fucking with someone. Despite his skin color his lips were pale when he turned to her.

"I want you out of here when I get back home."

"What? What do you mean?"

"Pack your things and get out!"

"But Arthur, you can't . . ."

He raised his hand and for a moment she thought he would strike her.

"You've lied to me. What you've done is worse than if you'd been unfaithful."

"It's all of them lying!" she cried. "That fucking hag Gunhild, she's made it all up, you have to believe me. I love you."

His face was tense and closed.

"And the name lust?" he said in a hard voice.

List, she thought, but it wasn't funny; sometimes she could joke with him and laugh when he said a word wrong. He had used to laugh too, and topple her onto the bed. "Just you wait and see what I'll give you for daring to tease me."

He looked like a stranger standing there in his subway uniform. She had thought it made him look sexy but now all of that was gone, only despair remained.

85

"She's written those names herself, she hates me. I'm a threat to her, I'm so much younger. She can't stand me."

He took his shoulder bag. His sketch pad stuck up out of it; when things were quiet he liked to draw.

"It's enough now, Jannike." The exact words the hag cunt had said to her, that last day at work. "You know what we've talked about before, you and I. And now it's enough."

Jannike had started laughing, a strange, gurgling sound.

"And just what do you mean by that?"

Red blotches had appeared on Gunhild's wrinkly chest. "Don't pretend to be stupid."

"I don't. I don't understand what you're talking about, you're imagining things. Making things up. You're a mythomaniac, that's what you are."

She was happy about that word; it had come to her at exactly the right moment.

"If you prefer I can get all the others in. Hold a staff meeting. But I suspect it wouldn't be very enjoyable for you."

She felt strong and indifferent. She cut her laugh off, as with a knife.

"Let me tell you something," she said, smacking her palms together. "Nothing at this place has been very enjoyable. Ever! And as I'm sure you know, it's always the boss who sets the mood."

Then she walked out.

The pharmacy bag was on the kitchen sink. Her dizziness had passed. She took out the two cardboard packs and looked at them. The angry red triangles that meant danger. Dextromordiphene. She pronounced the word aloud to herself, moving her lips very deliberately. Carefully she opened one of the packs and pulled out a blister strip, each cell containing a little pink, oval pill.

To be swallowed whole, she read.

She took down two tumblers. Her mother had given Jannike her old ones, the chipped ones. She had decided to throw them away but when Jannike moved out they came in handy. In one glass she poured hot water. In the other a little silver rum. While she fingered two of the pills out of their protective foil she felt her mouth go a bit dry, but nothing more. One pill in each glass, a spoon to stir. Wait for a little while, two minutes, ten.

Yes!

She shouted the word standing in her kitchen. YES! It worked. The pills were entirely dissolved, both in the water and in the rum. No trace of them left, nothing at all.

But of course, she thought. Of course they have to dissolve, how else could your body absorb them?

That night she slept well for the first time since moving to the apartment. She dreamt of flying, of Arthur and her sailing around above downtown Stockholm, dressed in white shifts. It was delightful.

A couple of days after he had thrown her out she had gone to the Old Town to look for him in the ticket booths. She couldn't find him. She asked a young guy in one of the booths.

"Excuse me, do you happen to know when Arthur's shift is supposed to start?"

He gave her a cold stare.

"Why don't you ask him yourself?"

She fell silent. Lost her words.

"You're holding up the line," he said. "Do you want a ticket or not?"

She felt like grabbing hold of his booth and toppling it. Could it be that Arthur had warned his coworkers about her? "If some skinny broad comes looking for me, don't speak to her."

Was that what had happened?

For a moment her anger turned towards Arthur, writhing within her, but then it stilled and again centered on her place of work. Gunhild and her former fellow workers. The list of names. Their hands holding pens, quick, flourishing movements. All of it on the sly, to push her away.

She hurt when she thought about it. And even Marja. Her name had been there, at the bottom of the list, as if she had hesitated until the very last moment but then finally had signed after all. Marja Hammendal. Marja, with whom she'd sometimes had gone to the movies. Marja, who had cried herself out at her place when she had quarreled with her husband.

Those times she had felt motherly. Sat there holding Marja's hand, pulling out tissue papers for her.

"It'll pass," she had comforted her. "You'll be friends again tonight."

Marja, who at last had started laughing. "You're so kind and wise, such a wonderful pal, what would I do without you?"

Even Marja.

She went four times to the Old Town subway station. Arthur was never there. He had been transferred. Systematically she began checking all the inner city stations. It was an unreliable method, since she didn't know his work schedule. But finally she succeeded. At the Rådmansgatan station and at two twenty-five in the afternoon. Coming down the stairs she already saw that it was him. She waited for a moment while the hallway emptied. Then she walked up to him and showed herself.

His beautiful, beautiful face, his mouth. Those eyes that had regarded her with so much love. Not now. No longer.

"Where do you want to go?"

As if he'd never before seen her.

"But Arthur, love . . . It's me."

They had all let her down. Deserted her. In a sudden jerk she lifted one of the two glasses and emptied it down the drain. Then the other. Ran the faucet at full.

At that moment the doorbell rang. At first she thought not to open. Then that crazy, wild thought that it might be Arthur.

It wasn't. It was Inga-Lisa. She had on a black turtleneck sweater that made her face seem older. Her eyelids shone, green metal. She looked like a snake or a lizard.

"Hi, honey. So you're back now."

Jannike stepped aside and let her in.

"I just wanted to hear how it went. Was the nice doctor real good to you?"

"Yes. He gave me the same as you, Dextromordiphene."

"Great. Then you'll soon feel better."

"Yes."

"How about coming along to my place for a cup of coffee? I was just going to make some."

Jannike accepted. Her friend's apartment looked as if a tornado had just passed. The place was full of boxes filled with Christmas decorations, candlesticks, Santas, ornaments made from straw and crackers. One box was overflowing with different-colored tinsel.

Jannike made place for herself at the very edge of the couch.

"What are you doing?" she asked.

"Just sorting some stuff. You end up with so much junk. I sure won't celebrate another *Fanny and Alexander* Christmas." She took a painted ceramic Santa with furiously red cheeks. Held it out to Jannike. "Ever seen an uglier thing?"

Jannike smiled uncertainly.

"Got it from my mother-in-law. A hundred and eighteen years ago. I've kept it all, can you imagine? But now it goes."

"What? Are you going to throw it away?"

"Well, I've always believed the kids might want it. But no fucking way. I never even hear from them any longer. Can hardly remember if I ever had any."

Jannike had heard it before. Inga-Lisa had two grown children, a son and a daughter. They didn't seem to put a high priority on keeping in touch with their mother.

Inga-Lisa pressed her lips together.

"The fuck with all that. I won't torture you with any more old nostalgia. I'll carry it all down to the garbage room. And then I'll be rid of it. Unless you happen to want it?"

Afterward she thought it had been part of the plan. As if some divine director sitting up among the clouds had pointed a knobby finger. Do this. Do that. While Inga-Lisa poured the coffee and chain-smoked cigarettes Jannike rummaged about in her boxes. She found several things that could be useful to her. Small things, which wouldn't be hard to carry. And best of all, a Lucia nightgown which fit her perfectly and a Lucia crown to go with it. Inga-Lisa was carried along by her enthusiasm and got her a new battery for the crown. She put it on Jannike's head and twisted one of the electric candles.

"Yes. It works."

"Can I still take it? Are you really sure?"

"Of course, honey. Everything you don't want is for the garbage bin."

She didn't ask what Jannike wanted the Lucia outfit for. She was great in that way, a true friend and comrade. As opposed to Marja and the others.

Early on Saint Lucia's Day she fixed the mulled wine. She warmed it in a pot she had borrowed from Inga-Lisa and poured it into a large thermos jug. She had borrowed that as well. It looked like one of the thermos jugs at work. Once she had jokingly painted eyes on it, making it look like a mad penguin. Of course Gunhild had failed to appreciate the humor. "We're having a board meeting, are you out of your mind?" As if the board members didn't need something to laugh about.

Over the weekend she had washed the Lucia gown and ironed it and the wide, red sash that went with it. The one said to symbolize the blood of the saint. She folded it neatly and put it in a paper shopping bag. In another she put her ten small Christmas presents. They were things Inga-Lisa had let her take from her boxes, nothing remarkable, but still. Santas, candlesticks, stars made from straw. She had taken great care and the presents had turned out beautifully, with ruffled strings and labels where she'd written the names of her ex-colleagues and the words *Merry Christmas* in her very best hand.

She put the thermos with the mulled wine upright into her knapsack and braced it with towels so it wouldn't fall over and start leaking.

Later, as she sat on the commuter train, it felt as if she was now one of them, one of all those going in to the city to work. Tired, pale faces, the aisles full of slush. The outside temperature this Lucia's Day morning was just around the freezing point and wet snow was falling. She took one of the free dailies and since she got on at the first station she got a seat. She leafed through the paper disinterestedly while some school teens with glitter in their hair were messing about, having celebrated all night. She smiled at them. As opposed to them, she was absolutely sober.

Thank heaven, the lock code remained the same. She took the elevator to the top floor of the building and continued up the half stair to the attic door. Up here, behind the elevator's control cubicle, she changed her clothes. She had been shivering from the cold while she walked from the train station. Now she no longer felt cold. She put her garments in one of the paper bags and pushed it close to the wall. Then she tied the red ribbon around her waist and put the crown of lights on her newly washed hair. In the glass pane of the elevator well she could see her own reflection. She twisted one of the candles and the crown lit up. So far everything had gone according to plan. She cleared her throat and sang softly.

Then in our darkened house,
Walking with gleaming lights . . .

After that, she glided slowly downstairs.

There was a wreath of boxwood on the door to her former place of employment. The smell of cat pee was persistent. It had been the same way all the previous years. That they never learned, that they didn't get lingonberry wreaths instead. They didn't smell at all.

It was a quarter to nine in the morning. Jannike steadied her grip on the thermos bottle and rung the bell.

Marja opened. Sudden worry flashed across her face.

"Who . . . oh! It's you!"

"Hush!" Jannike put a finger across her mouth. "I'll leave in a few minutes, I just wanted to . . ."

She held out her paper bag with the small presents.

"I wanted to ask all of you to forgive me," she mumbled and managed to make her voice sound just as thick and full of regret as she had planned. "I brought some mulled wine as well. Please, Marja, help me out."

Marja's bad conscience. It radiated from her. It came to her help. It was Marja who went out to the others and convinced them

91

all to come to the conference room. All of them were there, all ten of them; it hardly happened every day, but on just this day it did, everything went her way. It was also Marja who went to the canteen to get ten cups.

Jannike stood straight and calm. She paused for a moment on the threshold of the conference room, watched all of them sitting there, her former coworkers. Gunhild looking stiff and wary, Sylvia in a new hairdo. Evy, fatter than before, her breathing a dull rattle. Someone had lit the tea lights and the Advent candles. The room smelled of dust and old papers.

Jannike had intended to give a short speech, but it didn't work out that way. And perhaps that was just as well. Perhaps it was more striking this way. She passed from chair to chair pouring her mulled wine, without trembling or spilling a drop.

"Cheers, and Merry Christmas," she said and saw them lift their cups and drain them. They smacked their lips and smiled cautiously at her.

"And please forgive me for all the things I've done."

Marja said:

"But how about you, dear, aren't you going to have some mulled wine yourself?"

She looked Marja straight in the eye.

"No, you see, I've quit," she said softly.

Then she brought out her gifts, passed them out one by one.

"I wish you a wonderful Christmas," she said, leaving the office with the empty thermos cradled in her arms.

Born Inger Wilén in 1944, Inger Frimansson grew up in many different towns around Sweden. Though she started writing fiction in her teens— and at nineteen won a nationwide contest with her novella—she worked for many years as a journalist before finally publishing her first novel in 1984. For the next dozen years she wrote nongenre novels, though often incorporating strong thriller elements. Not until 1997 did she publish a clear-cut psychological thriller: Fruktar jag intet ont (I Shall Fear No

Evil). *Her second thriller,* Godnatt min älskade (Good Night, My Darling, *1998), won the Best Novel of the Year Award from the Swedish Crime Fiction Academy; in 2005, Frimansson again won that award for* Skuggan i vattnet (The Shadow in the Water). *Few dispute that Inger Frimansson is Sweden's finest writer of psychological thrillers in the noir tradition; her novels have been published in fifteen foreign countries, including the United States. In addition to her adult novels, she also writes for younger readers.*

PAUL'S LAST SUMMER

EVA GABRIELSSON

*To readers of crime, Eva Gabrielsson is known only as the life compan-
ion of Stieg Larsson, whom she met during an anti–Viet Nam War rally
in Umeå when they were both eighteen. They remained inseparable until
Larsson's death in 2004; in 2011, she published* There Are Things I
Want You to Know about Stieg Larsson and Me, *a book largely about
her struggle to live on after his death. But Eva Gabrielsson is a writer in
her own right. Just like Larsson, she was an active science fiction fan in
the 1970s, writing for fanzines and copublishing two. Later on, apart from
her writings on architecture, she translated Philip K. Dick's Hugo-winning
novel* The Man in the High Castle *into Swedish, wrote essays for feminist magazines, and published a book criticizing the treatment in Swedish
law of unmarried couples.*

*Eva Gabrielsson moved to Stockholm in 1977, where she stud-
ied architecture. She went on to work with computer-aided design at the
Ohlsson & Skarne building company; later still she was a secretary of the
governmental Building Cost Delegation, led a sustainable building project
in the county of Dalarna, and has developed manuals for the Build-Live-
Dialogue, a cooperative project to develop a sustainable Swedish living
style involving the national government, a number of local government*

areas, and a number of major corporations. One of her continuing projects is to write a book on the architect and city-planning head of Stockholm, Per Olof Hallman, who put his unique stamp on important parts of Stockholm as well as on numerous other Swedish cities and towns. Devotees of crime fiction may be interested in knowing that Eva Gabrielsson's research on Hallman influenced Stieg Larsson's Millennium novels—all the good guys in the books live in areas planned by Hallman.

Her contribution to this book is her first published work of fiction. It is a low-key story about a seemingly not very dramatic event. But it raises important issues, and asks us to examine both our conscience and the way we treat our fellow men.

PERHAPS THE UPWARD SLOPE TO THE CHURCHYARD WAS A LITTLE TOO steep after all. But Paul Bergström stubbornly set his jaw and continued walking, firmly if slowly and a bit unsteadily, supported by his cane. In honor of the day he wore his best tweed jacket and a trench coat bought in the 1970s, which he used in the summer.

"What your head lacks your legs better make up for, as they said when I was young. But now both my legs and my memory are going. Being eighty isn't easy. The down slope of life but still you have to go uphill, nothing fair about it," he grumbled to himself.

Finally he was on the graveled path winding among the graves, stepping carefully, his bouquet in a firm grip. "Now where is Emma's grave," he mumbled, trying to find the red granite stone somewhere among the linden trees. In the greenery, nothing seemed familiar. He stopped to get his wind and get a better look. The white stone church blinded him. "I'd really appreciate a tiny bit of revelation right now," he said hopefully.

Sitting in the cool church vestry, Louise Alm was considering her Sunday sermon. She lit a candle, wound her long hair around her

97

index finger, chewed her pencil, and finally began noting down random thoughts.

Her congregation was a mixture of young and old. Lately, they had begun worrying markedly more about the future. More of them had asked to see both her and the lay worker. It was a time of life crises for persons of all ages, and unfairly enough many of them seemed to land simultaneously on the same weary and insignificant person, as she saw herself. Louise felt insufficient. She was only forty, with much less life experience than many of the older members of her congregation. While the younger lived lives she was hardly able to comprehend, despite her two children. She was constantly uncertain about her own role. How was she supposed to be a shepherd to this flock of wildly careening individuals? Perhaps what she had felt to be her life's calling was hopelessly out of date in this era of egotism.

The candle suddenly fluttered as the doorway was blocked by an elderly man, clearly lost and with a bouquet of flowers in his hand. There were tears in his eyes.

"Can I help you in some way?" Louise asked, putting her pencil down.

He really looked desperate.

"Could you come?" he said. He held out a trembling hand, dropping his flowers.

"I'm sorry. My name is Paul Bergström."

"You are very welcome. I'm Louise Alm and I'm the vicar. We have met before, though perhaps you don't remember it right now." She stood, went up to him and shook his hand. Then she picked up his flowers.

Together they walked out in the churchyard and up to a small red granite marker with room for more names than the three already cut into it. Next to the red stone stood a smaller black one. They looked at them silently for a long while. Louise waited, uncomprehending, next to Paul. His breathing was rapid.

"I visit more graves than people nowadays," Paul said when at last he had regained some of his composure. "But even so I don't think anyone should have to visit his own grave while still alive."

"I'm sorry, I don't understand," Louise said.

"That black one," Paul said, pointing. "It has my name on it, though no dates."

"That can't be. How strange. Maybe it's been delivered here by mistake," Louise tried.

"Oh, no. I haven't even ordered it," Paul said.

Squaring his shoulders, he searchingly tapped his cane on the stone, as if to see if it was real. It remained, immobile, dark and frightening.

"And I'm not even supposed to rest here once the time comes," he went on. "I'm to be buried with Adele, my wife. And Emma is here, as she should be, with her husband and their daughter."

"But then why on earth is your stone here?" Louise said.

"I have no idea," Paul said, and started to cry again. "It frightened me."

"Please calm down, Paul. I'm sure there must be some reasonable explanation," Louise said. "Let me walk you home. Somehow I'll get to the bottom of this."

"Thank you," Paul said, wiping his nose. "That's very kind of you. Could you hand me Emma's flowers? After all, it's for her sake I went here."

Louise stopped to admire Paul's wooden house and its garden, full of apple trees.

"I built it myself, back in the nineteen fifties," Paul said. "Had to do it all on weekends and holidays, of course. Then I married Adele. But she died ten years ago."

"I remember you from Emma's funeral," Louise said. "That's when we met. And I knew she wasn't your wife."

"No, she never was. But we lived together for five years. Both her husband and her daughter died in a car accident eight years ago. Only her granddaughters are left now. Nice girls. You can see them in the photos on my living room bureau."

On the kitchen table was a pile of junk mail, a few magazines and a smaller pile of letters, some of them left unopened for more than a month, to judge from the postmarks. On the windowsill, a forlorn geranium wilted in abandonment. If anyone had had green thumbs, it must have been Emma. Louise pushed the piles of paper aside to make room for the coffee and cinnamon buns Paul began to set out. In the middle of it all the doorbell rang. Paul went off to the door and returned with more mail and a large parcel.

"That was Johan, the mailman. He usually checks to see if I'm in, so I won't have to walk out to the mailbox if I should get heavy or unwieldy things. It's hard to carry things nowadays, when I need my stick and often get a bit dizzy."

"What service," Louise said, while Paul sorted the new mail into the piles for junk, advertisements of interest, and letters. He put the parcel in a pile of its own. Most of his mail seemed to be bills.

While they had coffee, Paul praised his kind mailman. "Though one thing was a bit strange," he said. "Johan wondered about my lodger. But I've been alone here since Emma died."

"Yes, time must seem to run slow nowadays," Louise said. "How are you doing?"

"Well, when I don't speak to Emma's photo, I mostly talk to the birds in my garden. It does get a bit monotonous. Adele and I never had any children, you know. But of course I see my brother's children. And while Emma was still alive, her girls looked in on us fairly often."

"Maybe your mailman was suggesting that you should get a lodger, not saying that you already had one," Louise said.

"Oh, no. He said that someone is having his mail forwarded from my address."

"He couldn't be talking about Emma's mail?" Louise said.

"No. He didn't mean her. I asked him about that. But he couldn't remember the name," Paul said. "But I suppose they have too much going on at the post office nowadays to remember every small thing."

Louise suspected that Paul must have misunderstood what the mailman had said. Or misheard. Or simply was getting a bit senile. Which might explain the tombstone as well. But she felt that those things should wait until he seemed ready to talk about them. Meanwhile, they could always deal with his mail.

"Maybe we ought to open your letters?" she said, taking a bun.

"Yes, I suppose so," Paul said. "I simply haven't been able to do a lot of things since Emma passed. To think it's already been three months. Time flies, it really does."

There were a few bills that ought to have been paid weeks ago, solicitations from various charities, a few letters of condolence from Emma's relatives and a letter addressed to someone named Carl-Edvard Palm.

"Well, isn't that what I said," Paul said in a firm voice, putting the letter aside. "They have too much to do at the post office nowadays. No question about it. Carl-Edvard doesn't live here, now does he?"

"I seem to remember his name. Didn't he go to Emma's funeral as well?" Louise asked.

"Oh, yes, Emma was his mother-in-law. He used to be married to Emma's daughter, the one who died in a car accident. He lives in the house they had at the other end of town, but with his new wife. So the post office really has messed up," Paul said.

"Well, at least that's one mystery solved," Louise said.

Fortified by two cinnamon buns and very strong coffee with cream, Paul was clearly in better shape. He walked into his bedroom and returned with a binder full of receipts and account statements from his bank. To Louise's surprise, he said thoughtfully:

"Well, as you can see, there was no unopened bill for any tombstone. But I thought perhaps you might help me look through this binder as well, just to make sure that I haven't mixed anything up. Could you spare the time?"

"Of course," Louise said, impressed, and dismissed the idea that Paul might be senile. She began leafing through years of orderly bills and receipts.

After half an hour they were in complete agreement. There was no invoice for a tombstone, and the bank statements for the last seven months were in complete accordance with the bills accounted for in the binder. Nor were there any unexplained bank drafts or payments that could account for the 10,000 or so kronor such a stone would have cost.

"Well, that didn't make us any the wiser," Paul said.

"It really is very strange," Louise agreed.

"The stone wasn't there two weeks ago," Paul said. "So it must have been ordered fairly recently. But not by me, as I've said. And I certainly haven't paid for it either."

"No, I'm sure you haven't. I just don't quite know how to proceed with this," Louise said, "but if you want me to, I can easily find out which companies deliver tombstones to my church. Do you want me to give it a try?"

"God bless you," Paul said.

It was the first time Louise saw him smile.

Not until she got home that day did it strike her that the letter to Carl-Edvard Palm had been printed with the unmistakable logotype of the tax authority. And the tax authority, if anyone, should have the correct address of whomever they wanted to communicate with. After all, they were responsible for the national registration of citizens—if they had a wrong address for someone, that person might even get out of paying taxes. And the government certainly didn't allow that to happen. She suspected there was at least one more phone call for her to make.

Two days later, Louise returned to Paul. She stopped at his mailbox to pick up his mail before ringing his doorbell. Today it seemed his friendly mailman had been too rushed to bring Paul's mail to his door. Paul was in, waiting for her.

"Hello again," she said, "and here you are. Today's crop, but mostly advertising."

"Thank you," Paul said. "Come on in. I hope you have something to tell me."

Louise did. According to the tax authorities, Carl-Edvard Palm really was registered as a resident at Paul's address. The change had been made two months ago, and it was Carl-Edvard Palm himself who had requested it. At the same time, according to the mailman, whom Louise also had talked to, he had put in a request to the post office that all his mail should be forwarded from Paul's address to the house where he lived with his wife.

"Carl-Edvard never told me anything about this," Paul said.

"I can't understand it either," Louise said. "But the mailman has done nothing wrong, except delivering that letter from the tax people here instead of sending it on to Carl-Edvard's house."

"It's very strange. I suppose I ought to call him about it," Paul said.

"Wait a bit," Louise said. "I have more to tell you."

Paul suddenly looked frightened, and his eyes shifted warily. Louise suspected that the thought of the tombstone was haunting him.

"I'll fix some coffee," she said. "You just sit back and relax."

But Paul refused to be distracted. He sat rigidly and didn't move until Louise brought the coffee. Then he fetched a small bottle of schnapps from the corner cupboard, put a lump of sugar in his cup, added some schnapps and topped it with coffee.

"Today I need something stronger," he said. "It's all right now. Please go on." He lifted his cup and drank. "I'm sorry, I really am a bad host. Would you like some as well?"

"No thanks," Louise said. "I'm fine with just coffee." Though truth to tell, she, too, would have preferred something stronger. For what she knew filled her with uneasiness. She began talking. Since she was the vicar, the stonecutters had been very forthcoming.

"The fifth stonecutter I talked to delivered the stone with your name on it in early June. They remembered it well, since they'd thought it very peculiar not to put any dates on it."

"So I was right when I said I never ordered it, even if I've been a bit muddled," Paul said.

"Yes, you were right. It was ordered and paid for by a small company right here in town," Louise said, trying hard to sound calm.

"But what do I have to do with them?"

"Nothing at all, I gather," Louise said.

The stonecutters had sent her copies of all the paperwork. Everything seemed perfectly all right. Yet it was all wrong. She wondered how to tell Paul what she had found out.

"Actually," she said, "I think you should get someone to help you with this."

"Well, I suppose I could always ask one of my nephews," Paul said.

"Great. This sort of thing can be very demanding."

"Yes. But I'd really appreciate getting this thing fixed," Paul said.

While he went out in the hallway to make his phone call on the land-line telephone he kept in his old-fashioned way on a low teak bureau, Louise got out an envelope where she had put the photocopies of the invoice and the payment receipt she had received from the stonecutter, as well as the copy the tax authorities had given her of Carl-Edvard Palm's change of address. She quickly wrote a short explanatory note, adding her greetings and her phone numbers. The company that had ordered the tombstone was a real estate agent, and she had found out who owned it. But she preferred not to tell Paul. It was a matter for his nephews to take care of, not something to upset an already upset old man with.

"If you just give me his name and address, I can mail this to him," Louise said when Paul returned.

"Please. My nephew Gunnar will take care of it for me. He's always willing to help out when I need it," Paul said.

A few days later, Gunnar Bergström phoned Louise and asked her what really was going on. His uncle Paul hadn't been able to explain it very well.

"I'm afraid I probably can't explain it either," Louise said.

"Well, anyway, thanks for sending me those copies," Gunnar said. "It seemed pretty nasty. We've asked the stonecutters to remove the black stone. They'll pick it up today, and if there's any more trouble, they will have it out with Carl-Edvard Palm."

"Good. Nobody will miss it," Louise said. "Does Paul know that it was Palm who had it set up?"

"No, I just told him there had been some mistake," Gunnar said. "And I've called the tax people and told them that Palm doesn't live in Paul's house, or at his address. Now it's their job to sort it out.

I called Palm as well, but I couldn't get him to say anything sensible. He gave me some kind of tribute to Emma and Paul and their great love. When I asked him to explain in what way the tombstone and his address change were connected to the great affection for Paul he professed, he got abusive. But I don't want to talk about him. Mostly I wanted to thank you for caring about my uncle."

"It was no trouble at all. He is a good man. Let's keep in touch," Louise said.

Less than a month later, Louise had to prepare a funeral. In her world, life was in constant turmoil, beginning and ending without notice. Paul had passed away, and his nephews had asked her personally to officiate. When Gunnar Bergström called, she was in her vestry. He was cleaning out Paul's house.

"I know that my uncle came to care for you. If it feels right, you are very welcome to come by and pick out something to remember him by," Gunnar said.

"I'll be happy to. And we could talk about the ceremony without being disturbed," Louise said.

A little later, she sat with Gunnar in the by now familiar kitchen. Habit had made her check the mailbox on her way in, but this time it had been empty. On the other hand, the kitchen table was even more full of papers than usual, serving as storage for all the insurance policies, bills, subscriptions and private documents Gunnar had found in drawers and cupboards.

"It feels strange and a little solemn to be here without Uncle Paul," Gunnar said. "So today it seems right to use his best china, the set he only used on special occasions. He kept it in that showcase cupboard. Do you think you could get cups?"

"Of course," Louise said, pulling up a chair to stand on. "It's a little rickety," she added, balancing two cups and saucers in one hand and a carefully sealed envelope in the other. "This was wedged in next to the plates. I think you'd better take care of it. It says *Deed of gift* on the envelope."

"In that case I'm pretty sure I know what it is," Gunnar said. "Just put it with the other papers."

⋆　⋆　⋆

When they had finally sat down, begun sipping their coffee from the flowery, golden-handled cups and picking out the hymns to be sung at the funeral, someone opened the door to the house. Carl-Edvard Palm stepped in, camera in hand. He walked straight to the kitchen but stopped at the threshold.

"How do you do," he said, obviously surprised. "So you are here?"

"How do you do yourself," Gunnar said. "Yes, I'm here with the vicar to arrange some practical things after my uncle passed away."

"Hello. I'm Louise Alm," Louise said, holding out her hand.

"A pleasure," Carl-Edvard said, introducing himself. "Well. Yes, I suppose there is a lot of paperwork at times like these. Too bad about your uncle, of course. My sympathies."

He remained irresolutely in the doorway for a moment. Obviously the others intended to stay put for quite a while, he realized. Oh well, he could always return when they had left. Now he just had to make sure not to make a wrong step. But, of course, he had brought his camera.

"Right. Well, I'll just go about my business, I suppose," Carl-Edvard Palm said, and disappeared into the living room.

Louise and Gunnar exchanged a bewildered look. Soon they could hear the sounds of furniture being dragged around, interrupted by groaning and moaning.

"He's a real estate agent and seems to be taking pictures of the house," Gunnar said when they saw flashes of light reflected from the living room. "Maybe he intends to put it up for sale."

"I think it's a pity that none of you want to stay in this nice house."

"Oh, but my brother will move in as soon as the estate is divided up. He took care of keeping it up ever since Uncle Paul grew too old to do it himself," Gunnar said. "I really don't know what he is doing here."

Louise went along with him into the living room. Palm was

busy trying to find angles where the photos would show the antique charm of the house.

"Would you mind telling me what you are doing?" Gunnar asked.

"Oh. Yes. Well, I assumed that the house will be put up for sale," Palm said. "And I thought it best to be prepared. I mean, so you can get going at the right time of year, when buyers are eager to find something quickly. Next month prices usually fall, when everyone is away on vacation."

"Right. But our meeting with the lawyer about the inheritance is set for the week after next, so nothing has been decided yet," Gunnar said.

"Oh. Well, I was only trying to help you out. After all, we're almost family. Or were."

"I think you'd better leave now," Gunnar said.

"Well, I can always come back. By the way, who is handling the distribution of Paul's estate? Would that be you, Gunnar?"

"No. It's a lawyer my uncle picked himself," Gunnar said.

"Indeed. May I ask you which one?"

Gunnar told him, and asked him again to leave. Palm left, obviously disgruntled. Gunnar and Louise returned to the kitchen.

"Palm has always been high-handed rather than helpful," Gunnar said. "But taking that kind of liberty is more than I'd expected even from him." He opened the window, and the slight breeze blew the lace curtains and the scent of apple blossoms into the room. "Obviously he has gotten hold of Emma's keys to this place," Gunnar said after a moment. "I ought to get them back from him. Though God knows how many copies there may be."

"I could ask Him," Louise said. "But I don't think He'll tell me."

Gunnar laughed.

Louise left, feeling ill at ease despite the little creamer she had picked as a memento. The one she and Paul had used so often during their many talks at the kitchen table.

Gunnar stayed on to clean up and sort through his uncle's papers. Then he phoned a locksmith and took all the relevant documents along to the lawyer.

★ ★ ★

From his office, a week after Paul Bergström's funeral, Carl-Edvard Palm cheerfully phoned the lawyer who was handling the estate.

"Carl-Edvard Palm speaking. This concerns the estate of Paul Bergström. His nephew Gunnar has told me that you will hold a meeting to shift the inheritance in a few days."

"Yes, that's correct," the lawyer told him. "It's set for next Tuesday."

"Yes. But the thing is, I don't seem to have received a notice to attend," Palm went on.

"No, I'm sure that is also correct," the lawyer said in a neutral voice. "Since you aren't entitled to any share, you aren't notified. But we have notified your two daughters."

"What? What! There must be some mistake," Palm exclaimed. "Are you sure your papers are in order? Have you looked through his house? Really looked carefully?"

"Certainly," the lawyer said. "Everything is being done according to Mr. Bergström's will."

"Oh, no, I'm not buying that, I know there's something fishy going on," Palm told him angrily. "But you'll be hearing from me, be sure of that!"

"Thanks for calling," the lawyer said. But Palm had already hung up.

"The shit has hit the fan," he said aloud. "I'd better check up on it."

But at the front door of Paul's house, he discovered that his key no longer fit the lock.

The following week, Paul's two nephews and Emma's two granddaughters came to the lawyer's office to attend the shifting of the estate. After the meeting, Gunnar phoned Louise.

"I just wanted to tell you that I and my brother get the house, and that the girls get fifty thousand crowns each."

"Well, I suppose that was expected. So I hope everyone is satisfied," Louise said.

"Not quite everyone," Gunnar said. "There is a drama behind it. That envelope you happened to find turned out to contain another will none of us had ever heard about. In that one, our uncle left his house to Carl-Edvard Palm, and a hundred thousand to Palm's daughters. It seemed perfectly legal and was correctly witnessed. It was dated the week after Emma died."

"I understood that Paul was in a very bad way back then," Louise said. "He could hardly have been in a state to make any important decisions. Did he really understand what he was signing, that he was disinheriting both you and your brother?"

"No, not likely. But he often said that he wanted to give the girls some money. Though only money."

"I'm sure he did," Louise said. "But that thing about the house sounds suspicious."

"So it was. My brother and I went with Uncle Paul to show him that the black tombstone was really gone," Gunnar said. "And while we were talking he remembered that Palm had turned up with some papers to sign concerning gifts to Emma's granddaughters. We searched, but couldn't find anything. That made Uncle worried that his deed had been lost, so in the end I went with him to the bank where he wrote a new will and put it in his safe-deposit box. He never showed me what he wrote, and only his lawyer was authorized to open that box. I never saw his will until today, and I didn't know about that other one until you found it, even if I suspected something. But the fact is that Palm's attempt to swindle my uncle failed only by pure chance. Imagine that. Pure chance."

Gunnar and Louise fell silent. Neither of them felt like saying anything more.

Later that day, Louise stopped for a moment on the church stairs. In the dusk she saw that someone had put fresh roses on Paul's grave. It warmed her heart to know that others also remembered him. There was something deeply hopeful in all these small, visible proofs of concern for others. Louise walked down to the grave. There was a small, unsigned card tied to the bouquet. She read it.

From those who thought of Paul,
unlike his greedy relatives who sabotaged his last will.

Louise read the words over and over again. Unbelievable. Did that Realtor imagine that he could abuse the graveyard as his private battlefield? It could hardly be anyone else. She had had enough. She tore the card into pieces, walked away and stopped by the churchyard gates with her hand full of shredded paper. Her heart was pounding in anger. She threw the pieces of paper into the wastebasket at the bus stop before getting on the bus to go home. She was still upset when she reached her house and stood for a while outside her door.

This was far from over, she realized.

A sudden impulse made her go back to the church. She sifted through the wastebasket, retrieving the torn card. When she sat down in her vestry she felt lost. Why had she come back here?

She lit a candle to calm herself. The pieces of paper were spread on the table before her, almost illegible now after being smeared by ice-cream wrappers and the damp remains of some un-identified fruit. She looked at them for a long time. The dirt on them matched the dirty thought behind them.

She thought about the deadly sins, of all the holy scriptures that had warned generation upon generation of what unbridled passion could do to society and to men. That warning was always timely.

She nodded to herself. The flame fluttered in the draft from her hand when she took her pen to start writing her next sermon. She would talk about greed.

Carl-Edvard Palm was sitting on his porch, red both from sunburn and fury. His new wife was equally furious but less red. She used sun lotion. The only ones chirping with joy today had been his daughters.

"Do you know what the girls told me when we had lunch? The old bastard wrote another will just a couple of weeks after I had gone to all the trouble to help him out," he had told his wife.

"But how could he do something like that?" his wife said incredulously.

"That's what you get for trying to fix things for a senile old childless fart," he said.

"And you worked so hard," she said in an injured tone.

"I stood all the costs, I did all the work, and what did it get me?" Palm said. "Not a damned thing, that's what."

"It's really unfair," his wife said.

"I won't even get the fee for selling the house. It seems one of them actually means to live in it. Can you imagine? It's all come to nothing," he said bitterly.

But perhaps something could be salvaged, after all. He drove to his office, made a photocopy of the stonecutter's bill and payment receipt for the black tombstone and wrote out a bill. To the sum and his rate for helping out, he added the highest-allowed market interest. It came to quite a decent amount. On his way home, he mailed the bill to the estate of Paul Bergström.

Born in late 1953 in Lövånger, a town of then only a few hundred (now some 750) inhabitants on the far north coast of Sweden, Eva Gabrielsson studied at Umeå University, where she met her life-long companion, Stieg Larsson, in 1972. She later studied architecture at the Royal Institute of Technology in Stockholm, and has worked as an architect, project developer, and government expert on issues concerning sustainable building and maintenance. She lives in Stockholm.

THE RING

ANNA JANSSON

Anna Jansson was born and grew up in the important medieval trad-ing town of Visby, founded in the tenth century, on the island of Gotland, which lies in the Baltic east of both the Swedish mainland and the much smaller island of Öland. She began publishing crime novels in 2000, and in her first book introduced Maria Wern, a young police woman who has remained the protagonist in fourteen novels and a very few short stories, including this one.

In the first few novels, Wern works on the mainland but accepts extra assignments on Gotland during her summer vacations; by the time of the seventh novel, however, she has moved there permanently. In Anna Jansson's novels, considerable attention is given not only to the crimes com-mitted and the police investigations, but also to Maria Wern's problems as a committed professional trying to juggle her work, her two children, her romances, and private life into some semblance of functioning order.

In 2010, Anna Jansson also began writing a parallel series of crime novels for young adults, starring the eleven-year-old Emil Wern, Maria Wern's oldest child who, inspired by his mother and his reading, sets up a private detective agency.

Anna Jansson is one of Sweden's most popular crime writers. Her bestselling novels have also been filmed for both TV and cinema release, with Maria Wern portrayed by leading actress Eva Röse.

WHEN HE SAW THE BEER CAN TAB GLEAM UNDER THE THIN ICE COVERING the pool of water he understood that it was the Lord of the Rings. In the magical brightness of the streetlight the secret was revealed to him as it had been when Elrond ruled Rivendell and Gandalf was still called the Grey. Deep within his boy's heart he had anticipated that something like this would happen.

"Today, Tuesday, December the twelfth, Fredrik Bengtsson is chosen to be the Ring-bearer," he says out loud to himself. At the very edge of his consciousness he can hear the school bell giving its second call to class. The school yard is empty. The ring resting in its coffin of ice looks deviously inconspicuous, but nevertheless it will soon change the world.

Next to the bicycle stand there is a sharp stick. Fredrik is still in pain from the previous recess, when Torsten attacked his back with it and yelled "piss your pants" so the girls in his class could hear it. The wooden sword is the tool he needs. Liberator of the Ring. With a single stroke, the invaluable power is his. Fredrik takes the Ring in his hand and puts it on his finger in the name of Gandalf and the elves and the surly dwarves. It doesn't feel special, not to start with. But then, when he looks at Torsten's new, cool bike in the stand, with a hand brake, twenty gears and double shock absorbers, something happens within him. His teeth grow sharper and his eyes shrink to small, glowing fires. Rough, black hair slithers out of his hands and his nails grow into claws. The Ring-bearer does something Fredrik Bengtsson in class 1A would never dare. He steals a bike.

Downhill the bike is going much too quickly. The street is all ice. Streetlights pass by dangerously fast. Fredrik tries to brake by pedaling backwards, then in a panic tightens the hand brake and crashes. Thanks to his gloves he doesn't skin his hands on the asphalt, but he gets a tear on his knee. The bike's fender is dented and its enamel is scratched. If he hadn't worn the Ring he would surely have cried from fear and pain, but not now.

The Ring-bearer looks forward. The forest road calls to him. There is a whisper in the frosted crowns of the trees. A whisper of legends. He mounts his steel steed and enters the labyrinth of the black tree trunks. By the frozen flow of the creek is a village of small, gray cottages covered by turf roofs. At the far end, just where the pasture begins, there is a grassy hillock with a small door of decaying wood. That's how hobbit houses look. Now he has to be watchful. Fredrik crouches down behind the compost bin and pulls the bike down with him. There are black riders. You have to be careful. Just as Fredrik pulls off the Ring and puts it in his pocket he sees the door in the grassy hill open and a dark figure emerges and disappears towards the forest. He glimpses a face. Good or evil? Enemy or friend? He waits for an eternity of shivering seconds. The morning sun quietly filters down through the branches and eats the shadows. Supported by the bike he sneaks closer to look into the earth cellar. The door is slightly ajar. There is no trace of the roundness and friendliness characterizing hobbit homes. The walls are rough and the cold sticks to his body. Fredrik gropes farther in and his foot hits something on the floor. Something looking like a sack of potatoes, yet doesn't quite. He fumbles in his pocket for the cigarette lighter he took from his big brother's jacket earlier in the morning. With the slim flame in his hand he bends down, looking through the smoke of his breath straight into a pale, yellow face. Two eyes stare glassily at him. A mouth gapes with a toothless upper jaw. The dentures have fallen to expose much too pink gums. He stands mesmerized for a few

116

immobile seconds, then runs towards the light. Runs through the forest while his thoughts scatter like frightened birds.

"You're late again, Fredrik Bengtsson." His teacher has that peremptory wrinkle between her eyebrows. Everyone in class turns towards the door. Accusing eyes follow him to his desk.

"I've been to the boys' room."

"Piss your pants," Torsten hisses from his corner by the bookcase.

Detective Inspector Maria Wern watches as the slender woman's body is encased in a black plastic bag. The technician closes the zipper and rises clumsily, one hand to his back. Nobody has spoken in a long while. The silence of the forest makes it feel like a memorial grove. A place where mortality is natural, and yet isn't. The eye is offended by the brownish-red stain on the cement and by the child's bike dropped outside the door of the earth cellar.

"A woman wants to speak to you, Wern."

Police officer Ek points to a white Saab. The car has driven along the gravel road straight up to the cordoned-off area.

"Her name is Sara Skoglund. She says she spoke to you on the phone earlier today."

Maria takes a deep breath, tries to chase the images away and calm herself before entering the car with the upset old lady.

"Ellen Borg," Sara says, pointing to the cottage of the deceased, "and I live in the same apartment house. We always play bridge on Mondays. Last night she asked me if I could give her a ride to her cottage. She's gone here for the last few months. Every Monday after bridge. We agreed that I'd pick her up today, at two in the afternoon, but I was a little delayed. Ellen doesn't have a phone out here, so I couldn't call her."

"At what time would you say you got here?" Maria asked, taking out her notepad.

"Almost three, I think. The door was unlocked, so I went in. I called . . . but she didn't answer. Mostly she puts her key under the flowerpot on the stairs when she walks down to the village. But this time it was still in the lock. Then I saw that bike someone had left outside her potato cellar. I wondered about it and walked over there. And then . . ."

The woman's face crumples in emotion. Maria gives her time to recuperate before continuing her interrogation.

Night falls. Fredrik lies in bed, listening to the slowly ebbing sounds. The TV is turned off, but for a while yet he can hear the CD player in his older brother Leo's room. A horse voice penetrates the walls. The electric guitar claws at the wallpaper, scratchy, full of sadness, and beautiful. Leo is in love. Therefore he listens to uncompromisingly heavy bass rock ballads. Love hurts, he says, throwing himself down on his bed to stare at the ceiling, and Fredrik tries to understand what is hurting him so. Of course it would have been best if they could have been in love together, just as they both had chicken pox at the same time. He had felt snug listening to Leo reading *The Lord of the Rings*. Fredrik's room feels very lonely, especially when it's dark and Mom isn't at home. But Leo wants to be left alone in his agony. He showed that very clearly when he threw an empty Coke can at his baby brother's head just a short while ago. An Advent star lights up his window. It's at least a small comfort when so much is scary, and soon they'll celebrate Saint Lucia's Day in school. Fredrik has been given a verse he is supposed to know by heart. He practices until his head is spinning. In the whirlpool of sleep he lets go of reality. There are dachshunds under his bed, black slimy spirits of dead dachshunds. If Fredrik puts his legs over the edge of his bed they'll bite him and he'll be infected by death. That's why he's running through the forest without resting. They're snapping at his pant legs. He kicks out to get loose. Runs out into the cold, black water of the creek and jumps downstream on the ice floes. That's when he sees the face under the ice. Gray hair floating like a halo of dust and eyes staring at him from that yellow face, accusing and sly. Fredrik screams but the sound is stuck in his lungs, frozen. On the opposite bank, where his salvation is, he sees Torsten with his broken bike. His fear is greater than he can bear. Fredrik stops struggling, sinks, and is carried towards the dam by the icy creek water. He is so horribly cold that he wakes up. Then it all feels very lonely and wet.

"Leo! Wake up, Leo!" Fredrik shakes his older brother's shoulder.

"What is it?"

"The dachshunds have peed in my bed and I'm cold."

Maria Wern sits slumped in front of her office window, looking out at the falling snow without seeing it, lost in thought. What did Ellen Borg do in her cottage on Monday nights? The little house lacked every modern convenience. To get a cup of coffee you first had to break the ice, carry water and set a fire in the woodstove. The bedding was raw and damp and the floor cold as ice. Staying there in the summer might be charming, but in the middle of winter? Her musings are interrupted by Ek's voice on the intercom.

"You have a visitor."

A tall, thin man in a black overcoat tells her his name is Ludvig Borg. His thinning hair is parted in the middle and his eyes, peering behind wire-frame glasses, are very dark blue. Last night, Arvidsson and Ek had performed the difficult task of telling him that his mother was dead. Surprisingly, they had found Borg in his mother's apartment. He was passing through and had walked in using his own key.

Maria asks him to sit down and gets two cups of coffee. Ludvig declines milk and sugar. He wraps his thin hands around the cup for warmth. Despite his woolen coat he seems to be cold.

"She really was murdered?" is the first thing he says when at last he speaks.

"Yes. There is no doubt about it. Someone hit her from behind with a blunt object."

"A burglar?"

"Perhaps. Do you know of anything in her cabin that might attract a thief?"

"I can't believe there was anything. My mother wasn't well off. She had her pension. It doesn't come to very much when you've worked your whole life in a post office. She could hardly manage when they doubled the real-estate tax on her cottage a couple of years ago. She absolutely refused to sell the cottage. For a while she

119

even considered giving up her apartment to live there full time instead. I don't know how she managed to keep both."

"Yes, I remember. I read in the papers about the new estate evaluations. It seemed ill advised. Many elderly people had to sell. Do you know if there are any year-round residents left in the village, or are the houses only used in the summer nowadays?"

"Only well-to-do people can afford those houses now. The last resident to move out was the old grocer's wife. I don't think she sold her house, but now that she's living in an old people's home she rents it. I believe some nurse is living there in the summer. In the winter, there is nobody at all."

"I'll kill whoever broke my bike," Torsten says slowly and looks at the Lucia celebration boy attendees.

They're standing in the schoolyard in their long white shirts, holding their star-spangled paper cone hats in their hands to save them from being wafted off by the wind. Torsten stares them in the eye, one after the other, his own eyes half lidded, sucking his lower lip in to make a threatening face. Fredrik feels his stomach heaving, but tries not to listen. He wasn't able to eat any breakfast, just drank some water. There is a beast living in his stomach, and it refuses to eat human food.

"Whoever took my bike will get a hell of a beating from my dad. He won't be able to walk for a fortnight. They took my fingerprints!" Torsten says and holds out his thumb. "There's no escape!"

Here is their teacher with the school's Lucia, Ida, and her maids. It's time. The girls flutter in their long white robes. The tinsel coiled in their hair and tied around their waists gleams in the moonlight. With her wavy long hair Ida looks like an elven queen. Her hair must be very soft. Fredrik would like to touch that long, blonde hair, but he doesn't dare. In her crown of lingonberry sprigs, candles burn. Their teacher will sit at the front with a bucket of water. Last year the Lucia set fire to a curtain.

The assembly hall is full of parents and children. But Fredrik's mom can't come. She works nights again. Fredrik raises the stick with its paper star and sings though there is a big, nervous lump in his throat. Then there is silence. This is when he is supposed to recite. His teacher nods. The darkness in the hall is full of gleaming black eyes. Fredrik opens his mouth, but there are no words. Torsten jabs him with his star-boy stick and grins. His teacher tries mouthing something. Fredrik's whole body freezes up. He has to pee, he suddenly feels. The star on Torsten's stick is jabbing his armpit. There is not a sound in the hall and everyone hears the splashing which echoes from the hardwood parquet of the stage.

At dawn, Maria Wern is woken by a two-voiced Lucia song. Krister fumbles for his glasses, wraps the blanket around his naked body and opens the front door. Emil and Linda come padding out into the hallway and listen raptly to Krister's pupils, who stagger in more or less unsteadily after a night of revelry. Maria puts on coffee to serve them. Most of them look as if they need it after their sleepless night. One boy throws up on the stairs to the house, two of the girls fall asleep locked in the bathroom and a third suffers from frostbitten toes in her much too thin pumps.

"Is there really any point at all to teach class on December thirteenth?" Maria asks her husband in the kitchen once the Lucia train has left them to haunt other victims among their teachers.

"Someone has to look after them. Lots of things happen on Lucia nights that need daylight soul-searching and emotional processing. Conflicts become open, love turns sour, they have fights and get drunk. It's a busy day for teachers. As for cops, I suppose. I suspect you'll have your hands full today," Krister says and caresses her cheek.

"I wouldn't be surprised."

Maria helps her children dress while tidying the living room. She gathers a whole pile of forgotten items—a sweater, a CD, a bag of chips and a lot of tangerine peel. Emil is to be dressed as a gingerbread man and Linda will be a Lucia. At the day care center all the girls get to be Lucia. Linda's wire crown is a little too big. When she pushes it to the back of her head she looks more like a deer or an elk than a queen of light. Emil has a battery candle. When he puts it in his cheek it glows red through his skin. Linda tries to do the same with her crown, gets one of the candles down her throat and throws up on her white, newly ironed gown. Quickly and despite her loud objections she is turned into a Santa. Maria puts together the flower arrangement she is giving the day care staff, puts it on the washer, feeds the cats, and turns on the dishwasher, and they finally leave, still in darkness.

Detective Captain Hartman passes around the plate of saffron buns and gingerbread. It's been a reasonably calm night. No traffic accidents. A drunkard smoking in bed has been hospitalized with burns. Two teenagers are sobering up in the drunk tank. Their parents have been contacted. Bredström's jewelery has suffered a broken shop window, but nothing's been stolen. On the whole a calm Lucia night. Ek throws himself onto the staff room couch; the surge of the cushion almost makes Maria drop her coffee cup. He looks a bit hungover. No doubt the night has been personally rewarding.

"What did Ellen Borg's apartment look like?" Maria asks and puts down her coffee cup at a safe distance from Ek.

"Ordered and clean. A hell of a lot of knickknacks. A couch full of embroidered cushions, you know. She had a telescope mounted in her bedroom, pointed at the bedroom window of the apartment opposite hers. Want to bet if she knew everything there was to know about her neighbors? Then we found money. She had cash hidden away everywhere in her apartment, in the most unbelievable places. All in all, close to a hundred thousand."

"Her son says she was living at the edge of starvation. Are the forensics guys done out in Bäckalund?" Maria asks.

"Yes." Hartman holds the thermos in his hands. "Are you going back to her cottage?"

"Yes, right now."

The forest road is black and cheerless. Huge drifts of snow have fallen overnight, but here and there the branches of the trees have caught the snow and the ground is bare. The contrasts create a feeling of mystery. Maria steps out of her car and shades her eyes against the rising sun in the east. Why did Ellen Borg suddenly start going to her cottage on Monday nights, in the middle of October? Did she go here to see someone? According to Sara Skoglund, Ellen didn't have many friends, but this was where she was born and grew up. Perhaps there was someone here her friends in town didn't know about. She's a little odd, Sara had said. She doesn't get along at all with her daughter-in-law. Ludvig always comes to see her alone. How does it feel to leave an active life at the post office, where you know most things about most people, to become a pensioner? To sit in a one-room apartment with your newspaper and see very few people?

Maria is just about to step over the police tape when she catches a movement behind the curtains in the neighboring cottage. It's the one Ludvig pointed out, the one belonging to the grocer, a larger log cabin with a porch. A woman's bike is leaning against the gatepost. Maria walks over and knocks on the door. The ice crystals of the snow crust glitter in the sunlight. Snow crunches under her feet. The door is opened by an attractive blonde, at a guess just over twenty-five. She is enveloped by warmth. Maria hears crackling from the woodstove.

"Maria Wern. I'm with the police. Could I ask you some questions?"

"Lovisa Gren. I'm a school nurse." The woman's handshake is firm. "It's cold outside today. Please come in. I suppose it's about that awful thing that happened to Auntie Ellen."

"You're right."

Maria enters and brushes snow from her feet. They sit down by the kitchen table next to the woodstove. It's an unpainted gateleg table, adorned by a pewter tankard full of dried rowanberry twigs. On the wall above is a hanging edged in blue. The artfully embroidered letters reproduce an old proverb: A SMALL TUFT WILL OFTEN OVERTURN A BIG LOAD.

"When did you last see Mrs. Borg?"

Lovisa leans her chin on her hands, thinking.

"I honestly don't know. Probably sometime last summer. Yes, it must have been on Midsummer's Eve."

"When were you out here last?"

"At midsummer. Then I went abroad. Here it just rained all the time."

"Does anyone other than you ever come to this cottage?"

"No, I would hope not. I rent it all year."

Maria unbuttons her coat to let the heat reach her body. Her hands are red from the cold. It feels good to hold them out to the fire.

"How would you describe Ellen Borg? What kind of a person was she?" Maria asks.

"To me she mostly talked about illness. Sometimes I wished I had never told her I was a nurse."

"I can imagine. And now you've come to your cottage?"

"Yes. I read about the murder in the paper and wanted to make sure nobody had broken in."

"And all is as it should be?" Maria looks around with a friendly glance. Lets her glance take in the bedroom and the tousled bed.

"Yes. I slept here," Lovisa says apologetically. "And I haven't made up the bed yet."

"You're not easily scared. Have you ever met Mrs. Borg's son?"

"Ludvig. Yes, he was here last spring. He comes to plant potatoes for her. She hasn't been able to do it herself for a long time, but she did want fresh potatoes for midsummer."

"So what did you think about him?"

"I don't really know."

"You can tell me," Maria says. "I couldn't miss that undertone."

"I guess he's a bit of a show-off," Lovisa says with a laugh. "You know, always the shiniest car. Wants you to know he's done well. He is some kind of financial wizard."

Ellen Borg's little cabin is all tidiness and orderliness. The spice jars have handwritten labels and stand in perfect lines. The towels underneath the embroidered towel-rail cover have been ironed with perfect creases. The plastered brick hood above the fireplace is perfectly white, as if no fire had ever been set. Everything is in order, except for a single detail. There is a pair of binoculars on the kitchen table. The instrument lies at an angle to the tablecloth. Did the old woman spend her summer spying on her neighbors? Perhaps, but what could there have been to see in the middle of winter? Maria puts the binoculars to her eyes to check the definition. Through the kitchen window she can see clearly all the way to the main road. Not bad. Since Ellen Borg's cottage is the last one in the area, her kitchen window overlooks all the other houses. Maria walks through the cottage again, returns to the fireplace in the living room. Wouldn't she have used every source of warmth, given how cold it was outside? Maria gives in to a sudden impulse and puts her arm up inside the fireplace. Feels the bricks. One of them is loose and can be pulled out. She brings it along to the window. Underneath the brick, a black notebook is tied in place with string.

Fredrik hides his wet clothes under the bathtub, quietly so as not to wake his mother, who sleeps in the room next door. The blush of shame still burns his cheeks. Perhaps it's a burn he will have to carry all of his life. How will he ever be able to go back to school after this? Will they let you have home schooling if you've peed your pants? They ought to. There was a guy in third grade who had home schooling after breaking his leg. Peeing your pants is much worse. There is a great loneliness in that realization. Fredrik puts his hand in the pocket of his dry pants, feels the cold surface of the Ring against his fingertips. In a sense he is in an emergency. So he puts it on his finger. Evil doesn't overwhelm him all at once. He hardly even notices it creeping in as he thinks about what to do next. His thoughts veer off on a forbidden tangent, pull him in through the closed door of Leo's room. For a while he stands in the persistent deodorant smell, staring at the new poster that has appeared on the wall. A girl in string panties on a motorbike. Fredrik thinks it's a funny picture. She looks like a giant baby with a too-small diaper. She peers at him over her shoulder, her eyelids half shut and her lips open and pouting, as if someone has just grabbed her pacifier.

Leo's cell phone is on the aquarium. It has a tiger-striped shell. Fredrik takes it, weighs it in his hand and almost feels a little like a grown-up. Hello, this is Bengtsson speaking, Fredrik Bengtsson. In the contact list there are girls' names. Fredrik keeps punching and suddenly someone answers. It feels as in a horror movie. She can't see him. He is evil. Evil people pant in telephones to frighten girls. He's seen that on TV.

125

"Hello, is anyone there?" She actually sounds scared.

Fredrik pants heavily and shudders at his own awfulness. And there is a pleasure in frightening someone, a feeling of power. It makes you want more. When the first girl hangs up on him he goes on to the next and the next again until only his grandmother's number remains. Then he quits and puts the phone back on the aquarium without looking. Where he had thought would be glass is open water and the cell slowly spins down to the bottom like a hunting tiger shark. It looks cool. The doorbell rings.

Miss Viktorsson and Mom are in the kitchen and have closed the door. Fredrik looks at his watch. It's ten. Mom has slept for only two hours after her night shift. That's not good. He knows that from experience. She is speaking in her night voice, the soft, whispering voice they use at the hospital. His teacher, on the other hand, speaks loudly and clearly. She uses words like difficulties and concerned. Then she says ill and school nurse. Fredrik doesn't need to hear any more. What do you do at the school nurse's office? You have an injection or someone is counting your balls. Both are equally horrible. What if you did that to all the old men in parliament, had them line up alphabetically and . . . they'd be sure to write about that in the paper. Just as they did about murders. Fredrik doesn't want to think about the dead lady. Or about the bike. Or about who had come out of the earth cellar. The beast in his stomach moves again. It doesn't want to be disturbed by those kinds of thoughts. Sickness fills him so quickly that Fredrik can't get to the bathroom fast enough. He throws up on the blue hallway carpet. All that comes is some acid yellow water. Now the kitchen door is opening. He can't stay here. Quickly he grabs his jacket and steps into his boots.

"Fredrik. Freeeedrik!" His mother's voice echoes in the stairwell.

But he doesn't turn. His feet hardly even touch the asphalt while he flies away into the forest. Once he is hidden by its darkness he removes the Ring from his finger. It's cold. He didn't get his mittens, or his cap. It would have been simpler to walk on the forest road. But someone might find him there. It's better to move among the trees, where there are places to hide. His feet ache from cold in the thin rubber boots. Thin smoke is rising from one of the chimneys down in the old village, but he can't see anyone. A longing for warmth overpowers him. Fredrik runs down to the little cottage with the porch. The door is locked. But out here nobody is in the habit of locking for real; people just lock their doors to let visitors know if they're in or out. The key is under the juniper twigs on the stair. When he silently sneaks into the hallway, the heat envelops him. For a moment he stands immobile, his back to the wall, listening. Then he slides into the room. On a chair is a rolled-up sleeping bag. Fredrik takes it and makes himself a small nest on the floor under the bed.

Detective Captain Maria Wern pulls her long, blonde hair into a ponytail and climbs into the patrol car. Hartman is already seated behind the wheel.

"So how do we proceed from here?" he says, eyes in the rear mirror. The Bäckalund school shrinks as the car accelerates, then disappears behind trees.

"We'll take two of the absent pupils. The two Bengtsson brothers. One of them is in high school, the other in first grade. The older has a cold and is at home, the other one disappeared during the Lucia pageant. His teacher thinks he had something wrong with his stomach. Do you know the way to Lingonstigen?"

"Yes, I do. Anything else new?"

"I talked to the forensics guy this morning. He found surprisingly little. No fingerprints. No murder weapon. The ground outside the earth cellar was frozen, and it didn't start snowing until the afternoon on December twelfth. So the only footprints to be found are Sara Skoglund's, and they fit in with what she told us. Time of death has been fixed at just after eight in the morning."

"What about that notebook you found? Anything in it?"

"Numbers, just numbers. I suspect it might be time listings—dates, hours, minutes. None of the numbers are higher than fifty-nine. Then there are some kind of symbols. They look more or less like the ones used to indicate curses in Donald Duck comics, if you know what I mean."

"Do you think any of the numbers relate to December ninth?"

"I think so. We'll have a full analysis in an hour or so. But Hartman, there's one detail that doesn't fit. Maybe it means nothing, but I just can't let go of it. Let's go to Bäckalund."

The sound of Leo's voice wakes Fredrik. At first he believes he must be at home, in his own bed, but the smell is all wrong. He smells dampness, mice droppings and resin and something else, something cold and unknown. Before answering his brother he looks around. Sees two pair of feet, very close to each other.

"You can't phone me. I thought we agreed about that," the woman says peevishly, wagging her right foot.

"I haven't phoned!" Leo says in a surprised tone of voice.

"Really! Then who was panting on the line when the display showed your number?" she says angrily, her voice rising.

"I don't know. I forgot my cell at home this morning, so I haven't had it all day. I tinkered with my car down in the garage. Maybe Fredrik has sneaked into my room."

"Anyway we can't keep meeting like this. I hope you understand that," the woman's voice says.

"But I have to see you, Lovisa. I love you," Leo whimpers in a voice Fredrik has never heard before.

The smaller feet take a step back. The larger ones follow.

"You're just horny. It'll pass. Go now and forget about me."

"I can't!"

"You have to. A school nurse isn't allowed to have a relationship with a student."

"But you said you loved me," Leo says, hopelessly.

"Maybe I did, but it's over. And Ellen Borg saw us. She had a little black book where she wrote down every time we met here. She wanted money to keep quiet about it."

"But she's dead now."

"Right. And if you ever say a word about any of this to anyone, I'll tell them you did it. Tell them you killed her. In a very safe place I have a hammer with your fingerprints and Ellen's blood on it. Whenever I want to, I can plant it somewhere and tip off the police.

And do you really think anyone would believe anything you might say after that?"

"You can't. I never thought . . . How could it have my fingerprints?"

"You put them there when you helped me put up the hanging."

"But how could you just . . . kill her?"

"You have no idea what I can do."

The feet belonging to Leo move across the door. The house echoes from the sound of the door being slammed. Fredrik tries to be quiet but the sobs in his throat force themselves out. A hand grabs his hair and pulls him out on the floor while the sound of Leo's car dies away. She grabs him by the scruff of his neck as if he were a kitten. A stream of words pour out of the school nurse, but he can't make them out through the roar of the waterfall inside his head. Passively he goes along with her movements and lets himself be led down through the hatch in the floor into the damply cold cellar darkness. He hears her lock the hatch. There is only darkness. And cold. And silence.

Detective Captain Maria Wern knocks again at the door and waits. Behind her, Hartman steps back and slaps his arms against his sides for warmth. Smoke is rising from the chimney of the gray cottage with the porch.

"What do you want this time?" Lovisa says when she opens the door.

Her cheeks are very red.

"Is it a bad time?"

"No, it's all right."

Lovisa leads the way in. Her movements seem nervous and jerky to Maria. They sit down at the kitchen table. Lovisa bites her lower lip. Maria waits for a moment without speaking.

"So what is this about?" Lovisa says in a shrill voice.

"Did you pick these rowanberries yourself?"

"Yes, I did. What's that got to do with anything? What do you want?"

"You said before that you hadn't been here since midsummer. Was that true?"

Lovisa stares at the table, rubs her hands against her thighs. Then she meets Maria's gaze. "I may have been here once or twice in October. I'm not really sure."

Maria is silent. So is Hartman. Lovisa lowers her eyes.

"Was that all you wanted to ask?" she says with a strained smile.

"Yes, for now. We may be back again later."

Maria rises without haste. Glances out the window at the white-rimed trees. A half-eaten red apple is lying on the snow, abandoned by magpies. Long icicles hang from the edge of the roof. Then she turns to nod at Hartman, who follows her into the hallway. Lovisa remains sitting. Suddenly she gives a jerk. There is a scratching sound from below them. A weak, small voice is calling for mommy.

"If it's easier for you to tell me that way, you can put on your Ring and become invisible," Maria Wern says and turns on the recorder.

"But what if I slip away?"

"I trust you," Maria says, and her eyes are kind and very serious.

"I don't think I want it any longer," Fredrik says. "You can have it."

Anna Jansson is originally from Gotland, Sweden's largest island, situated off the east coast in the Baltic, close to sixty miles from the mainland. She was born in 1958 and initially trained and then worked for twenty years as a nurse. When her family bought its first computer in 1997, she began writing stories and finished two novels before finding a publisher for her third, Stum sitter guden (The God Sits Mute), *in 2000. That book introduced Detective Inspector Maria Wern with the Gotland police force, who has been the protagonist of all Anna Jansson's fourteen crime novels. Her 2006 Maria Wern novel,* Främmande fågel (Strange Bird), *was the Swedish nominee for the Glass Key Award given annually to the best crime novel published in the five Nordic countries. Beginning with that book, the Wern novels also began to be produced as TV miniseries. Jansson is one of Sweden's most popular crime authors; her novels have also appeared in translation throughout Europe. In addition to her adult writing, she also publishes books for young readers.*

THE MAIL RUN

Åsa Larsson

Åsa Larsson is one of Sweden's finest crime novelists. Her first novel, Sol-storm (Sun Storm), *won the Swedish Crime Fiction Academy Award for Best First Novel in 2003; she went on to win the Academy's Best Novel of the Year Award for her second novel in 2004 and for her fifth in 2012. Larsson's novels are contemporary and feature a recurring heroine, public prosecutor Rebecka Martinsson. But the following story is very different.*

"The Mail Run" is a historical story set in Kiruna, home of Åsa Larsson's paternal grandfather and where she herself lived from the age of four until leaving to attend college. Kiruna is a mining town at the extreme north of Sweden, built on a major iron ore deposit, which had been impossible to mine profitably before a railroad was finally built in 1891 and the newly formed Luossavaara-Kiirunavaara AB (LKAB) staked out large tracts in the area. The mining town, earlier called Luossavare and basically a haphazard collection of sheds, was renamed Kiruna in 1900, as a more modern town began to be built, financed, and run by the mining company. Larsson gives an insightful, humorous, and tragic image of this Swedish frontier outpost a century ago. A town of mainly railroad men and miners, with a mixed population of Samish, Finnish, and Swedish descent, was in the grip of fundamentalist religious groups, where the most important one

was the Laestadians, characterized by their severe lifestyle, ecstatic services, and extreme piety. This conservative Lutheran strain still exists in Sweden, Finland, and the United States, though it has long since broken up into several splinter groups.

Here, then, is a tale of what might be called the Swedish frontier a century ago, with sheriffs and gunmen, set not on the sunbaked western plains but in a company town built on a northern mountain, where the mean temperature throughout the year is around twenty-nine, where the sun for two months never rises above the horizon, and where snow covers the ground, often more than two feet deep, from October to early June.

BÄCKSTRÖM'S ASSISTANT NEVER QUITE BECAME HIMSELF AGAIN AFTER-wards. Before it happened he had been a cheerful type. One of those who sang while he worked. Throwing two-hundred-pound sacks on his back while winking at the girls and tucking snuff under his lip. He became more serious afterwards. Surly, even. Never joked with the girls at Hannula's general store when he came to pick up goods. Began to lose half his pay at cards. Bought liquor from the bootleg-gers at Malmberget and sold it to the miners, young boys with more money in their pockets than sense in their heads.

But about this thing that happened. It was December 14, 1912. Bäckström, the hauler, and his assistant were on their way to Gällivare. Their sled was full of grouse intended for the train to Stockholm. But the train didn't run between Kiruna and Gällivare due to the amount of snow on the tracks. The snowstorm had lasted for three days and was only now starting to abate. But the restaurant keepers in Stockholm didn't want to wait.

Bäckström delighted in the winter evening. Huge, soft stars of snow fell slowly from the heavens. Almost sleepily they came to rest one by one on top of the outer pelt of his wolf's- fur coat, gath-ered on top of his Russian fur cap like a white hillock.

The moon found a rift between the snow-filled clouds. It wasn't particularly cold out, though of course his assistant was freezing, dressed as he was in only rough homespun and knitted clothes. But the hauler's assistant wrapped the reindeer skin around himself and was soon shouting his love to the mare, who really was the best in the world. Lintu, which means *bird* in Finnish. And wasn't she just like a long-necked crane? So beautiful! Now and then he gave her an encouraging lash when she stepped off the wintry road and risked sinking into the deep drifts. The sled remained right-side up, but all the newly fallen snow made it hard going. The mare steamed from exertion, though her load was light.

Hauler Erik Bäckström let his eyes follow the falling snow upwards, to the sky. A faint smile played over his lips as he thought that perhaps God's angels were a bunch of women doing needlework. Not very different from his own dead mother and the women in his childhood village. Perhaps they were sitting there crocheting in God's old cabin, dressed in their long skirts, their long hair pinned up and covered in head cloths. They had certainly been busy at needlework while alive. No matter how many socks and sweaters, caps and mufflers they made, it was never enough. They had spun, knitted, woven and mended. But now, carefree in the hands of the Lord, they could knit snowflakes. With gnarled hands that had carried well water to the cows during painfully cold winter mornings and had rinsed washing in holes cut through the ice, they were knitting all these stars, absently letting them fall to the floor.

Which is no floor, the hauler thought philosophically, but the vault of sky above our heads.

"What are you smiling about, sir?" the assistant asked, panting.

He had jumped off the sled and was trudging through the snow beside the mare, who was the light and joy of his heart, to help her manage an uphill slope. In his pocket was a cube of sugar, which he gave her.

"Nothing, really," Bäckström replied, happy about the freedom you enjoyed in your own mind, after all. Even a workingman who was also a businessman like himself could think the most girlish thoughts without risk.

His assistant jumped back up on the sled. Brushed the snow from his pants. Wrapped his muffler around his head all the way up to his ears.

Aside from occasional snorts from their horse, the silence was as deep as it can only be in a wintry wood during snowfall. The runners slid soundlessly over the soft, new snow. Only just before meeting the other sled did they hear the horse bells.

Both Bäckström and his assistant immediately recognized the mail sled.

They called a loud greeting to the postman, whom they both knew very well indeed.

"Hello, Johansson!"

There was no answer. The postman, Elis Johansson, sat deeply hunched over in his sled and gave no reply no matter how loudly Bäckström and his assistant called.

The mail horse trotted on in the opposite direction and Bäckström and his assistant continued on towards Gällivare.

"Was he drunk?" the hauler's assistant asked, looking back over his shoulder. He could no longer see the mail sled, only the black silhouettes of trees in the weak moonlight that managed to escape between the snow-laden clouds.

"Nonsense," Bäckström replied angrily. Johansson, never. He was a deeply devout Laestadian and a teetotaler.

"Maybe he was deep in prayer," the assistant said mockingly.

Erik Bäckström did not reply. Shame over his recent fanciful speculations about God stopped him from defending Johansson the way he should. But he knew that Johansson was a hardworking and capable man. His faith was serious and grounded in scripture. He would never speculate freely about heaven the way Bäckström just had.

And Johansson kept his faith to himself. He never said a word if others had a drink, for instance. Many of his Laestadian brethren dared to do just that. They might be a guest in someone else's home, decline a swig but then glare indignantly at those who accepted the bottle. "That shot will soon feel lonely," they'd preach. "It wants company, so they get to be two. Then they start arguing and a third is sent down to intervene. And then it's boozing."

No, Johansson wasn't like that. He left others to their own. Bäckström felt an urge to smack his young assistant.

But the assistant soon got going again. Talked a blue streak about all the hypocrites and liars and drinkers among the Laestadians. Everyone knew it. There were those who went to prayers and asked forgiveness of God and their brothers just to keep sinning as usual come Monday. And really: What, if not strong drink, could make a man sleep so deeply while seated in a sled?

His harangue was interrupted when the horse suddenly stopped dead. She shied backwards a step. Her neck stretched and her eyes rolled back.

"Easy, girl," the assistant cooed.

"What's gotten into her now?" Bäckström wondered, swinging his whip.

The horse didn't move. Her nostrils widened. She snorted. Muscles hard as steel wire under her skin.

The hauler's assistant put a hand on Bäckström's arm to stop him from delivering yet another lash with the whip.

"Lintu is a good horse," he said softly. "Sir shouldn't whip her in anger. If she stops like that, there's a reason for it."

He was right. Erik Bäckström dropped the whip, fumbling for his rifle under the box. *Wolf pack* is what he was thinking now. Or a bear that had been wakened from its winter sleep.

He prepared himself for the mare suddenly kicking over her traces. Turning round to bolt. Maybe tipping the sled over. And if he fell out of the sled and was left alone with the wolves, he sure wanted his gun for company.

"Is there anything up there?" the hauler's assistant said, peering through the falling snow.

"What?" Bäckström said. He couldn't see a thing.

"It's a man! Wait a moment."

The assistant jumped out of the sled and ran on for a few paces. Now Bäckström too could see that there was something lying across the road.

The assistant ran, but then stopped himself and walked slowly the last few feet to the body lying across the middle of the road.

"Who is it?" Bäckström called.

The body was lying on its stomach, face down in the snow. The hauler's assistant bent down low and looked from the side.

"It's Oskar Lindmark," he called to Bäckström, who was now standing in the sled, peering up ahead. "And I think he's dead."

Oskar Lindmark was mailman Johansson's twelve-year-old errand boy.

"What do you mean?" Bäckström called back. "Has he fallen from the sled and broken his neck, or what?"

"No, I think . . ."

The handyman leaned down over the body and fell silent. Was it blood, all that black stuff? All colors disappeared in the faint, weak moonlight. Snowflakes fell in the dark puddle and dissolved.

"Hey, there," he said, putting his hand on Oskar Lindmark's back.

Then he resolutely turned the body. Pulled on an arm until Oskar Lindmark flopped over on his back. Still thinking that Oskar might not be dead. That he needed air.

Oskar's face was as white as the snow itself. Eyes open, mouth as well.

Is it blood? the hauler's assistant wondered, pulling his mitten off and touching the black on Oskar's forehead.

Yes. Maybe. It was wet. He looked at his fingertips. Rubbed his index and middle fingers against his thumb.

Suddenly Bäckström was standing beside him.

"Is he dead?" the assistant asked. "I think he is."

"Oh Lord," Bäckström said in a choked voice. "Of course he's dead. Can't you see that his skull is completely smashed in?"

And that's when the hauler's assistant saw. He stood up quickly. Backed away from the body.

Bäckström turned in the direction of Jukkasjärvi.

"Johansson," he called desperately into the forest.

The snow caught his voice. It carried nowhere. They could stand there yelling in the forest to their heart's content.

"Put the boy in the sled," he said to his assistant, who was shaking with terror, steadying himself against a birch tree so as not to fall down.

"I can't," the assistant trembled. "He's all covered in blood. I can't touch him."

"Get a grip on yourself, boy," Bäckström roared. "We have to turn the sled around and catch up with the mail run."

Then together they dragged the dead boy and laid him on top of the grouse. Bäckström thought that the blood would seep through the sacks and stain the white birds. Then he thought that the restaurant keepers down in Stockholm never needed to know what kind of blood it was.

In the Kiruna police station, county sheriff Björnfot and his acting parish constable Spett were sitting at opposite sides of a desk. Outside, snow was drifting down in the glow of the electric street lamps. The police station was equipped with a proper tile stove and Spett had been feeding it birch logs all day. On a rag carpet on the wooden floor, his dog Kajsa was chewing on an elk jawbone.

Sheriff Björnfot was writing up the day's events in his log. It didn't come to many lines. He was the older of the two men, had served for a number of years in Stockholm, where he had met his wife, and moved back to Kiruna with her and their two daughters only a year ago. He was a sensible man and didn't have anything particular against writing up records or taking down witness interrogations, tasks that had seldom been performed during the time when Spett alone had been in charge of the station.

Spett, who was unmarried, was darning a sock. On the tile stove damper, another pair of his socks had been hung to dry. Björnfot overlooked this. When he had taken up his duties in Kiruna, Spett and Kajsa had been living at the police station. In order to keep the peace he turned a blind eye to certain habits that remained from those days.

They were both broad-shouldered men of considerable strength. Spett was wiry, while Björnfot had an impressive stomach. "Diplomatic talents and physical strength" was what the mining company, which paid the salaries of the town police force, wanted in its servants of justice. The ability to break up troublemakers, in other words. Because there were a lot of those in town. Socialists and communists, agitators and trade union organizers. Not even the religious people could be trusted. Laestadians and Bible thumpers, always on the edge of ecstasy and senselessness. In Kautokeino, a group of newly converted Laestadians—in their eagerness to put an end to sin and liquor sales—had killed both the sheriff and the local shopkeeper, set fire to the vicarage and beaten the vicar and his wife. This happened before the sheriff was born, but even so, people were still talking about the Kautokeino uprising. And then there were all the young men, navvies and miners, just kids, really, migrating here from all over. Far from their fathers and mothers, they spent their wages on drink and behaved as could be expected.

But for the moment, the cell in the corner of the room was empty and Björnfot closed his log and thought of his wife, who was waiting for him at home.

Kajsa rose from the carpet and barked. A second later, there was a knock at the door and Erik Bäckström, the hauler, stepped in. He didn't even take the time to say hello.

"I've got postman Johansson and Oskar Lindmark in my sled," he said. "They're as dead as can be, both of them."

Parked in the courtyard were the mail sled and Bäckström's sled. Bäckström's assistant had draped blankets over the horses. Johansson lay in the mail sled and young Oskar Lindmark in Bäckström's sled.

Spett swept away a few curious passersby who had stopped at the opening to the courtyard.

"There's nothing to see here," he roared. "Keep moving, before I lose my temper!"

". . . so when we found Oskar Lindmark lying in the snow we realized that something must have happened to Johansson,"

Bäckström said. "We put Oskar on the sled and turned around and caught up with Johansson. His horse was just trotting along. Of course it knew the way from earlier trips. Good Lord, when we halted it and saw that Johansson was shot . . ."

He shook his head. Looked at his assistant who stood a few steps away, pale as paper and holding Lintu's reins. She exhaled calmingly on him, as if he were her half-grown colt. Don't be frightened, my boy.

"So we tied the mail horse to our sled," Bäckström finished. "And came here at once."

Sheriff Björnfot climbed up on the mail sled and took a good look at Johansson. Turned him over.

"Shot in the back," he said thoughtfully. "And you found him sitting up."

"Yes."

"And young Lindmark on the ground?"

"Yes. With his face in the snow."

Björnfot felt in Johansson's pockets. Looked around in the sled.

"Where is his pistol?" he asked. "I'm not saying he wasn't a peaceful man, but he must have been armed when he was traveling on duty."

Bäckström shrugged his shoulders.

"We didn't see any gun," he said.

"And the letter box is broken," sheriff Björnfot went on. "So it was a robbery. But it seems strange to think that someone would shoot him with his own gun."

He switched sleds and examined the wound on young Oskar Lindmark's head. He leaned down over the boy, holding his lantern very close to his face.

"It's snowing," he said. "Was it possible to see any tracks?"

"No," replied hauler Bäckström. "But of course it was dark. And we were upset."

"Come here and take a look," Björnfot said to Spett.

Spett came closer.

"Now this looks like frozen tears," Björnfot said, touching Oskar Lindmark's face with his finger. "And look at his muffler.

Given the light clothes he has on, he should have used it to cover his face."

"So?" Spett said.

"What I'm thinking," Björnfot said, "is this. Perhaps the killer shot Johansson, and the boy ran. Crying. And pulled his muffler away from his face to be able to breathe more freely while he ran."

"Maybe so," Spett said thoughtfully. "But why wasn't he shot as well?"

Björnfot pulled his hand over his face in a gesture that meant that he was thinking. His hand passed over his large mustache and down over his mouth. His fingers and his thumb followed the opposite sides of his jaw until they met at the tip of his chin.

"We have to talk to the postmaster," he said. "Ask what kind of mail they had to deliver. And then we have to tell Johansson's widow. And Oskar Lindmark's parents."

Spett regarded him silently. Kajsa also quit her sniffing around the runners of the sleds, sat down in the snow and gazed at him. Her tail struck a pleading rhythm against the ground. Björnfot knew what their looks meant. They didn't want to bring mournful tidings to crying widows. They wanted to follow the trail of blood.

"Yes, yes," Björnfot sighed, turned to Kajsa. "You talk to the postmaster, I'll talk to the families."

At that, Kajsa gave a happy bark. She rose on all four and ran to the archway. When she was out in the street, she turned and gave her master a summoning glance. Her pointed ears were turned forward.

Come on, she seemed to be saying. We have a job to do.

Hauler Bäckström had to smile despite the harrowing events of the evening.

"Look at that," he said to Spett. "Before you know it, she'll be ironing your shirts."

"She's too smart for that," Björnfot commented, watching his younger colleague disappear into the street, following his dog.

When Björnfot arrived home shortly after eleven that night, the lights had been turned off and the sheriff's house was dark. He found his wife sitting at the kitchen table.

"Hello," he said, carefully. "Are you sitting in the dark?"

He immediately felt stupid. Of course he could see that she was sitting in the dark. She often did. Said it saved them expensive kerosene. Now she slowly turned towards him. Smiled, but only as though her polite upbringing compelled her to.

Björnfot thought of Spett and Kajsa. How simple that bachelor life seemed. He lit the kerosene lamp hanging from the ceiling as well as the one on the table.

She didn't reply. Instead she asked:

"Would you like something to eat?"

She got out bread and something to put on his sandwiches. Set a fire in the stove as well. That disturbed him. It was as if she was telling him that there was no need for a fire just for her sake. He asked about the girls. She told him that they were asleep.

"What's that?" Björnfot asked, nodding to a parcel on the sideboard.

"Sheet music from my mother," she replied without looking at it.

"Aren't you going to open it?"

"I don't have anywhere to play," she said without emphasis. "I can't understand why she would send them to me. Will three sandwiches do?"

He nodded without finding anything to say. He wanted to remind her that she was welcome to use the piano at the community center whenever she felt like it. As well as the piano at the company school. But what good would it do? She had answers to everything and he was tired of hearing them. One of the pianos was too out of tune for her to stand it. The other was guarded jealously by the headmistress of the company school, who always found it convenient to appear just as Mrs. Björnfot sat down on the piano stool. And since it was the headmistress who played at commencements and gave lessons, her interest in the keyboard took precedence. Always.

"You could at least open it, take a look," he tried. "Wouldn't it be nice to see what it is? And I'm sure your mother has written you a letter."

"Open it if you want to," she said, still in the same light tone. Thin as autumn ice on cold, black water.

Björnfot looked at the parcel. Would it lie there all through Christmas, spreading malaise? He was seized by a longing to throw it in the fire.

Instead, he chewed his sandwiches dejectedly. His wife watched him with vacant eyes. Not in an unfriendly way, but he still felt that he was being punished. He just didn't know for what.

He thought of Elis Johansson's widow, whom he had visited. Her silent reaction when he had delivered the news of her husband's death. Six children in a two-room apartment. The ones old enough to understand had gathered around her. Stared at him, dressed in dark fabrics, as the Laestadians usually dressed themselves and their children. Eyes like deep wells when he told them. Mrs. Johansson had stood there before him, she also simply dressed in a long, gray skirt, a kerchief and a simple cardigan. Nothing ostentatious. No frills. Their home had also been simple, no curtains, no pictures on the walls. She hadn't cried. But he had seen her mouth and the wings of her nose widen in fear.

What will become of her now, he thought. Will she be able to support the children on her own? Will she have to give up some of them? Of course they wouldn't be able to stay on in the apartment, since it belonged to the Postal Administration. She had asked if he wanted some coffee, but he had declined. Her frightened eyes were more than he could stand. And the sobs of Oskar Lindmark's parents were still ringing in his ears.

He had longed for home, for Emilia and the girls.

Now he wished he had returned home earlier. So that the girls had been awake. They enlivened things.

Why can't you be happy? he wanted to ask.

The girls were healthy. They had food on the table. Dresses of bought fabrics. She had recently purchased new lace curtains. How could she feel that everything was so miserable all the same? When the Female Lecture Association had courted her and offered her membership, she had declined on some pretext he could no longer remember.

"I'm not the pioneering sort," she had said at some point.

You don't know what a pioneer settlement is, he had wanted to answer. In this mining town we have streetlights, shops. A public bath! But he had kept quiet. The words between them were growing more and more scarce.

After they had gone to bed, he lay awake for a long time. Stared up at the darkness under the roof and thought about Oskar Lindmark's crushed head. About postman Johansson's widow. He longed to touch his wife, but refrained for fear of being rejected.

"Are you aslcep?" he asked.

She didn't reply. But he could tell from her breathing that she was awake.

When he woke up it was still dark. It took him a while to realize what had awakened him. Someone was throwing snowballs at the window. The pocket watch on his nightstand showed a quarter past five.

Spett and Kajsa were waiting for him. They were accompanied by hauler Bäckström.

"Get dressed and come along," Spett called. "Bäckström has something to show us."

They walked together in the falling snow through the town. Kajsa was sometimes ahead of them, sometimes behind them. Plowing her pointed nose through the snow, which was light as down. Sometimes she snorted and took a small, joyful leap.

Björnfot felt frozen in spite of his winter uniform and coat. Even so, it wasn't as cold as it could be in December.

Lights were lit in many homes already. Women had risen to light fires. Now they were preparing breakfasts and lunch boxes for their husbands. After that, they had their own jobs to go to. The insides of the kitchen windows were fogged up.

When they arrived at Bäckström's property, the hauler led them into the carriage shed. They went up to one of the sleds inside.

"An hour ago, one of the mares arrived home alone dragging this sled. Someone had borrowed her without asking permission and then just left her somewhere. But she found her way home on her own. Stood outside the stable in the cold, waiting to be let in. And when I took a look at the sled . . ."

He finished his sentence by pointing at the floor of the sled.

An axe. Spett bent to pick it up. The blunt end of the axe blade was covered in blood and hair.

"Who is capable of doing something like that?" Bäckström wondered. "And besides, I also found these." He held out his hand, showing little red pieces of a broken seal.

"Is that a mail seal?" Spett asked.

"We'll bring them to the station to have a closer look," Björnfot said. "Did you speak to the postmaster?"

"Yes," Spett said. "He said that Johansson had a very valuable delivery in his sled. It was insured for twenty-four thousand kronor. Probably worth twice that. And he was armed. The postmaster was certain of that."

"Someone has driven this horse to the limit," Bäckström said. "Her back has been beaten and she had sweat so much that a sheet of ice covered her coat of hair. My assistant has rubbed her off and covered her in blankets. I'll be glad if she doesn't fall ill and die on me."

"Yes," Björnfot said, thoughtfully. "The horses have been through quite a lot since yesterday. I wish they could speak."

"That they can," hauler Bäckström said. "Though perhaps not of such things."

At that moment, the door to the carriage shed was opened and a boy poked his head in. He was around ten years old. Dressed in an oversized leather jacket. A running nose poked out of a knitted gray scarf. Clumps of snow hung like grapes from his knitted mittens.

"There you are, sir," he said to sheriff Björnfot and managed something that resembled a bow. "Your wife told me . . . I ran there first, then here . . . They've caught you a robber, Sheriff. They're waiting for you outside the police station."

In the street outside the police station, four men were waiting for sheriff Björnfot and acting parish constable Spett. They were all around twenty years of age. Three of them wore heavy clothes against the cold. One was dressed only in pants and shirtsleeves. Two of the heavily dressed men were holding the thinly dressed one. One of them was twisting his arm up behind his back. The other had pulled his mitten off and was holding the lightly dressed man's neck in a firm grip.

The last one, who had both hands free, called out in greeting as soon as he caught sight of Björnfot and Spett.

"And here comes the police authority. We've brought you a present."

The speaker was a big man, easily as large as the arriving servants of justice. He was blond. His eyes shone, blue as spring snow.

The man being held captive was delicate, almost spindly, with shoulders like a bottle. He had brown, greasy hair. His eyes were dark and full of terror—like swamp water in his pale, frozen face. His lip was swollen and split. One of his eyes was swollen shut and his nose was red and puffy. It seemed as if the man in his shirtsleeves had tried to stop his nose from bleeding, because the sleeve of his white shirtsleeve was stained red all the way up to his elbow.

"Here's your murderer," the big man said, shaking hands. "My name is Per-Anders Niemi. I work at the post office. The postmaster told me what happened last night. So all I had to do was to think it over a little. Who knew about the valuable delivery? And when Edvin Pekkari didn't show up to work on time this morning, I though . . . well, why not surprise him with a visit?"

"Are you Pekkari?" Björnfot asked the man being restrained by the others.

"Answer," the man holding the spindly one by the neck said and punched his temple with his free hand.

Pekkari didn't answer.

"That he is," Per-Anders Niemi said. "He works at the post office, too. As a mail carrier. As I said, he knew about the insured letter. And we found this at his place."

He hauled a pistol out of his pocket and handed it to Björnfot.

"It's Johansson's," he said. "I recognize it."

"But what about the money?" Björnfot asked.

146

"We didn't find it," Per-Anders Niemi said. "But then we didn't look all that carefully. We were more interested in turning him over to you."

"Did he resist?" Spett asked, scrutinizing Pekkari's battered face.

Per-Anders Niemi and his two friends smiled crookedly and shrugged their shoulders.

"We'll lock him up," Björnfot said. "After that, we'll search his place."

Pekkari gave him a frightened look.

"You can't lock me up," he croaked. "I'm innocent."

Per-Anders Niemi turned quickly and hit him in the stomach.

"Shut up," he screamed. "Goddamned killer bastard."

Pekkari sank to his knees in the snow.

"We can watch him for you," Per-Anders Niemi said to Björnfot.

"There won't be any watching," Spett said resolutely and snatched Pekkari as if he had been a sack of potatoes.

He walked into the police station, holding Pekkari by the scruff of his neck. Kajsa stood guard outside. After a while he came back out. Locked the door from the outside and demonstratively put the key in his pocket.

"He should be hung right now," Per-Anders Niemi growled.

"If anyone as much as touches the door while we're gone . . ." Spett warned.

"All right, boys," sheriff Björnfot said diplomatically, "now I'd like to take a good look at Pekkari's place. Not waste my time imposing fines on such splendid specimens of our citizenry as yourselves just for disobedience to the police. So if you'd be so kind . . ."

He finished his sentence by making a considerate gesture asking them to leave.

The men muttered a moderately insolent goodnight and slunk away.

Edvin Pekkari's apartment was on the second floor of a wooden house on Järnvägsgatan. A stuffy smell of boiled reindeer meat, old smoke and wet wool greeted sheriff Björnfot and acting parish constable Spett when they entered the house.

"Here it is," the landlady said, opening the door to a tiny room just under the sloping roof. She looked askance at Kajsa, but said nothing.

"Who does he share with?" Björnfot asked.

"He doesn't share," the landlady said. "Asked special when he moved in back in October. And since the windowpane is broken and the window is boarded up, he got it cheap. No, he doesn't know anyone and lives all lonesome. Is it true he killed Johansson and his waggoner lad? You'd never have believed it. He never made a fuss about anything. Paid his rent on time."

A bed, a chest of drawers, a small chair and a shaving mirror. Nothing more would fit in the room. It was quick work to search it. Björnfot went through the chest, pulling out all the drawers. Checked the coat hanging on a hook in the wall, felt its pockets. Spett kicked aside the rag carpets on the floor to check for a loose floorboard where you might hide a wad of bills. They found nothing.

"Hang it all," Spett said as they went back into the hallway.

"Are you done?" the landlady asked. "You can tell him from me that I'll be renting the room at once."

"What's up there?" Björnfot asked, pointing at a hatch in the ceiling.

"Nothing," the landlady said. "Just an attic."

"That we want to see," Björnfot said.

Spett got the chair from Pekkari's room, put it under the hatch and opened it. He folded down the ladder made fast to the hatch. They asked the landlady to bring something to light their way and she returned with a simple flashlight. Björnfot climbed the ladder, lamp in one hand.

When he had climbed a ways up the ladder and placed the flashlight on the attic floor, something suddenly rustled up there.

A rat ran across his hand on the edge of the hatch and he heard numerous others start running back and forth. Their shrill squeaks cut through the dark. He quickly backed down the ladder.

"Rats!" he exclaimed. "Nasty devilry!"

The landlady smiled, amused. Afraid of rats. Such a big man.

"Move over, Sheriff, and we'll let Kajsa up," Spett said.

Spett lifted the bitch and carried her up the ladder under his arm. Set her down in the dark. He stayed on the ladder, holding the lamp.

Suddenly the hunt was on in the attic. They could hear rats scurrying across the floor. As well as Kajsa's heavier but rapid steps. Then a mortal scream as she bit the back of one of the rats. After that silence, broken only by the crunching and slurping from Kajsa, eating her prey. The other rats had escaped and wouldn't dare show their ugly noses for quite a while.

The servants of the law climbed up into the attic. Kajsa swaggered about on the double flooring, fawning and swaying to the praise of her masters.

"You're really something, girl," Spett said proudly, but he wouldn't let her lick his mouth. It had been a rat, after all.

And Björnfot said that he was going to order a uniform for her the next morning.

They searched the attic. And this time they didn't have to search in vain.

"It's time to confess!"

Sheriff Björnfot was standing outside the cell in the police station, talking to Edvin Pekkari. In his hand he held a cotton bag, adorned by the Postal Service emblem.

"We found this in the attic above your room," he went on. "There is five thousand kronor in it. Can you explain how it ended up there?"

Edvin Pekkari didn't answer. Just sat on the farthest corner of the cot.

"You can improve your position by cooperating," Björnfot continued. "The examining magistrate is arriving tomorrow. If you hand over your haul and confess, it will count in your favor. There was supposed to be fifty thousand in the sack. Where is the rest of the money?"

"Listen to the sheriff," said acting parish constable Spett, who stood with his back turned, picking his dry socks from the tile stove damper and stuffing them into his pockets. "What good will the money be to you if they chop off your head?"

"I'm innocent," Pekkari said in a low voice. "I've already told you . . ."

Acting parish constable Spett turned around violently. Kajsa stood up, barking passionately.

"Johansson had six children!" he roared. "God knows what will happen to them now. Oskar Lindmark was twelve years old. Johansson's gun was found in your room. The sack with some of the money in the attic above your room. You knew about the money. I want you to tell me . . . Tell me how you stole the sled from hauler Bäckström, how you shot Johansson with his own gun, how you killed Oskar Lindmark with the axe. I can't take any more of your damned lies, so shut up until you want to confess."

He grabbed his uniform coat and his fur cap.

"I'm going out," he said to Björnfot. "I need some fresh air."

He pulled the door open and a man standing outside, on the verge of raising the knocker, lost his balance and stumbled into the police station. Spett caught him in his arms and kept him from falling down. It was a tall man with an impressive mustache. Borg Mesch, the town photographer.

"Mister acting parish constable!" the photographer exclaimed. "Now only the music is missing! But which of us should lead? You or me?"

Spett lost his ill humor and laughed. He put his coat back on its hook and let Kajsa out the door to take her evening walk on her own. Mr. Mesch dragged in the heavy cases holding his equipment. Then he put his hand in between the bars to introduce himself to Edvin Pekkari.

"May I take your picture?" he asked.

Pekkari pulled his hand back.

"No," he said. "I'm . . ."

He glanced at acting parish constable Spett and fell silent.

"Perhaps I could show you some photos," Borg Mesch said eagerly, anxious to break the silence.

He opened his briefcase and pulled out a bunch of black-and-white photographs. They were neatly wrapped in tissue paper and he showed them one at a time. Before showing the next picture, he carefully rewrapped the previous one.

"This one," he said, "just look . . . it's King Oscar II after the inauguration of the ore line up to the border. This is from the royal dinner with managing director Lundbohm. Important gentlemen. I photograph important gentlemen. That's my profession. Well, what more could I show you . . . oh, yes, this one . . . just look . . . the Kiruna Athletics Club . . ."

Spett and Björnfot had to come closer to look at the strong men of the athletics club, posing with folded arms in their black vests, with broad leather body belts and light-colored tights. On the floor in front of them were round iron weights with handles or fitted on steel bars.

"The one with the medals is Herman Turitz," photographer Mesch said. "Isn't it great that we have such an outstanding and versatile athlete in town . . ."

He fell silent and looked with interest at Pekkari.

"You actually resemble him a little. Would you be kind enough to turn your head a little away from me . . . no, in the other direction . . . Do you see, gentlemen? Can you see the resemblance?"

The photographer kept talking while, with surprising speed, he unpacked his equipment.

"Mainly it's your forehead. And your jawline. You have a phrenologically interesting forehead, Mr. Pekkari. A sign of inner strength, did you know that? So I told Mr. Turitz when I took his portrait. That in his case, one might have expected a herculeanly developed occiput. Which is what you find in most physically strong persons. But no, it's his forehead. Too bad, I should have brought his portraits along. You would have found them most interesting. Perhaps next time. I told Mr. Turitz that inner strength is more important to an athlete than bodily qualifications. It's his inner strength that makes him submit to the constant practice, the self-sacrifice necessary to win all those medals. The other day I heard that he had run through the deep snow all the way to Kurravaara for a training session. If you could . . . if you'd allow me to take a picture . . . perhaps you could come a bit closer to the bars. Yes, that's it. No, no need for you to look this way, keep your eyes down a bit just as you did. I can see a sadness in your expression, which I hope to do justice. Now, please hold . . ."

The flash was lit and burst.

Borg Mesch put a new glass plate in his camera and replenished the magnesium powder in his flash.

"Perhaps now you might come a little closer," he went on. "I would like to see your face here, between the bars. Just so. Do you think you might take hold of the bars as well? One hand high, the other below. Exactly. I don't doubt that you could have become an actor if you had wanted to, Mr. Pekkari. Just a moment now . . ."

Photographer Mesch quickly walked up to Mr. Pekkari and arranged the sleeve of his shirt so that all the bloodstains were clearly visible.

"Open your eyes a little more, Mr. Pekkari. So! Just so! You're a mind reader!"

Sheriff Björnfot watched Mr. Pekkari while he was being immortalized.

Now he was truly posing in front of the camera. He stood there, seeming to want to burst out of his cell. Eyes wide and hands clenched around the bars as if he were shaking them. Blood on his sleeve, a black eye and a swollen lip.

Kajsa barked outside the office. Spett let her in and she immediately sought out her moose jaw, lay down in front of the tile stove and began gnawing it. Photographer Mesch offered everyone Turkish cigarettes.

"Who is it now?" Spett wondered when the knocker sounded. "What an infernal running."

Photographer Mesch looked out the window. Dusk had returned. It was that time of year when daylight lasted only briefly at midday and the sun never managed to clear the horizon.

"Watch your language," he said with a wink. "For here comes the servant of the Lord."

★　★　★

The Eastern Laestadian preacher Wanhainen was simply dressed in black pants, a black worker's vest and a woolen coat. He was a working man, drove water around town on weekdays. The preachers were not like the priests who lived off the toil of their brethren. No, a Laestadian preacher supported himself. He was not superior, was not a burden to his siblings in faith, never leafed through Scripture with tender fingers looking for cloudberry-sweet words as did the state church priests.

He walked into the police station closely followed by the father of the murdered errand boy, Oskar Lindmark.

Wanhainen greeted them the Laestadian way, giving a half embrace with his left arm while simultaneously shaking hands in the Swedish fashion.

"*Jumalan terve.*"

God's greetings, in Finnish.

Björnfot and Spett both grew stiff and uncomfortable. It was the preacher's way to hold a handshake for so long, his eyes staring unflinchingly into those of the one he was greeting, that it seemed as if he had the penetrating eye of God. And to that came his way of ending his embrace with pat on your back that was slightly too hard.

Borg Mesch kept his good humor, even responded to the greeting, though Spett thought that his reply sounded like a teasing "*Jumalalle terveisiä,*" Greetings to God.

Oskar Lindmark's father also greeted them, but mostly kept his eyes on the floor.

The preacher turned to Pekkari.

"The boy you killed," he said, "his father is here to forgive you."

He put his hand on the father's back, pushing him towards the cell.

"As I myself have been forgiven," Oskar Lindmark's father said in a thick voice, "I want to forgive you."

"Are you ready?" the preacher asked in an unctuous voice. "Are you willing to let go of your thoughtless life and receive redemption from your brother? What is bound on earth is bound in heaven and what is released on earth is released in heaven."

Edvin Pekkari was drawn to the bars by a power he was unable to resist.

Maybe what he saw in the teary, sincere eyes of the father was the image of his heavenly maker.

He was unable to stop himself from seizing the knotty hands of Oskar Lindmark's father. And while he held them, tears streamed down both their faces.

Borg Mesch rigged his camera and immortalized the moment.

"God's forgiveness," the preacher said. He too seized Pekkari's hands through the bars.

In that moment, the door burst open. In strode the Western Laestadian preacher Jussi Salmi. East and West were adversaries in faith ever since the Laestadian congregation had split in two. Preacher Jussi Salmi in a roundabout way had learned what was happening in the jailhouse and had therefore brought the widow of postman Johansson, who belonged to his congregation. His red cheeks and the fact that he had removed his mittens showed that he had been in a hurry. He greeted the policemen with the same embrace and a "God's peace."

Johansson's widow also mumbled a "God's peace." Spett noted that she showed the same interest in the floorboards as had Oskar Lindmark's father.

"*Jurmalan terve,*" preacher Wanhainen said, carefully wiping tears from his cheeks with a cloth handkerchief. "This evening, Pekkari has been absolved of his sins."

His statement made preacher Salmi grind his teeth. It was ignominious to arrive late and also to have lost the race to redeem Pekkari. But he refused to let himself be disheartened. He tore off his coat and pointed at Johansson's widow.

"This mother," he said tremulously to Pekkari. "This woman, who has lost her husband. This mother of fatherless children has come here to forgive you. She has not traveled as a gentleman, in a sled with bells . . ."

154

Here he made a brief pause while his opponent Wanhainen blushed in vexation.

Preacher Wanhainen and Lindmark's father had indeed arrived in a horse-drawn sled. And it was true that Lindmark's horse had a bell around its neck. What pride. Vanity of vanities!

". . . but tonight she has left her little ones to walk on foot through darkness . . ."

What followed was a soulful sermon on the widow who had suddenly lost her provider and who would now have to trust to God and, of course, her congregation siblings. The sermon rambled this way and that, touching on the widow's mite and the camel and the eye of the needle and that many are too great in their own eyes to enter the Kingdom of Heaven, but the true God was the God of the poor, indeed, the God of the widow. And Now Here She Was.

Preacher Wanhainen mostly looked as though he had a mind to throw both the Western preacher and the widow out into the snow. Oh, if they had only walked, in the fashion of pilgrims.

"To lose your only son . . ." he tried.

But his words fell on bedrock. Now the hands of the widow and of the murderer had also met between the bars.

He asked her to forgive. And without being able to make herself meet his eyes, the widow whispered that if indeed he was truly sorry, she forgave him. Then she turned to her congregation preacher and said that the little ones were all alone at home. That she must return.

Through the window, acting parish constable Spett saw her enter the street. In the glow of the streetlight he saw her bend down and wipe her hands on the snow, as if she wanted to wash them clean. Then she hurried off.

Back by the cell, the preachers were now deep in a dispute concerning the vanity of the world and the fact that East Laestadian women were permitted to wear hats.

Spett turned around.

"Out," he roared. "It's bedtime for converts and sinners both. You are welcome to return tomorrow after the hearing."

When all visitors had disappeared, Spett leaned against the bars and spoke to Pekkari.

"Now that you have received absolution from God, perhaps you might tell us where the rest of the haul is hidden."

Björnfot, who was busy shining his boots in preparation for the next day's trial, stopped rubbing the leather and raised his head.

But young Mr. Pekkari gave no reply. Without a word, he backed into the corner of his cell and lay down on the cot, his back to the two policemen.

The trial was held the next morning. It had stopped snowing but the wind had picked up during the night and now a storm was brewing. It lifted the newly fallen snow, whipping it madly across the mountain and along the streets in town. You could hardly see your own hand in front of your face. The wind took your breath away.

In spite of this, people had plodded down to the courtroom. Word had spread about the atrocity. Everyone wanted to get a look at the murderer, as well as hear more about the shudder-worthy deed. And watch the shiny buttons, uniforms and store-bought boots of the servants of justice. The kind of footwear poor folk could only dream about. The crowd wore large, homemade shoes of reindeer skin, which they stuffed full of hay.

The presiding judge, Manfred Brylander, regarded his courtroom. Today's audience was filling it to the brim; people were even jostling one another outside in the hallway. And it was growing warm, of course. The usher had been feeding the stove all morning. The steam was rising from wet woolen coats and furs. On the floor, snow had melted into small lakes. You could smell the odor of sour fat from peaked shoes. A number of dogs lay at the feet of their owners, adding to the musty smell of poverty filling the room. Manfred Brylander wiped sweat from his brow, banged his gavel and called upon women, children, and youths to leave. So they did, but the crush grew no less. Some of those in the hallway managed to squeeze in. The women and children remained in the hallway, out of his sight.

He glared at the audience. There were the Laestadian brethren, like gloomy ravens on the branches of a spruce. The Eastern brothers looked askance at the Western and vice versa. There was the indignant public, Lapps, Swedes, and Finns, all wanting to see the murderer pay with his life.

Per-Anders Niemi and his friends sat in the front row. They had caught the killer and enjoyed admiring glances and slaps on the back. A few people even snuck them a coin, or a piece of dried meat.

"Will it ever begin?" Per-Anders Niemi called out, well aware that he would never be ordered out of the room.

Kiruna, judge Brylander thought. A town of rebels and agitators. The room seemed full of an electric power. Something vibrating, waiting to be let loose. He could see it in their burning eyes. He feared that the mere sight of the accused would make the entire crowd explode. He looked at sheriff Björnfot and acting parish constable Spett. Dressed in uniform and stiff-legged, polished and brushed. The sheriff let his hand rest easily on his service gun.

"Any outburst and I'll clear the room," judge Brylander warned, but without looking at Per-Anders Niemi.

The district police superintendent, Svanström, was serving as prosecutor. There was no defense attorney. After all, the accused had declared himself willing to confess.

The prisoner was brought in. His hands and feet were chained and he rattled a bit when taking his seat at the place of the accused. His large prison uniform made him look smaller than ever.

The proceedings began. Svanström presented the strong evidence pointing to Pekkari. Johansson's service gun, which had been found in Pekkari's room, and the mailbag with part of the stolen money, found in the attic above his abode.

"Do you admit," asked the judge, "that on December fifth, and without leave, you borrowed a sled from hauler Bäckström, that you drove it in the direction of Gällivare, that in cold blood you shot mailman Johansson and killed his errand boy Oskar Lindmark with an axe? That you then broke open the mailbox and stole an insured parcel?"

Pekkari whispered something inaudible.

"Louder!" the judge urged.

Pekkari said nothing. Then a man in the audience stood up. It was Oskar Lindmark's father. He remained silent. Just stared at Pekkari until the judge ordered him to sit.

But then Pekkari began to speak.

"I confess," he said in a steady voice.

"This is a most serious crime, and I must urge you to reply honestly to the questions of the court," judge Brylander admonished him. "Did you perform your actions alone?"

"Yes," was the answer.

"Did no one accompany you in the sled?"

"No one but the devil!"

There was a ripple through the audience. Someone blew his nose, someone gestured quickly with his hand. Someone else muttered something and half rose in his seat. It was like drifting snow pushed across the frozen crust by a gust of wind. Judge Manfred Brylander had heard of the religious ecstasy of the Laestadians, their *liikutuksia*. He had never seen it with his own eyes. What did it take for something like that to start in this flock of ravens? Had it already begun? He lifted his gavel but didn't strike the table in front of him.

"Did you not have anyone else with you?" he asked the accused.

"No one except the devil," Mr. Pekkari said.

Now his voice rose and he called out from the stand like a preacher.

"I obeyed him. At Tuolluvaara I wanted to turn back. But he whispered in my ear. Urged me on. I had not yet found safety in the blood of the lamb."

Now the flock of ravens was sobbing in the benches. Embracing each other. Giving God's redemption to the brother closest to them.

"I did it," Mr. Pekkari called out, raising his shackled hands and shaking them to heaven in despair. "Young Oskar Lindmark. He was on his knees before me, begging for his life. He spoke of his mother. He clasped his hands. He turned his face towards me and I beat him to death."

Sheriff Björnfot leaned towards acting parish constable Spett. "Come along outside for a while," he said curtly.

Out in the street, Björnfot began walking quickly. The storm hit them. The wind whipped along the streets. When Spett called to Björnfot to slow down and wait, his mouth filled with snow. Turning his collar up and buttoning his coat was a chore. Snow blew in at his neck and between the buttons. Kajsa ran along behind him, sheltered from the wind by his legs.

"He didn't do it," Björnfot yelled.

Although they walked close together, his voice was lost in the wind. Spett had to strain to hear him.

"What do you mean, sir?" Spett called back.

Björnfot pulled Spett into a doorway. They stood inside, in lee of the wind. Snow had already formed a hard crust on their clothes. Kajsa was biting her paws, ridding them of clumps of snow.

"Damn it, Pekkari is innocent," Björnfot said, out of breath. "You saw Oskar Lindmark. He was wearing mittens. There's no way he could have kneeled and clasped his hands and talked of his mother."

"Well, Pekkari is exaggerating. I suppose he enjoys the attention, now that . . ."

"Right," Björnfot said. "He enjoys the attention, as you put it. The back of Oskar Lindmark's head was crushed. He was hit from the back. If he'd been on his knees, facing his killer, he would have been hit here."

He pointed to his forehead.

"Pekkari's lying. Why doesn't he say where the rest of the money is?"

"I suppose he's hid it and hopes to get away with life. Then maybe to escape . . ."

Björnfot shook his head. The icicles in his mustache jingled.

"He doesn't know. It's that simple."

"Then why would he confess?" Spett wondered distrustfully.

"I don't care!" Björnfot snapped. "But who else knew about the insured parcel? Who . . ."

"Who found the gun in Pekkari's room?" Spett asked with clenched teeth. "Per-Anders Niemi did."

They remembered Per-Anders Niemi and his friends, delivering the badly beaten Pekkari to the police station.

"I'll rip his head off his shoulders," Spett growled. "It'll be a deliverance for him to confess. And those tail-wagging friends of his . . ."

"But first, we'll take a look at his room," Björnfot said, opening the door.

The wind tore at it. Kajsa looked at the two men.

Do we have to go back out into that? she seemed to be saying.

Postal assistant Per-Anders Niemi rented a room in an unplastered brick house on Kyrkogatan.

"He shares it with a friend," said the landlady who opened the door for Björnfot and Spett.

"Was he home on the evening before last?" Björnfot asked as he stepped into the room.

"Don't think so," the landlady said. "He spends most of his time with his fiancée. She rents a room of her own."

She gave the policemen a knowing glance.

The rag carpets on the floor were overlapping to keep out the cold. The two beds were separated by a hanging piece of cotton. There was a washstand with a bowl and a jug. Next to a portrait of King Oscar II on the wall hung a shaving mirror, brown with rust. Beside each bed stood a valet stand. A yellowed undershirt and a pair of socks hung on the one by Per-Anders Niemi's bed.

Spett and Björnfot tore the covers off both beds. They lifted the pillows and the horsehair mattresses. They rolled up the rag carpets and examined the floorboards just as they had done in Pekkari's room. When they'd turned the room upside down, they searched the attic. And found nothing.

"Are you finished?" the landlady asked, glaring at the mess in the room. "Can I make up the beds again?"

Björnfot seemed not to hear her. He was gazing out the window at the white curtain of snow. He had been so certain. Now he suddenly felt unsure. Perhaps Pekkari was guilty after all. Perhaps he just didn't want to admit killing Oskar Lindmark from behind. That was a base deed, after all. Perhaps he wanted to add drama to what had happened.

Kajsa settled down on the floor with a disappointed sigh.

"I suppose we'll have to take a look at where his friends live," Spett suggested.

Björnfot shook his head.

"I don't think he's the kind of man who trusts his friends . . ."

He turned to the landlady.

"What's the name of his fiancée? Where does she live and work?"

Majken Behrn was the fiancée of postal assistant Per-Anders Niemi. She was nineteen years old. A girl with round cheeks and curly hair who attracted customers to Hannula's General Store, where she worked as a sales clerk. When Björnfot and Spett asked her to put on her coat and hat and come along, Björnfot knew that they were on the right track.

She didn't ask what it was all about. Hurried to get her coat on. Didn't even take the time to remove her apron. As if the wife of shopkeeper Hannula might forget that she had been picked up at work by the police if she was just quick enough about it.

"Perhaps you can guess what this is about," Björnfot began as they started off along the street.

But it wouldn't be quite that easy.

Majken Behrn wound her scarf several times around her neck as protection against the snowstorm and shook her head.

"Your fiancée, Per-Anders Niemi: did he spend the evening before last in your company?" Björnfot yelled over the wind.

"Yes," she yelled back. "I'll swear to that."

Then, quickly, she added: "Why do you ask?"

"It's regarding a double homicide," Spett said bitingly. "And I'll ask you to remember that, miss."

They fell silent and struggled on through the storm to the house where Majken Behrn lived.

★ ★ ★

It was a pleasant room, Björnfot thought as he looked around. Woven curtains with knit fringes. Between the outer and the inner windows, Majken Behrn had put *Cladonia stellaris*, the white lichen beloved by reindeer, against the damp. In the lichen, she had placed little Santa Claus figurines made of yarn. On the wall in the bedstead alcove hung a paper Christmas hanging depicting a farmyard house elf feeding red apples to a horse.

There was a plain wooden chair on each side of a drop-leaf table covered by a spotless embroidered tablecloth. A coffee pot stood on an iron stove with a hotplate. Over the pot handle a small, crocheted kettle-holder hung neatly.

Kajsa shook off snow to the best of her ability. Then she found a tub of water on the floor in the alcove and drank noisily. Spett and Björnfot searched the room. Looked in drawers and everywhere. Nothing.

She doesn't even ask us what we're looking for, Björnfot thought. She knows.

Spett called for Kajsa to come. When she didn't appear, he went over to the sleeping alcove.

"What's that she's drinking?" he asked.

He saw that the tub held a piece of clothing put there to soak.

"I hope you haven't put any lye in the water," he said.

"No, no," Majken Behrn assured him, suddenly blushing. "It's just. It's nothing . . ."

"What are you washing?" Björnfot asked when he saw the color rise in her cheeks. Spett pulled the garment out of the tub. It was a pair of men's breaches. Even though they were wet, you could see that the legs beneath the knees were stained with blood. Björnfot turned to Majken Behrn. If her face had been red a moment ago, it was now white as linen.

"Those are your fiancée's trousers," he said sharply. "And it's Oskar Lindmark's blood."

Majken Behrn was breathing harshly. She fumbled blindly for something to hold on to.

162

"Tell us everything," Spett said. "If you do, you may save yourself. Otherwise you'll be sentenced as an accomplice, I can promise you that."

Majken Behrn said nothing. But she turned slowly, pointing to the iron pipe leading to the stove.

Spett dropped the wet pants on the floor. He hurried to the stove and grabbed the iron pipe with his huge fists.

"How?" he said.

Majken Behrn shrugged.

"Don't know."

Spett tugged at the stovepipe and the middle part of it came loose.

"There's something stuck inside," Spett said, peering down into the loose pipe.

Majken Behrn turned in alarm to Björnfot.

"Don't tell Per-Anders. He'll kill me."

"He won't be killing any more people," Björnfot said calmly as Spett began unfolding a thick wad of bills with his sooty hands.

Majken Behrn was standing by the window. She looked at her engagement ring. At the white frost ferns on the windowpane.

To know something, yet not know, she thought. How could you explain that?

The night before last she had suddenly awoken. Per-Anders was standing by the iron stove. He was twisting the pieces of the stovepipe together. "What are you doing?" she asked. "Just go back to sleep," he said.

Then he came to her in bed. He was cold. His hands like two winter pikes. "Soon, now," he whispered in her ear before she went back to sleep. "Soon I'll buy you a fur coat."

In the morning, he had awakened before her. Told her not to light a fire in the stove to make coffee. She mustn't touch the stove for a few days, he said. And his pants were soiled. He asked her to wash them for him. "I helped the cobbler with his Christmas pig," he said. "He sure bled all over me. I asked if I could have the head to bring you."

She laughed and pretended to shudder. Later, when she heard about the two murders, she stopped laughing. But she said nothing. Perhaps didn't want to know. Lit no fires in her stove.

"And he, Edvin Pekkari," she said to herself, forgetful of the presence of Spett and Björnfot, "he was such a nasty man. Never said a word. Didn't even say hello when you went into the post office. But stared at me as soon as he thought I wouldn't notice. In that way, you know. The whites of his eyes all yellow. It could have been him. It should have been him."

Sheriff Björnfot threw open the courtroom door. Judge Manfred Brylander lost his way in the middle of a sentence. People turned their heads.

"Pekkari is innocent," Björnfot called out, striding up to the bar. "Release him!"

"What are you talking about?" judge Brylander exclaimed. He had grown vexed and worried when Björnfot and Spett left the courtroom. His thin hair now lay sweaty and flat on his head. He was gasping for air like a clubbed fish.

"I've got the money from the robbery in my hand," Björnfot called, holding high the parcel he had found in Majken Behrn's stovepipe.

"And this," he went on, lifting his other hand, "is the murderer's trousers. Stained by Oskar Lindmark's blood."

All the spectators gasped in unison. Theirs was a joint inhalation of horror at the sight of the wet pants in Björnfot's hand, and perhaps an inhalation of rapture at the amount of money known to be in the parcel he held.

Per-Anders Niemi rose quickly. Before anyone managed to stop him, or even realized that he ought to be stopped, a few quick steps had brought him to the side door at the front of the room, the door through which the accused Pekkari had been brought in only an hour before.

"Stop!" sheriff Björnfot roared, but by then Per-Anders Niemi was already out of the room.

Outside the doorway he ran straight into the hard fist of acting parish constable Spett.

It took only a second or two. Then Spett walked in, holding Per-Anders Niemi by the scruff of his neck.

Björnfot looked around for the men who had helped Per-Anders Niemi bring Edvin Pekkari to the police station. One of them was crouched down in his seat like a sinner at the altar. Björnfot grabbed his hair and pulled him to his feet.

"I'll talk," he whimpered.

"You'll shut up!" Per-Anders Niemi yelled, trying to pry himself loose from Spett's closed hand.

"No," his friend cried in desperation. "I want to speak. I haven't slept since it happened. Per-Anders told me about the money. Said we should rob the mail sled. But only that. He never said anything about killing anyone. We took the sled since the hauler was gone. We stopped at Luossajokki, turned the sled over and pretended that its runner had broken. We had mufflers up to our ears and caps pulled down low. They'd never have recognized us, we didn't need to . . . Per-Anders hid behind a tree, since the postman knew him. They stopped to help us. Oskar jumped out of the mail sled and bent down to look at the runner. Postman Johansson stayed in the sled, holding back the horse since it wanted to go on. Then Per-Anders slipped out from behind the tree. He jumped on the sled and shot Johansson in the back."

"With Johansson's gun?" Björnfot asked.

"No, with his own. We found Johansson's later and pretended to discover it in Pekkari's room when we rushed him. Even Pekkari though we found it in his drawer. Tried to tell us that someone else must have put it there. Sneaked in while he was sleeping."

"But after that," Björnfot said. "Out in the woods. When Per-Anders Niemi had shot mailman Johansson."

"The shot made the horses go crazy. Our horse reared up and tried to run, but the sled was turned over and stuck in the snow. The mail horse bolted. Per-Anders Niemi was standing in the sled, holding on, and called out to me. The boy, he said. Get him!"

Per-Anders Niemi's friend tottered. In his mind, the scene was played out again. The sheriff had to grab hold of him to keep him from falling down.

Oskar Lindmark's face is pale blue in the moonlight. He is kneeling by the sled to look at the runner that is supposedly broken. Eyes wide. He hasn't understood what has happened, though the shot has been fired and the mail horse has neighed in panic and bolted. The mail horse is running, though not very fast in the loose snow. Per-Anders Niemi is standing in the mail sled, yelling:

"I have to break it open to get the money. The kid! Get him. Don't let him get away!"

They stare at each other, Per-Anders Niemi's friend and Oskar Lindmark. Frozen in fear of this deed that lies before them. The grown man's mind calls out: I can't!

Their horse rears up, trying to get loose. And suddenly Oskar Lindmark jerks. He gets to his feet. Stumbles, but doesn't fall. Runs off like a hare in the moonlight.

"Get him," Per-Anders Niemi roars. "If he escapes in the woods we're done for." His friend takes the axe. And goes after the boy.

The snowflakes dance so beautifully in the air. As though they can't make up their minds whether to fall or rise. Clouds float across the moon. Like a woman's behind in a smoking sauna, fat and shiny. Hiding and revealing itself in a dance of veils. The shadows of the trees on the snow are now sharp and black, now soft and almost invisible. Not even if the moon is entirely hidden by clouds will Oskar Lindmark get away. It's easy to follow his footprints in the snow. But still Per-Anders Niemi's friend runs so hard that he can taste blood. His feet sink down in the snow, but since he can run in Oskar's tracks he is gaining on him. And he is just a little boy. Oh, God. Per-Anders Niemi's friend has soon caught up with him. He raises the axe and strikes the boy's head before he manages to turn around. The boy mustn't look at him; he wouldn't have been able to endure it. Now Oskar Lindmark

166

lies before him, face down. His feet are still running, like those of a sleeping dog.

The man hits him over and over, because of those feet.

Per-Anders Niemi's friend kept his eyes on Björnfot.

"Lindmark ran. But I caught up with him quickly. I hit his head with the back of the axe. He died in the snow. I walked back to the sled and managed to get it right side up on the road. Held the horse until Per-Anders came trudging up with the money. He had Johansson's pistol. My pants were bloody. It drove me insane, that blood, so Per-Anders said we could switch. He put on my bloody pants and gave me his clean ones. Outside town we jumped off, lashed the horse and walked home, each to his own place. The snow was coming down heavier. We knew all the tracks would soon be gone."

The third man who had come along when they took Pekkari to the police station suddenly stood up.

"It can't be true!" he exclaimed, looking in horror at Per-Anders Niemi and his friend who had just confessed to the awful deed. "You damned bastards. I believed you. When you came to me and said we should search Pekkari's room. When you said that you suspected him. You bastards!"

The room grew deathly silent. Then Spett spoke up.

"Out, all of you," he cried. "There will be a new trial here tomorrow. But now. Get out! Get out!"

People rose from the benches, as if stunned.

Nobody spoke. They had sat there, willing an innocent man's death. Guilt pulled a thick blanket over the courtroom. The Laestadian brethren looked awkwardly down at the ground. Nobody looked at Edvin Pekkari.

Pekkari, who stood up by the bar, still in chains, and who called out:

"But I did it. Can't you hear me? I am guilty. I AM GUILTY!"

The snowstorm lasted for three days. Then it went on its way to ravage other places, leaving Kiruna in peace under a soft, white blanket.

Horses pulled snowplows and drifts cracked fences. Birch tree branches bent all the way down to the ground under their snowy loads.

Björnfot and Spett stood at the railroad station, watching Edvin Pekkari board the southbound train. The mining company had ordered men to shovel snow from the tracks. People were moving back and forth over the platform, passengers and goods.

Pekkari with huddled shoulders and a knitted cap. He carried all his belongings in one suitcase. Nobody was going with him. Nobody had come to see him off.

"So, I guess he's moving out, then," Spett said.

Björnfot nodded.

"Why the devil did he confess?" Spett wondered.

"Who knows," Björnfot said. "Perhaps the attention," he said. "He became famous overnight. And before that he was a loner nobody wanted to know."

He thought of when they had searched Pekkari's room. Not a single letter in any of the drawers. Not a single photograph.

"He would have had his head cut off," Spett protested. "It's senseless."

"The evidence pointed to him. Perhaps he imagined that he had done it. That what everyone said was true. Who can know?"

Spett snorted incredulously, then laughed at Kajsa who was greeting the train conductor and trying to invite him to play. She ran a few crazy turns, spattering him with snow.

"Well," Björnfot said, stroking his moustache. "People talk about the mystery of God. But I'd say people can be just as great a mystery."

"I thought that only applied to women," Spett said.

Speaking about women made sheriff Björnfot remember to check his watch. He had arranged to meet his wife at one o'clock. It was time to get going.

"But admit that it's strange," Spett said before Björnfot hurried off. "The Laestadian brethren, I mean. They could forgive Pekkari for being a cold-blooded killer. But they couldn't forgive him for being a simple liar."

"People are a mystery," Björnfot said again and bid him good-bye for now.

She stood waiting at the street corner as he came panting up the hillside. Her dark, wide eyebrows under the ermine hat. Her hands in the white muff. Her long, black coat had a rim of snow.

"Just wait!" Björnfot said cheerfully and linked his arm through hers.

The walk to the new music pavilion took only three minutes. He had borrowed a key. On the stage up front was a Steinway grand piano.

"It's yours every Thursday from two till half past three," he said. "Nobody will disturb you."

She looked at the grand piano. Felt herself lured into a trap.

She thought of her first trip up north to Kiruna. In Gällivare, the train conductor had come up to her and inquired whether she had someone to "answer for her."

"What do you mean?" she had asked.

"You can't travel to Kiruna by yourself," he had replied. "You must have a man to answer for you. Or at least a certificate stating that a man will meet you up there and answer for you."

"Answer for me?" she had exclaimed, but at that moment Albert and the girls had entered the compartment. They had just been outside, taking a walk on the platform during the stop.

The conductor had excused himself, checked their tickets and gone his way.

Albert had defended him.

"It's not like Stockholm," he had said. "It's a mining town. But they don't want it to turn into another Malmberget, full of drunkenness and . . ."

He had stopped talking and glanced at the girls, who were following their discussion with rapt expressions.

". . . and women who oblige with this and that," he said. "They want to keep that kind of womenfolk out. There's no need for you to take offense."

"In Finland, women are allowed to vote," she had said. "Here, we're not allowed to take the train."

Kiruna was a town belonging to men. The gentlemen and their businesses. And of course the sheriff was always invited when this or that was to be discussed.

How he polished his boots when he was invited to visit managing director Lundbohm. Spat and buffed. The director himself sometimes turned up for meetings dressed as a navvy.

She had expected something else from this town of the future. Something that felt modern. But the women here sighed devoutly in front of the altarpiece painted by Prince Eugén.

And she suffered poverty badly. All those women and children whose cheekbones stuck out from their faces like mountaintops. From hand to mouth, all the time. All those women whose men came to harm in the mines. The child auctions. They had them in Stockholm as well. But here, it was all so close. It affected her badly.

Albert had a five-year contract as sheriff. She couldn't understand how she would bear it. Nowadays she could hardly stand him either. His heavy breathing when sleeping. His table manners had begun to annoy her. She felt ashamed of herself. But what did that accomplish? Sometimes she wished that she would come down with some illness. Just to escape it all.

He opened his uniform coat and pulled out the parcel with the sheet music her mother had sent her.

"I can't," she said. "My fingers are frozen stiff."

He dropped the music. Took her hands in his.

"You don't want to?" he said, pleadingly. "Don't you have any feelings left for me?"

She gave in. Loosened herself from his hold and sat down at the piano. Struck a chord. Hoped for it to be out of tune. It wasn't.

I'll drown here, she thought.

And at that moment, her fingers dove down onto the keys.

They landed on the opening chord to Debussy's *La Cathédrale Engloutie*.

★   ★   ★

The piano can't lie to Debussy. The first tones sound one by one. But the grand piano keeps the promise it made from the start.

Now the cathedral bells are ringing down in the depths of the sea. She strikes each key distinctly. Oh, these pealing sounds. The storm tears the surface. Waves rise high. The bells below toll and ring out.

Her touch is hard and demanding. Furious.

Her fingers aren't long enough. Her arms aren't long enough. Her coat arms are tight as a straitjacket. She sweats. Her back hurts when she stretches.

Then she looks at Albert. He is smiling, but below that smile is worry. He doesn't understand this music. It frightens him. She frightens him when she shows him this side of herself.

Abruptly, she stops playing. Her hands land in her lap. She almost wants to sit on them.

"Go on," he says.

Why, she wants to ask him. You don't understand.

And as if he could see right through her, he says:

"I'm a simple man . . ."

His voice thickens. The thought of his crying scares her half to death.

". . . but if you knew how proud I am of you, my songbird. When you play. I wish I could . . . I'm really trying . . ."

He is unable to go on speaking. His lips compress and the muscles under their skin twitch.

She looks out the window. A squirrel runs along a branch. Snow loses its grip and falls to the ground. It is light outside. Beyond all the white, the sky is colored rose.

Her heart is not as heavy as before.

I'll try to be happy, she decides. Thursdays from two until three-thirty. Maybe that's what I need.

She smiles at him. Then she puts her hands on the keys again and begins to play. She picks Schubert's Impromptu in G Flat Major. It's lyrical and she knows that he likes it very much. She looks at him and smiles. Goes on playing tunes he appreciates.

Now he is smiling back at her, his heart happy. As if she were the returning sun.

He is a good man, she thinks. He deserves better.

She is miserable in Kiruna. Sometimes she thinks she'll go mad.

But he is a good man. And soon it will be Christmas.

Åsa Larsson was born in 1966 in the university town Uppsala, roughly fifty miles north of Stockholm. At four she moved with her family to Kiruna, a mining town some 750 miles farther north, where she grew up; her paternal grandfather Erik August Larsson, who lived there until his death in 1982, was a cross-country skier who won one gold and one bronze medal at the 1936 Winter Olympics, but who later renounced sports and became a preacher in the Firstborn Laestadians congregation, noted for its highly traditionalist and conservative pietism.

Åsa Larsson grew up in the strict Laestadian faith, to which her parents also subscribed. As a student, however, she gradually rejected the extreme views of the Laestadians, returned to Uppsala to study law and went to work as a tax lawyer. But the harsh landscapes of the extreme north and issues of faith and religious conflict remain important and recurring themes in her fiction.

She published her first novel in 2003, Solstorm (Sun Storm), *which won the Best First Novel Award from the Swedish Crime Fiction Academy; it also introduced her recurring protagonist, prosecutor Rebecka Martinsson. Her second novel,* Det blod som spillts (The Blood Spilt, *2004), won the academy's Best Novel of the Year Award, as did her fifth novel,* Till offer åt Molok (Sacrifice to Molok, 2012). *Larsson's novels have been extensively translated; she now writes full time and lives in Mariefred, a small town fairly close to Stockholm, with her husband and two children.*

BRAIN POWER

STIEG LARSSON

Stieg Larsson's first and only professionally published works of fiction were the three novels known as The Millennium Trilogy, *which he began writing in the summer of 2002, shortly before his forty-eighth birthday, and that after his death in late 2004 became an international publishing phenomenon, selling so far a total of more than seventy-five million copies in some fifty languages.*

What few of Stieg Larsson's readers may know, however, is that he had dreamed of becoming a fiction writer for most of his life. By age ten he was already writing stories; in his teens, he tried his hand at novels and also published a handful of stories in mimeographed science fiction fanzines published by himself or others. Later on he worked on at least one very ambitious science fiction novel which never satisfied him and that he finally discarded.

As noted, Larsson's first literary love was science fiction, but in his early teens he also became fascinated by crime fiction. He favored the hard-boiled, grittier crime stories: Dashiell Hammett, Raymond Chandler, Ross Macdonald, and Peter O'Donnell were early favorite authors. And when he began publishing his fanzine stories at seventeen, he sometimes combined his two favorite genres, writing suspense or crime stories in a science fiction mode.

The story presented here initially appeared in the third issue of Sfären, a fanzine copublished by Larsson and his close friend Rune Forsgren. That issue—fewer than fifty mimeographed copies—appeared in April 1972. For all practical purposes, this is the first time the story is published.

"Brain Power" is an early work by the teenager who would turn into the man who wrote The Girl with the Dragon Tattoo. *But the story shows that even the very young Stieg Larsson had a talent for storytelling; it shows that at seventeen he was already concerned with issues such as the abuse of power and the abrogation of civil liberties by the elite, and it shows his interest in building both suspense and narrative through a series of disclosures, only gradually letting the reader in on what is actually happening.*

What we get then is not only a very early glimpse of the storyteller who gave us Lisbeth Salander, but also of his love of both science fiction and crime fiction, of his joy in writing, and of his lifelong dedication to the causes of justice, compassion, and civil liberty.

Mr. Michael November Collins
Sector 41
Aldedo Street
8048 New York 18-A-34

Mr. Michael November Collins, that's me, and the letter with my name and address on its envelope arrived in the morning, dropping from the mail tube to the breakfast table.

Judith, my wife, picked it out of the basket, read my name and handed it to me. Even before opening the letter I saw that it wasn't an everyday one. There was no postage on it, just a stamp informing me that postage was paid by the government—or the taxpayers, whichever you prefer. My getting mail from the government was hardly a common thing. It had only happened a single time before, two years ago when I'd managed to run myself into a gold medal at the Olympics and the President had sent me his congratulations. That was in 2172. Now was 2174, but the world record I set then still held.

I slit the envelope open.

175

Michael November Collins 46-06-18

> Mr. Collins is called upon to report for medical examination at the office of Dr. Mark Wester, Boston University, State Research Facility, on 74-08-24. This is a Governmental request.

That was the entire text of the letter, apart from an illegible signature above the single word "Assistant."

I was still staring in confusion at the letter when Michael Junior and Tina came to say goodbye before rushing off to the school lift. While I was hugging the children, Judith came up, took the letter from me and told the kids to hurry.

"What's the meaning of this?" Judith asked.

"No idea, honey. I guess I'll just have to go there and find out."

"But why would they want you to have a medical examination?"

I pulled her close, smiled and gave her a kiss.

"Maybe it's something about my fitness. I do hold a few world records, you know."

"But why at the government's request?"

"Your guess is as good as mine." I shrugged. "But I guess in time they'll tell me why."

"Doctor Mark Wester," I repeated.

I was standing by the information desk in the central rotunda of Boston University, speaking to the attendant.

"Where can I find him?" I asked impatiently.

"I'll phone his secretary. It may take a while. As you perhaps don't realize, Boston University is no ordinary university, but a state research center, and formalities usually do take a few minutes."

"No, I didn't know. Perhaps you can enlighten me by telling me why I've been asked to come here?"

"For a medical examination. It says so in your letter."

She picked up her phone and tapped a number.

"Mary? Hi, it's Information. You're expecting a Mister Michael November Collins today. He's here now."

Silence.

"Oh, okay, I can send him right up."

She gave me a smile and pointed to a uniformed man seated inside a glass booth. "Talk to the man in there. I'll give him a call, and he'll show you to Doctor Wester." She lifted her phone again, and I began walking across the hall. I saw that she'd finished her phone call before I was even halfway across. The uniformed man rose, left his cage, came to meet me and shook my hand.

"I understand you're here to see Mark Wester."

"That's right."

"Fine. I'll show you to him. Please follow me."

While walking along in his footsteps, I began feeling a steadily growing apprehension. My imagination was telling me that something was wrong. I couldn't put my finger on exactly what made me feel that way, but that only added irritation to my unease. Twice along the way we had to stop when uniformed guards asked us for access permits, but both times my guide sent them away by pointing to me and saying, "He's here to see Doctor Wester."

I grew steadily more bewildered, and finally couldn't refrain from asking him why I had been requested to see Wester. But the man knew nothing more than the girl at the information desk. Finally, we arrived.

An assistant, whom I assumed to be Mary, asked me to sit down on the couch and said that Doctor Wester would see me in just a minute or two. After three minutes, a man of around fifty came out of an inner office. He was fairly heftily built, and all of his visible skin was darkly tanned—a real tan, I mean, not the disgusting coloring you buy at the chemists. He looked to be in great shape.

"Thanks for coming in," he said and held his hand out. I shook it.

"Perhaps you'd like to tell me why I'm here," I asked.

"Didn't they put that in the letter? You're to have a medical examination."

"That's what they wrote. I just don't understand why."

"Oh, that. Well, you'll understand why in a short while. All depending on the results, of course."

177

"Oh. Really? Well, in fact I'm not sure if I have any great wish to be checked. I'm extremely fit. In my line of work, I have to be."

"Certainly. I know you're incredibly fit, but what I want to find out is how your innards are doing."

He laughed, patted me on the back, and showed me into his office.

"I didn't know Boston University is a state research center. Don't you have any students at all any longer?"

"Yes, but we're all about specialized education nowadays. Not much of what we do is known to the general public."

"So what are you doing?"

"I really shouldn't tell you, I suppose, but I suppose you could sum it all up by saying that we're doing biological research."

"And what's that got to do with me? Where do I come into this?"

"Unfortunately, I'm afraid I can't give you any details until we have finished testing you."

"Really? Well, how about getting started at once, in that case? I'd really like to get this over and done with, so I can get back to Judith and the kids again."

"Oh, that's true, you're married, of course," Wester said, scratching his head.

"So I am. To the most wonderful woman in the world," I said, smiling.

"Good for you. Personally I have neither wife nor children, and I suppose I'm getting too old to start thinking about those things. At any rate I'm happy that you agree to our examinations."

"So when can we start?"

"Tomorrow."

"Tomorrow? I had believed it could all be done today."

"We're talking of extremely thorough and complex examinations, and I'm afraid the procedure will take some time. But don't worry. We have arranged a private room for you here at the university. And you can always phone your wife."

"Exactly how many days are we talking about here?"

"It's difficult to say. But it might be up to a week. It depends on if everything works out as it should."

"A week! What kind of examinations are we talking about here? I want to know what this is all about. Why am I here? How are you going to test me? And why?"

"I've already said that I can't tell you until we have the results."

"In that case I'm not going to go along with any tests at all," I said firmly.

Wester smiled.

"Please, there's no reason to get all worked up about this. I assure you that the tests will be absolutely harmless."

"That doesn't change anything," I said. "I still want to know the reason for them. That's not negotiable. I won't cooperate otherwise."

"You've misunderstood, I'm afraid. It's not a matter of cooperating or not. You *will* cooperate. That's an order."

"Whose order?"

"The government's."

"Damn the government," I said and grew angry. "I'm not cooperating."

"You don't have a choice."

"I certainly do. I'll simply stand up and walk out the same door I came in." I stood up and walked away from him.

"Please take a look at this paper," Wester said just as I was grasping the doorknob.

"Why should I?"

"Because it's of great concern to you."

"So long," I said, opening the door.

"It's an order signed by the president . . ."

I hesitated.

"It demands your absolute obedience. If you refuse, you will be arrested for obstructing the government."

"Is this some kind of joke?"

"Hardly. You can be punished by up to twenty-five years in prison and fined twenty-thousand dollars."

I stared at him, mouth open.

"I don't believe you."

"Read it yourself."

Slowly, I closed the door. Slowly, Wester had adopted a threatening attitude.

"Well, how about it?"

"It doesn't look as if I have much of a choice, does it?"

"No, not really."

"Can I phone my wife?"

"Of course. You are free to do whatever you like."

"As long as it doesn't contradict what's in your orders, you mean?"

"Exactly. Someone will escort you to your rooms."

"Where I'll be under guard?"

"Just to ensure your safety, of course."

"Of course . . ."

Mark Wester certainly hadn't exaggerated when he told me that the tests and examinations to be performed were complex. For four days I did nothing except be shuffled from one room to the next, in each of which different doctors did their best to discover any ailments. In vain I tried to explain to them that I was as fit as a fiddle—to use an old and tired cliché. Nothing helped. They examined me from top to toe, from the inside and out. The first day they put me to a number of physical tests and fitness tests. They checked, double-checked, triple-checked and then, just to be sure of not having overlooked even the slightest detail, did a final check.

The second day I was X-rayed; they tapped my spine and asked me to stick my tongue out and say, "Aaaah!"

That was all they did that day, and so I actually got a short breathing pause. They had given me a luxurious suite of rooms, and I was truly living just as comfortably as I normally spent my time wishing I could live. I phoned Judith every night and tried to explain to her that I had to stay put for a while. I never mentioned Wester's threats about jail time and fines. She kissed me over the phone and wished for me to come back home.

From the first time I was taken to my suite of rooms and for my entire stay at the university, two hefty uniformed guys from the university security force had stuck to me like glue. Just to ensure my safety, of course.

If I'd been hoping for the rest of the examinations to be no harder than those during the second day, I was hugely mistaken. During the third, fourth, and fifth day they practically turned my entire body inside out, scrutinizing every nook and cranny. They checked me for everything from athlete's foot to lung cancer.

On the sixth day it was finally all over, and Wester came to my rooms to tell me that I would be allowed to go home over the weekend, but that I had to return on Monday.

"Why?" I asked. It had become a routine question.

"We'll take your appendix out."

I turned in my hospital bed, discarding mt half-read comic book. I really didn't like my situation. The operation had been performed twelve days ago, and since then the doctors had pumped me full of vaccines against every conceivable illness.

I was bored and mad as hell. Mad because they more or less forced me to do whatever they felt like. Mad because I no longer felt like a free citizen of the United States. Mad because they refused to tell me what it was all about.

I sighed and picked up my comic book again.

In the afternoon, Mark Wester entered the room and sat down on a chain by the bed. His face was serious, and I realized that something must have happened, something that meant that everything was no longer going according to his plans—whatever they might be.

"You'll be discharged from this ward tomorrow."

"Hooray," I said, cheerful, for once.

He remained sitting, silent, hardly saying a word for perhaps five minutes.

"I guess you'd like to know what all this is about," he said at last.

"Man, that was the smartest thing I've heard you manage since I came here."

Wester took no offense.

"Have you ever heard of Hans Zägel?"

"Professor Hans Zägel, you mean?"

"Yes."

"Could anyone have failed to hear about him?"

Professor Hans Zägel was the foremost scientist of our time. He was born in Germany, but when the Russians occupied Germany in 1936, he escaped to England, later on to the United States. There could hardly be anybody not aware of Hans Zägler, and I felt slightly insulted that Wester had asked me if I had heard of him. Compared to Zägler, Einstein was a nobody.

"No, I suppose you can't have failed to hear about him. Do you know how old he is?"

"Around eighty-five, I guess," I said.

"He's eighty-six. Do you know what kind of research he is doing?"

"This and that, if you are to believe the news. He seems to know most everything within all areas of natural science. I suppose physics is his field of specialty. After all, he did build the first photon spaceship."

"True, physics is his main subject, but for the last ten years he has mainly concerned himself with biology."

"Hold on. What does Zägel have to do with me?"

"I'll tell you in a moment. Do you read any science fiction?"

I gestured towards the pile of magazines I had spent the last few days reading.

"Have you read anything about brain transplants lately?"

"I guess the idea pops up in some story now and then. Why?"

"What do you think about brain transplants in reality? Do you think they might be possible to perform?"

"No way," I laughed. "That's impossible."

"You're wrong. Hans Zägel has performed several successful brain transplants. The first one six years ago."

"But, dear God, that's impossible. There are just too many nerves that would have to be spliced together. It's just not possible!"

"Professor Zägel has performed one hundred forty-five transplants, forty-six of them on humans. With the help of his computer, he has developed a risk-free method. A computer, incidentally, that he himself constructed."

"I find this very hard to believe."

"I understand your doubts, but I assure you it's all true."

"How?" I asked, still doubting him.

"Professor Zägel makes the necessary incisions. Opens the cranium, and so on. After that, he performs the rest of the operation aided by his computer. It keeps track of all nerves that have to be spliced and makes sure that none of them are forgotten. The nerve splices are performed with a laser."

I scratched my head.

"If he's really managed all that, he's even more amazing than I thought. But why haven't you published anything about this?"

"That's what Professor Zägel wants until his work is entirely done."

"And when will it be done?"

"In nine or ten years' time."

"Now I'm not sure if you're pulling my leg or telling the truth, but I certainly would like to see some kind of evidence. Would it be possible for me to meet Professor Zägel?"

"No, unfortunately not."

"And why not?"

"He is dying. He is an old man. His heart is giving out."

I lay back in bed without answering, feeling sorry for Zägel.

"And where am I supposed to enter this?" I asked at last.

Wester slowly stroked his beardless chin.

"I assume you'll agree that Zägel's brain is the most distinguished on earth, possibly the finest ever known?"

"Sure," I nodded. "He's brilliant."

"And would you agree that when such a brain is put at the service of mankind, that brain becomes the most important one on earth?"

"Yes, of course. Too bad he's going to die."

"Now listen. To speak plainly, the world can't afford to lose a brain like Professor Zägel's."

"Everyone has to die sometime."

183

"Professor Zägel's work is almost finished. He needs, perhaps, another ten years. That's all the time he needs."

"And where do I enter into all this?" I repeated patiently.

"Professor Zägel needs another ten years to finish the greatest work ever performed in the history of mankind."

"And . . ."

"What we wish for is to find someone willing to give him the time he needs."

"Where do you want to get with all this? Nobody can stop death."

"No, but it can be postponed. We want you to let Professor Zägel's brain borrow your head in order for him to finish his work. We want you to be his new heart and body."

I just stared stupidly at him. There was a long pause before I managed to reply.

"You're insane," I whispered hoarsely.

"To Professor Zägel, it's a matter of life or death."

"What about me, then? What about my life? I'll never agree to it!"

"You have to. Professor Zägel has no more than a week left to live."

"The answer is no. To me, Zägel is welcome to die this instant, if that's what he wants. My life is more important to me than his. How could you even suggest something like this?"

"You have no choice in the matter. Professor Zägel is too important."

"You can't force me!" I stood up and grabbed Wester's jacket.

"Pull yourself together, for God's sake!"

"Pull myself together?" I cried back at him. "Do you really expect me to commit suicide just to save Zägel's life?"

"Professor Zägel's knowledge is of paramount importance to all of humanity."

"I won't do it. Is that why you've been testing me these last weeks? What made you pick me instead of anyone else?"

"That's self-evident. You are as fit as anyone on earth. Your physique is phenomenal. Professor Zägel himself picked you out three months ago . . ."

"So he's picked me. He's chosen his own salvation. I'm supposed to save Zägel's life by means of his own discovery. But you'll never make me do it."

"You have no choice. The president himself has approved the plan."

I sat silent for a few seconds, then shot up and tore the door open, attempting to get out of the university. But I didn't manage more than five steps before the guards posted outside my door had caught me. I yelled and cursed, kicked them to make them release me. One of them twisted my arm hard behind my back, and the pain made me scream.

"Don't hurt him!" I heard Wester call out.

So I did have one small advantage. They couldn't hurt me, but I had no scruples as far as they were concerned. When all is said and done, I am one of the world's foremost athletes. I aimed a kick at the stomach of one of the guards, and hit home perfectly. He doubled up, and before the other one had a chance to stop me I kicked him again. The second guard held me in a hard grip around my body, locking my arms to my sides, but I slammed him hard against the wall. I heard him moan when the back of his head struck the marble, but I was unable to pity him. I was fighting for my life. He refused to let go, but when I threw myself down, his body flew forward, above my head. Now my hands were free, and with all my strength I drove my fist against his temple.

Jumping across the first guard, who had started to rise, I ran towards the exit. Wester tried to catch hold of me after a couple of steps, wanting to stop me, but I pushed him violently aside. "Bastard," I cried, and ran out the revolving door.

I ran along the hallway and down the stairs until I reached the ground floor, where I paused for a second or two while trying to remember if I should go left or right to get out of the building. I decided on left and was halfway down the hall when I heard the loudspeakers warn that I was escaping. They urged everyone to try to stop me, but warned people to be careful not to harm me. Suddenly I was back in the rotunda and saw the huge glass doors leading to freedom.

I began running but was immediately seen by the receptionist at the information desk. She stood up, yelling at me to stop, but of course I ignored her. She screamed for the uniformed guard who had helped me find my way on that first day to stop me, and I saw him closing in on me at an angle. He was closer to the doors than I was, but I was faster. I knew that if I could only make it out the doors, I could outrun anyone who tried to catch me.

Perhaps being a champion runner wasn't such a bad thing after all. The guard almost reached me, but missed by a few inches.

I threw myself out the doors and began running across the lawn. I was dressed only in my pajamas and was barefoot, so I had to choose the lawn. I made it out of the campus block. I ran across the street and saw a man just getting into his car. He was putting his key into the ignition lock when I threw the door open and tore him out on the pavement.

"Sorry, buddy, but this is life or death," I told him.

The car didn't start on the first turn of the key, but on the second try it began spinning. The guards were sixty or seventy feet away when I started accelerating and I assumed that they noted the plate number. I drove for six blocks, then turned towards the main road. I had to stop for a red light, and while I waited for traffic to pass by I realized that I was shaking from fear. I felt empty inside, unable to realize how I—I, of all people—had ended up in this nightmare.

"Fuck you, Mr. President," I muttered. "And to think I voted for you. Next time I'll vote for the Democrats . . . if there is a next time."

When I woke up, Wester was leaning down over me. The shock from the injection they'd given me was slowly abating, and I was able to start thinking again. I tried to rise, but found that leather straps tied me to the bed, so I let my body relax.

"What . . . how?" I asked.

186

"The police caught you. You shouldn't have tried to run."

"No, of course not. I suppose I should just urge you to operate as soon as possible?"

"The operation will be tonight. We don't dare let Professor Zägel fight his body any longer. He might die at any moment."

"Let's hope. Is there really no way you could pick someone else?"

"No. It's too late, and regardless of that you are the one we need. Your excellent physique makes your chances to survive the operation better than anyone had during any of Professor Zägel's previous procedures. And besides, this time I'll be operating, and it will be my first time. I want the best chance possible to succeed, particularly given the importance of this operation."

"My life is important to me. I have a wife and two children. I'm responsible for them and have to take care of them!"

"Don't worry about your family. The state will take care of them in the best way possible. They'll want for nothing."

"But I don't want to lose them. I don't want to die!"

"I'm sorry, but there really isn't any alternative."

"But why try to stop the inevitable? Zägel will die anyway, sooner or later. Even at best, I won't live for more than fifty or sixty years."

"Professor Zägel can put those fifty or sixty years to immense use. And please let me ease your mind. You won't feel anything at all during the operation."

"And what will you do with my brain afterward?" I asked him ironically. "Donate it to medical research?"

"No, of course not. We plan on freezing it. In a few years, perhaps when Professor Zägel has perfected his method, we'll try to find a suitable body for it. Maybe you'll even get your own body back, though I doubt the government will agree to that."

"I doubt it, too. Zägel will still be important. And what will you do when my body wears down? Find him another?"

"Perhaps. That will depend on how worn-out his brain is becoming."

"Don't you have any feelings at all?" I didn't even try to hide the loathing I felt for him.

"You have to understand why we're doing this. Look at it from our perspective. We do what we truly believe is best for the state. In addition to his medical work, Professor Zägel is also engaged in designing robots to cancel the Russian defense shields."

I spat at him, but Wester didn't even react.

"I'll leave you now. Next time we meet will be in the operating room. Your wife has been permitted to see you for two hours. You will be entirely undisturbed during that time, and how you spend it concerns nobody else."

Wester opened the door. Two guards entered the room. They undid my restraints and left before I had time even to rise. After a few minutes the door opened again, and Judith walked in. She had tears in her eyes and threw herself into my arms.

"Michael," she gasped. "Why, Michael? Why you?"

"They just picked me. Do you know what will happen?"

"They've told me. But they can't do it, Michael, tell me they can't do it!"

I sighed. "I'm afraid they can. I did my best to get out of here, but I only got a few blocks away before the cops picked me up."

"But the police are supposed to protect people's lives."

"They do exactly as the government tells them. And in this case, Zägel's life is more important than that of an athlete. Judith, promise me to take care of Junior and Tina. Make sure they get the best of everything."

"Oh, Michael, can't you stop it somehow?"

"How?"

She made a helpless gesture. I held her close and kissed her. For the first time I realized how unbelievably lucky I really had been to find a wife like Judith.

"Where are the kids?" I asked her.

"They weren't allowed to come. They're too young to understand this kind of thing, they told me."

"Too young . . ." I felt bitter.

"I'll take care of them."

I pulled her down on the bed.

"Michael . . . Wester, that man out there, he says they might be able to freeze your brain and wake it again later."

"But my body will be ten years older, or even much more than that. At the very least I'll have lost years of my life. And besides, I don't believe they'll give me my body back even when Zägel has finished his work. He would still have maybe fifty years left to live in it, and I suspect the government won't feel like wasting those years on me."

I kissed her again, softly at first, then hard and demanding.

"We have two hours. Would you? One last time?"

I began undressing her. We touched and teased each other, fondled and urged each other on. Finally we tumbled down on the bed and made love more tenderly and intensely than ever before. It was my last time, and I had never before felt a greater passion, never before realized how much I truly loved living. My last time. I could hardly assume that Judith would live in celibacy for the rest of her life because I was no longer there. Perhaps she would marry again. In that case, who? I couldn't bear thinking about that.

We melted together.

Afterwards we lay talking. Judith smoked one of her cigarettes. I caressed her thoughtfully. Strangely enough, neither of us felt any despair or fear despite what would happen. We were both very calm and spoke mostly of things in the same way we used to do when I was going off to some training camp and would be gone for a couple of weeks. We talked just as if I would be back after a while.

They let us stay together for more than two hours, but after three, one of the guards knocked on my door, stuck his head in and told us to get ready to say goodbye. We dressed, or at least she did, and we said our goodbyes. Then we sat holding each other until they came back in through the door.

They closed the door behind Judith, and one of the men stayed inside trying to talk to me. I didn't want to. I just lay on my bed, staring at the ceiling, remembering Judith's lips.

At half past four the other guard came back and told me to make myself ready. I had half an hour. He wondered if I would like to talk to a priest, but I told him no. Then a nurse came and shaved my head.

I was hungry, but they wouldn't allow me to eat. At five sharp a nurse rolled in a hospital bed and asked me to lie down on it so she could roll me off to surgery.

"The hell I will," I told her. "I've got legs to walk on, and if this is my last trip, at least I'll walk it myself."

None of them objected. I stood, put my shorts on and followed the nurse. The guards walked behind me. When we stepped into the hallway, I thought of trying to escape again, but I knew it would be pointless. They would have caught me in a few minutes. So I stepped into the lift instead. Another hallway, more swinging doors. Then I stood in the operating room. There were half a dozen people, all of them busy preparing for the operation.

Mark Wester came up to me. He nodded and asked me to lie down. There were two operating tables in the room. A man already lay on one of them. I assumed him to be Zägel, and for a second or two I was filled with the thought of rushing up to him, crushing his head, beating his brain to a pulp. Wester broke the spell by grabbing hold of my arm and walking me to my table. I lay down and someone covered my body with a mauve sheet.

"Let me thank you for all your assistance and cooperation," Wester said. "Thank you."

I felt the sting of a needle in my arm.

The last thing I remember was hating him. Hating him. Hating . . .

Born in the small town of Skelleftehamn in 1954, Stieg Larsson grew up at his maternal grandparents' house in a village of less than fifty inhabitants, only rejoining his parents at the age of nine after the death of his grandfather. He moved out to live on his own at sixteen and from eighteen until his death was in a relationship with fellow political activist and science fiction fan, and later architect, Eva Gabrielsson. They were both active in science fiction fandom throughout the 1970s. After moving to Stockholm in 1977,

Larsson worked as a graphic artist with a news agency during the 1980s and 1990s, but simultaneously became known in Sweden as a leading opponent of racist and totalitarian views, on which he published several books in addition to being the Scandinavian correspondent for the British antifascist Searchlight *magazine. In 1995, he was involved in founding the similar Swedish magazine* Expo, *of which he was the editor from 1999 until his death. Hoping since his teens to break through as a fiction writer, Larsson in 2002 began writing a series of crime novels taking their basic theme from his feminist and antitotalitarian convictions. He died of a sudden heart attack in November 2004. By that time, he had finished and sold the three first novels featuring journalist Mikael Blomkvist and expert hacker Lisbeth Salander, and was working on further books in the series. The three finished novels, called The Millennium Trilogy, were published in Sweden in 2005 to 2007 and made publishing history. They have appeared in more than fifty countries, selling a total of seventy-five million copies to date, making them the best-selling adult novels in the world during the first decade of the twenty-first century; they have also been made into both Swedish and American feature movies. The first novel in the series,* Män som hatar kvinnor (Men Who Hate Women, *but in English published as* The Girl with the Dragon Tattoo) *was awarded the Glass Key as the year's best crime novel in any Nordic country by the Nordic Crime Fiction Society; the second,* Flickan som lekte med elden (The Girl Who Played with Fire), *received the best novel of the year award from the Swedish Crime Fiction Academy; the third,* Luftslottet som sprängdes (The Girl Who Kicked the Hornets' Nest), *again received the Glass Key. The novels have also received numerous awards in other countries.*

AN UNLIKELY MEETING

Henning Mankell and Håkan Nesser

Henning Mankell and Håkan Nesser are two of the giants of modern Swedish crime fiction, both also known and highly respected for their non-genre work.

Henning Mankell published his first crime novel (and his eleventh book) in 1991. It introduced his recurring protagonist, Detective Inspector Kurt Wallander of the Ystad police. He has since returned in ten further novels and one story collection, which have made the small town of Ystad—situated on the south coast of Sweden, where it was founded as a fishing village in the late twelve century and with just over 18,000 inhabitants—internationally famous. In one of the novels, Before the Frost *(originally published in 2002), the main protagonist is Wallander's daughter, Linda, newly graduated from the police academy.*

Håkan Nesser's first crime novel was Det grovmaskiga nätet *(The Mind's Eye), which appeared in Swedish in 1993. It introduced Detective Chief Inspector Van Veeteren in the fictitious town of Maardam, placed in an also fictitious, unnamed country in Northern Europe and with similarities to the Netherlands, Sweden, Germany, and Poland. Van Veeteren is in his early sixties at the start of the series; in the first five novels he is on active duty, but in the later ones he has retired from the police and instead works as an antiquarian bookseller but still assists in police investigations. He is a sullen, cynical man and an avid chess player.*

After ten Van Veeteren novels, Håkan Nesser changed venue and has written six novels featuring a Swedish police Inspector of Italian descent, Gunnar Barbarotti, and several stand-alone novels. Like Henning Mankell, he is widely translated. Together, the two authors have received one Best First Novel Award and no less than five Best Novel of the Year Awards from the Swedish Crime Fiction Academy.

"An Unlikely Meeting" is their only collaboration, a fascinating metafiction of a strange night in the lives of their two most famous protagonists. Readers should also know that Håkan Nesser is tall, thin, with dark, thinning hair, while Henning Mankell is short, heavily built, with fairly long, white-gray hair.

SUDDENLY WALLANDER REALIZED THAT HE NO LONGER KNEW WHERE HE was. Why couldn't she have come to Ystad instead? On the freeway, somewhere north of Kassel, he had doubted if it was even possible to drive on any longer. The snow had come down very heavy. Already then he had known that he would be late for his meeting with his daughter. Why did Linda have to suggest that they should spend Christmas together somewhere in the middle of Europe?

He turned on the roof light in the car and found his map. In the beam lights the road stretched empty. Where had he made a wrong turn? Around him was darkness. He had a sudden premonition of being forced to spend Christmas night in his car. He would drive blindly along these unknown continental roads and he would never find Linda.

He searched the map. Was he even anywhere at all? Or had he crossed some invisible border to a country that didn't even exist? He put away his map and drove on. The snow had suddenly stopped falling.

After a dozen miles he stopped at an intersection. He read the signs and searched the map again. Nothing. He made a sudden decision. He would have to find someone to ask. He turned off towards the town the road signs claimed to be closest.

The town was larger than he had expected. But its streets were deserted. Wallander stopped outside a restaurant that seemed to be open. He locked his car and realized that he was hungry.

He stepped into the dusk.

The restaurant was a breath of a Europe that hardly existed any more. Frozen in time, a strong smell of stale cigar smoke. Deer heads and coats of arms shared the brown walls with beer posters. A bar, also brown, empty of patrons; shaded booths, similar to the pens in a barn. At the tables shadows leaned over glasses of beer. In the background, loudspeakers. Christmas songs. Holy night.

Wallander looked around without finding an empty booth. A glass of beer, he thought. Then a good description of how to drive on. Then a phone call to Linda. To tell her whether he'd make it tonight or not.

One of the booths was occupied by a single man. Wallander hesitated. Then made up his mind. He walked up and pointed. The man nodded. It was okay for Wallander to sit down. The man sitting opposite him was eating. An old, sad-faced waiter appeared. Goulash? Wallander pointed to the other man's plate and beer glass. Then he waited. The man opposite went on eating with slow movements.

Wallander thought that he might start a conversation. Ask about the way, ask where he was. He took the opportunity when the man pushed his plate away.

"I don't mean to disturb you," Wallander said. "But do you speak English?"

The man nodded noncommittally.

"I've taken a wrong turn somewhere," Wallander said. "I'm Swedish, I'm a policeman, I'm on my way to spend Christmas with my daughter. But I'm lost. I don't even know where I am."

"Maardam," the man said.

Wallander recalled the road sign. But he had no memory of having seen the place on his map. He told the man his destination.

The man shook his head.

"You won't get there tonight," he said. "It's far. You're off course."

Then he smiled. His smile was unexpected. As if his face had cracked.

"I'm a policeman, too," the man said.

Wallander gave him a thoughtful look. Then he held out his hand.

"Wallander," he said. "I'm a detective. In a Swedish town called Ystad."

"Van Veeteren," the man said. "I'm a policeman here in Maardam."

"Two lonely policeman," Wallander said. "One of them lost. Not the most amusing of situations."

Van Veeteren smiled again, nodding.

"You're right," he said. "Two policemen meeting only because one of them has made a wrong turn."

"Things are as they are," Wallander said.

The waiter put his food on the table in front of him.

Van Veeteren lifted his glass, toasting him.

"Eat slowly," he said. "You're in no hurry."

Wallander thought of Linda. Of his having to call her. But he realized that the man who also was a policeman and who had a weird name was right.

He would spend his Christmas Eve in this strange place called Maardam and which he suspected wasn't even marked on his map.

Things were as they were.

Nobody could change that.

Just as so many other things in life.

Wallander placed his call to Linda, who of course was disappointed. But she understood.

After the call, Wallander stayed on outside the phone booth.

The Christmas songs made him sad.

He disliked sadness. Particularly on Christmas Eve.

Outside, the snow had begun falling again.

★　★　★

Van Veeteren remained sitting in their pen, his eyes fixed on two crossed toothpicks. How strange, he thought. I almost could have sworn that I wouldn't need to exchange even two words with anyone until the Christmas dawn's early gleaming . . . and then this guy suddenly turns up.

A Swedish policeman? Taking the wrong road in a snowstorm?

Just as unlikely as life itself. And that he himself was sitting here certainly wasn't the result of any planning. Quite the contrary. After the obligatory Christmas lunch with Renate and the afternoon best wishes telephone call to Erich, Jess and the grandchildren, he had crawled into a bubble bath with a stout beer and Handel turned up full. While waiting for the evening to come.

Christmas Eve chess with Mahler at the society.

Just like last year. And the year before that.

Mahler had called shortly before six. From the hospital up in Aarlack, where the old poet was stuck with his even older father and a broken thighbone.

A pity for such a vital ninety-year-old man. A pity considering the gambit he had thought of while taking his bath. A pity all things considered.

When despite all he had finally arrived at the society in the whirling snow he had also realized that it was no use to him without Mahler. He had driven on a few blocks towards Zwille and finally walked into the restaurant without any expectations. Regardless of everything else he had to eat. And perhaps drink.

The Swedish policeman returned with a sad smile.

"Did you reach her? What did you say your name was, by the way?"

"Wallander. Yes, it's fine. We just postponed everything until tomorrow."

There was a sudden soft warmth in his glance and there could hardly be any doubt about its origin.

"Daughters aren't such a bad thing to have sometimes," Van Veeteren said. "Even if you can't find them. How many do you have?"

"Only one," Wallander said. "But she's all right."

"Me too," Van Veeteren said. "And a son too but that's something else."

"Doesn't surprise me," Wallander said.

The sad waiter appeared, asking about what was to follow.

"Personally I prefer beer when alone," Van Veeteren said. "And wine with company."

"Ought to think about where to spend the night," Wallander said.

"I've already done that," Van Veeteren stated. "Red or white?"

"Thanks," Wallander said. "Red it is, then."

The waiter again disappeared into the shadows. A brief silence fell at the table while an Ave Maria of unknown origin began playing from the speakers.

"Why did you become a policeman?" Wallander asked.

Van Veeteren studied his colleague before answering.

"I've asked myself that question so many times by now that I can't remember the answer any longer," he said. "But I'd guess you to be ten years younger, so maybe you know?"

Wallander gave a half smile and leaned back.

"Yes," he said. "Though I'd have to admit that there are times when I have to stop to remind myself. It's all this evil; I'm planning to exterminate it. The only problem is that it seems we have built an entire civilization on it."

"Or at least some major supports," Van Veeteren said, nodding. "Though I would have thought Sweden to be spared at least the worst aberrations . . . your Swedish model, your spirit of consensus . . . well, it's what you read about, anyway."

"I used to believe in all that, too," Wallander said, "But that was a few years ago."

The waiter returned with a bottle of red wine and a few pieces of cheese, courtesy of the house. Ave Maria ended and muted strings began playing.

Wallander raised his glass but stopped in the middle of moving, listening hard.

"Do you recognize that?" he asked.

Van Veeteren nodded. "Villa-Lobos," he said. "What's the name of it?"

"I don't know," Wallander said. "But it's a piece for eight cellos and one soprano. It's damned lovely. Listen."

They sat without speaking.

"We seem to have some things in common," Wallander said.

Van Veeteren nodded contentedly.

"So it seems," he said. "If you play chess as well I'll be damned if I believe you're not just something someone's made up."

Wallander drank. Then he shook his head.

"Damned badly," he admitted. "I'm better at bridge, but hardly a champion at that either."

"Bridge?" Van Veeteren said and cut off a third of the Camembert. "Haven't played that in thirty years. Back in those days we used to be four."

Wallander smiled and gave a slight nod towards another table.

"Back there are a couple of guys with a deck of cards."

Van Veeteren leaned out of the booth to check.

Wallander was right. In a booth a few yards away two other men were flipping cards back and forth, looking bored. One of them was tall, thin and slightly stooped. The other one was almost his opposite: short, heavy and with a dogged expression. Judging from wrinkles and hair they were both close to fifty years old.

Van Veeteren stood.

"All right," he said. "It's only Christmas once a year. Let's make our move."

Less than ten minutes later the bidding was under way and after a further twenty-five minutes Wallander and Van Veeteren had won a doubled bid of four spades.

"Vagaries of chance," the shorter of the two men muttered.

"Even a blind hen sometimes finds a grain of corn," the taller one explained.

"Two," Van Veeteren said. "Two blind hens."

Wallander shuffled the cards with slightly unpracticed hands.

"And what do you two do for a living?" Van Veeteren asked, accepting an offered cigarette.

"Writers," the tall one said.

"Crime novels," added the shorter one. "We are fairly well-known. At least back home. Or at least I. We lost our way—that's why we happen to be here."

"Many have lost their way tonight," Van Veeteren said.

"Crime writers often lose their way," Wallander noted and began dealing the cards. "I suppose that's another pretty rotten line of work."

"I don't doubt it," Van Veeteren said.

They were about halfway through the next hand—an undoubled three no trump contract with the fairly well-known author as declarer—when the waiter appeared unasked from the shadows. He looked pained.

"Might I just inform you," he said subserviently, "that we'll be closing in ten minutes. It's Christmas Eve."

"What the heck . . . ?" Wallander said.

"What the hell?" Van Veeteren said.

The tall crime writer coughed and waved a dismissing index finger. But it was the short, well-known one who spoke.

"In that case, might I just in turn inform you," he said without the slightest tone of subservience, "that there is at least one advantage to being a writer . . ."

". . . even one who has lost his way," the tall one interjected.

". . . and that is that we are the ones writing your lines," the short one continued. "So I'll ask you to damned well repeat that entrance!"

The waiter bowed. Disappeared and after only a few seconds reappeared, armed with a bunch of keys. Bowed again and cleared his throat.

"On behalf of the host I would like to wish you all a Merry Christmas. Please feel free to serve yourselves from the bar, and should you feel hungry, there are cold cuts in the refrigerator. Lock up whenever you leave, but please don't forget to put the keys in the mail slot."

"Excellent," Van Veeteren stated. "Perhaps there is some common sense and good in the world after all."

The waiter retired for the last time. When he disappeared through the entrance they briefly heard the whistling of the snowstorm, but then the winter night again enfolded the little restaurant in the town that was missing from the map.

Common sense? Kurt Wallander thought, sliding a trey towards the king and jack already on the table. Good?

Well, if there was, perhaps on Christmas Eve.

And in the company of fictitious poets.

Poets, my ass! he thought after a second. Eight novels and not even a fucking line of blank verse!

Tomorrow, he would see Linda.

Henning Mankell was born in Stockholm in 1948. He began writing at an early age, but was also interested in the theater and initially worked as a stage director; from 1984 through 1990, he was in charge of the Växjö theater. During the 1960s, he was politically active on the far left, largely in sympathy with the Maoist groups in Sweden as well as Norway, where he lived during most of the 1970s. Currently, Mankell and his fourth wife, Eva, daughter of movie and stage director Ingmar Bergman, have homes in the southern Swedish town Ystad, on the Swedish island Färö, and in Maputo, Mozambique. Mankell published his first novel, Bergsprängaren, in 1973, and has since written more than thirty novels as well as plays, short stories, juveniles, and an autobiography. His first crime novel, introducing Detective Inspector Kurt Wallander in Ystad, was Mördare utan ansikte (Faceless Killers), *published in 1991; it won both the Best Novel of the Year Award from the Swedish Crime Fiction Academy and the first Glass Key for best crime novel of the year in any of the Scandinavian countries. In 1995, the fifth Wallander novel,* Villospår (Sidetracked), *received another Best Novel of the Year award. In Sweden, a total of thirty-five Wallander films have been released, covering all Mankell's novels as well as more than twenty based on original stories by the script writers. In*

202

Britain, the BBC has produced twelve adaptions of the Wallander novels starring Kenneth Branagh. Mankell's work is published throughout the world.

Håkan Nesser was born in 1950 in the small town of Kumla, which also houses one of Sweden's high-security prisons. He studied at Uppsala University and from 1974 until he became a full-time writer in 1998 was a gymnasium (approximately equivalent to high school) teacher of Swedish and English. His first novel was Koreografen (The Choreographer, 1988); *with his second,* Det grovmaskiga nätet (The Mind's Eye, 1993), *he published his first crime novel and the first of ten featuring Inspector Van Veeteren in the fictitious city of Maardam; the novel received the Best First Novel Award from the Swedish Crime Fiction Academy. The second and fourth in the series* Borkmann's punkt *and* Kvinna med fodelsemärke, (Borkmann's Point, 1994, *and* Woman with a Birthmark, 1996) *received the Best Novel of the Year Award; the seventh,* Carambole (Hour of the Wolf), *won the Glass Key for best crime novel published in Scandinavia during the year 2000. In 2006, Nesser introduced a new protagonist, Inspector Gunnar Barbarotti, a Swedish policeman of Italian descent; for the second Barbarotti novel in 2007,* En helt annan historia (An Entirely Different Story), *Nesser for the third time won the Best Novel of the Year Award. A further three Barbarotti novels have followed. Nesser has also written stand-alone crime novels, set in Sweden as well as in London and New York, and is an internationally acclaimed author.*

AN ALIBI FOR SEÑOR BANEGAS

Magnus Montelius

Magnus Montelius is an environmental consultant who spent many years in Africa, Latin America, and in the Eastern European countries that were part of the Soviet Union before 1991. He now lives with his family on Stockholm's south side. His first novel was published in 2011 but is set in 1990 and is concerned with the political history of the previous decades. Montelius grew up in a family where many members had been active on the radical left, particularly during the 1960s and 1970s, and he wanted to portray both that intellectual environment and its relationship to the surrounding world and its realities. Mannen från Albanien (The Man from Albania) *was a very strong first novel: a political thriller of the last period of the ColdWar, based on meticulous research and personal insights.*

Both before and after that book, Montelius has written occasional short stories. As in his novel, he uses the personalities of his characters as the starting point for the events that follow. His story here displays both his careful sense of story, his humor, and his skill in portraying characters.

THEY WERE ALONE IN THE SMALL INTERROGATION ROOM. THE DEFENSE lawyer regarded him under heavy eyelids. His face was red and bloated and his hair a bit unruly. It had probably been a tiring holiday. Welcome to the club, Adam thought.

"So you mean," the lawyer sighed, "that you are absolutely innocent of these charges."

Adam nodded.

"But you did make a complete confession to the police?"

"It's complicated."

The lawyer looked even more tired. He obviously didn't believe Adam, nor was he in the mood for any complicated stories. But even so, Adam thought, he had to tell him what really had happened. And start at the beginning.

Señor Banegas carefully sipped his wine toddy and glanced around appreciatively. He and Adam were the only guests in the Hotel Reisen bar, not particularly strange since, after all, this was the night before Christmas Eve.

"It's not a bad plan, is it?"

Adam couldn't get a word out. Actually, it was the most idiotic idea he had ever heard.

Banegas smiled crookedly. "Of course it entails a certain amount of inconvenience. And to me, personally, considerable cost. But love, my dear friend, is worth any sacrifice."

Señor Banegas was the Honduran secretary of state for infrastructure, a successful retailer of favors and favors in return. He had arrived with a delegation a little over a week ago. The absurd time of year had been chosen to coincide with Christmas shopping, and the delegates had all brought their wives.

Banegas twisted his grizzled mustache. "Adam, I tell you this most seriously. We never know where and when a great love will overwhelm us."

But Banegas was strangely reticent about the object of his passion.

Adam felt as if the minister read his thoughts. "We are gentlemen, you and I. So I know that there is no need for me to name the young lady. That is well. As I have told you, my wife is the problem." He sighed. "She is crazy, and I use the word in a strictly clinical sense."

Adam was prepared to agree. During his trips to Honduras he had met Mrs. Banegas at receptions. A round woman with staring eyes who seemed to watch every movement her husband made.

"When I told her that we would stay on an extra week, just she and I, to celebrate Christmas in Stockholm, she was at first overjoyed. But then she became jealous and suspicious. Why had I decided on such a thing? Was I going to meet someone? I tell you, she is crazy."

"Well, not totally off the mark, anyway. And is this where I enter the picture?" Banegas spread his arms.

"Exactly. I explained that it would unfortunately not be possible for me to spend all my time in her company, no matter how happily I would have done so. But that my good friend Adam Dillner laid claim to part of my time for meetings concerning a transaction between the Honduran government and the company represented by him. And that I could hardly refuse, which she also realized. In my country, this would have been entirely normal. Not here, naturally. But she doesn't know that."

He was right, of course.

Banegas fished a paper out of his inside pocket and put it on the table. "I took the liberty of writing the schedule you have set me, since I thought it would add a nice touch. I used your company letterhead."

Where had he gotten hold of that? "If I may say so, this looks like a very busy schedule."

Banegas solemnly put his right palm over his heart. "My friend, I am in love." In a more subdued voice, he went on: "I must implore you to stick entirely to our little subterfuge. Explain to your family that you are meeting an important client and, of course, stay away from home during the periods set out in the schedule. As I have told you, my wife is unstable and might very well decide to check on your absences from home. It is a most reasonable precaution."

Adam looked at the schedule. In fact it was highly unreasonable that he would have to spend such a large part of the days between Christmas and New Year's shuffling around in the snowstorm to prevent Mrs. Banegas from breaking her unfaithful husband's alibi. There were more conventional ways of making business contacts with Central American customers that worked perfectly well. Still, right now Banegas' insane wife happened to be just what Adam needed.

"Grampa, Grampa, Grampa!"

Max and Ada ran a set course around the living room, through the hallway, past the kitchen, and back again. Adam walked up to the kitchen island to pour himself some more wine.

Kattis gave him a glance. "Adam, we'll have a nice evening tonight."

His mother-in-law entered the kitchen, an empty wineglass in her hand. She stumbled on the carpet, muttering under her breath, bent to the bag-in-box wine container and wrinkled her nose. "Don't you have anything Spanish? A Rioja?"

The plane she was on had lifted off from Málaga less than ten hours earlier.

Kattis removed a baking sheet full of gingerbread from the oven. "Adam, would you look?"

But his mother-in-law had already forgotten it all and refilled her glass. "I think I'll make some toffee tonight, by the way. The poor little ones have hardly had any Christmas candy at all."

"We're trying to cut back on sugar."

"Adam, dear, you really shouldn't jump on board every new health bandwagon."

"It's hardly—"

Kattis let go of her rolling pin. "That's a great idea, Mother!"

Grandma called out to the living room: "What do you say, kids, do you want some of grandma's toffee?"

They screamed back. Hopelessly, Adam verified that they were always willing to sell their souls for some melted cane sugar.

"There, you see," Grandma said, staggering back into the living room.

He turned to Kattis.

"Adam!" she growled.

In the living room, Grampa was in the middle of playing something with Max and Ada while Grandma was leafing through some old Swedish family magazines Kattis had put out for her. When they entered, Grampa poured a whiskey and sat down in the couch, arms spread across its backrest. "Katarina told us about your Mexican, Adam," he said.

"Honduran."

His father-in-law waved an impatient hand. "That's what I said." He glared at Adam. "What I don't understand is how anyone, a husband, can abandon his wife almost the whole Christmas holiday just to play tourist guide to some Colombian."

"Hond—"

"When he has two small children and his wife's parents have come to visit—"

"Daddy, it's okay. Adam and I have talked about it. It's his work."

210

"Haven't we come any further despite all our talk about equality? And Adam, what's so important about this—Honduran?"

Adam hesitated. "We are trying to get a road project, the new highway from Honduras to Nicaragua. This Banegas fellow—"

His father-in-law slowly shook his head. "Adam, Adam, Adam. That's so out-of-date. Why don't you build a railroad instead?"

Grandma put her magazine down and turned to Kattis. "Daddy is the chairman of the Torremolinos Environmental Club. We have become activists."

"That's great, Mother!"

Adam half-heartedly began to describe the infrastructure of Honduras, but his father-in-law interrupted him again.

"They don't need a new road to Nicaragua, Adam. What they need is a road away from climate disaster."

"God, how well you put that, Göran!" Grandma exclaimed. "Why don't you write it down, Adam?"

He rose slowly. "I think I'll lay the table."

When he stood in the kitchen, he heard his mother-in-law's voice. "He never listens to a word we say."

Tomorrow was Christmas Eve, but according to Banegas' schedule he would still be away for a few hours to explain the traffic solutions used on the Southern Link expressway. He could hardly wait.

Thanks to the Banegas scheme, he could spend several Christmas Eve hours in a coffeehouse on Nybrogatan. He brought a book he had given himself for Christmas, but most of the time he just sipped his coffee and looked at the last-minute shoppers rushing past outside. As for himself, he had no more shopping to do, no other tasks to perform than to serve as an alibi for a horny minister of infrastructure.

On Christmas Day, Banegas hadn't dared make any entries on his schedule, and Adam spent the entire day with his family and in-laws. It was worse than usual. Kattis' family had introduced so many traditions that the holidays became rigidly directed performances. Every detail was sacrosanct and their order must not be changed.

211

Mostly it was all about games. After ten years, Adam was still unable to see any point to them. They played Hide the Pig Santa, the Almond Race, and something which seemed mainly to involve everyone hitting everyone else's head with tiny sandbags his mother-in-law had dragged along from Spain for the occasion. He wanted to refuse to get involved but knew from experience that everything would just get worse if he didn't join in. Since he was the only one unaware of the rules he always lost, to his father-in-law's undisguised delight. Adam sadly observed that as opposed to himself, his children always joined in with great enthusiasm.

The evening ended with a quiz on the lives of members of the clan. Though he always got what the others considered unusually easy questions, he had so far never managed a single correct answer.

"But Adam," his mother-in-law exclaimed, "you had the same question about Aunt Lotta's rusty old Audi last year!"

Tomorrow was the day after Christmas. That was when they were supposed to have their traditional waffle breakfast in front of the TV. Followed by a combined outdoors walk and new quiz competition, then a lunch with Kattis' sister in Australia attending via a computer link, and after that a family game called Where Is the Krokofant, named for a disgustingly sweet candy bar.

Luckily, Banegas had a full schedule.

Adam decided to install himself in the cafeteria of the Museum of the Mediterranean. According to the schedule, he was showing Banegas biogas refueling stations. In the evening they were doing something even more silly; he didn't remember what. It didn't matter.

He was deep into his book when his phone rang. It was Banegas.

"Adam, we have a problem. It is extremely important that we meet at once."

Every protest and demand for further explanations was met by hissed objections.

"We really must meet, I'm waiting at the Hotel Reisen bar."

Adam plodded through the snow on the bridge to the Old Town. What had he gotten himself into?

212

Banegas seemed perfectly calm and sat comfortably with a wine toddy. His whole demeanor suggested that it was far from his first. He went straight to the point.

"We have a problem with tonight's activity."

We?

Banegas went on. "I chose the visit to the Hammarby Lake City since my wife refuses to travel by boat. Now it turns out that you can go there by land. Which you failed to tell me." He glared at Adam. "And of course my wife has found that out and insists on accompanying me."

Why, oh why had he gone along with Banegas' plan?

"Adam, it just won't do. And so at the last moment you have changed our schedule and instead arranged for us to go to the opera."

"Opera?"

"My wife hates opera. As an extra precaution I have also decided that Señor Harald Thorvaldsson of the Export Council will join us, and that after the performance we will have supper at the Gyldene Freden restaurant to discuss business." He held up Thorvaldsson's calling card, as if it were a winning lottery ticket. "That's when he gives me this, which will further strengthen the credibility of our story."

It was hard enough to get hold of any of the Export Council functionaries during normal office hours; to convince one of them to spend the day after Christmas at the opera with a Honduran secretary of state would probably be humanly impossible. But, as Banegas would probably have said if Adam had bothered to object, his wife didn't know that.

Banegas pulled out their schedule. "So I would like to ask you to make the necessary change to our little program." He gave Adam a pen and added kindly: "You can do it by hand."

As in a trance, Adam struck out the visit to Hammarby Lake City and wrote in the opera performance according to Banegas' instructions. "Don't forget to write that Señor Thorvaldsson will accompany us."

When that was done, Banegas conjured up a ticket to that night's performance of *Don Giovanni* and ceremoniously tore it apart along the perforation. "Here's your ticket, Adam, I leave nothing to chance."

"Is that really necessary?"

"I insist."

Outside, Banegas embraced him. "Adam, how will I ever—" The Honduran was cut short as they both lost their footing. Arms around each other, they bounced down the snow-covered steps to the sidewalk. Adam managed to loosen his grip and keep his balance, but just as he imagined all was well he felt one of his feet crack the ice on a pool of water and his shoe immediately filled.

"God *damn* it!"

Banegas gave him a reproachful look. "My dear friend, I don't know what that was all about, but there is no need to worry. Here we both are, and none the worse for wear." He glanced down at Adam's feet. "Well, sorry about your shoe. But I assume you must agree that it's a minor problem." He checked his watch. "Sorry, I really can't chat any longer. Remember that according to our schedule we are having supper after the performance. Make sure not to get home earlier than midnight."

The minister hurried off towards Kungsträdgården park.

Back at his house, the windows glowed in the night. Adam hid behind the snow-laden lilacs. According to the program he shouldn't be here, but there was no helping it. His foot felt frozen stiff. In the washroom there were rubber boots and a laundry basket with warm socks; the key to the cellar was in the third right-hand flowerpot in the greenhouse. Perfect.

Then he saw it. The door to the cellar was open. The kids must have been playing down there again. How many times had he told them . . . And besides, there had been a lot of burglaries in the area lately. Silently he sneaked across the lawn, cursing under his breath every time the cold water in his shoe splashed his toes.

He walked soundlessly through the cellar and was just about to start digging in the laundry basket when he saw the man. His heart skipped a beat and he had to bite his lip not to scream. Wasn't that . . . Yes, something metallic gleamed in the thief's hand! Adam's eyes flickered wildly around the room and stopped at a board left over from their renovation. Perfect. He grabbed it, slipped forward. His temples throbbed. I'll fucking show you!

Slap that thing out of his hand with the board. Get the bastard. He lifted his arm, felt his foot slip on the floor. He lost his balance but completed the blow. No, a little too high, straight to the head. And much too hard! A nasty, dull sound and a jolt he could feel all through his arm and body. The man collapsed to the floor and made a rattling sound.

Fuck, how bad had he hit him? He couldn't . . . A thin, red trickle of blood ran from his ear and joined the blood on his cheek. Adam frantically looked for some sign of life. He couldn't . . . Warily his shaking hands turned the body. That's when he recognized the familiar face, burned hazel by endless hours on the golf courses in Torremolinos. An unlit flashlight rolled from a slack hand. He felt his cartoid artery. Nothing. No no no, say it isn't true! Anything, just not this! Suddenly he heard the rhythmic yells of his children upstairs.

"Where's the Krokofant? Where's the Krokofant?"

Get rid of the board, find socks, put on boots. Fuck fuck fuck. He ran across the lawn, through the woods, to another subway station. Just to be safe. Threw his shoes in a building-site container. Then he threw up on the platform. It just couldn't be true. At the pub in the main railway station he downed a pint of beer and immediately ordered another. At least it made his hands stop shaking. What had he done? But it was an accident! Sure, but still!

While running through the wood he had promised himself at least to consider it. But halfway through his third pint he made up his mind. What good would it do? Confessing wouldn't bring Göran back to life. But it wasn't the thought of jail that frightened him, it was the reactions of his children. What would they think of him? He would forever be the man who had killed their adored Grampa. And Kattis? No, no, he would keep silent.

The two police officers waiting in the living room were dressed in civilian clothes and unobtrusive. The body had already been removed, the older one whispered, a kindly man who reminded Adam of his company's personnel officer. His colleague was a younger woman who wore an inscrutable expression and her hair in a ponytail. She scrutinized Adam from head to feet. Did he have any stains? He had checked so carefully! The personnel officer cop took him aside.

"A horrible thing. I understand you are all in shock." He went on to explain the circumstances with which Adam was already much too familiar. "We have had reports of a number of burglaries in this area. Your father-in-law must have left the door open and been surprised by them. He was playing some game with the children, aah . . ."

The young police woman checked her notes. "Where's the Krokofant?"

"Exactly," the policeman went on. "These international burglar gangs are no Sunday school boys. They used as much violence as necessary to be sure of getting away. Unfortunately they may already be out of the country."

Adam slowly shook his head, angrily clenching his jaws to hide his relief.

"Of course we hold no preconceptions," the young woman added. Adam said nothing. He much preferred her older partner.

Adam spent the rest of the evening trying to comfort Kattis. His mother-in-law took care of the children and managed to be both strong and tender despite her own grief. Had he misjudged her all these years? Before the police officers left they had wanted to know where he had spent his evening. Just routine, the man assured him self-consciously. Adam told them about his visit to the opera and showed them the ticket Banegas had given him. The policeman excused the necessity for such formalism. The woman said nothing but carefully noted the seat number in her little book. No, Adam didn't like her at all.

That night he got no sleep at all. Would the police contact Banegas? And what had that policewoman been looking at all the time? He had to get hold of Banegas before the police got to him. At eight in the morning he sneaked out into the garden to call Banegas' cell. No answer. He called again, several times, until nine-thirty. He didn't dare phone their room at the hotel, given how suspicious Mrs. Banegas was.

Finally he decided to go to the Grand Hôtel. He waited in the lobby for at least an hour. Suddenly he got a glimpse of Mrs. Banegas, hurrying out alone through the revolving doors. Strange. According to their schedule, there were no imaginary educational field trips until three o'clock. At this hour, Banegas ought to be keeping his wife company. Could he be busy with the police?

Nonchalantly, Adam stepped into an elevator. On the third floor he found room 318.

"Señor Banegas," he hissed while knocking. "Señor Banegas, it's me. Adam."

No reply. Adam tried again. "Héctor! Open, it's important."

He waited for another minute and was just about to knock again when he heard someone clear his throat behind him. A tall man in the hotel uniform, buttons gleaming.

"Are you looking for someone?"

Adam made a half-hearted attempt to explain.

"Hotel policy is that all callers must announce themselves at the reception. And your friend doesn't seem to be in. If you give me your name, I will inform him that you have been here to see him." He gave Adam a strange look. "Your *full* name."

Adam thought for a second and decided on "Jonas Lindgren," an old classmate who had always gotten into trouble. The uniformed man followed him all the way out to the street.

Kattis had decided to leave for Spain that day, bringing her mother and the children. They had to get away from the house for a while, she said. Adam told her that he understood and promised to take care of all the practical details, whatever they might be. When he had waved them off in the departure lounge at Arlanda airport he felt sweat begin to seep out on his forehead. But not because of what Banegas might say; what filled his mind was the memory of the blood trickling from Göran's ear. It was an accident, he mumbled, a little too loudly. People around him seemed to look suspiciously at him.

When he got home he was unable to eat and instead poured a large whiskey. He had heard that some of the neighbors were going to start patrolling the area at night after what had happened, but that they didn't want to ask him to join. Nobody wanted to ask anything of him. Out of sympathy. His conscience was surging over him and he began pondering whether he should begin building water mains in Sudan, give all his money to homeless or join a monastery. But it passed. What did any of that have to do with Göran's death? Maybe he could just sign up to be a Homework Help instructor with the Red Cross. It had just been an accident, after all.

He lay down on the couch, pulled a throw over himself and tried to read. When the doorbell rang, he didn't know how long he had slept. It was the two police officers. Something seemed to have changed. Now the young woman stood in front while her male partner stood to one side behind her, his head slightly bent. And it was she who spoke first.

"Could we come inside, we have a few more questions."

They asked about his evening with Banegas, about the opera and the supper. Adam answered to the best of his ability and kept to the schedule. What might Banegas have told them?

"Have you spoken to him?" Adam tried to smile. "He can be a bit confusing sometimes, maybe the Swedish police would make him nervous if . . ." He fell silent. Something was obviously wrong, enormously wrong. The two police officers exchanged a glance. The woman cleared her throat.

"He is dead."

"Dead?" At first, Adam felt immensely relieved. His worries about what Banegas might say had been totally needless.

"Banegas was found murdered on Kastellholmen," the police woman said. "Beaten to death with a blunt object. We estimate the time of death to between ten p.m. and midnight. In other words, shortly after you left the opera."

Adam had nothing very satisfactory to say and chose to give an uncertain nod.

"There are a few details we find confusing. We thought you might help us fill in the blanks."

Was this when he should insist on having a lawyer present? Or was it too early? Would it seem suspicious instead?

Before he had reached any conclusion, she went on: "Maybe we could do this down at the precinct."

They took turns questioning him. The older policeman seemed anxious to explain that it was all just routine, nothing to worry about. He had a kindly smile.

His female partner didn't. She pulled out Banegas' schedule. "Do you recognize this?"

Adam nodded.

"What happened to your supper? At the Gyldene Freden they have no memory of you, and there was no reservation made in your name."

Adam managed to strain out an answer he felt reasonably satisfied with, about having forgotten to reserve a table and that anyway it had turned out Banegas had preferred to go for a walk on his own. If he had said anything else earlier, he must have mixed things up. She silently wrote down what he said. Then her partner took over and explained that of course this was no interrogation, but would Adam consider helping them out by staying on for a couple of hours?

In fact, only around three-quarters of an hour passed before the police woman returned. "Your schedule says that Harald Thorvaldsson at the Export Council was supposed to join you at the opera."

Damn it!

"However, when we spoke to Mr. Thorvaldsson he denies that any such thing was ever even considered on his part. In fact, he dismissed it very firmly."

The answer Adam managed this time was less satisfying. She put a few resulting questions, and Adam got himself still more entangled. After a while she suggested that they could take a break and continue later. He declined to have a lawyer present.

When he was brought back into the room, the kindly police-man was gone and the woman in the strict ponytail questioned him alone. As before, she wasted no time on small talk or smiles. "We have had an interesting conversation with a member of the Grand Hôtel staff. The day after the murder someone tried to gain access to the room where the Banegas couple stayed. That person acted nervously and gave a name that turned out to be false. However, you were identified from the photo we took in connection with out other investigation."

Adam's efforts to explain were torn to shreds by her furious counterquestions. He needed to sleep and clung to the single point which seemed to speak in his favor. "But why would I have anything to do with Señor Banegas' death? It's absurd!"

"Actually, we've learned a reasonable motive from his widow. It seems that you have spent a long time discussing some major road construction project. But Banegas had already given the commission to some American consortium. He was going to tell you before leaving for home."

What a bastard! "But you don't kill anyone because—"

But she wasn't interested in Adam's reasonable objections. They let him go home to sleep but brought him back again the next morning. At first, the atmosphere seemed more relaxed. The kindly policeman said that they accepted Adam's statement that he had left for home immediately after the opera. Adam said that he was glad to hear it, and the policeman seemed pleased as well. But the female officer remained silent and resolute throughout. Without any warn-ing, she asked:

"So could you tell us why you didn't get home until two hours later? And wearing rubber boots?"

Suddenly the interrogation veered off on a new, horrible track.

The lawyer looked up from his notes. "So that was when you decided to confess to the murder of Banegas?"

Adam nodded. "I just can't bear to be convicted of murder-ing Göran, my father-in-law." He thought of Kattis and the children and closed his eyes. "This way I get an alibi for that."

"But now you claim that you had nothing to do with Banegas' death?"

"That's what I've been telling you. But on the other hand—"

The lawyer held up a deprecating hand. "One thing at a time. Let us focus on the crime you have been arrested for."

He summed up the situation in a few tired platitudes and looked at his watch. "We'll see," he said. "Complicated. Must consider strategy, consult my colleagues."

A police officer arrived to return Adam to his cell. He was led along a corridor and past the open door to a room. In the room was a sobbing, rotund little woman dressed in black. She was leaning her head against the shoulder of a woman officer, but despite that Adam immediately recognized Mrs. Banegas. She glanced up at him. Her sly eyes shone triumphantly and her mouth curled in a superior smile.

She really was crazy.

Magnus Montelius was born in 1965 and returned to live in Stockholm after many years as an adviser on water and environmental management in both Africa and Latin America; he has also worked extensively in Eastern Europe and the former Soviet republics. He began writing in earnest in 2009, winning a short story competition that year and another one in 2011. In 2011 he also published his first novel, Mannen från Albanien (The Man from Albania), *a universally praised spy thriller set during the 1960s and 1970s, which has been sold to eight countries and will become a Swedish feature film. Magnus Montelius is at work on his next novel.*

SOMETHING IN HIS EYES

Dag Öhrlund

Many of Dag Öhrlund's Swedish readers may be surprised by his story for this book.

After starting to write for publication at fifteen, Dag Öhrlund worked as a journalist, essayist, reporter, and photographer for many years before turning his hand to fiction. His first novel, written in collaboration with Dan Buthler, was published in late 2007. Since then, the writing team of Buthler and Öhrlund have produced a further seven novels, while Dag Öhrlund alone has written one. All of them are crime fiction, but of a kind not common in Sweden: Dag Öhrlund, both on his own and with Dan Buthler, writes what may perhaps best be characterized as hard-boiled, action-oriented crime novels. All but one of the Buthler and Öhrlund collaborations share the same protagonist, Criminal Inspector Jacob Colt, and in most of the novels Colt is pitted against the same villain, psychopath, and serial killer, Christopher Silfverbielke, a man who—in Dag Öhrlund's phrase—"actually does the things other people just imagine doing."

The Colt-Silfverbielke novels have become very popular indeed in Sweden, perhaps because their villain's total break with the strong sense of consensual social control dominating Swedish society appeals to an otherwise seldom revealed wish to revolt that may well smolder within many

Swedes. But the stories have also made their authors' names synonymous with action-packed plotting, inventive gruesomeness, and, unfairly, with the callousness and misogyny characteristic of their recurring villain.

"Something in His Eyes" shows very different aspects of Dag Öhrlund's writing and concerns.

THE SCREAM BURST FROM LENYA THE MOMENT SHE LOST CONTACT WITH the balcony rail and fell.

It seemed strange to her that so many thoughts could pass through a brain in only a few seconds. An icy wind burned her cheeks.

Her life became a movie. As a small child she toddled around with Azad. Of course they squabbled, like all siblings, but she didn't love anybody else the way she loved her big brother.

He was God, and Love, and everything else, even though she wouldn't truly understand that until much later.

Would he ever forgive their father, after this?

A second or two later, her thoughts ceased as her head hit the asphalt.

Lenya Barzani died instantly.

If any angels lamented, her father's howl from the balcony drowned them out.

Detective Captain Jenny Lindh's fingers tightened on the steering wheel as she fought back nausea.

Her car was stuck in traffic on the Essinge freeway leading downtown. The line of cars inched forward a few feet at a time through the heavy snow, and the wipers were hard put to keep the windshield clear.

Right now, Jenny hated everything.

She'd gotten the call a few minutes earlier. A patrol car had been sent to an apartment building in the suburb of Tensta after a witness had reported seeing a lifeless girl lying on the ground. In the midst of the blizzard, they were scarce on patrol cars, field investigators and everything else.

So Lindh got the job.

As if I didn't have enough problems, she thought.

Her life, as the 'burbs kids would say, had gotten *totally fucked over* about a week ago.

That night.

Jenny had felt sick during the night shift. She excused herself by saying she must have caught a bug, and left for home several hours early.

She didn't want her colleagues to know she was pregnant.

At least not yet.

She managed to grab a Kleenex just in time, catching the small gob of vomit that came up as the images returned to her mind.

Cursing under her breath, she rolled down the window, threw out the slimy tissue and was blasted in the face by a whirl of snow.

Daniel and . . . the whore.

Yeah. She had looked like a whore. Blonde, a bit too fat, in a lace bra and black garters, moaning and riding Daniel on the bed.

Their bed. *Her* bed.

The nausea that had been tormenting her for hours was forced aside as she stood immobile in the doorway. It was replaced by rage, kindling in her stomach and working its way up her throat to her mouth.

She had screamed. Seen the slut's eyes bulge as she slid off Jenny's husband's cock and tried to cover herself. Seen Daniel sit up, raise a hand in some kind of defense.

"Jenny, it's not what you think . . ."

The stupidest fucking sentence she had ever heard.

That was when she had drawn her gun.

DAG ÖHRLUND

It had been a funny sight: Daniel and the whore, practically naked, racing out of their home as she aimed at them. Tumbling around in the snow outside as they tried to get dressed.

For no discernible reason, the line of cars slowly dissolved. Jenny Lindh pulled out a cigarette, lit it and wondered if she had any pain relievers in her handbag. She had been up drinking whiskey until two in the morning, and her head was pounding.

Yeah, sure—she shouldn't drink while she was pregnant.

Yeah, sure—she had taken up smoking again two days ago, even though she knew better.

Who cared? She would have an abortion. Her marriage was over. Her picturesque life had ended. Her dream of a good life with another cop had turned into a pathetic game of roulette where her money was on the wrong number.

Clara, her only support, had made the difference between extinction and survival. Tough, smart Clara, who had always been there. Who always had answers, could comfort and encourage. And who had an outlook on men and relationships that was completely different from Jenny's.

Everlasting love is fucking bullshit. So I'll help myself, get laid, have fun and move on!

Clara was one of a kind.

Smacking her hand against the wheel, Jenny shot the car into the left-hand lane and sped up. Her right hand fumbled for the rotating blue light, managed to get it up on the roof above her and turned it on.

Get the hell out of my way!

Sixteen minutes later, she stood outside the blue-and-white police tape and observed the scene in front of her.

The first thing that struck her was the ugliness of the building, and she wondered who had thought it up.

Had *anyone* been thinking?

Roughly forty years ago, the politicians of a small country called Middle-of-the-Road suddenly realized there weren't enough homes.

One million apartments.

It took them ten years to build that million, and here in front of her was one of the results.

It looked awful.

The first patrol on the scene had cordoned off an eighty-by-eighty-foot area. The forensics team's gray-blue Volkswagen van was parked just outside the police tape. A tent had been erected close to the building to cover something that had to be the body, in order to stop the press photographers from taking pictures.

A man dressed in a coverall and boots came plodding up to her through several inches of snow. As he approached, she recognized him as Björkstedt. A reliable workhorse who had been investigating crime scenes since forever.

"Hi. You can come in if you want."

"Thanks, Anders." Jenny lifted the tape and slipped under it. "So what have we got?"

"Balcony girl, model One A."

"Which means?"

"No footprints, no other tracks anywhere near her. She must have died from the fall alone. The neck is bent at an unnatural angle."

"So, broken?"

"I'm no medical examiner, but yeah, I'll bet my next paycheck on it."

"Anything else?"

"She wasn't wearing outdoor clothes, just jeans and a T-shirt. Her cell phone fell out of her pocket. It's crushed; must have ended up under her body when she landed."

"Can I have a look at her?"

"Sure."

Björkstedt turned and walked ahead of her through the snow. She had to crouch to enter the tent, where a strong lamp cast a cold light on what, until recently, had been a living teenager.

The girl was on her stomach with her head turned to one side. Her face had stiffened into an expression that was anything but peaceful. There were scrapes and bruises on one cheek, but the rest of her face was unmarked.

Lindh pointed to the marks. "What do you think?"

Björkstedt shrugged. "She hasn't been moved. You can see that the snow has been pushed aside by her cheek, and there's blood. So she could have gotten the scrapes when she hit the asphalt, but they could also have been caused before she fell—I can't swear to either."

"Do you know anything about her?"

Björkstedt jerked his thumb at the building. "I talked to our colleagues. Lenya Barzani, seventeen years old. Lived on the fourth floor. The uniforms are up there."

She nodded. "Thanks."

"Sure."

Jenny left the tent, her boots leaving a straight track in the snow up to the police tape closest to the main entrance.

My husband cheated on me with a whore. In our bed.

A seventeen-year-old girl is dead, maybe murdered. Gotta focus. Damn, it hurts!

Head pounding, she took the elevator to the fourth floor while fumbling for painkillers in her pocket. From inside the shaft, she could hear a commotion that got louder the higher she rose.

She opened the elevator door and stepped out into chaos, pushing aside a woman who flailed her arms and cried. Distressed neighbors spoke loudly in a language she didn't understand. Uniformed colleagues patiently kept them from entering the apartment they were guarding.

Lindh showed the colleagues her badge, pushed through the throng of upset people, and stepped into the hallway where she was met by yet another uniformed policeman.

"Hi. Jenny Lindh, criminal investigations. What have we got?"

The officer consulted the small notebook in his hand.

"The dead girl is Lenya Barzani, seventeen. A Kurd from northern Iraq. Her father Schorsch is in the living room. Nobody else was here when we arrived. We've had a look around. The living room and balcony are a mess; one of the techs is out there now."

"Thanks."

Jenny walked past him, into a long hallway. A bedroom door stood open to her right; she paused and looked inside.

It was a typical girl's room. A Justin Bieber poster on the wall; a vanity table with a laptop squeezed in between lipstick, deodorant and perfumes. A speaker with an iPhone dock; a teddy bear and pink pillows on a sloppily made bed. A pair of jeans, a spaghetti top and some underwear discarded on a chair.

Lenya's room?

She kept walking. The doors to the other rooms were closed, and the hallway led her into the living room.

The man on the couch might have been sixty. He was dressed in brown pants, a beige shirt and a brown knit sweater. He sat slumped over with his head in his hands, sobbing. Next to him sat a female cop, her hand on his shoulder, trying to speak calmly to him.

He's barefoot. The floor by his feet is damp. Why?

Lindh gave the policewoman a quick nod, saw the kitchen doorway and walked in. She dug a couple of aspirin out of her pocket, put them in her mouth, turned on the faucet and filled her cupped hand. The unpleasant taste filled her mouth as one of the tablets dissolved, and she gazed at the small pool of water in her hand as if it were a mirror.

We should have had an entire life together. We were happy. We had bought a house. We were going to have a baby.

You betrayed me. So I wasn't good enough?

With a jerking motion she threw the water into her mouth, then refilled her palm, shut her eyes and swallowed. She stood there for several seconds, her eyes closed, while the water ran from the tap and the policewoman spoke softly to the man on the couch.

Focus, Jenny.

She pushed back a stray strand of hair and looked around.

An ordinary kitchen, except for the large fabric decorations on the walls. Images, probably of some religious significance. Writing she didn't understand. Kurdish? She went into the living room. The policewoman was still there, her hand on Schorsch Barzani's shoulder. Through the window, she could see the squatting technician working outside. Jenny opened the door, and he looked up at her.

"Hi. Jenny Lindh, criminal investigations. What's it look like?"

230

He swiped a plastic-gloved hand across his forehead.

"Well, there seems to have been some kind of scuffle. The snow's been kicked away, and a couple of flowerpots have fallen and broken. That chair has lost a leg. Right now I'm taking casts of the shoe prints. And I've bagged a few fibers."

She nodded, and was just about to close the door. Then:

"How long would you say it takes to fall from here to the ground?"

The technician's eyes lost focus and stared into space.

"Fourth floor . . . maybe nine seconds."

"Thanks."

She closed the door.

Nine seconds.

Her head was still pounding, but the pain seemed to be abating. Jenny sat down opposite the man on the couch. She met the policewoman's gaze.

"Has he said anything?"

The woman shrugged. "That she jumped of her own volition. He's devastated. He tried to stop her."

"Had they argued earlier?"

"No, not according to him."

Oh, really. So a smiling, carefree Lenya had walked past her father on the couch and told him she was going to jump. He had stood up, followed her and tried to stop her, but his strength hadn't been enough to restrain a seventeen-year-old girl.

In fact, he hadn't even had the strength to drag himself down to the courtyard where his daughter lay dead.

"I want him detained for interrogation on reasonable suspicion."

Jenny leaned forward.

"Schorsch . . . ?"

No reaction. She tried again.

The man slowly raised his head. His face was red, swollen from crying. His eyes were wet, his gaze both empty and despairing.

"Schorsch, you'll have to come with us to police headquarters. I want to have a little chat with you there. Do you understand me?"

He made a resigned gesture.

"Why no talk here?"

"For practical reasons."

"You cannot think . . . ?"

"I don't think anything, but I need to talk to you where we won't be disturbed."

She went on.

"Where's the rest of your family?"

Again the resigned gesture. "Azad is at a friend's . . ."

"Who is Azad?"

"My son."

"And your wife?"

"She and Lara are with my cousin Naushad."

"Who is Lara?"

"My daughter."

"How old is she?"

"Fourteen."

Something in his eyes when he mentions her name.

"Okay, I understand. Now, would you please come with us . . ."

The police building at Kronoberg is colossal. Covers a whole block. Gray and ugly. It holds more departments, corridors and officials than most people could ever imagine. In one of the interrogation rooms, somewhere near the middle of the building, Jenny Lindh is sitting at a table opposite a sixty-two-year-old Kurdish man.

The man looks weary and worried. He twists his hands. He stopped looking around a long time ago; his empty stare is fixed in front of him.

Jenny Lindh has activated the recorder, has pointed the microphone at Schorsch Barzani.

She intends to conduct a short routine interrogation in accordance with paragraph 24, section 8 of the penal code, then ask the prosecutor to arrest Schorsch.

But their conversation drags on, and it makes Jenny feel ill at ease. Neither an interpreter nor a defense attorney is present. She would have felt better if there were.

Schorsch doesn't want to stop. They talk for almost an hour. About Lenya. Schorsch. The whole family. About their escape from Hawraman in northern Iraq. About their request for political asylum, and how they were allowed to stay, many years ago. About their life since then.

Lindh is still suffering from a dull headache. She tries to push her personal problems aside, tries to understand what Schorsch is telling her.

It's bullshit, of course. The same old nonsense. Of course he was the one who threw his daughter from the balcony, like other Muslim men have done to their daughters or sisters. Because the girls became real Swedes after they came here—no longer wanting to live by Muslim rules, they went to dances, lit cigarettes, fell in love with boys. Broke all the rules.

That's obviously what happened. Schorsch Barzani murdered his daughter because she broke his rules. Shamed her family.

The police have seen it before. A hundred times. Famous cases have been debated in the papers. Fadime Sahindal, a twenty-six-year-old Kurdish woman from Turkey, had been threatened and beaten by her father, who finally killed her with two shots. Being in a relationship wasn't her only crime: she had also let the public know how Kurdish men treated their women.

Pela Atroshi, a nineteen-year-old Kurdish woman living in Sweden, had been murdered on a visit to her family's home in Iraq, for besmirching the family honor. Her father's brothers got a life sentence, but years later her father confessed that he was the one who killed her.

Jenny Lindh makes a face. She hates the concept of *honor killing*, and cannot for the life of her understand why both politicians and feminists use it. To her, the word *honor* has a positive connotation, and she thinks it should be called culture killing, or even ignominy killing.

There is no honor in killing someone. Least of all in killing your own daughter.

It's unacceptable in a modern, Western society. Maybe *they* put religion and respect first, but *we* put the law above all.

Jenny Lindh realizes that after all her years of police work, she is full of prejudice, based on what she has seen and experienced.

It's what they do to their women, those Muslims. Force them to obey and to veil themselves. Forbid them from showing their faces and loving whomever they choose.

She looks back at Schorsch, who has fallen silent after a long story about himself, Lenya and the rest of the family.

He keeps repeating that he loves her. That he has loved her since she was born. That she can't be dead.

That he did everything he could to stop her.

Jenny lets his words sink in. On her recommendation, the prosecutor has already decided to arrest Schorsch. She studies him for a few seconds before calmly saying:

"Schorsch, you'll have to stay here for a while. Right now, you're suspected of murder."

Barzani meets her eyes, in surprise and despair.

Then his expression changes.

And there is something in his eyes that she doesn't understand.

A few hours later she learns that Magnus Stolt has been assigned to lead the investigation, and with a grimace she drives to Solna to find him at the west Stockholm prosecutor's office.

Stolt barely even looks up when she enters his office and greets him.

Asshole.

He's well-known among the police, and most of them think that Dick would be a more suitable last name. Magnus Stolt is the man who gave bitterness a face and nurtures his preconceptions as if they were vulnerable hothouse flowers. He is generally disliked, not particularly successful in court, and Jenny Lindh wonders why he gets to stay, when there are so many good public prosecutors.

"Hi."

"Hello. Take a seat."

He shuffles through plastic folders and papers. As if to show her how busy he is. Finally he takes the top folder from the pile, pushes his glasses onto his forehead and looks at her.

"It's Tensta, right?" He glances at the printed-out interrogation protocols. "Scho . . . well, Barzani, right?"

Lindh nods without speaking.

Stolt gives her a crooked smile.

"I see that he's denying all charges. And, as we know, they always do. But—I'll have him put in custody and then you can keep working at your leisure."

His voice is nasal and his tone is superior. She can understand that he rubs people the wrong way.

Stolt stands up, closes the office door and sits back down. Twirls the arms of his glasses between his fingers.

"Conduct a formal interrogation at once. But make sure his lawyer and an interpreter are present, or the defense will be screaming their heads off later. What more have you done?"

"The technicians are working hard out there. We've impounded the girl's laptop and given it to forensics. Operation door-to-door is in full swing, and we're waiting for the rest of the family to come home so we can do preliminary interviews with them."

"I see. And how many are they?"

"The wife and Lenya's sister and brother."

Stolt raises an eyebrow. "That's all? There's usually at least seven or eight of those people."

Those people.

"I think . . ." Jenny pauses midsentence.

"Yes?"

She thinks Stolt looks annoyed. That bothers her. Right now she would like to have his support.

". . . he's innocent."

"Why?"

Jenny shrugs. "A gut feeling."

His glasses fall back onto his nose as he keeps shuffling through his papers. "Tell your gut to calm down until we have the autopsy report and the results from forensics."

Jenny Lindh stands up and leaves the prosecutor's office.

In a fourteen-by-eight-foot holding cell, Schorsch Barazani pounds his fists against the wall until they start bleeding, and howls in pain and despair.

★ ★ ★

That night, Jenny Lindh drinks too much again. She wanders slowly through her house, *their* house.

This was where the love of her life should have flourished.

This was where their child should have grown up.

The drunker she gets, the more aggressively she declutters. Furious, she tears his clothes from the closets and throws them on the floor, rips pages from photo albums, dumps framed photographs and small mementos into a cardboard box.

Deep in a closet drawer, she finds the dildo they shyly purchased from a sex shop a long time ago. In disgust she flings it in the garbage without removing the batteries.

She feels sick, throws up in the toilet and drinks more wine before she continues getting rid of everything that was her, their, life for five years.

Everything has to go.

Him. The child. The house.

Jenny Lindh has no idea what will happen next.

The next morning, she has an impulse. She returns to the apartment, which has been sealed off. The family had to spend the night somewhere else.

Where do you stay when you've been thrown out of your home? With friends? A homeless shelter?

Jenny takes a deep breath. She's got a long day of interrogations ahead of her.

The crime scene technicians have combed the apartment, and Jenny doesn't actually know what she's doing here. She won't find anything they missed.

She just wants to look. Feel. Try to understand.

At ten o'clock, she conducts a long, investigative interrogation of Schorsch. He's been saying all along that he doesn't need a defense attorney, because he is innocent, but they appointed one anyway. He also declined help from an interpreter, but nevertheless one is sitting beside him.

Magnus Stolt enters the room just before they begin.

Jenny drinks cold water from a plastic cup to ease her sick feeling. She starts the interrogation coolly and calmly, as usual. As time passes, she notices more and more signs of the prosecutor's annoyance. He sighs deeply, occasionally tapping a pencil against the table. Schorsch Barzani is distraught and worn out. His eyes are red and what little gray hair he has left is standing on end. He sticks to his story.

All he did was try to stop Lenya from jumping.

As he utters the words, Stolt makes a sound like a snort, and the defense attorney looks at the prosecutor in surprise.

Barzani answers every question and the interpreter never needs to intervene. Yes, of course Schorsch has kept his daughters on a tight rein. Forbade them to get piercings or tattoos, told them to be proud of their origins and to live by the *Book*. He has tried to restrain himself, allowing them to dress as they liked, listen to pop music and even go to dances. But he has used his right to choose whom they will marry.

"What *right*?" Stolt suddenly asks.

Barzani looks surprised, spreads his hands and explains the duties of a father. The prosecutor sinks down in his chair, drags a tired hand across his face and fixes his gaze on a point far away.

Jenny continues asking questions in a calm voice. No, Schorsch really has no idea why Lenya was so upset. When she was on her way to the balcony he had asked her why, and she had said that it was none of his business. She had opened the balcony door in her stocking feet, letting in the cold, and he had followed her. Lenya had grabbed the railing and begun heaving herself up. Schorsch had grabbed hold of her and pulled her down. She had clawed his face, hit him and kicked wildly so that the flowerpots broke. In vain, he tried to hold her, but she had been stronger.

She'd heaved herself up—thrown herself over.

Schorsch bursts into tears again, and Jenny lets the next few questions wait. She throws a quick glance at the prosecutor, who rolls his eyes before leaning across the table and making a half-hearted attempt to hide the irritation in his voice.

"Wouldn't it be better just to confess, Barzani? This doesn't look good, and it's such a relief to just come clean."

The interpreter translates and Schorsch Barzani shakes his head, burying his face in his hands.

"I . . . I loved her," he sobs. "I would never . . ."

The interrogation ends at 11:42.

Early the next morning the lobby guard from the police station calls Jenny Lindh to tell her that a group of men want to talk to her.

"It's about Schorsch Barzani."

She asks what they want, but the guard doesn't know. According to him she has two choices. She can either come down and try to calm this perturbed bunch or he'll have to request some uniformed officers.

Jenny sighs and takes the elevator down.

The guard was right. The men, five Iraqi Kurds who are friends of Schorsch Barzani, are very upset. They can all swear that Schorsch had indeed done everything to defend the Barzani family honor, but he was certainly no murderer and should be released immediately.

Patiently, Jenny tries to explain to them how the Swedish justice system works.

She gets no response. The men tell her that they want to talk to the *man* in charge of the investigation.

Jenny tells them that she is in charge and is greeted by incredulous stares. The men confer quietly for a moment in their own language and then demand to speak with the *man* who is her superior officer.

Jenny tells them that her superior officer is Lena Ekholm—a woman.

This doesn't diminish their agitation. Once again they call for the immediate release of Barzani. When Jenny firmly explains that they will be moving forward with the investigation, the group becomes more strident and starts shouting in a mixture of Swedish and their own language and Jenny can no longer subdue them. Some uniformed officers enter the building and there is a bit of a scuffle as

238

the Kurdish men are forced outside. One of them resists so violently that he is arrested.

She slowly shakes her head.

Why does it have to be this way?

Three weeks later Jenny Lindh is sitting in a one-bedroom apartment in a new suburb, thinking about life.

Everything's happened so quickly. The house was sold. She left almost all the furniture in it behind; the mere thought of keeping anything that might remind her made her sick. With the help of friends, a van and IKEA she put together a new home in a few days.

The rest wasn't as easy.

The abortion.

It was mandatory that she speak with a psychologist first, and of course she broke down. A five-year relationship, promises of undying love, memories of adventure and intimacy—it all came together as she faced the decision of whether or not she really wanted to get rid of the child in her belly.

The child.

When it was over she steeled herself, took only a couple of days' sick leave while the bleeding was at its worst.

Better to bury yourself in work than to stare at a wall wallowing in memories that aren't worth remembering anymore.

Daniel had made some awkward attempts to contact her. He had used words like *respect* and *adults* and said that they should at least try to talk to each other.

Jenny texted him saying that he a) could take his whore and go to hell, and b) should contact her lawyer if he wanted anything else.

Very mature, Jenny, she thinks and bites her lip, as she stands in front of the mirror trying to put on her makeup. Her tears smear her mascara and she has to redo it.

It's high time she spent an evening drinking wine with Clara.

At work she downs cup after cup of strong coffee and winces at the burning sensation in her stomach.

Once again she carefully sifts through the material surrounding Lenya Barzani's death.

The CSI and computer forensics reports are coldly formal, just like the autopsy report from the pathologist and the evaluations from SKL, the state crime lab.

The technicians indicated that they found footprints from both Lenya and Schorsch Barzani in the snow on the balcony, and that there were numerous signs of a struggle. They found traces of Lenya's blood. After scraping her fingernails they detected evidence of her father's skin under them. Samples taken on the first day Schorsch was examined showed traces of Lenya's DNA in wounds on his cheeks. Jenny searches for the major points in the pathologist's long report. Lenya's neck was broken, her skull and brain sustained injuries. Her face was swollen where there had been bruising. Her left arm was broken. The pathologist was unable to determine whether all of these injuries happened simultaneously or in brief intervals. Theoretically she may have sustained some of her injuries before falling from the balcony. Her lungs indicated that she was a smoker, but apart from that the girl was healthy. Neither drugs nor alcohol were found in her blood or any traces of semen inside of her.

The computer forensics experts easily accessed Lenya's laptop and went through her files, e-mails, and Facebook account. Their report included an attachment of about a hundred pages of documented conversations between the girl and her friends, as well as a printout of something that looked like a diary.

Jenny spent hours absorbed in reading the printouts. The e-mail exchanges between Lenya and her friends revealed that Schorsch had been very strict with both Lenya and Lara. Granted—just as he had admitted—he had allowed them a certain amount of freedom in choosing their clothes and activities, but he made himself very clear when it came to the most important thing of all: their choice of boyfriends.

There was no mistaking that Lenya was in love with a boy named Joakim. The e-mail exchanges between him and Lenya were intense, and she gushed over him to her girlfriends.

Meanwhile, she expressed her deepening distress in her diary.

240

Several years earlier, her father had explained that she was to marry Rawand, his cousin Naushad's son. The fact that her chosen husband lived with his father in Badinan, in northern Iraq, did not make things less complicated.

In a private Facebook exchange, Lenya had told her friend Ebba that her father had discovered her relationship with Joakim and gone ballistic. He had subjected Lenya to a long and rigorous interrogation. After that he grounded her and said she could not go anywhere at all without either her father or Azad as chaperone.

And not only that. Her diary also disclosed that Schorsch had ordered his wife, Runak, to bring Lanya to Haval, an Iraqi in Tensta who claimed to be a doctor. The purpose of this visit was to determine whether or not Lenya was still a virgin.

Lenya described the encounter as disgusting. Her appointment with Haval took place in an ordinary apartment, and Lenya got no impression that he was actually a trained doctor. Her mother had looked away as the man poked around her genitals with his fingers. Lenya described the experience as both painful and deeply humiliating. In her text messages, she told Ebba that she had never had sex with Joakim or anyone else, but that her hymen had broken a year or so ago during ballet practice.

When Schorsch received the "doctor's" report he had become even more furious and grounded Lenya indefinitely. This took place about a week before her fall from the balcony, and during that time, Lenya's brother had met her at school each day to walk her home.

Jenny put the papers down, drank some coffee and sighed deeply. Would she ever get used to these cultural differences?

Lenya's mother, Runak, and an interpreter are sitting across the table from Jenny.

Runak, weary from lack of sleep and worn out from crying, answers Jenny's questions only briefly. She knows Schorsch well after all these years. He loves his daughters and would never harm a hair on their heads. Runak wants to know when Schorsch can come home and cries hysterically when she gets no definite answer.

Two hours later, at Jenny's second interview with fourteen-year-old Lara, instead of an interpreter, a woman from social services in Tensta is present.

Jenny gets no clear answers to her questions. She leans across the table, and smiles at the girl.

"Are you afraid of something or someone, Lara? I promise that nothing is going to happen to you."

The girl is silent for a moment. Then she shrugs her shoulders, looks Jenny in the eyes and says:

"How can you promise anything? You don't even understand what this is all about."

You're right. How could I ever understand?

"Then tell me, Lara. Explain it to me so I can understand."

The girl just stares down at the table, silent.

Her interrogations of Azad Barzani don't go much better. He replies laconically to some questions, and answers others with a shrug of his shoulders or not at all.

"But, Azad, do you think that Lenya was afraid of your dad?"

"Why would she be?"

"Is it true that recently Lenya wasn't allowed out by herself? That your father told you to meet her at school every day, to make it impossible for her to see Joakim?"

"Who's Joakim?"

"Lenya had a boyfriend named Joakim, didn't she?"

"She didn't have a boyfriend."

"But we've already spoken to Joakim, and he said that he and Lenya were in a relationship."

"He's lying."

Not once during the questioning did Azad meet her gaze, and Jenny knows that he will never tell her anything.

Another world. A world of men with a concept of honor that differs from the Swedish one. For a moment she considers letting some male colleague take over the interrogations.

But—no way in hell!

She is Detective Captain Jenny Lindh.

★　★　★

The next day, Jenny questions Lenya's best friend, Ebba Green. Ebba isn't afraid. She confirms much of what Jenny has already learned from the computer printouts.

Lenya was definitely afraid of Schorsch. Her father had a terrible temper and was constantly setting up new rules for Lenya. She was hardly allowed to use makeup, always had to wear pants instead of skirts and having a boyfriend was out of the question—she was set to marry the older man, Rawand, in Iraq. Ebba said that they had talked about this a million times and Lenya wanted nothing more than to get away from home. But how would she do that? She was seventeen, a high school student, with no other place to live and no job. And besides, even if she had escaped, Schorsch, his friends and his relatives would have found her and brought her back home.

According to Ebba, Schorsch was a family dictator, and both the Barzani sisters were afraid of him. Lenya had even said that she feared for her life, that her father would kill her if he discovered that she had a boyfriend. And her mother, Runak, would never dare to stand up to Schorsch.

After all, she was only a woman.

The interrogation transcripts were typed out and entered, along with all the other investigation reports, into the DurTvå system —a computerized log of pretrial investigation material.

Shortly before lunch the next day Jenny gets a call from the prosecutor who curtly tells her she should report to his office immediately with an update. Slightly annoyed, she drives to Solna again, hurries along the corridors to Magnus Stolt's office and takes a seat in his visitor's chair. The prosecutor pushes his glasses up on his forehead. "Did you get anything from the door-to-door?"

"Hardly. Nobody seems to have seen or heard anything. It was midmorning when it happened. I suppose most people were at work."

He gives a short laugh. "Work? People in that area are hardly known for working themselves to death, are they? You know the type—the ones who are said to enrich our culture."

His voice drips with sarcasm. Lindh has heard it before, in paddy wagons, in the corridors of police headquarters. *Cultural Enrichers. Camel jockeys. Dune coons.*

If the police, with their special training, can't accept these people as citizens, then how can the rest of the population be expected to do so?

Jenny has seen on the news that populist, right-wing extremist parties have gained considerable support in recent years. Jackboots.

She shudders.

You can't hate people just because of their origin.

Stolt shuffles through his piles of paper and pulls out some that are marked with a yellow Post-it note.

"You're saying that nobody has seen or heard anything. But here's a transcript from a witness named Pettersson who says that he heard shouting and arguing, and that he saw the father and daughter fighting on the balcony."

"That's true. But for one thing, that man is obviously an alcoholic. He reeked of liquor when we spoke to him. And for another, he keeps changing his story around. You can see from the transcript that he's confused."

"But it says here that he even saw the father throw his daughter from the balcony."

Jenny takes a deep breath.

"But if you read on, it says later that he isn't sure about that. I suspect the defense would rip him to pieces pretty fast if you put him on the stand."

Stolt looks irritated and puts the papers down.

"Do another door-to-door. Without any witnesses or supporting evidence I won't be able to charge him with murder."

"But what if he didn't do it?"

The words slip out before she's had time to think.

Jenny notices a small muscle twitch near his eye. Stolt pulls his glasses back down over his eyes, leans over the desk on his elbows and fixes her with his stare.

"If he *didn't* do it? Get a grip, Lindh. Read the interview with her best friend. Lenya feared for her life. This is just one more honor killing and I'm gonna put Barzani away for life. Stone Age behavior is not acceptable in this country."

Jenny Lindh stands up. As she leaves his office she hears him say quietly: "*Fucking Hajjis.*"

She turns around and looks at Stolt.

"Did you say something?"

He forces a smile.

"No, no. It was nothing."

The next morning Jenny interrogates Schorsch Barzani again. As she is about to start, in comes the prosecutor, out of breath and with his face showing clear signs that he's under pressure. Both the morning papers and the tabloids are still headlining Lenya's death so maybe Stolt has been fielding phone calls from police headquarters as well as from politicians. Jenny's heard what can happen when a case becomes politically sensitive. The next election is closing in. The center/right-wing coalition government is under attack from the opposition and will resort to any tricks to stay in power. Statistically significant opinion polls show that support for the populist, anti-immigrant party has reached two-digit percentages. Not only does that mean that it will become more influential, but it will likely continue to hold the balance of power in parliament in the little country called Middle-of-the-Road.

A political disaster.

And now an immigrant girl is dead. Again.

Her father is suspected of murder. Just like so many fathers before him.

The result of this trial could have major political consequences.

Will the small, but democratic country allow immigrants from different cultures to murder their daughters in order to "protect their honor"?

It seems to Jenny that Schorsch has become smaller, hunched over. When she asks her questions about that particular day, the point at which Lenya died, he sticks to the same story as before.

He had been watching TV when she walked past. He followed her onto the balcony and yes, there was a fight when he tried to stop her from jumping.

As before, she asks why he didn't leave the apartment and run down to the courtyard after Lenya fell.

He shakes his head slowly.

"It was like . . . I paralyzed. No could move. I just sat, no could understand."

Prosecutor Stolt squirms in his seat, gives Jenny an irritated look that says: *Get going damn it—c'mon, sink him!*

But she asked her questions again and again and received the same answers. Asked about the family's escape to Sweden, about Lenya's childhood, about how Schorsch thought his daughters should conduct their lives. Asked what he was doing during the minutes and seconds before she fell. Asked why he was barefoot.

And sure, he is a cliché that would make any xenophobic Swede smirk. A typical *Muhammad*, dominating his wife and daughters, writing his own laws and administering whatever punishments suit him.

But then they return again and again to that moment when Lenya walked out onto the balcony.

And Schorsch gets that look in his eyes.

Jenny is becoming increasingly more convinced of his innocence.

Granted—through his dominance and tyranny, she feels certain that he made Lenya afraid of him. Maybe even systematically broke her spirit, contributed to her suicidal thoughts. If the prosecutor can prove that, it might lead to Schorsch's conviction. Jenny doesn't know if any similar case has ever gone to trial before.

But she does know that there is a world of difference between *causing someone's death* and *murder*.

Jenny Lindh gives it one last try. She makes an effort to sound more determined, looks Barzani in the eye and says:

"Schorsch, isn't it time for you to confess? You threw Lenya from the balcony, didn't you?"

The tired, gray-haired man looks at her in surprise. This woman who had been so kind to him up until now. After a few seconds he bursts hopelessly into tears.

The defense attorney lays a gentle hand on his shoulder, and between sobs Schorsch manages to reply:

"No . . . I . . . loved her . . . !"

Magnus Stolt closes his notebook irritably and quickly leaves the room.

And Jenny Marina Elisabeth Lindh covers her eyes with her hand and wonders why the hell she ever became a police officer.

The pressure on her is increasing. Stolt wants a report at least twice a day and Jenny has little news to give him. Operation door-to-door number two yielded no better results than the first one. The witness Pettersson has been questioned again, numerous times. And every time there are discrepancies in what he's seen, heard, and experienced. It is obvious that he greatly enjoys the attention and loves responding to questions. The problem is that he gives a different answer each time.

And that he reeks of booze.

Jenny questions Joakim Merker, the boy who was supposedly Lenya's boyfriend. She had spoken to him previously a few times on the phone; now everything is formal and official.

Joakim is eighteen years old, a senior in high school majoring in media studies. He gives a calm and quiet impression, and Jenny likes him from the start.

He tells her that they met in school about six months ago. Then one thing led to another, they continued seeing each other, they took walks, went for coffee, talked—*like things we usually do.*

And it turned into love.

Of course Joakim can't tell her the exact day he fell in love with Lenya, or she him. He remembers certain days and dates when they said or did something special. Like the time he wanted to buy her a ring from a shop at Hötorget in Stockholm, but she couldn't accept it for fear her parents might see it and ask what it meant.

The boy tells his story. Every once in a while, Jenny tosses in a question or two. She is absolutely convinced that he is telling her the truth.

Yes, they had hugged and kissed, eventually made out a little. In doorways, on footpaths, in places where they could avoid being seen. Even in the basement of Joakim's house. And yes, Lenya had come with him up to his room, but his mother or siblings were always at home, so . . . no, they had never gone any farther.

Yes, they had wanted to. But Lenya wouldn't dare.

Before Lenya, Joakim had had two girlfriends, both of them Swedish. He had had sex with one of them. Lenya had told him that she was a virgin, sworn that she would happily give herself to Joakim, that she loved him and wanted to live with him for the rest of her life.

But then she also told him about the rest, and sorrow clouded their romance.

If Schorsch found out that she had a boyfriend, both Lenya and Joakim could end up in big trouble, she had said. And if her father discovered that they had had sex, she'd be killed.

Maybe Joakim, too.

At first, he hadn't believed her.

Slowly, she convinced him to believe her and helped him to understand.

But she couldn't make him accept it.

How do you kill love when it's at its strongest? How do you say good-bye because someone else refuses to respect your love?

How, when you're only seventeen or eighteen?

You can't.

They had continued meeting in secret. Hugged, kissed, caressed.

But nothing more.

Joakim had been happy and somewhere deep inside he hoped that one day, all of it would be resolved. He had even suggested to Lenya that they could explain everything to Schorsch, and Joakim could ask him for his daughter's hand.

That day, the look on Lenya's face was filled with sorrow and she just shook her head as tears welled up in her eyes.

That had only been a few weeks ago.

One morning she had arrived at school completely beside herself, pulled Joakim into a corner and told him what had happened. Somehow—she didn't know how—Schorsch had found out about their relationship. From now on she would be watched and they could no longer see each other. Azad would pick her up at school every day, so all they could do was communicate secretly via cell phone texts and e-mails—unless those things were also taken away from her.

Joakim had comforted her as best he could, but he felt a burning pain in his chest as he watched Azad walk away with Lenya after school, without so much as a glance back from her.

The next day, during their first break, she told him what her father had said the evening before:

If he found out that they were seeing each other outside of school, both she and Joakim would die.

He had been shocked, not wanting to believe what she'd said. Then he had thought about it and discussed it with his closest friends. Wondered if he ought to report Schorsch to the police or what? After all, this was Sweden in the year 2012.

After the interrogation, Jenny shook hands with Joakim and thanked him. She told him that he would be called as a witness at the trial.

After he left she made a cup of strong coffee and felt grateful that she was no longer seventeen.

Then thoughts of Daniel and the whore came back to her, and once again she hated everything.

Ebba Green sat on a park bench, staring at nothing while she took quick, nervous drags on her cigarette.

Old son of a bitch. Asshole.

The trial had ended a week ago. She had been called to witness and told them everything she knew. So had Joakim.

Then came that neighbor, the guy who said he'd seen the old bastard hit Lenya and throw her down.

The bastard's lawyer had tried to break the guy, but this time he was sure of himself.

He had witnessed the fight and seen how Lenya's father heaved her over the railing.

This morning she had read online that the bastard had been convicted of murder and sentenced to life.

Serves him fucking right.

Slowly she pulled out the crumpled piece of paper she had been keeping in her jacket pocket for weeks.

Lenya's letter.

It had arrived the day after Lenya died. Ebba had been more than surprised to see the neat handwriting on the envelope.

Lenya's handwriting.

Usually they kept in touch only via texts, e-mails and chats, and in fact Ebba couldn't recall ever having received a real letter, a paper letter, from any friend before. She read it for the thousandth time:

> Ebba, I love you! I love you and Jocke and Gusse and Anna and Mariana and Linnéa, but I can't take it any longer!
>
> My old man is never going to change. There's no hope for me, they'll force me to go to Iraq and get married. Just can't take it! I want Jocke and no one else.
>
> There's no other way out than what I'm about to do. Not sure if I'll cut myself or jump or what. But I'll do it. Sending you this as snail mail since I know you'd try to stop me otherwise.
>
> Love you forever, give this to my darling Jocke afterward, I've written to him on the back.
>
> XOXO, Lenis

She had let Joakim read the letter. He remained silent for a long time afterwards. Finally he said that they would have to take it to the police. Lenya had committed suicide after all, but now her father had been convicted of murder.

Ebba tore the letter from his hand and ran away.

She'd never let the bastard get away with it.

She pulls out her lighter, watches the flame flutter in the wind, then catch hold of the paper, obliterate it.

Ebba drops the letter on the ground, witnesses the flame devour Lenya's handwritten lines. Tears come to her eyes and when only ashes remain she rubs them into the ground with the sole of her shoe.

*   *   *

Jenny Lindh has taken some time off, is sitting in the silence of her apartment and looking out the window.

The trial had been tumultuous at times and in the end the judge had to remove the Kurdish men who continued to protest loudly as the prosecution presented its case.

She had listened to all the witnesses and been very surprised by the neighbor, Pettersson. He had appeared on the stand in a clean shirt and suit, was clean shaven and did not smell of liquor. Now there was no doubt in his mind about his testimony. He had seen a violent fight that ended with Schorsch Barzani lifting up his daughter and throwing her over the balcony railing.

And when the verdict was handed down, she had observed Schorsch Barzani very closely. As if he had felt her gaze, he turned to face her.

There was something in his eyes . . .

Translated by: Angela Valenti and Sophia Mårtensson

Dag Öhrlund, born in 1957, began writing professionally in 1972; for more than thirty years, he was a journalist and professional photographer. In 2007, he published his first crime novel, Mord.net (Murder.net), *co-written with Dan Buthler. The novel introduced Criminal Inspector Jacob Colt, who also appears in most of Öhrlund and Buthler's later novels. However, the lasting success of the writing team was the criminal they introduced in their second novel,* En nästan vanlig man (An Almost Ordinary Man, *2008), murderous psychopath Christopher Silfverbielke, a charming, attractive, and immensely rich stock broker who also enjoys degrading women and killing people regardless of sex. So far, he has appeared in five novels that have made their authors two of the most popular Swedish crime writers currently active. Apart from the Jacob Colt and Christopher Silfverbjelke novels, Buthler and Öhrlund have also written the first book in a projected series with mainly American protagonists,* Jordens väktare (Guardians of the Earth, 2011). *On his own, Dag Öhrlund wrote the hard-boiled thriller* Till minne av Charlie K. (To the Memory of Charlie K., 2012).

DAY AND NIGHT MY KEEPER BE

Malin Persson Giolito

Malin Persson Giolito as far as I am aware is the only Swedish second-generation crime author: her father is noted criminologist and leading crime fiction novelist Leif G. W. Persson.

The young Malin Persson did not plan a writing career. She studied law, graduating from Uppsala University, was employed by the Court of Justice of the European Union for two years, then was invited to join one of the most prestigious Swedish law firms, Mannheimer Swartling, where she worked from 1997 through 2007. Until 2001, she worked at the Brussels office, after which she transferred to the Stockholm office. She had also married Christophe Giolito, and in 2000 she had her first child, taking six months' maternal leave; gradually she realized that she was given both less and less-challenging work at the law firm. After the birth of her second child, she was informed that she'd never make partner, and, before the birth of her third child in 2006, she was told that she would have no work to return to after her maternity leave.

Her experiences at Manheimer Swartling inspired her to finally live up to her secret wish of also writing fiction. Her first novel, Dubbla slag (Two-front Battle), *is about a young lawyer, Hanna, headhunted for a prestigious law firm, who after having children finds herself rejected and ridiculed at her place of work.*

Though her first novel was not crime fiction, her second was: Bara ett barn (Only a Child) *was published in 2010, and her third followed in 2012,* Bortom varje rimligt tvivel (Beyond All Reasonable Doubt). *In both of these, the protagonist is lawyer Sophia Weber, who in representing her clients is also forced to become a legal detective. In these novels, Malin Persson Giolito shows herself to be not only an excellent storyteller, but also a writer deeply concerned with such important issues as the abuse of justice, the prejudging of accused persons in popular media, and the distortion of justice for political reasons. She is one of the clearly rising stars of contemporary Swedish crime fiction.*

In the following story, which is at heart about a moral problem, in typical fashion she presents different viewpoints as well as different possible interpretations. She speaks in a low voice, but it is more than worth the effort to listen hard.

THERE WAS NO FRAGRANCE OF CINNAMON, OF SEALING WAX, OF BUBBLING toffee or grilled ham. Only of stressfulness and rancid calories. The wind brought sounds from a tombola booth and a shrill, electronic version of "Jingle Bells." The cloud cover was sagging with repressed rain.

The woman held her daughter's bare hand in one of hers and a pen in the other. Her son sat in his stroller. At the entrance to the city amusement park, and at a couple of popular museums, they gave you little ribbons to fill out and fasten around the wrist of your child. They called them identification bracelets. But they had nothing like that at the Christmas market. Writing your phone number on the hand or arm of your child instead was a tip the woman had found in a parenting magazine.

I shouldn't be here, she thought. It was a mistake. But the kids had been quarrelsome, teasing, snatching each other's toys. One of them had pulled the other one's hair, they had yelled in chorus and she had decided that they must do something, or they'd all go mad. Stroll for a while among happy families, buying cornets of home-made fudge and letting the kids gorge themselves on sweet buns. It could have been an excellent idea.

Now she longed for home. Longed to get back to the apartment, lie down on the couch and nap while the kids watched the children's channel.

Instead they were here, and returning home without pushing the walker even once around the square would feel like failure. Besides, her baby boy would probably fall asleep on the bus and if she allowed him to sleep now she would never manage to get him into bed tonight. She tightened her grip on her daughter's hand. It was hard to write on the girl's thin skin and she had to press down pretty hard to get the ink to stay. When the child protested her mother yanked her arm.

"Be still . . ." she muttered. But she couldn't think of anything more to say. She went on writing. A muscle twitched under one of her eyes and she blinked.

One turn. Just a single turn around the square, then she could go back home. With a bit of luck they'd fall asleep early. Then the evening would be all hers. A few hours of peace and quiet. She deserved that.

When all ten digits of the phone number were done the mother drew her thumb over the ink. It was already dry. And as soon as she let go of her daughter's hand, the child's chapped thumb found its way into her half-open mouth. The girl hardly sucked, just let her thumb rest in the corner of her mouth. Her mother shook her head but said nothing.

"Mommy," the boy in the stroller complained. "Moommyyy!"

The woman's son was only a little over a year old. In a crowd like this, there was no way for her to let him rove on his own. But he hated his stroller, hated every second of sitting still. Now he twisted with all his strength, furiously trying to escape the harness that tied him down, bumping up and down in his seat. The stroller swayed. The girl stood by, thumb still in her mouth, while her mother pulled a couple of clasps tighter and tried to force the boy down on his seat. He kept trying to squirm free. His mother gave up, started walking and shook the stroller hard a couple of times to make her son slide back down.

The girl's boots were both too hot and too big. Her heels scraped the gravel when she walked. Her snowsuit zipper was pulled down and her collarbone showed. The pale, blue shadow of a vein fluttered with her heartbeat.

"Walk properly," her mother said. "Can't you lift your feet?"

"One turn around the square," she repeated under her breath. "Just one turn."

If only the square hadn't been so crowded. The rock candy stand was far away, the waffle stand looked closed. But on a two-foot-high platform maybe thirty feet away sat a middle-aged man with a flopping false beard and a bright red felt cap. Next to his easy chair stood a stuffed reindeer. The prop animal had black eyes of glass and a basket full of smoked sausages hung like a saddlebag across its back. A handwritten sign proclaimed that the sausages cost twenty kronor and that Santa wanted to know what all good children wanted for Christmas.

With a vague sense of relief, the woman halted the stroller. Her daughter no longer believed in Santa Claus, and her son probably had no idea of who he was or what miracles he supposedly worked. But this was better than the alternative. She dug out a painkiller from her handbag and swallowed it dry. It stuck in her throat and she closed her eyes against the pain, putting her fist to her chest.

This is when it happens. They stand in line. The woman tries calming her son with a cracker she's found at the bottom of her handbag. But the boy refuses to be coaxed. Instead he snatches the cracker, sharp nails scratching his mother's wrist, and throws it at the man standing in line before them. And when his mother has brushed crumbs from the stranger's coat and apologized fervently, her daughter is gone.

The woman turns around. Many times. Looks in all directions. Calls out, first in a low voice, then louder; the third time her throat hurts.

Where is she, she thinks. She can't be far; she was here a moment ago. Just a few seconds, can it even be a minute since she saw her last?

At first she is irritated. Angry.

"Be still!" she screams at her son. Her handbag keeps sliding off her shoulder, she claws at it. And she feels very tired. Exhausted. "Why," she whispers to herself. Not frightened, just dejected. "Why, why, why?" It isn't fair. What's she supposed to do now?

She asks the man in line next to her to take care of her stroller. Her son's wide eyes watch the stranger while she squeezes through the crowd, calling and calling, jumping high to be able to see farther ahead.

Which direction should she choose? She chooses them all, a dozen feet this way, a dozen that. But she finds nothing and then she has to return to her boy and already on the way back fear sneaks up on her, suddenly pushing everything else away, her angry thoughts, her tiredness and gloom. Fear hugs her close, envelops her with its poisoned smoke.

Where is the girl? Where is her daughter? How can she just be gone? Why can't she find her?

And when she fumbles her phone out to be certain of hearing its signal when someone calls the number written on her daughter's hand, she sees that the display is all black. The battery has run down. It's dead.

She presses a few buttons, shakes it, but it's pointless. Her daughter is gone and the phone won't ring and fear has to duck because now terror runs up her back, with sharp talons and pointed teeth.

My daughter is gone, she thinks. Swallowed by the sluggish crowd of shoppers and by something totally unknown.

Her son starts twisting in his stroller again. But less furiously. His mother's terror is infectious. High above the clouds finally loosen their grip. The rain pours down. The crowd disperses as people hurry off, take cover by the stage and close to the canvas roofs over the stands. The mother remains in the open, looking into the gray curtain of water. But no girl is left in the rain. No child remains on the square. She is gone.

Her name is Petra, the mother who has lost her child. She is dressed in jeans and a thin down jacket. Her hair is dyed. She is on parental leave from her office work. Actually she isn't really a single parent, or at least wasn't supposed to be, but her boyfriend has left her and she doesn't know how to find him. He left almost four months ago, and when she phones his cell he never answers; all she gets are his parents or some friend, and once his brother. They all say the same thing: he needs to be left alone and that he'll be in touch as soon as he can. What they mean is that they want nothing to do with her. She and her kids should leave them alone, all of them. She has had to pay her rent alone since he left and she hates him, hates his parents, his whole family and every one of his worthless slacker friends. She couldn't call him. Not even if her phone worked.

Where is the kid? How is it possible to disappear so quickly?

Petra doesn't know what to do. Where should she turn? Whom should she talk to? She needs help. But how to ask for it? Should she try to seem calm? Would anyone listen to her if she did? Will she have to scream or at least cry to make them understand that it's serious? Before she has made her mind up she feels a hand on her shoulder. She probably looks frightened, for the man who stood in line in front of her offers to help search. He tells her to ask the Santa Claus for help.

"Tell him what's happened," the man says. And he says, "It'll be all right." He must see that she needs to be calmed. "Don't worry," he says, "she'll soon be back."

But there's no need for her to worry; she does that without any conscious effort. The images appear faster than she can explain what has happened to the false-beard Santa. They trip over each other, those pitiless images. Her daughter is little, only four years and nine months; she still wears a diaper at night, still stubbornly sucks her thumb.

Is there any deep water close by, Petra thinks while Santa Claus, whose real name is Magnus, phones someone who will put out a call on the improvised speaker system in the square.

"My daughter's name is Emma," she says.

"Emma," the loudspeakers crackle. "Your mother is waiting for you beside Santa Claus."

"She can't swim," Petra whispers. A lake, a canal, a river or just a creek? The water doesn't even have to be deep. A child can drown in eight inches of water.

But they're in the middle of the city. Where could she drown here? The fountain is turned off during winter and she can't get down to the harbor; it's much too far, more than an hour's walk. Of course Emma can't walk that far on her own and, even if she could, someone would find her before she got that far.

Still the images crowd Petra's thoughts. There are no limits to the disasters possible, no end to the number of accidents that can happen. Falling down? Easy to see her daughter lose her balance, see her body fall headlong, perhaps from a height. An empty playground, a tree, a slippery swing, a wall, a rock, a jungle gym. Or down a manhole in a street, the darkness below swallowing the child, silencing her wordless cries. Squeezed to death, beaten to a pulp, bones crushed, chest caved in, suffocated in some cramped space. Death is always quick, even if dying can be painful, excruciating, drawn out. There is no merciful transition from living child to no longer breathing child, from growing child to decaying corpse.

The rain has abated and the crowd is moving again. Another announcement rasps from the speakers. "Emma, who is four, is looking for her mother. Emma is dressed in a blue snowsuit and has blonde hair. Her mother is waiting by the main stage."

The man who has helped her search is back. He looks sad, but now his children are hungry and tired and he has to go home.

"It will be all right," he says again and leaves Petra. Her mind runs on, her thoughts wild.

The square seems small. The crowd, the stands—it's such a limited area. Why would her daughter want to stay here? Only a few feet away the wild city begins. The parking places, the streets, the cars, the badly lit thoroughfares. Has Emma walked there? It isn't very far. In the throng it's not easy to see if a child is alone.

Run down, run over, dusk is early this time of year. Her reflector disc, a luminous rabbit, is stuffed in the pocket of her dark blue snowsuit. Emma will never remember to pull it out so drivers can see her. Why should she? She hasn't learned to watch for traffic before crossing streets. Emma can't judge distances, can't find her way. If she starts walking you have to tell her to turn around, or she'll just keep going straight ahead. How could she ever find her way back to a place she's left? She is only four.

Magnus, the Santa, has stopped asking about presents, turned his chair over to Emma's mother and rid himself of both cap and beard. Nobody stands in line in front of his stage; they've all switched to the Social Insurance Office grab-bag stand. Dark has fallen, the streetlamps are lit. The lanterns outside the Red Cross stand flutter forlornly.

Magnus is staying with Petra. They are waiting for the police. A couple of adults have left their stands to help search. Magnus paces, feels worried. The boy, Emma's brother, has fallen asleep in his stroller and Emma's mother sits frozen in her chair.

They don't talk of the things that can happen to a lost little girl. There is no need. Those thoughts live their own lives. That statistics and probability and experience all say that Emma will soon be found means nothing.

Petra just sits there. Is it shock that makes her immobile, Magnus wonders. He clenches his hands, opens them. His joints feel swollen. He thinks of his own mother. She was always worried. Always.

Is it her thoughts that make her like this? The stories she's read and heard and can't fend off, of what really does sometimes happen? Is she thinking about the children who never return home? Or who are found but harmed for life, with invisible scars that never heal? The children abducted, away from cars and precipices but into hidden recesses, locked up by someone they should never have met. Human monsters with strong arms, heavy bodies, cellars, incomprehensible desires, and strangling hands.

Why isn't she searching, Magnus wonders. He feels an urge to shake her, slap her. She is just sitting there, staring. He clears his throat. Leans towards Petra, crouches down, puts a hand on her knee. Tries to sound authoritative. Decisive. His voice quavers as if

261

it were breaking. Petra doesn't even raise her eyes when he says that Emma won't return on her own. He knows how important it is to act quickly, the first hour has already passed and they are approaching the steepest part of the slope to disaster. Yet here she sits, the child's mother, letting the minutes pass.

"I have to charge my cell phone," is all Petra says.

And Magnus takes out his own, puts in her SIM card instead of his own. They watch the phone while it searches for a provider. But there are no missed calls for Petra, no texts. Instead the police arrive.

There's a routine way to do this. It tells you which questions to ask and which observations to make. Police officer Helena Svensson even has a checklist in her pocket. She could pull it out and mark it off, but instead she squats down beside the chair where the mother, Petra, is sitting. She speaks in a low voice. Unless she manages to keep the mother calm, she won't get any answers. And right now nothing is more important than for her to get reliable information.

Helena Svensson takes this seriously. She asks about Emma's length and weight and what she wore. Petra doesn't have a photo of her.

"It doesn't matter," Helena soothes her. "I'm sure we won't need one."

Then she takes Petra's arm, stands with her and asks her to show her exactly where they were when Emma disappeared. Six of Helena's colleagues are already searching the area. The dog patrol is busy elsewhere but has promised to come as soon as possible. The square is badly lit, but the flashlights of the police are sweeping the ground, their swaying beams of light dissolving the December dusk. When Petra tells her that she doesn't know where Emma's father is, that she hasn't heard from him since he left four months ago and that she doesn't even know if he still has the same phone number, Helena excuses herself to step aside. A phone call later, her colleagues at the precinct have been informed.

Helena knows the statistics. Statistics are held in high esteem at the police academy. Around seventeen hundred children are reported missing each year. Helena knows that most of them turn up. Even before the police arrive at the scene most return by themselves, without any drama at all. Occasionally it takes longer, and that makes it important to act before the cold gets too severe, the darkness too impenetrable. Children can get lost in the night, fall asleep and freeze to death. And Helena also knows that if a child is in fact abducted, it is almost always by one of its parents.

Helena wants to know more about Emma's father. She can hardly contain her excitement. What happened when they separated, does his family live in Sweden, what's his profession, what does he do or not do. At that Petra gets angry. Almost screams at Helena not to be such a fucking idiot, does she really believe Petra doesn't get what she's after?

"Emma's dad hasn't kidnapped his daughter," Petra spits. "If he'd wanted to see her I sure wouldn't have stopped him." She breathes. "I do it all on my own, it's all on me. He doesn't contribute a dime, never changes a diaper, it sure isn't him wiping vomit or cooking, picking them up or dropping them off, dressing them and undressing them. If he wants her he can have her for as long as he wants." Petra is getting breathless. She is falling to pieces. "Take her, I'd say if he ever asked, just take her and keep her."

Helena nods to calm Petra. She's worried; there's nothing odd in her screaming, anyone this scared would scream. But Petra refuses to calm down, she's losing control. And her loud voice wakes her son.

"I have to get home," Petra says when the boy tenses against his harness and tries to rise. "You have to call me when you find Emma, but I've got to get home. I can't stay all night. He has to have a new diaper and I have to feed him and I can't stay any longer to answer your stupid questions."

Helena is surprised. It's true that you can very seldom predict how anyone will react to extreme stress. She learned that at the academy, but nobody has prepared her for this. Nobody has told her how to cajole a mother to help look for her missing child.

But Helena finds a new diaper in the stroller and offers to change the boy. That calms Petra down a bit. Someone gives the boy a banana to eat and when that's finished a female Salvation Army soldier gives him a sweet bun. Petra sits down in Santa's chair again, sipping hot coffee, and Helena walks off to call in. She wants to know if they've got hold of Emma's father.

But Helena never makes the call. People start calling to each other and though she can't hear what they're saying she knows it from their voices and their bodies. Then her colleague Stefan is walking towards her, holding a child in his arms; he is smiling and she returns his smile. Now they're all smiling, all gathering around Stefan. Applauding. The darkness seems to recede. Maybe they weren't truly worried as yet, but now they feel happy in a way they had hardly expected.

He found her less than thirty-five feet from her mother, deep under the improvised stage. He had to crawl in with his flashlight and backing out was even harder, but he managed and got Emma out. She had fallen asleep and her snowsuit smelled of pee. When he started pulling her out she woke up but didn't cry.

Helena feels a lump in her throat. She laughs again, calls out to Petra.

"Let's go to Mommy," she whispers to Emma. "Mommy is waiting for you."

When Stefan steps up on the stage with his smile and his precious burden, Petra rises from the chair. But she takes no step towards him, just puts her arms around herself. She can see that he has her daughter. But she asks nothing, not is she fine, is she hurt, is she alive. Nothing.

"She was asleep," Stefan says. "But she's fine. I guess she was just hiding."

Emma has turned her face and sees her mother. But she doesn't hold out her arms to her. Instead she turns back, pressing her nose to Stefan's chest. He tries coaxing her, doesn't she want to go to Mommy? She doesn't. Her thin arms are tight around the strange man's neck and Helena's smile stiffens.

But it's not really strange, she thinks. The girl must be frightened; she just woke up, everything is scary, she's so small. Not strange at all.

Petra is no help.

"Damn kid," she growls. Her eyes are black. Then at last she lets go of herself and tears the child from Stefan. Emma starts to cry. She fists her little hand and puts it in her mouth and there is no sound, but tears trickle down her cheeks. "Have you peed?" Petra says when her fingers feel the wet snowsuit.

"I didn't mean to, Mommy," her daughter whispers. "I didn't mean to."

"Let's leave," Stefan says, taking Petra's arm. Helena Svensson agrees. It's perfectly natural that the girl is afraid, with the high-powered flashlight shining into her hiding place and all the strange adults looking at her; it must be overwhelming. And Petra is in shock, of course she is numb. People react differently to extreme stress. Helena learned that at the academy. None of this is really out of the ordinary. Nothing is strange, everything is quite normal. Petra will soon calm down.

Now the boy too has started to yell. He screams very loudly but it's good that they're crying; children who cry and scream are seldom badly hurt. When they're silent is when there's cause for alarm.

"Have you peed?" Petra says again and this time she almost screams and Emma starts crying harder and now they have to get away from here, have to get into a warm apartment, and the children must get some food and dry clothes because now it is raining again, hard. Helena feels her pulse racing, her hands sweating. How could anyone calm down in this chaos? And if she gets this upset, is it strange that their mother can hardly contain herself? It must be a thousand times harder on her.

It's been a tough afternoon, Helena thinks, and everyone is jumpy.

"Let's go to my car," Helena Svensson says at last. "I'll drive you home."

But the mother doesn't seem relieved. She wants to fend for herself, take the bus home. "Why do you want to tag along?" she asks. "I can manage on my own. Don't you think I can manage? Anyone could lose a kid for a little while. She's back now. You don't have to check up on me. I'll manage, I always have."

Helena Svensson has to insist. When they get to her car someone has called an ambulance. It's parked next to Helena's patrol car and Helena asks them to turn off their flashing blue lights. One of the paramedics takes a look at Emma and certifies that she doesn't seem to be harmed, doesn't need any treatment. She has scratches on one knee and a few bruises, one over her ribs and a couple on her arms. But nothing is broken. And she is hardly black and blue. She confirms it herself: it doesn't hurt.

Petra is standing beside the girl while she's examined.

"I guess she must have hit something crawling around in there," Petra says, glaring at the bruises. Then turns to Helena. "It makes no difference how many times I tell her. She never listens. And she's so clumsy. Always running into things or falling down. If she'd just listen . . ."

The bruise on her ribs is yellowish, not even blue any longer.

And Helena thinks: Those aren't recent bruises, she didn't get them today. She glances at the paramedic. But he just slides his hand across the girl's downy back, pulling her shirt back down. Then he pats Emma's cheek. The examination is done.

Children always hurt themselves, Helena thinks. Always. At day care, for instance. She must have hurt herself at the day care center.

"I'll help you get settled," Helena says to Petra. "You could use some help." And for some reason she can hardly understand she goes on, to forestall any protests. "There are some questions I have to ask you for my report, and if we can do it at your place you don't have to come down to the precinct. I'm really sorry I have to; I know you'd prefer to be left alone, but those are the rules."

Petra just nods. Now she looks tired again, exhausted.

Helena's partner drives. Petra and the children are in the backseat. When they arrive, her partner waits in the street and Helena enters the building with Petra and the children. The apartment is small but tidy. You can see all the rooms from the hallway. A bar of butter is lying on the sink in the kitchen but the beds are made, the living room floor is empty of toys.

Both children run off when their shoes and snowsuits are off.

"I'll shower her after you leave," Petra says, calmer now, and puts Emma's snowsuit in the laundry basket by the apartment door. "Take your jeans and panties off," she calls to her daughter.

Helena nods. The apartment is neat. Warm. Ordinary.

Helena shuffles her feet. Mumbles a few questions. Petra replies. She doesn't ask her in. Walks into the living room and Helena hears her turn the TV on. She considers following her, but doesn't.

"I'm hungry, Mommy," Emma calls from the TV couch and Petra walks into the kitchen. Helena stands on the threshold, watching Petra pour frozen meatballs into a frying pan.

Helena can't think of anything more to say and retreats into the hallway. They agree to talk again next day. Just to follow up.

"Bye, then," she calls to the children.

"Bye," they say.

She can hear their mother lock the tumbler and put the door chain in its slot.

Helena Svensson walks down the stairs and out in the street. It isn't relief at having left that makes her turn around and look up at the apartment building, trying to find the windows of the apartment where Petra and her two children live. It's a different feeling. A jarring one.

Her partner waits in the car. He is older than her. At least fifteen years on the force. He wants to get home. As soon as he's let her off he will. Have dinner. Watch TV. Be with his family.

"What did you think of her?" Helena asks carefully. "The mother. Didn't she seem a bit . . . angry?"

"Who the hell wouldn't be angry?" her partner asks. He laughs and Helena feels her cheeks redden. He thinks she is silly, it's unmistakable. "Kids getting lost. Anything could have happened. She might have been stuck down there under the stage. Unable to get out, what do I know? And I guess she was embarrassed, too. Got half the cops in town out just because her kid fell asleep thirty feet away. Of course she felt ashamed."

Helena nods. Of course she did.

"Just let it go." Her partner turns in at her street. "We did something good today, Helena. Think about that instead. It sure doesn't happen every day. Now let's go home. It's fucking Christmas. Smile and be happy. This was one of the good days."

Police officer Helena Svensson goes to bed early. A large cup of tea on her bedside table. She leafs through a glossy magazine. A recipe for gingerbread cupcakes, a home decoration article full of embroidered silk cushions. A famous actress talks about her family Christmas traditions. She wants to teach her children the joy of giving.

Helena turns pages, reads, starts over again when she is done. She is wide awake. Unthinkingly reads the same article again and again, unable to concentrate on how to make a sugar-frosted Christmas garland out of spruce twigs. Her mind is full of dirty yellow bruises and a little girl clinging to Stefan's neck.

Even at the police academy they talked about it. About the worst threat to little girls not being a dirty old man with his pockets full of candy and an imaginary puppy in the trunk of his car. The dirty old men are few. Many more children have mothers who can't take it any more, have fathers who never help out, are always told that they are hopeless and clumsy and stupid. And get bruises even if they never dare climb a tree.

The apartment where Emma lived was warm. Her mother wasn't a drunk. She cooked meatballs and kept a laundry basket by her door, had bought detergent and booked the laundry room.

Let it go. That's what her partner had said. And why shouldn't she? Petra already led a tough life. Alone with two kids. She certainly doesn't need to get social services on her back. And Helena has other things to worry about.

Tomorrow was another day. Her shift would start at eleven and the weather forecast said it would be cold. Cold drove the homeless to places where they became visible, into stairwells where landlords complained about their smell and into shopping malls where they didn't fit in with the Christmas decorations. Tomorrow would be a hard day and tomorrow night even worse. She can't worry the small stuff like this. She'll burn out before finishing her first year.

Helena throws the magazine on the floor and switches off the light. She turns on her side and kicks at the covers to get her foot free.

Let it go? Is that really what I'm supposed to do? Is that really how it's supposed to be? When it's soon fucking Christmas. Was this really one of the good days?

Born Malin Persson in Stockholm in 1969, Malin Persson Giolito is the daughter of celebrated crime author and professor of criminology Leif G. W. Persson. Herself a lawyer, she worked for ten years at the Stockholm and Brussels offices of the international law firm Mannheimer Swartling; in late 2007, she accepted a position with the European Commission, the executive body of the European Union. She lives with her husband Christophe Giolito in Brussels. Her first, noncrime novel, Dubbla slag *(Two-Front Battle),* was published in 2008; it has so far been followed by two crime novels that have established her as one of the most interesting young Swedish crime writers. Her novels are carried by strong characterizations and serious, topical themes: in her second book,* Bara ett barn *(Only a Child),* crimes committed against children; in her third,* Bortom varje rimligt tvivel *(Beyond All Reasonable Doubt),* miscarriage of justice.*

THE MULTI-MILLIONAIRE

Maj Sjöwall and Per Wahlöö

For thirty-five years, Maj Sjöwall and Per Wahlöö were the indisputably best known, most highly regarded, and most read of all Swedish crime writers. Their ten police procedural novels featuring Detective Inspector Martin Beck and his team of investigators, initially published in Sweden 1965 through 1975, were translated worldwide; won numerous awards, including the Mystery Writers of America Edgar Allan Poe Award for best novel; were made into movies in the United States, in Sweden, in the former Soviet Union, in Germany, and in the Netherlands; and have remained in print throughout the world.

Maj Sjöwall and Per Wahlöö met in the summer of 1962. Wahlöö was a well-known writer and journalist, thirty-six years old, married, and with a daughter. Sjöwall was twenty-seven, a journalist and magazine art director, twice divorced, and with a six-year-old daughter. The attraction was instant but the situation was difficult. They met in bars, worked together, wrote together. Within a year, Wahlöö had moved in with Sjöwall. Their first son was born nine months later. They never married, but in Sweden their romance, one that had started out as virtually a public scandal, became envied and almost legendary: they were inseparable. A year after they met, they began planning a series of crime novels in which they would apply their common, radically leftist perspective. The series title, The Story of a Crime, in fact was meant to refer to the political agenda of the novels: the crime referred to was society's abandonment of the working classes.

They wrote their novels in longhand, alternating chapters. They would then switch, editing the other's work as they typed the final copy.

Apart from their ten novels, Maj Sjöwall and Per Wahlöö had time to do very little collaborative writing. For most of their time together, for economic reasons, they had to keep their day jobs. But they did work on movie scripts and occasional shorter nonfiction and fiction. All told, they published only three short stories. These stories follow a similar pattern: the authors are themselves present as observers and relate to their readers what they have heard and seen. "The Multi-Millionaire" is the only short work by Sjöwall and Wahlöö to reflect both the psychological and, by implication, political concerns that drive their ten famous crime novels. It is the story of an unusually successful con artist.

A FEW YEARS AGO, WE MADE THE ACQUAINTANCE OF A DOLLAR MULTI-millionaire. You don't meet multi-millionaires every day. Particularly not in dollars. When all's said and done, there is something special about dollars.

If you consider the place where we met, perhaps the occurrence wasn't all that strange. It happened on board the *Queen Elizabeth* —the real *Queen Elizabeth*, the one nowadays moping around as a hotel somewhere in Florida—and not only that, but in first class, where they probably had more than one millionaire. There were also a lot of blue-haired American ladies and tottering English lords. But we particularly remember our man because he told us a story. A story complete with a moral.

From the poop deck we watched as we sailed out to sea under the Verrazano-Narrows Bridge, and when Ambrose Lighthouse had disappeared in the sun haze we went to the bar and that's where we first saw him.

He sat alone at a table, his back bent in its light blue cash-mere pullover as he brooded over a double whiskey. It was fairly early in the morning. He gave us a cursory glance as we each climbed on one of the bar stools. The three of us and the man behind the bar were the only ones in the room and it was still more than an hour to lunch.

The man looked close to sixty; later we learned that he was forty-two.

At the same moment we were ordering drinks the man dropped his pack of cigarettes on the wall-to-wall carpet. Then he fixed the bartender with his violet-blue stare and said: "Please hand me my cigarettes."

The barman went on mixing our drinks.

"My cigarette pack fell to the floor. Please hand it to me," the man on the couch said.

The bartender vigorously stirred our drinks and pretended not to hear.

"Shall I blow my top?" the man asked.

Unconcerned, the bartender rattled the ice while the man on the couch sat immobile, staring hard at him with his truly conspicuous violet eyes.

We started to get interested and awaited further developments.

The man in the light-blue pullover slammed his glass down on the table and said, "Okay, I'll blow my top."

So he did. Which meant that he got furious. He stood up, heaped abuse on the bartender, behaved like a hysterical five-year-old and left the bar with quick, mincing steps, leaving his pack of cigarettes on the carpet. The bartender didn't bat an eyelid. After a while a bar assistant arrived and put the cigarettes back on the table.

"A loathsome man," we said.

The bartender's face was sphinxlike.

For this trip we had been seated at the table headed by the purser and the ship's doctor. At the table we met the man from the bar again. Not at lunch, when his chair was empty, but at dinner. He was in a bad mood, since he had been expecting to sit at the captain's table. After all, he was a multi-millionaire.

The crossing took four days, fifteen hours and twenty-five minutes.

This isn't a very long time, historically speaking, but aboard a large ship it can feel rather long.

Since there were relatively few first-class passengers on the trip and meals tend to be many and long and we also sat at the same table, we came to talk a lot to the man who was a multi-millionaire.

We even learned his name: McGrant. That he was an American there was no reason to doubt for even a second.

When we asked him where he lived, he raised his eyebrows in great surprise and said, "In McGrant, of course."

And so it was. He came from a town called McGrant somewhere in Mississippi or Kentucky or whatever state it was in. His great-grandfather was a Scot and had come there and founded the town and then it had been passed on to his heirs. Quite simply he owned the town that bore his name: the bank and the department stores and most of the buildings and, indirectly, also almost all of the land. It was a fine town, he said, of around ten thousand inhabitants, and they all lived in their own houses and were white, even the servants, and of course he also had control of the local party organization.

He liked his Bentley, he said, but he liked his Rolls-Royce better, even if both of his Cadillacs were more American, and he regarded us as friends of his since we shared our bread and our salt and Cunard's peculiar desserts, which looked like swans made from jelly pudding, and sat at the same table.

He threw indignant glances at the elderly, stodgy peers at the captain's table and said that of course he couldn't have known we would end up at the same mess table that first time in the bar when he delivered his first fit of rage and let his pack of cigarettes fall to the long-suffering deck in the old *Queen*'s barroom.

We listened to him in badly hidden amazement and watched his antics in sadness mixed with terror.

He never opened or closed any door, never sat down in a chair unless someone pushed it under him and never retrieved any of the objects that with regular and usually very short intervals he let fall from his hands. And however fast the servants were he would tell them off. That was part of the system, an integrated component of his method.

If any of us, or any other passenger, in some way tried to help him along, he was put off.

Somehow that was inappropriate.

We wondered: How can any person become like him?

And he must have read that question in our eyes, for that was when he told us his strange story.

The beginning wasn't so strange. The story of the single son of an inhumanly demanding father. And the son, who within a year would take it all over but who first had to prove himself capable of making his own way. What was strange was the rather particular method.

Suddenly one day his father had said: Here's a ticket to San Francisco. Go there and stay for a year and fend for yourself and come back and take over the town of McGrant. (He ought to have added that he himself would probably die from heart failure within that year, and so indeed he did, that is, die.)

McGrant junior had no other choice than to do as his father demanded. With a couple of dollars in his pocket and a bag with the bare necessities of clothing he took the train to San Francisco. It was a very long way and he had never before been on the West Coast and he knew nobody in the city.

"But I made do," McGrant said. "Of course I made do. And more than that, I lived well that whole year in San Francisco."

"So you got yourself a job there," we suggested.

"A job?" said McGrant, flabbergasted, and looked unsympathetically at us with his round, violet-blue eyes.

It was the third day, a stormy day, and in the afternoon through our binoculars we had sighted Fastnet Rock far away in the northeast quadrant. The swell of the Atlantic was heavy and green and pitiless and manropes had been stretched all around the ship.

We three had been the only diners in the mess—rumor had it that even the ship's doctor was seasick in his bathtub, where he observed the swell of the sea by watching the water in his bath rise and fall—and now we were having coffee and brandy in the very thinly populated salon.

★ ★ ★

"No," McGrant said. "No, I certainly didn't get a job, but I did learn how to live in San Francisco. And since you are friends of mine I will tell you how I did it. Perhaps knowing it will come in handy at some point."

And we listened.

"So I arrived in San Francisco without a cent in my pocket," McGrant said.

"Without a cent?"

He raised his eyebrows in a very surprised manner above his violet-blue eyes and said: "Don't you really know how to do it?"

No, we said. We truly really didn't know.

And so he told us:

"I came to San Francisco without a cent in my pocket and I had only one chance."

"San Francisco," he said, "is one of the toughest towns in the States, and that makes it one of the toughest towns in all the world."

"Really?" we said. "And how do you get ahead there," we said. Questioningly.

And then he told us his story.

It went like this:

"So as I said, my dear father sent me to San Francisco without a cent in my pocket."

"And then what happened," we said.

"It was morning, early morning, when I arrived in San Francisco," McGrant told us. "I was broke and hungry and since I wasn't used to either I didn't know what to do. I walked out of the railway station and saw the line of cabs and it felt strange not to be able to get into one of them and go to the best hotel in town. I stood there with my little bag and I thought: You're all alone now, and you have to manage this.

"But I didn't know how."

"That's when I caught sight of him. A short, shabby man stumbling along on sore feet along the opposite sidewalk. He was carrying a sign saying: EAT AT FRIENDLY—THE FRIENDLY RESTAURANT!, and below that, in smaller letters, it said: *TRY OUR GREAT HOMELY FARE—IF YOU'RE NOT SATISFIED, YOU DON'T PAY!*

"As I already told you, I was hungry, and the little money my father had given me for travel expenses I had already out of old habit spent on drinks in the dining car. I decided to do as the sign suggested and I decided that I would certainly not be satisfied. "As it turned out, the friendly restaurant happened to be just halfway down the first block on the next crossing street. The dining room was huge and full of breakfast eaters. I sat down at the back of the room and ordered a square meal of ham and eggs, toast, butter, cheese, jelly, juice, coffee, well, basically all I could think of. Now I should mention that I really don't eat much, as you may have noticed already, being my friends at the purser's table. I eat like a bird, always have."

We nodded. He certainly hadn't indulged much in the way of solid food during these few days.

"At any rate, all the things I had ordered were brought to my table and when I'd just tasted a small sampling of each I was absolutely full. So I called to the waitress, pointed to my seemingly untouched breakfast and declared that it was the worst meal I had ever been served. She got hold of the head waiter. He was sorry that I wasn't satisfied, assured me that of course Friendly would stand by its promise and asked me to sign my name to the check. I wrote the first name that popped into my head: G. Formby. I've always liked the banjo. When I walked to the door, full of food and happy, I noticed that many of the guests had left their tips on the table, you know, coins half hidden under a plate, the we do back in the States. It was an easy thing to snatch those coins on my way out."

"Well, it wasn't a bad start. The money I found under the plates was enough to rent a room. And can you imagine how surprised I was when I glanced out the window and the first person I saw was an old man carrying exactly the same sign as the one I'd see outside the railway station: EAT AT FRIENDLY—THE FRIENDLY RESTAURANT! *TRY OUR GREAT HOMELY FARE—IF YOU'RE NOT SATISFIED, YOU DON'T PAY!*

"Naturally I went to a phone booth and to my considerable delight I found that Friendly was a huge chain of restaurants with at least a hundred outlets in the San Francisco Bay area. I immediately realized the enormous possibilities hidden within this fact. Obviously I became a faithful patron of these eateries, and the coins I found under most plates meant that I never needed to be penniless. On the contrary, my capital began growing, slowly but surely.

"One day a man at the table next to mine spoke to me. He was a shabby creature whom I of course hardly could start talking to. What he said was:

"'This is a great trick. Too bad you can only pull it a couple of times a year. The checks you sign are collected in some office somewhere, and they keep track of the names. If you sign too often they put you on their blacklist, and they just won't serve you any longer.' "I stared at him. Most probably he was an imbecile. After watching me sign the check with a dignified and dismissive expression, he sadly wiped his mouth and said:

"'I know another good trick, but you can only do it once a year. At Parsley's. They give you a free cake on your birthday. And then you can sell it. But you have to be able to document that it's really your birthday.'

"Without dignifying him with a glance I rose to leave, increasing my capital with a further five quarters on the way out."

"I was now faced with a problem, but solved it immediately. I could hardly get in touch with my father, but instead I could write the authorities in McGrant and tell them to send me a hundred identity cards with my birth date left blank. In McGrant, that kind of thing was handled by the sheriff, and since he was up for reelection only half a year later, I had the cards in three days. He had mailed them special delivery.

"After that, everything became much easier. I picked my cakes up at Parsley's, which was also a major trade chain, and sold them to those Friendly restaurants I had already used up.

"Perhaps I haven't told you that I genuinely dislike walking, while at the same time disdain on principle so-called public transportation, possibly, and I really mean just possibly, with the exception of this kind."

McGrant fell silent and made a sweeping gesture encompassing the *Queen Elizabeth*'s lounge, where the fifth Earl of Something, strongly marked by age, senile decay and general stupidity, was just giving a lecture on Lord Nelson and the Battle of Aboukir to a sparse audience of commandeered ship's officers twisting uneasily in their seats. The old man seemed totally oblivious of the swell.

"Well," McGrant continued, in passing letting his coffee spoon fall to the floor, "in brief, this is what I did. I phoned all the major car retailers in town and told them that my aunt had asked me to buy her a car. A luxury car, but that she wanted it thoroughly tested. Then I set up meetings with the salesmen in the lobby of one of the largest hotels. After that I let myself be chauffeured around for a week or so, taking in the nearby sights. When the salesman began to seem nervous and started hinting that I ought to make my mind up, I would of course have come to realize that his particular car just wouldn't do for my discriminating aunt. After that, I turned to the next outlet. At one point, I believe when I was riding a Daimler, I had already been driven around for ten days and had to let my poor aunt pass away from a heart attack on the eleventh."

"Yes, my friends, that's how I lived during my year in San Francisco, most brutal of all great cities. And if you should ever happen to find yourselves there, at least you know how to cope. When the year ended I took a train home, and you can trust me when I tell you that this time I had plenty of dollars in my pocket. Unfortunately my father never got to see my proud return, since he had died a week before."

McGrant was a careful man. At an intimate moment he showed us his medicines—around a hundred—and his cash. In spite of his checkbooks and bank accounts and credit cards and the fact of his trip being prepaid, he always carried a wallet full of bills in large denominations and from every Western European country.

"You never know what may happen," he said.

And of course that's true.

He disembarked at Cherbourg and on the quay a black, chauffeured limousine waited for him.

The last piece of advice he gave us was:

"Don't tip the bootblack when you get to Southampton."

We last glimpsed him as he minced out from the dining room, on his way palming a few dollar bills left under a plate by some gullible American.

Otherwise, the trip was as such trips usually are. Schools of flying fish and porpoises and a whale blowing. By the way, the captain was named Law.

And we won a prize in designing the funniest hat in a competition. Everyone who entered did. McGrant didn't enter. He was up on deck, telling off the cabin steward for allowing his suitcases to be wrongly packed. Incidentally, it wasn't his cabin steward.

Per Wahlöö was born in 1926, began working as a journalist in 1947, and continued writing—though gradually emphasizing theater and movie reviews and features—for newspapers and magazines until 1964. He published his first novel in 1959 and a further seven until 1968; they express his strong political convictions as well as his concerns about social justice and abuse of power. These themes are also central to the ten crime novels he wrote in collaboration with Maj Sjöwall, born in 1935 and a journalist, editor, writer, and translator. Wahlöö and Sjöwall met and began living together in 1963; in 1965, they published their first cowritten novel, Roseanna, *which began their ten-novel series The Story of a Crime, starring the detectives working under Chief Inspector Martin Beck at the homicide commission of the Swedish national police. The fourth novel in the series,* Den strattande polisen (The Laughing Policeman, 1968), *in translation won the 1971 Edgar Allan Poe Award for best crime novel published in the United States. Sjöwall and Wahlöö also wrote movie scripts, short stories, and essays. The last novel in their series,* Terroristerna (The Terrorists), *was not yet published when Wahlöö died in 1975, at the age of forty-eight. The Sjöwall-Wahlöö novels were published around the world and have never been out of print. All of them have been made into feature films or adapted for TV, and more than twenty-five additional movies have been based on characters from the novels; in Great Britain, the BBC has produced a radio dramatization of the ten books. As Maj Sjöwall has noted, she and Per Wahlöö failed in changing the face of Swedish society, which was the task they set out to accomplish. But they did, most emphatically, change the themes and directions of Swedish crime fiction.*

DIARY BRAUN

SARA STRIDSBERG

When her first novel was published in 2004, Sara Stridsberg was recognized as a major literary talent; her second, in 2006, confirmed her position as perhaps the foremost new voice in Swedish literature. Since then, she has gone on to publish a third novel, again hailed by critics, as well as writing several stage plays performed at the Royal Dramatic Theater in Stockholm, the stage closest to a Swedish national theater. The lead in her second play, Medealand (Medea's Land, *performed 2009), was played by Noomi Rapace, who became an international star when she player Lisbeth Salander in the Millennium trilogy.*

  Stridsberg's novels and plays explore the personality, inner and outer conflicts, and treatment of extraordinary women. Her first novel, Happy Sally, *was inspired by the life of Sally Bauer, who, in 1939, became the first Scandinavian woman to swim across the English channel, and draws parallels to a present-day admirer wanting to repeat Bauer's feat. Her second,* Drömfakulteten (The Dream Faculty), *was inspired by the life of Valerie Solanas, author of* The SCUM Manifesto (*which Stridsberg has translated into Swedish); her third,* Darling River, *was inspired by Vladimir Nabokov's iconic novel* Lolita, *and in parallel stories both completes and gives alternative readings of the Dolores Haze* character, in Nabokov's novel viewed only through the eyes of Humbert Humbert. Stridsberg's first play again revolved aroundValerie Solanas; her second takes the theme of Euripides' Medea, but is set in the present and the protagonist is an immigrant woman, abandoned by her husband and denied the right to stay on in her new country; her third, Dissekeringar av ett snöfall (Dissections of Snowfall, 2012), is loosely based on the life of the Swedish Queen Christina, expected by her court to let the men around her rule while she married and bred future kings, but raised by her father as a prince and with no wish to renounce her humanity in order to be what men consider a woman.

In the following story, Stridsberg is inspired by one of the mythologized women of the twentieth century, a woman both known and unknown to us all, who was not only a witness to, but in a sense also an accomplice in, and certainly a victim of, one of the worst crimes ever committed.

THE CURTAINS LET IN LIGHT BUT NO IMAGES. THE LANDSCAPE OUTSIDE is a desert. The rhythm of the train is convincingly and seductively lulling. He has written you that you must pull down the curtains in your compartment when the train passes the places you have talked about. So you pull down the curtains or you lean your head against the window glass and watch the other passengers in the compartment and their luggage when the train pulls close. A woman alone with cheap luggage and her face turned to the corridor. A man with an armful of sunflowers in a paper bag. The compartment is sunfaded with burnt-through leather seats that must once have been elegant, but which are now splitting along their seams and letting out spongy upholstery. Politics bores you, always has bored you to death. The sun-bleached curtain separates you from the world and the earth. You are going back to the house on Berghof. Insubordinate sunbeams sneak in through tears in the fabric. A patch of blue, bulging sky. The beauty of this country. Wheat and roses.

How should I describe you? Sweet as a box of chocolates. A kind of dreamy beauty, an expensive small piece of jewelry. The Munich girl falling for a pair of famous blue eyes. For a long while you were retouched out of all public photographs since your love has the notion that he shouldn't be seen in public with any women. So. Your rabbit fur disappears from the image. Your ash-blonde hair, your mother-of-pearl nails, all your devotion will afterwards be re-touched out. As if you had never been there or as if you are a ghost who on her own has invented your decade-long love. Occasionally a single woman's hand is visible on his forearm, but the body belong-ing to it is gone. As late as June of 1944, the British intelligence ser-vice believes you to be his secretary.

Further descriptions of you from literature: mild, naïve, dreamy, romantic. I add your longing for death to the catalogue. Since it must be there. Your inclination for the underworld. Absolutely.

"About twenty-four years of age, brunette, attractive and un-conventional in her dress. Occasionally wears Bavarian leather shorts. In her spare time, walks two black dogs. Protected by operatives of the RSD during her walks. Always without makeup, on the whole gives an impression of inapproachability."

—*From a Special Operations Executive document*

The spring smells of ashes and greenery just come into leaf. Long, lonely walks, rambling conversations about the weather and the dogs, sleepless nights. Obersalzberg, the small set piece, a utopia of purity and beauty. Still no public displays of affection. Hamburg transformed into a sea of fire, its people ashes. It's your birthday. Money in an envelope. No greetings, not a kind word, nothing, but your entire office looks like a florist's shop and smells like a funeral chapel. You ought to make use of the shelter, but instead you stay in the house, dancing with your mirror image, get up on the roof after each raid to see if any fire bombs have fallen. The crowns of the trees bend down towards the water as if in prayer. You write: *They say that my country is burning. All will be well. It will be all right. Dragonflies dive down at our picnic. My bathing suit is gold and silver.*

You have never been as happy as now. After all the years of waiting he is finally yours. He has grown strangely old and stern, but at least today he is cheerful. Blondie sings like Zarah Leander. She sounds like a mad wolf. It's snowing even though it is April and throughout the night you drink wonderful champagne, full of promise, toasting his last birthday. The next day all of the presents from the ranks of the people are sent away due to the risks of poison. You wear the dress he loves, the navy-blue sequined silk one. When you are dead, a German journalist writes of it: "Her taste now was more mature and she could carry off clothes that were chic, not just lovely and youthful." Then Munich falls and he is off again to the underworld.

You and your silly little cousin wait every day in your bathing suits for the mailman in Obersalzberg who drives you down to the lake and the beaches, the happy waterfall, the fairy-tale beach by the ice-cold blue lake. Sometimes you take off your bathing suits to swim nude between alps. You imagine the officers doing nasty things to themselves while they watch your naked body. That thought appeals to you. The assassination attempt in Berlin fails, but all the sunlight disappears. Days pass. All the tender letters and carrier pigeons. *Pull the curtains down my dear when the train passes the places we talked about. Pull the curtains down my dear . . .*

You order a new dress for Christmas. It's to be something special and more, something to amaze everyone. Miss Heise nags you about her perennial bills. It would be best if they could be obliterated once they are paid. It would be best if they just disappeared. You don't want anyone afterwards to study your correspondence with you seamstress. Your dresses are your secrets. You hold a slip and a diamond brooch up against death. Snow falls like sugar cubes on the city. There is no longer any hope for a future.

A cherished meeting with a sister in Wassenburgerstrasse. A few pieces of jewelry handed to Gertraud when you are both temporarily in the shelter beneath the house, a necklace and a bracelet. You say, "I don't need them any longer." The decision has been made; we leave all of this together, where you go I will go, where you are buried I too want to be buried.

His birthday gifts for your last birthday: a Mercedes, a diamond bracelet, a pendant set with topazes. You have a birthday celebration in the marbled room. I don't know which dress you chose to wear for this last night in the house, but I imagine it to be extravagant, I imagine you in cream and embroideries and throughout with a brandy snifter in your hand. You pick clothes and jewelry to bring along from your enormous closet, the rest you will have to give away now. You make sure that the dogs will have somewhere to live. One last time, trying out everything, once more enjoying your image in the huge, mirrored bathroom. The flocks of jackdaws take wing from your heart, leaving it empty.

The sheets in the night train sleeper are white and fragrantly clean. Outside are the wastelands. When you arrive at Berghof there is still snow. The train to the underworld will leave at 8:14 p.m. He can no longer stop you since you are not afraid of death, since you long for it. The only thing frightening you is that your body will be disfigured, violated by strangers once you can no longer defend it, dress it, adorn it. Now you leave the window of your compartment naked despite his warnings. Anyway it's dark outside. Earlier in the day a weak sun was shining. Ominously weak.

The lack of natural light underground amazes you. That disgusting neon light, artificial and sinister. From now on it is always claustrophobic night. You dream of huge scenic windows. In your dreams strange tropical animals roam in slow motion through the garden above. Your miniature suite next to the chart room comprises a bedroom, a closet, a bathroom and toilet. Even Blondie has a small room to herself and her pups. It isn't far to the climbing roses in the garden and yet you can't go there because of the grenades. The cities are gray and wasted now, dead and crushed, occasional shreds and climbing roses, people resembling clouds.

The apartment underground smells of marmalade and metal. You watch movies, drink sparkling wine, eat fruits and sweet cookies, you prepare for death, write wills. A black sunlight radiates through the windows. The night is a tomb. Not all birds sing. In a letter to your sister, you write, "Destroy all my private correspondence, particularly the bills from my seamstress, Heise. Bury the blue leather notebook. Wait until the last to destroy the films and the albums. The telephone lines are all dead now. I hope Morrell landed safely to bring you my jewelry."

You order Moët et Chandon. You order cakes. Cocaine drops for his bad eye. New promotions. The pretend war goes on. Paper swallows across the office floor illustrate devastation. You call into the wind. Mrs. G. is given a brooch. Afterwards it is still pinned to her dress. It looks like a fallen butterfly. Now death is keeping you busy, it is your only conversational subject. To do: Change dress. Fix nails. Paint mother-of-pearl. Life is a beauty pageant and you are the foremost exhibit underground where you have free access to his luxurious bathroom. A. still washes and irons your clothes. You change your dress several times a day, always wearing elegant, gossamer underwear. You dance alongside the dead. A brimstone butterfly gone astray into the tunnels.

The silver-fox stole gleams like a cloud in darkness. How you have loved that stole. A garment made for a movie star. A boa for the future. For all your silly dreams. You give it away, too. It has lost all value for you. You put it in the arms of a secretary, Miss T., convincingly say, "Take it. Use it. Enjoy."

The best way to die is to shoot yourself through the mouth. Memorandum: *My husband dislikes being seen in the nude. For that to happen would be a defeat to him. Please bear this in mind*

The underground wedding resembles none of your dreams. But yet. An elegant, navy-blue sequined dress and black suede Ferragamo shoes. No flowers, no songs, no incurable diseases, but champagne— the cellar is still full of fabulous, immortal drops. For the very last night your are dressed in carbon dioxide and night. Thirty-six hours of marriage under the earth. A political testament in four blueprints. The bride of night in poisoned veils. Your closet is like your love, a black circle without end. The king's first and last wife.

And I want my death to be painless. Nothing of all I wished will turn out as I wished, but that I do want. A painless death. I thought about dying in my silver-fox stole. I think about this and that. Everything passes, everything ends.

Thirty-six hours after the wedding all that remains is a last, dizzying farewell. The patterned fabric of the couch under your nails, your favorite couch. In the distance the sound of a diesel-powered fan, and the scent of his sweat. You sit like children, legs up in the couch. You listen to his continuously more disjointed talking, his chest close to your ear and in it you can still hear the beating of his heart. How you loved him, dizzyingly much. The garden, fire, love, the underworld.

The dress with black roses will be your last dress, the one leading to eternity. There are thirty-seven roses, you have let him count them one last time. One rose for every hour you were a wife, and one extra. For nothing. For all you will now never be. The pink curlers are thrown on the floor of your bedroom. Hair newly set. Just a whiff of powder and a little lipstick, since he still hates makeup. You have showered in perfume to drown the odor of sweat.

A last, flaring memory. You are riding your bike through the woods to meet him by a lake. You are young and his eyes are blue like gemstones. A box of cookies on your baggage carrier. A dead pheasant smeared across the road. The feeling that a cloud is following you. A light in those blue stones you will never afterwards be able to forget. Afterwards your bodies will be burned outside in the garden. The small brass tube that held the cyanide looks like a discarded lipstick. A glass phial full of dark-brown fluid. The searing smell of bitter almonds. Breaking the glass phial between your teeth and swallowing the dark-brown fluid. Soviet grenades fall around your burning bodies. And Blondie. Doctor Stumpfegger takes care of her. Your loved one was unable to do it himself. He put the glass phial into your mouth, in bewildered trembling tenderness, but he was unable to do it to her.

Sara Stridsberg, born in 1972 in the Solna area of Stockholm, is a writer and translator. After a number of highly regarded essays, for which she in 2004 received the annual award of the Swedish Essay Fund, she also in 2004 published her first novel, Happy Sally. *Her second novel,* Drömfakulteten (The Dream Faculty, 2006), *was a fictional, impressionistic work based on the life of Valerie Solanas. It was a finalist for the Swedish August Award for best novel of the year and received the Nordic Council Literature Prize for best novel in any Nordic country. Her third novel,* Darling River, 2010, *was again a finalist for the August Award. In 2006,*

Stridsberg's first play, Valerie Jean Solanas ska bli president i Amerika (Valerie Jean Solanas Will Be the President of America), *premiered at the Swedish national stage, the Royal Dramatic Theater in Stockholm, which also staged two of her later plays. Her book of collected stage plays,* Medealand (Medea Country, 2012), *made her a three-time finalist for the August Award. In 2013, she received the Dobloug Prize awarded by the Swedish Academy for outstanding work in the field of literary fiction. Sara Stridsberg is one of Sweden's foremost contemporary authors.*

REVENGE OF THE VIRGIN

Johan Theorin

Johan Theorin is a journalist and author. He was born in Gothenburg, but grew up in the sparsely populated mining country of Bergslagen. Since his childhood, he has spent every summer in a cottage close to a barrow grave in the northern part of Öland, a long, narrow island of 518 square miles in the Baltic, between two and three miles off the eastern coast of the Swedish mainland. The island provides the setting for most of Johan Theorin's fiction, including this story.

Öland in Swedish simply means "island land." The island is separated from the mainland by the Kalmar Strait; its landscape is dominated by the Stora Alvaret [the Great Alvar], a barren limestone plain covering some 138 square miles and overgrown by sparse, stunted trees and an immense diversity of other flora. Öland was settled around 8000 BC, and the island offers a vast number of burial grounds, barrows, and Iron Age ring forts and artifacts, as well as the ruins of more modern keeps and other buildings: it is a lonely, windswept, and often mysterious place, full of history, legends, and stories. Even today, Öland has a population of only around 25,000 people; the largest town, Borgholm, probably named for a castle built there around 1270, has only some 3,000 inhabitants.

In the middle of Kalmar Strait is the small island of Blå Jungfrun [the Blue Virgin], only about a quarter of a square mile but rising to a height of almost 290 feet above sea level. Blå Jungfrun is partly naked rock, partly dense hardwood forest. It holds numerous caves and an ancient stone labyrinth, as well as other remains; it is surrounded by the remains of numerous wrecked ships, some of which are visible from the surface of the sea. According to Swedish folklore, already documented in the 1550s, Blå Jungfrun was the place where witches went on Maundy Thursday to meet with Satan and celebrate the witches' sabbath. Another, still living legend says that anyone removing a stone from the island will suffer bad luck until the stone is returned.

In this barren and magical setting, Theorin sets his novels of mystery, violence, humor, and wisdom. His first novel was published in 2007, and received the Best First Novel Award from the Swedish Crime Fiction Academy; his second won both the Crime Fiction Academy Best Novel Award and the Glass Key Award given by the Scandinavian Crime Writers' Association to the best novel published during a given year in any of the five Scandinavian countries. Theorin is one of only seven Swedes who have won this award during its twenty-two-year existence. He has also twice won awards from the British Crime Writers' Association.

One of the recurring central characters in his novels is fisherman Gerlof Davidsson, who also plays a lead role in this story; he is based on Theorin's maternal grandfather, sea captain Ellert Gerlofsson. "Revenge of the Virgin" is set in the 1950s, and Johan Theorin wants his readers to remember that at that time, the dangers of smoking were much less known than now, and smoking was much more common.

GERLOF WOKE IN A CRAMPED AND COLD WOODEN HOUSE. THE WALLS AND windows shook and rattled. The house was his own, his old boathouse, and it moved when gusts of wind pushed up from the beach to howl like a lost, unholy mare.

When he lifted his head from his camping bed he also heard the sound from the waves at the beach. It wasn't a roar, not yet, just a rhythmical rattle when they broke on the gravel.

There would be a storm today, it seemed. Gerlof didn't worry about his boathouse—his grandfather had used it for twenty years, then his father for thirty and now he had used it another ten years. He knew that the house and its foundation of stone would stand, no matter what winds blew in across the coastline. So the best thing for Gerlof would be to just stay inside. He had a day off from the sea. His boat was moored in Borgholm harbor, waiting for a new anchor.

But Gerlof had to get up. He, John Hagman and the Mossberg cousins had put quite a few nets in the strait last night, and they had to be emptied as soon as possible. Otherwise the storm would blow the nets out into the strait—along with all the fish that had been caught in them overnight.

Only one thing to do. Sighing, Gerlof sat up in his boathouse.

"Up ev'ry day, bad weather or fair," he muttered to himself and put his stockinged feet on the linoleum.

The floor was icy. The fire in the small iron stove at the foot of the bed had gone out during the night.

"John?"

Gerlof bent to the other narrow bed and shook his friend's shoulder. Finally John raised his head.

"Wha'?"

"Wake up," Gerlof said. "The fish are waiting."

John coughed, blinked his eyes and looked at the window.

"Can we put out?"

"We have to. Or do you want to lose the nets?"

John shook his head.

"We shouldn't have laid them yesterday . . . Erik was right about the weather."

"Just a lucky guess," Gerlof said.

"Might well go and get stormy tomorrow," fisherman Erik Mossberg had said in his dialect the evening before, when he'd come down to the beach. His cousin Torsten waited with Gerlof and John by the boats.

"Really?" Gerlof said. "Did they say so on the radio?"

"Nope. But on the way here I stepped across a viper. It lay on the stairs and hardly wanted to leave."

"I suppose it had eaten its fill," Gerlof said. "Are snakes supposed to become experts on what happens in the atmosphere just because they lie still?"

"It's proven true before," Erik said. "I've seen snakes before when there was a storm brewing, and more than once."

Gerlof just shook his head and put the nets down on the floor of the boat. He believed neither in portents nor prophecies.

But a little later, when they had launched their two wooden crafts on the glassy water and begun to lay their nets over the railings, Gerlof had peered north at the Blue Virgin on the horizon and seen that the granite cliff had changed its color. It had darkened from blue gray to black and seemed to have risen above the waters of the strait, as if it floated in the air.

The weather was still fine. The sun shone on the sea and the May wind was soft and almost warm, but when Gerlof had thrown in the last of the net floats he realized that Erik had been right. A storm was coming. He didn't believe in vipers, but the changed appearance of the Virgin had told him so. And when he rowed back to shore the cliff was no longer visible—it had disappeared in a pale, white mist.

Harder winds were coming.

Half an hour after they woke up the next morning, John and Gerlof were down at the beach along with Erik and Torsten.

The boats were ready, but despite the gale drawing closer John and the two cousins persisted in smoking a cigarette each on the beach before setting out.

Gerolf checked his watch in irritation, but the smokers just smiled.

"If you smoked too, you'd be less cranky in the mornings," Erik said, blowing a white cloud into the wind.

"Tobacco isn't healthy," Gerlof said. "Pulling a lot of thick smoke into your lungs? Sooner or later, doctors will start warning people not to do it."

The other three smiled at his prophecy.

"I'd be bedridden without my cigarettes," Torsten said. "They keep me healthy . . . they rinse out your throat!"

After their smoking break they walked down to the boats. Gerlof and John pushed their old Öland gig onto the water and stepped down in it. Then they pushed out past the breakers, each using one oar, and finally raised the small spritsail.

As the wind caught the cotton canvas and the seventeen-foot gig began making way across the sea, they heard a dull whining behind them, as from a large, bad-tempered bumblebee. Erik and Torsten Mossberg had started their new outboard. The motor made their rowboat speed up and determinedly plow straight ahead, white foam mustaches at its prow.

Gerlof didn't want an outboard, not while there were oars and sails. They used no gas and the long-keeled gig was easy to sail. It lifted effortlessly from the waves, kept a straight course and beat to windward as steadily as a Viking ship, which the Öland gig was, in a way. At least they were related.

When John and Gerlof had reached their nets they let out the sail and let the boat drift freely. Their three nets were north of those of the cousins, who had laid four on the night before. The cork floats holding the nets up were called *läten* on northern Öland and were marked by small, white pennants fluttering hard in the wind.

Gerlof pulled up the first *läte*, then began hauling the net on board with long, even strokes. The net twisted around his legs, coiled down like wet hawsers into the wooden crates.

The catch was good this morning. The first struggling flounder appeared after only a couple of yards, followed by many more. But the wind increased and while he pulled up the nets Gerlof was continually forced to try to stand steady in the rough waves lifting and pulling down the gig.

He felt relieved when the nets were all out, lying like huge balls in their crates. The balls moved, for the flounders kept struggling.

Gerlof gently worked loose a fourhorn sculpin that had managed to get stuck in the loops of yarn and threw it back in the water.

"How many did you make it?"

"Eighty-six," John said.

"Really? I made it eighty-four."

"Then I guess it's eighty-five."

That was fine—Gerlof's wife Ella in Borgholm had wanted flounders for the weekend, and their daughters liked them, too. Time to get back to land and home to the family.

The wind had risen steadily, as had the waves. Of course, here in the strait they never grew to the steep hills of water and pools of spray Gerlof and his boat had met farther out on the Baltic, but they were closer together and made the gig's broad planking shudder.

He would have preferred to turn the boat and get back ashore as quickly as possible, now that the nets were up, but when he put his hand to the tiller he felt John's touch on his shoulder and heard a question through the wind:

"What's that over there? In front of the Virgin?"

Gerlof turned his eyes northward and saw something narrow and black move in the strait, around a nautical mile from the Blue Virgin—an object seeming to roll helplessly in the foaming sea.

"Looks like a rowboat," he said.

"Yes," John said, "and it's empty."

Gerlof shook his head. He couldn't see a head sticking up out of the boat, but he had seen enough small and large crafts at sea to know when one of them was loaded or not, so he said:

"Not quite empty. There's something in it."

Or someone, a human? His glass was still lying in the wheelhouse on the boat down in Borgholm, but when the waves lifted the rowboat he could still make out something long and light within it. At this distance, it looked like a person who had lain down, or fallen, and been covered by a tarpaulin.

Without saying anything more Gerlof set the spritsail again and set off to northwest. John sat in the bow and didn't object. Every Ölander knew that if someone in a boat was ill or in distress that person must be helped, no matter how hard the wind.

Fifteen minutes later they were within hailing distance of the rowboat, which now and then disappeared in the waves. Gerlof cupped his hands.

"Ahoy," he called. "Ahoy over there!"

Nothing moved in the boat, but Gerlof saw that the tarpaulin was dry. That meant the rowboat couldn't have drifted for very long in the strait.

Behind them, a rattling outboard came closer.

"What's up?"

The Mossberg cousins had followed and reached them. Erik gave more gas, yawed narrowly across a wave and went up alongside the rowboat. Gerlof was envious at how easy it was with the outboard.

Torsten stretched out his arm and caught hold of the boat's railing. In the calm of a trough he crossed to the rowboat, stood up and threw a rope to his cousin. Now the two boats were tied together.

Finally Torsten bent down, lifted the tarpaulin and looked at what was underneath it.

"It's just rocks!" he called to the others.

"Rocks?"

Gerlof turned his gig round. It closed the distance to the rowboat a bit, and he saw that Torsten was right: in the bottom of the rowboat was a large pile of rounded rocks. They looked like water-smoothed beach stones.

Gerlof had no more time to consider their strange find. A huge wave broke against his boat, drenching both fishes and fishermen in ice-cold spray.

He shook himself and blinked at the wind. Now the waves had grown to sloping walls. There was a storm in the Kalmar strait, no point in denying it.

Gerlof tried turning his gig around to catch the waves on the aft quarter, but suddenly there was a short bang and an extended, tearing sound. The boat straightened and the sail lost all power. When he raised his eyes there was a large tear in the canvas.

"*Pöt!*"

John cursed in the Öland dialect and held on to the gunwhale as the boat heaved on a wave. He rushed forward to take in the torn sail.

At the same time, Gerlof let go of the tiller for a couple of seconds to get the oars in. When he was done, John took over between the oarlocks and started rowing, but it was hard work for him to make steerageway.

"The waves are steering us!" Gerlof yelled through the wind.

"What?"

Gerlof cupped his hands.

"It's too late to turn back . . . We might as well make the Virgin, until it lulls."

"What about this one?" Torsten called from the rowboat. "What do we do with it?"

"Tow it!" Gerlof said.

After all it was a solid boat, and Ölanders have taken care of lost property adrift on the sea since time immemorial.

★ ★ ★

Laboriously they made their way north and saw the Blue Virgin grow in front of them, immobile and heedless of the storm.

Gerlof was always amazed that the strangely round island cliff rose here, just a few nautical miles from the coast of Öland. The Blue Virgin was older than Öland, millions of years older.

The island of witches. And indeed the waters around it looked like a boiling cauldron.

It was to this island the witches came at Easter, according to popular belief, to revel with Satan himself. The place had been in bad repute for centuries. In fact it had another name, an older name than the Blue Virgin, but saying it out loud meant bad luck. Gerlof didn't intend taking any such risk, for out here on the waves he was more superstitious than ashore.

He turned the tiller to make the gig run parallel to the steep rock, dancing in the water. John stayed on the seat, fighting the oars.

"Can we make landfall in this wind?"

"Not here!" Gerlof said. "The east side is better."

There were no natural harbors on the Virgin, just rocks plunging into the sea—but on the opposite side of the island the wind was less hard. The sea was calmer there as well, though choppy and foaming close to shore.

Gerlof had taken the oars and both steered and paddled, closer and closer to the granite. The gig rolled back and forth in the water, but John was used to waves and managed to jump from the prow at the right moment. He landed, kept his balance by the heels of his boots and was ashore, almost dry-shod and with a rope to make fast the boat.

Shortly after him the Mossbergs' boat reached the shore thirty-five feet away and its outboard fell silent. Now there was only the deep rumble of the storm above the cliffs.

Well ashore, Gerlof blinked against the wind and looked searchingly up at the spruce growing on top of the island. No people were to be seen. Had the abandoned boat in the strait come from here? That's what he suspected. But who would have picked the island as their goal on a day like this? In bad weather, nobody willingly set off for the Virgin.

"Give me a hand."

The four fishermen managed to get their boats higher up on the rocky beach, then lifted out their nets and their catch and turned the hulls on their side against the wind, supported by a few driftwood planks.

They sat down in the lee of their boats to take a breather.

"Fine," was all Gerlof managed to say.

Before darkness fell, he realized, they would have to get up to the forest to get some spruce twigs in order to be able to sleep comfortably on the rock under their boats. Unless the wind fell.

After a while John got up to untangle the nets and take care of their catch. There were matches in the boat, as well as salt and ground coffee and a can of drinking water, so surviving on the island wouldn't be a problem.

At least not for the first week, Gerlof thought. He remembered an old legend he'd heard about three shepherds who hundreds of years ago had spent a summer on the Virgin, but who had been trapped there by a prolonged storm in the strait. First they had slaughtered their animals to survive, and when all the sheep had been eaten two of the shepherds had dined on the third.

He walked over to the cousins who were already picking the fish from the nets. They had let the abandoned rowboat remain bobbing in the water, tied by a piece of rope in its prow. The boat was too heavy to drag out of the sea while the pile of rocks remained in it, but if the wind turned the waves would quickly slam it to pieces.

"Should we bring the boat home?" Gerlof said.

"Sure, it could come in handy," Erik said. "But the stones should remain here."

"They make fine ballast."

"True," Erik said, "but they bring bad luck. The weather will never improve as long as they're still in the boat."

Gerlof sighed at the superstition.

"I guess I'll have to empty it, then."

He pulled the rowboat to a small cove and jumped down in it. Then he folded back the tarpaulin and began lifting out the stones. They were round and quite beautiful, pale gray and polished to large egg shapes by the water. He became even more convinced that they actually had come from the Virgin. Just as when he'd pulled up the flounders earlier in the morning he counted the stones before throwing them ashore: *one, two, three* . . .

Stone followed stone over the railing, back to all the others. *Twenty-nine, thirty, thirty-one* . . .

He had put his hand out to the thirty-second stone when he stopped himself. It was round and grayish white, but didn't quite look like the others. He turned it over and froze.

"Erik," he called into the wind. "Come take a look at this."

Both the cousins stopped gutting flounders and walked down to the water's edge.

"What?"

"Look at this," Gerlof said again.

What he held up to them wasn't a round granite rock.

It was a skull. A human skull, pale gray and with deep, black sockets. The lower jaw had fallen off, but the upper smiled broadly with white teeth.

Nobody on the beach said a word.

Gerlof carefully handed the skull to Erik Mossberg and looked down at the pile of stones in the boat.

"There's another one down there under the rocks," he said quietly. "And bones."

The cousins looked but said nothing. Erik silently accepted the second skull and put both of them on the flat rock, out of reach of the waves. Then he and Torsten and Gerlof together picked all the bones out of the boat and put them beside the skulls.

When they were done, two almost complete skeletons were laid out on the rock. Tall enough to have been adults, Gerlof saw. They had been dressed when they died, since there were pieces of pant fabric around their hips.

The mood on the beach was even more subdued than before.

"How old can they be?" Erik said.

"Difficult to say," Gerlof said. "What's left of their clothes looks modern . . . but I don't think they're really fresh."

"What should we do with them?" Torsten said.

Gerlof had no answer. He looked out across the empty sea, then glanced back at the island. He sniffed the wind and thought that he caught a whiff of smoke. And hadn't he seen something move as well, at the corner of his eye?

Now he saw nothing. He slowly walked over to John Hagman, who had quickly turned his back on the dead and gone to deal with the nets. Gerlof knew that John had a thing about dead bodies, as who hadn't?

"Are you okay?" he asked.

John nodded. Gerlof glanced back up the the Virgin and opened his mouth.

"I thought I caught a smell of . . ."

Then something clicked up on the cliffs and he heard a brief, whistling sound a few feet over his head.

"Down!" he yelled.

He made John duck. A second later another shot rang out from the cliffs—it really was a gunshot, no doubt about it. Gerlof even imagined seeing the second bullet hit the water not far from the shore, like a white strip of bubbles.

He also saw that the Mossbergs had heard the shots. They were lying down behind the hull of their boat now, while he and John were entirely unprotected on the cliffs. Gerlof quickly slid away towards a couple of mulberry bushes. Unworthy but wise. John followed him, and they stayed down.

"Someone's moving up there," Gerlof said in a low voice.

John stayed pressed to the ground behind him but tried to look.

"Can you see who it is?"

Gerlof shook his head.

"Stay here," he said softly. "I'll move a bit."

The bushes grew closer together there and, hidden by them, he slowly crept a couple of hundred feet north along the edge of the water. From there he went on, behind pines and boulders.

From a distance, the Virgin looked round and smooth, but close up the granite was full of cracks and steep rock faces. Gerlof certainly didn't mind; they gave him protection.

The wind blew cold and the island felt more dangerous than ever. There were no more shots, but Gerlof didn't relax. He moved in a wide circle towards the western side of the Virgin.

There he found an unknown rowboat pulled ashore. He saw it near the water from a long way off—it was made from pinewood and couldn't be missed. But no owner was in sight.

Gerlof went on at a crouch. A hundred feet above the boat he came to a precipice, and on top of it he found trampled-down lyme grass and a fresh cigarette butt.

He looked up at the forest and saw, or believed that he saw, a dark flow of hair billowing in the wind and disappearing among the firs.

A woman?

He thought of the mythological sea warden of the Blue Virgin, she who ruled the waters and the winds and who punished those who mocked her. That legend was older than those about cursed stones and witches' revels, but of course Gerlof believed in none of them. The sea warden would hardly sit on the grass smoking cigarettes.

He went faster, but tried to move as quietly as possible.

Then he was inside the forest, a labyrinth of boulders and twisted firs. Here were both tangled hazel shrubs and deep crevices, and it was easy to lose your way.

He stopped again to listen. Then he moved quickly, stepped around a thick maple—and almost collided with the person hiding behind the trunk. A woman in dark clothes. She sat looking down, and Gerlof was able to sneak up very closely behind her.

"How do you do?" Gerlof said calmly.

The woman gave a scream. She twisted round, saw that she had been found and threw herself forward, fists raised.

"Easy!"

Gerlof roared and stood his ground on the cliff, but didn't hit back. He just raised his palms.

"Take it easy!" he shouted again. "I won't hurt you."

Finally the woman lowered her arms, stopped fighting. Gerlof could ease his breath and take a step back. He saw that she was around thirty-five and dressed for a visit on the Virgin, in a warm woolen sweater and heavy boots. Her eyes were tense and nervous—but at least she didn't hold a rifle in her hands.

"What are you doing here?" he said. "Why are you sneaking around on us?"

She stared back at him.

"Who are you?"

"I'm from there," Gerlof said, pointing across his shoulder at the coast of Öland. "We've been out fishing and came here to get away from the storm . . . we're harmless."

The woman slowly relaxed her tense shoulders.

"I'm Gerlof Davidsson," he went on. "Do you have a name?"

She gave a short nod.

"Ragnhild," she said. "Ragnhild Månsson. I'm from Oskarshamn."

"Good, Ragnhild . . . How about us joining the others?"

She nodded without speaking, and Gerlof led her around the island close to the water's edge. He kept looking up at the top, watching for movement. If Ragnhild wasn't armed, someone else had fired the shots. But he couldn't see anyone up there.

When they got back to the eastern side, John and the Mossberg cousins had sat up behind the boats. They were smoking again, throwing nervous glances at Gerlof.

The woman looked at them without speaking, then at the bones and skulls placed on the cliff. Her eyes were still worried, but Gerlof saw no surprise in her face.

"We found those in the strait. At the bottom of a rowboat."

"An empty rowboat?" Ragnhild said.

Gerlof nodded.

"Have you seen them before?"

"I don't know who they are," she said finally.

Gerlof realized that she hadn't denied anything.

306

"And the rowboat?" he said, nodding towards the water. "Do you recognize it?"

Ragnhild Månsson looked at the boat bobbing by the beach and paused for a while before answering.

"It's Kristoffer's," she said at last. "My brother. It's his boat."

"And where is your brother?"

"I don't know."

The woman sighed, sat down on a boulder, then suddenly became more talkative.

"I came here for his sake . . . we were supposed to meet here today. I took my own motorboat from Oskarshamn and landed on the western side. Kristoffer was supposed to come from the opposite direction. He lives on Öland."

"The rowboat was out in the storm when we found it," Gerlof said. "Did he have a life belt, or a life vest?"

"I don't think so."

The cliff was silent.

"I think we could get our spirit stove going and make some coffee," Gerlof said. "Then we can talk."

Fifteen minutes later they had newly brewed coffee with biscuits. Gerlof handed a cup to Ragnhild and met her eyes.

"I think you should tell us more now, Ragnhild," he said. "My guess is that you know some things about the bones and the stones in your brother's boat. Or don't you?"

"Some," she said.

"Fine. We'll be happy to listen."

Ragnhild looked down into her coffee mug and drew a breath. Then she began talking in a low voice.

"My elder brother Kristoffer was a bird-watcher when he was young, or rather a bird lover. Back in the thirties, when we were teenagers, our family lived on Öland, near Byarum . . . closer to the Virgin than anyone else, I believe. So Kristoffer used to row out here to the island to look at the eiders and guillemots and all the other kinds of birds. Autumns and springs there was almost never anyone here. But when Kristoffer got here one morning he found traces of other visitors . . . And they were horrible traces, trampled nests and broken bird eggs on the rocks. People who hated birds had come to the island."

She fell silent, drank some coffee and went on.

"We didn't know who they were, but Kristoffer wanted to stop them. He brought me with him. That autumn we came often to the island, wanting to watch over the birds. It was a kind of an adventure. But one Sunday when we got here there was a strange boat moored by the old quarry. Kristoffer put ours beside it and then we sneaked up on the island. We heard loud screams from the birds . . . that wasn't a good sign."

Ragnhild turned her eyes upward to the cliffs.

"Up on the cliffs we met the people who were tormenting the birds. They were two young men, not much older than Kristoffer. Immature idiots. They had collected stones and broken branches and were throwing them at the black guillemots that were flying in flocks around them, terrified. The birds they hit fell with broken wings on the beach and in the water . . . I was heartbroken when I saw it. So I forgot to be scared, I just ran up to them and screamed that I would call the police. Which of course was a stupid thing to say out here. They just laughed, and one of them grabbed me."

She lit a cigarette and continued.

"Kristoffer yelled at them and then they caught sight of him as well. When they heard him they forgot about me for just a moment. So I tore myself loose and began running back down to the water, with Kristoffer beside me. They came after us and threw rocks at us, but we knew the terrain and were faster. Down at the beach we pushed their boat out, then jumped into our own. And then we rowed back to Öland, ducking the stones those guys on the shore were throwing at us. The last we saw of them was that they were standing like fools at the water, staring at their boat, which was drifting away from the island."

Ragnhild blew out smoke.

"We rowed back home to Öland," she went on, "and even before we got back a storm was rising in the strait. I remember thinking that the angry wind came from the Virgin, that it was the island that had called it up to take revenge on the bird haters. The storm increased almost to a hurricane during the evening and lasted for more than a week, nine or ten days. The Virgin was invisible in the mist, nobody could go there or get away from there. Kristoffer and I stayed inside, and we didn't dare tell anyone that there were people on the Virgin."

She lowered her eyes.

"Finally the wind in the strait slackened, and then we rowed back here. Kristoffer had brought one of our grandfather's old rifles. But the guillemots were calm and silent and there was nothing threatening left on the Virgin any more."

Ragnhild was silent for a few seconds.

"We found the two men almost at the top of the island. One of them lay sheltered by a large fir and the other one nearby, close to a boulder. The birds had pecked them . . . they no longer had any faces."

She was silent again.

"Do you know how they died?" Gerlof said.

She shook her head.

"I don't know if they had starved or froze to death, but dead they were. And then we panicked, I and Kristoffer. We felt like killers who had to cover up our crime. So we pulled their bodies down into a deep crevice and put a lot of beach stones on top of them. We carried stones for hours to fill that crevice. Then we rowed back home again . . . and a couple of days later we heard that two young men from the mainland were missing since the storm. They had taken their boat out, and police believed that it had gone down in the strait."

She sighed again.

"We tried to forget what had happened, but of course that was impossible, and I've been thinking about it for almost twenty years. And nowadays there are just more and more tourists coming to the Virgin every summer . . . sooner or later they would be found. So I and my brother decided to get the bodies today and sink them out in the strait in a tarpaulin weighted with stone. That's what we planned to do. But I was delayed on the mainland this morning, so I guess Kristoffer began without me. He must have fallen from his boat, or . . ."

Ragnhild fell silent and looked sadly at the empty rowboat. She had nothing more to tell.

But Gerlof did. He felt a smell in the air and looked up at the top of the Virgin.

"There is someone else on the island."

"How do you know?" John said.

Gerlof pointed to the middle of the island.

"There's a fire burning up there, and earlier someone shot at us."

"Shot at you?" Ragnhild said.

"Someone shot to warn us off."

"He said he would bring the rifle," Ragnhild said in a low voice. "Kristoffer, I mean. Just as a precaution."

Gerlof nodded.

"In that case your brother might still be here," he said, "if the sea pulled his boat out without him. I think we should take a look at the top of the island."

Ragnhild nodded quickly and stood up.

"But carefully," Gerlof added. "Make sure he knows who you are before he starts shooting again."

John and the cousins stayed down by the water and let him and Ragnhild start climbing to the top of the island.

As much as he could, Gerlof kept in the shelter of thickets and trees while he led the way up to the largest of the caves on the island. He had been there on earlier visits; it was called the Virgin's Chamber and lay on the east side of the island's highest cliff. The chamber was like a small church room hollowed out of the mountain and gave good protection against the winds.

Silently and carefully, Gerlof drew close to the opening. He hid behind a boulder to look into the chamber. It was dark inside, but the floor of the cave rose slightly and inside the narrow opening he saw a flickering light.

He stayed on behind his boulder, irresolute and still remembering the shots by the beach, but Ragnhild slipped closer and called out.

"Hello? Is anyone there? Hello?"

For a few seconds, all was quiet. Then an echoing reply came from the vault, a tired male voice.

"Hello yourself."

Ragnhild flew up and hurried into the chamber.

"Kristoffer?"

Fifteen minutes later Gerlof returned to the edge of the water, alone. Torsten, Erik and John stood smoking between their boats. They looked hard at the Mauser rifle Gerlof was holding, its barrel pointing to the ground.

"Her brother had this," he said. "I thought it better to take care of it."

"So her brother is here?" John said.

Gerlof nodded.

"He took shelter from the storm up in the Virgin's Chamber. He had loaded the stones and the skeletons in the morning, but his rowboat had drifted off in the storm. When he saw us on the beach he shot a couple of warning shots. He was upset, wanted to scare us off . . . I guess we'll have to try to understand."

The others nodded, not very willingly.

"And what are they doing now, those siblings?" John asked.

"They'll be leaving soon." Gerlof nodded to himself and looked at the two skeletons on the cliff. "My thinking is we bring these back with us to Öland and tell the police that we happened to see some bones sticking out of a deep crevice here on the Virgin. That way maybe we can solve an old disappearance without getting anyone else involved. Is that all right by you?"

The other three nodded again.

"You can hardly accuse an entire island of murder if someone happens to die there," John said. "Not even the Virgin."

The other fishermen dragged thoughtfully on their cigarettes.

"It's just one thing I don't understand, Gerlof," Erik said. "How you could be so sure there were others here on the island. Do you have second sight?"

Gerlof thought of praising his intuition or perhaps blaming the movements of vipers, but told them the truth.

"It was the smells."

"The smells?"

"I didn't notice any smells at all," John said, dropping his butt between the stones.

"You should have," Gerlof said. "I caught the smell of Ragnhild's cigarette smoke from the very beginning, down on the beach . . . and then the smell of her brother's fire up in the Virgin's Chamber."

"You did?"

"Oh yes, very clearly."

The three fishermen silently regarded Gerlof, but he just pointed at their glowing cigarettes.

"I told you to stop that . . . The tobacco is ruining your noses."

Johan Theorin was born 1963 in Gothenburg, Sweden's second-largest city and its traditionally largest seaport, but spent his summers on the island of Öland. As a student, he lived for two years in Michigan and Vermont. After working as a journalist for many years, he published his first novel, Skumtimmen (Echoes from the Dead), *in 2007; it received the best first novel award from the Swedish Crime Fiction Academy and the Crime Writers' Association John Creasey Dagger in Britain. His second novel,* Nattfåk (The Darkest Room, 2008), *won the bestnNovel of the year award in Sweden and in Britain the CWA International Dagger award. He has published a further three novels, the latest, Sommarboken, in 2013. Theorin describes his work as "a combination of dark crime stories and Scandinavian folklore and ghost stories." Theorin's stylish, dark, and intensely personal novels have gained him a huge Swedish and international following; he is one of the most highly regarded Swedish crime writers.*

MAITREYA

Veronica von Schenck

Veronica von Schenck is almost an atavism among current Swedish crime writers: her favorite character in fiction is Sherlock Holmes; her favorite crime author, Arthur Conan Doyle; and she is fascinated by the intricacies of plotting—planting leads in her work, letting her readers try to outguess her protagonists, and tying together the threads of the story. She came to crime writing after a number of other pursuits: she has been a live gamer, a computer game reviewer, editor of a computer magazine and of a Stockholm events magazine, and a recruitment consultant. She remains the last, part time, while writing; she lives with her husband and two children in a Stockholm suburb.

The protagonist of her first two novels was Althea Molin, a criminal profiler of half-Swedish, half-Korean parentage. She has also written three juvenile crime novels, all based on historical events, since the study of history fascinates her; in her juveniles, the reader is invited to explore both a historical period and a crime in the company of her two young sleuths, Milo and Vendela.

In her story for this book, Veronica von Schenck introduces a new protagonist who will be featured in her next novel. Stella Rodin reflects the author's fascination with history, artifacts, and solving problems.

STELLA RODIN SIPPED THE CHAMPAGNE IN HER GLASS AND LOOKED AROUND at the exhibition room. The slate-gray walls showed off the colorful modern art covering them like an old quilt. The dark suits of the male guests showed off the colorful dresses of the female guests. The overall effect was attractive and the room was filled. At the center of the show was Stella's father, Emmanuel Rodin. His glow competed with both his guests and his exhibits; he wore a light tweed suit with a burgundy vest, matching bowtie and pocket handkerchief. This was his favorite moment. To rule absolutely but with mild joviality one of the year's most important showings and auction afterwards. To introduce with flattery and generosity his experts to interested and inquisitive customers possessing extremely well-stuffed wallets. To personally extol the quality of paper used in Warhol's serigraphies. As for Stella, she loved art as passionately as did her father, but she hated this world. She had always been a black sheep, ever since day care. A girl as pretty as a doll and with a searing intelligence, who neither in day care nor since had had the sense of hiding her brain's capacity and hunger for knowledge and truth. Definitely unattractive. She had a way of shaming, irritating or frightening most of the people she met. Mainly because she had never quite learned to keep

315

her big mouth shut when someone stated an obvious lie. Her school years had been understandably painful, but had provided her with a hard shell. Instead of working in the family company atmosphere of flattery and hypocrisy (*We do this just because of our passion for art, not at all to make money, of course not!*) she had chosen to become a police forgery expert. It had made it possible for her to work with the art she loved, but in an environment a bit more tolerant of her abrupt personality and in her view at least slightly less hypocritical. But since her parents and her older brother, to whom she was close, still ran the auction house, here she was, reluctantly moonlighting as a poster girl for the family business. Her father had resolutely bribed her to do it. A beautiful, burgundy vintage dress with a tight waist, a boat neck and a flowing skirt with several petticoat layers. From the fifties. Dior. She stroked its crisp fabric. It was a bribe she had simply been unable to resist.

Stella walked up to her father and lightly kissed his cheek.

"Hi, Dad. An hour and a half, okay?"

"And what's so important for you to do then? Do you have a date?" he asked in a kindly but irritated voice. This was a discussion they had had innumerable times. It usually started with some disparaging comment about her choice of profession—working in a police laboratory wasn't her father's idea of a successful career for his daughter.

"Yeah. With a good book and my bathtub."

He sighed.

"Do you even understand how condescending that sounds to me? Don't you know how hard I—all of us are working for all this? The least you could do is to smile and act a little friendly, at least this one evening. It can't be all that hard."

Stella sighed.

"Okay, okay, I'll stay on."

After a full hour's worth of kissing cheeks and smiling, Stella was dead beat. She wasn't made to stand this much uninteresting human contact in a single day. She turned to the paintings to escape further platitudes, at least for a moment. She stood for a long while watching a Picasso all in shades of gray, for one of his pieces a strange but surprisingly anatomically correct portrait of a young woman named Françoise, if the title was to be believed. If she had happened to have an extra 50,000 dollars she would happily have made a bid for it, but considering her police salary she ought to be happy if she managed to put that much aside during her entire working life. She straightened the frame minutely; it had slipped slightly to one side. Earlier in the day she had helped her brother Nicholas hang the pictures. Even if she didn't work here she enjoyed helping him create the exhibitions, and he enjoyed having her there. It had almost become a tradition. She loved art intensely. Loved the craft of it. Was fascinated by the hours of single-minded energy and pure love given by artists and artisans to their work, by the combination of deep sorrow and exultant joy coexisting in a truly successful work of art.

Nicholas came up to her and put a hand on her shoulder.

"Someone named Carl Andreasen wants to talk to you. He's at the entrance. Isn't he your boss?"

With a worried frown, Stella looked searchingly towards the door. Yes, that was Carl, all right. A tall, gray-haired man with a crew cut and a lined face wrapped in a gigantic scarf he was trying to untangle himself from.

"Yes, it's him. What the hell is he doing here?"

She wove through the throng of visitors and reached him.

"Carl. What are you doing here?"

"I've got a job for you."

Stella caught her father's disapproving glance from the opposite end of the room.

"Okay. Come along," she said, pushing him ahead of her, away from the nosy, curious glances of the guests. Carl looked more like an aging soldier turned homeless than as a guest slightly late for the party.

Stella turned, snatched a second glass of champagne and brought Carl up to the library before he had time to object. She gave him the new glass and pointed to a chair. Carl sat down and Stella took the chair beside his.

"I never knew you were playing daddy's girl during week-ends." His voice was scornful and he put his glass down without touching it.

"So now you know." Stella smiled, amused at his lame attempt at provoking her. He usually did better. She and Carl were joined by a love-hate relationship to each other. She thought his thinking too traditional and formalistic, though despite that a good policeman. And he, as far as Stella could tell, considered her a troublesome pain in the ass who ought to keep her mouth shut, do as she was told and not stick her nose where it had no business to be—but despite that a good forgery expert. "Now tell me what you need my help with that's panicky enough for you come looking for me yourself even in a place that's so obviously uncomfortable to you."

"I want you to go to another cocktail party tomorrow. I hope that's not overtaxing your talents."

Stella raised her eyebrows but said nothing. He sighed and went on.

"We have a guy who's worked undercover for a long time in a smuggling ring. He's finally been invited to a party given by the head of the organization, an informal auction of what we believe to be il-legally imported works of art. Our guy needs a girlfriend."

"Doesn't sound too hard. Don't you have lots of boobsy po-lice officers who could help you out? It's been a long time since I did any police work outside the lab, as you very well know."

"It isn't your police field experiences I'm interested in. I want you to do what you do in the lab. Take a look at the art and tell us what it is and whether it's genuine. So simple even an academic like you ought to manage."

"But—if the guy you're after is in the antiques business, he might know who I am. I might blow your whole operation."

"I grant you your daddy is pretty famous. But I don't think my guy has gotten his stuff from your auctions."

She drank some champagne and gave him a searching look. He was far from as biting as usual. He must be really desperate. She was far from certain that it was quite as simple as he made it out

318

to be, but the idea of doing something outside of the lab for once sounded like fun. She gave him a brief nod.

"But what has your undercover guy been doing? I don't believe it's mainly about antiques. In that case you'd either have talked to me about it before, or your guy would know enough about it for you not to need me."

Carl looked vexed, leaned back in his chair and swung his foot.

"Mostly it's about drugs. And weapons. The antiques are just a sideline."

Stella watched him carefully for a moment. What he'd just said wasn't the whole truth either. She shrugged her shoulders.

"Okay, I'll do it."

"Good girl."

Stella followed him to the door—she didn't want to risk his starting to talk to any of the guests. A cold gust of wind, full of dancing snowflakes, sneaked in when she opened the door for him. Stella shivered and looked thoughtfully at her boss when he crouched down against the wind and slowly disappeared into the darkness.

"So what did your boss want on a Saturday? I imagined police forgery experts only worked weekdays." It was Nicholas.

"He wants me to play cop for real—do an undercover job. There's a private auction of illegal antiques of some kind tomorrow night," Stella said, her eyes still fixed somewhere far off in the wintry night.

"Cool."

Ali opened the limousine door for her. His black suit was a perfect fit and his smile was broad. He looked just as disgustingly healthy as always, Stella noted, with black curls, slim hips and broad shoulders. Those hips she remembered particularly vividly. They were very attractive when covered only by briefs. Without briefs as well, in fact.

"You look great, as usual."

"Hi, Ali. Long time. Good to see you."

Many years ago they had belonged to the same class at the police academy and been a couple during their years of study. But

319

when she decided to go for forensics while he went for investigative work, they separated. Though whom did she think she was fooling? The simple fact was that she had never been able to make any relationship work in the long run. He had been no exception.

"Jump in. I'll tell you about the party while we go there." He made an exaggerated bow, helped her into the back of the car and stepped in beside her. Another cop in civilian dress had been given the honorable job of driving them.

"Great. Where are we going?"

"Djursholm. The stronghold of snobbery and wealth."

"And here I was thinking we were bound for one of the dangerous hoods, given the badly concealed gun you're carrying under your tux." She snaked a hand in behind the small of his back to adjust his leather holster.

"Thanks," he said with an apologetic grin. "Did you see my mike as well?"

She studied him carefully but caught nothing suspicious.

"Nope, all fine—you're as handsome as ever."

"Thanks."

The sky was inky black when they stopped outside an enormous yellow mansion on a low hill. Stella walked carefully up the sanded path in her stilettos, holding Ali's arm. She savored the cold air, which brought her the scent of his warm body. He smelled of spice and recently showered skin. She snuck her arm deeper under his. He smiled, but she was very aware that his body revealed apprehension rather than any other emotion. She knew that he was not given to worry. On the contrary, he had a definitely exaggerated belief in his own abilities. Like most males, for that matter. Again, she was convinced that this assignment was far from as simple and harmless as Carl had wanted her to believe. Thick walls of chalk-white snow rose on both sides of the path. Lit torches were stuck in the drifts, their softly flickering light casting dancing shadows on the snow. It had stopped snowing only an hour ago.

"It'll work out fine," Stella said in a clumsy attempt at sounding calm.

Ali gave her an amused glance.

"Sure. But be careful with Peter. Don't irritate him. He's fucking unstable."

"Don't irritate him? How would I do that? I don't even know the guy."

"Please, just don't be yourself. You see . . ."

"Shut up and smile, you mean?" She was amused. A little put off deep down, but she certainly wouldn't let him see that.

"Right. And show him that magnificent chest."

"Got it. Smile. Flash tits. Almost makes you wonder why I spent seven years in college to get where I am now . . ."

"Seven!"

"Sure. Police academy, art, a few courses in England—"

He gave her a weak smile, shook his head and raised a hand to make her stop. "Sorry for asking."

Stella punched his arm.

"Hey. That hurt."

They had arrived at the house and a grave doorman let them in. They left their overcoats with another strict and unsmiling man. Stella heard a murmur of voices. On their way to the living room they passed a pedestal with a cracked and badly worn urn. Mediterranean. Roughly two thousand years old, she couldn't be more specific without inspecting it more closely. There were still traces of sand left on it. Beautiful and dignified in its pale patina.

"I understand why I'm here," Stella whispered to Ali and kissed his neck to make her whisper seem less suspicious. Or actually just because she felt like it. He shivered slightly.

They stepped into the huge living room and the rigidly directed performance began again. A nod here, a glass of champagne there. Twice in the same weekend was definitely too many for Stella. Shallow exchanges of pleasantries conveying nothing, meaning nothing and impossible for anyone to remember. Laughter and charming smiles but ice-cold eyes. Superficiality. Stella hated it, but she was a pro. At least tonight she had a job to do. As soon as the tenth smiling male with a forehead unlined as a baby's bottom had finished his platitudes and turned away, she pulled Ali over to an object placed on a smooth, white pedestal by one of the walls. The wall was made of glass. You could vaguely distinguish the fluttering torches on the terrace outside, but beyond them was only the impenetrable blackness of night. As she came close to the pedestal, Stella's heart beat faster. She saw an eight-inch-tall bronze statue. Its surface was black, dark with a satiny sheen, but the details were perfect. It depicted a crowned man sitting cross-legged. His right palm was raised to the viewer. His left rested on his thigh, holding a water pitcher. The almond-shaped, half-closed eyes were inlaid with silver and watched Stella kindly along his narrow nose. The statue was perfect. So beautiful that it stole her breath. She had to stop herself from grabbing it and trying to run off with it. She carefully caressed the curves of the statue and felt that there still were remnants of sand at its hollow base. Fury began to seethe in her.

"Ali, let me introduce you to Maitreya."

"Mai . . . who?"

"The next Buddha. This is a statue made in the first decade after Christ, I'd guess. Probably dug up somewhere in Afghanistan. And very recently."

"How do you know that?"

"It hasn't been professionally cleaned. There are still traces of sand on it, and there are scratches made by the clumsy fools who dug him up." She slid a fingertip across a deep scratch. It was impossible for her to understand how anyone could do something like this. It was an insult to the country, to history and to the present.

Stella saw Ali stiffen and look at someone behind her. Probably the famous Peter. She put on her most simpleminded smile and slowly turned around. Behind her was a tall man with an almost unbelievably huge stomach hanging from a body that seemed to suffer under its extra weight. He was dressed in a perfectly tailored gray suit and the hand holding his champagne flute was adorned by numerous golden rings. He looked at her, or rather at her plunging neckline, in the same way a cat looks at a herring before sinking its teeth into it. Stella pushed her chest out some more. After all, that was her task tonight.

"Ali, I see you've brought a little tidbit along tonight."

Ali gave a hearty laugh and put his arm around her waist. He seemed impressively at ease in this kind of situation, Stella noted.

"Absolutely. This is Stella, my girlfriend."

"So nice to see you at last." Stella held her hand out. He took it, pulled her close, and kissed her cheek instead. He smelled of liquor and expensive cologne, with a vague undertone of acrid sweat.

"I see you're admiring the statue. Are you going to bid for it, Ali?"

"It seems Stella has fallen in love, so I probably don't have a choice."

"It's adorable. Is it Indian?" Stella chirped in her most naïve and imbecile voice.

"You might say so. This little baby is around two thousand years old. It won't be cheap."

"Oooh, is it really that old?" Stella said with what she hoped was a surprised look and leaned closer to the statue. So at least he knew what he had, she noted.

"Oh, yes. There aren't many in this little shithole country that can compete with this collection," Peter said, then turned to Ali. "So what happened yesterday, did you get anywhere?"

"It's beginning to come together. They wanted us to talk about the last details tonight, if that's okay with you."

"Business on a night like this?" His eyes were suddenly hard; then he began laughing. "Why not? Tonight is all about great deals anyway, isn't it? Just remember to leave Stella with me when you abandon her for business. I'll take care of her, okay?"

Stella smiled and preened a bit while suppressing a sudden urge to throw her champagne in his face and respond with a couple of impolite words. She really appreciated the fact that normally her work didn't entail meeting a lot of people, she thought. She just wouldn't be able to handle that.

"How do you think he gets hold of things like these?" Ali asked her when Peter had walked off. Their eyes followed him as he moved away among his guests, like a good-natured absolute ruler among his subjects.

"Afghanistan has been more or less systematically plundered of its art objects during the last decade. Items like these are being sent abroad to finance the war. If he is in direct contact with people in the country and doesn't need any go-betweens, he's probably gotten treasures like this one very cheaply."

Ali sighed deeply. Stella took another look at the beautiful Maitreya. "The problem is that it's almost impossible to prove. A real auction house couldn't sell things like this, since we demand documentation of provenance. But how are we supposed to prove that it hasn't belonged to his family for a century? All he needs to say is that the paperwork was lost, or destroyed. Nobody can prove anything at all."

"Disgusting. At least I'm happy that we'll soon have enough to get the bastard for other things."

"His drug deals?" she asked.

"Yes. That's what I'm going to talk to him about later. With just a little luck he'll make me an offer. They're going to give me a job with the organization. We've beaten about the bush long enough." Ali glanced back at Peter. So this is what scares him, she thought, and almost immediately one of the waiters came up to Ali.

"Adam wants a word in his office on the upper floor."

"Back soon," he said to Stella and nodded at the waiter.

"Good luck," Stella said, squeezed his forearm slightly. He responded with a warm glance, then gave her a long, hard kiss. She responded. A little surprised, but why not, she thought.

"How about reliving some old memories later tonight, Stella?"

"Sounds fine."

He nodded and she studied his back while he disappeared toward a large, curved staircase. When he was gone she turned to the next pedestal. She spent a long time looking at the objects for sale. The room contained a veritable general store of epochs, religions and styles, with the fact that she felt convinced that most of these things had been dug up by clumsy idiots somewhere in Afghanistan during the last few years as their only common denominator. She also studied the buyers and realized that she recognized some of them.

They were accomplished collectors, knowledgeable in the history of art. She kept as far away from them as possible. The risk of any of them recognizing her as Emmanuel Rodin's daughter was small but real—and if any of them whispered something about it in the fat man's ear, the entire operation would break down. She sent Carl an angry thought. When Ali had been gone an hour, Stella began feeling restless. She went out on the terrace and took a deep breath of the painfully cold air. A waiter offered her a fur-lined blanket, and she gratefully wrapped it around her shoulders. A small group of people was outside, smoking in the flickering torchlight. The quiet was music to Stella's ears and she lowered her shoulders, trying to relax. Her cell rang in her purse. She walked farther out on the terrace to escape other guests possibly listening in, and took out her phone. The display told her that the call was from Ali's cell. She put on her wireless headset and answered.

"Ali, where the hell are you?"

The wet gurgling sound ran like a cold wave through her body.

"Ali, what's happened?" she whispered. The sound went on for a few seconds, then stopped.

Shakily, Stella replaced the phone in her purse without ending the call. She pulled her hair over her ear to hide her headset and went back inside. Without seeming to hurry she wove through the crowd. Behind her relaxed smile she could feel her heart beat hard and fast. She climbed the stair to the second floor without being challenged. The house was enormous. Carefully she opened the doors to a few rooms just enough to glance in. One of them held an intimately occupied couple, but she saw no signs of Ali. Just as she was going to round a corner she heard footsteps. She opened the door closest to her, silently slid in and closed it behind her while praying to the beautiful Maitreya downstairs that nobody had seen the door move. She held her breath and heard them clearly as they walked past.

"Take the body out with the kitchen garbage when the party's over. Just let it be until then."

When they were gone, Stella waited for two minutes before returning to the hallway. She still seemed to hear weak, rasping breaths through the headset. She must find him. Before it was too late. She continued in the direction the two men had come from and stopped when she saw a small, almost black mark on the floor outside one of the closed doors. Blood. Almost certainly, and put there by someone's shoe. She opened the door very slowly. The dark inside was impenetrable. As soon as the opening was wide enough for her to slip through she slid in, closing the door behind her. She turned on the light. A twisted body lay on the floor. Ali, a large, open wound in the middle of his chest. Blood had formed a pool on the floor around him. Stella went down on her knees beside him, feeling the sting of vomit in the back of her throat. She felt his neck, but there was no need. His eyes were staring blindly at the ceiling. Probably she had just imagined those last breathing sounds from her phone. Stella closed the call and carefully took Ali's iPhone from his hand. She put on the long, black gloves she had worn when they arrived, stretched her hand under his body and felt along his waist, underneath his jacket. Warm blood enveloped her hand. There it was. His gun. She pulled it out, took off her bloody glove and used it to wipe off the gun. She might need it before the evening was over. With a last look at Ali, Stella rose and went over to the window. Standing in darkness, she looked out into the black night. Inside she was cold and hard. She had no time to feel. Later, not now. She saw the fluttering flames of the torches on the terrace below. At last she drew a deep breath, took out her cell and phoned Carl. He answered almost immediately.

"Ali is dead. Shot," she said straight out.

"What? What are you saying?"

"What the hell have you put us up to?" she asked. "I want to know it all. Right now."

"We'll be there as soon as possible."

"No. Hell no. We have no evidence of anything. You'll never be able to prove a damned thing. We'll never get either Ali's killers or the damned fools who are plundering Afghanistan."

"Afghanistan? What's that got to do with anything?"

Stella gave an exasperated sigh.

"The antiques they're selling here tonight are invaluable art treasures from Afghanistan, dug up by assholes whose only thought is to get money to wage war. I'll get you evidence." She spoke quickly but with exaggerated clarity.

"It's too dangerous."

"You have to trust me. I know what has to be done. I want a backup force in place at a quarter past midnight. Not a second earlier or later. Okay?"

"Stella . . ."

"Did you understand me?"

"Yes. Okay. But . . ."

Stella heard footsteps in the hallway outside and ended the call. She stood immobile, breathing slowly. There was nowhere to hide in the room. The steps faded. Stella felt a rush of relief. She weighed Ali's gun in her hand and pulled out the magazine. It was fully loaded. Good. She wondered where to hide the gun. It was true that she did have large breasts, but nowhere near large enough for her to be able to hide a nine-millimeter pistol in her bra. On the other hand she wore enormous, flesh-colored "tummytuck" panties under the wide skirt of her 1950s dress. She slid the gun up inside her panties and carefully checked that it would stay there. It did. Peter's cell phone she put in the inner compartment of her purse, along with her bloodstained gloves. She put on more lipstick and straightened her shoulders, then crouched down beside Ali's body for the last time. Stroked his cheek. He looked very calm. She remembered his bubbling, ringing laugh. His special way of twisting his fingers in her hair to kiss her neck.

"I promise to find the bastard who did it," she whispered to him. Not only that, she would personally make sure that he regretted what he had done. Then she stood up, straightened her dress and went back down to the party, without looking back. Gladly accepted a new glass of champagne and sat down on a bar stool. Carefully, so that the gun wouldn't fall to the floor. She took out Ali's cell and sent the identical text to the last five numbers he had spoken to. "I know," she wrote. Then she let her eyes roam, trying to find someone just receiving a text message. She looked for a long time but saw no one. She resent her message. Peter was in the middle of the room, a giggling girl on his arm. Stella studied him, her anger carefully hidden.

Instead she hoped to look vaguely admiring. He was at the top of her list of suspects. She looked searchingly at him. He was large, boisterous and extremely pushy, particularly towards the female guests. He behaved as if he owned the place. That made Stella suspicious. Hold on, now, she thought. If he really did own the place he wouldn't have felt the need to behave as he did. Of course, the house might actually be his. But someone else was more powerful. Who?

Stella sipped her champagne, carefully weighing everyone in the room, one by one. At last she found him. A thin man of average height, light-skinned, with black hair and dark eyes. He was absolutely calm and relaxed. Polite but without the least interest in impressing anyone. He reminded Stella of her black tomcat, Sherlock. He, too, acted just that way: friendly, relaxed and condescending, as if he owned the world. In this case it might well be true. Both the dark-eyed one and the gray-haired man he was talking to turned toward her and looked at her. The dark-eyed man raised his glass to her in a silent toast. She returned the gesture and simultaneously recognized the gray-haired man. He was an art collector. One of Rodin's regular customers. Her cover was blown. Hell!

Time for a new plan. Stella slid off the stool, in the same movement returning Ali's phone to her purse. She too knew how to look as if you owned the world. It came easier to women. Tits out, sway your hips and you're fine. She crossed the floor, went straight up to the dark-eyed man and put out her hand.

"Stella Rodin. I want to attend the auction."

His velvet eyes smiled at her. His eyelashes were so dark that they looked painted. He took her hand, pressing it slightly.

"Markus From. Aren't you already at the auction? I assume you have an invitation."

"No. I came with someone else. I had hoped to be more discrete, but that plan didn't seem to work out. I represent a client of the Rodin auction house. Someone who is prepared to pay well for your objects. The Maitreya by the wall, for instance, would fit my client's collection perfectly."

"And how am I to know that you are who you claim to be?"

"I assume you already know."

328

Their eyes locked for a long moment. Stella's patience began to run out.

"You're very welcome to phone our office to get confirmation, if you want. I believe my brother is still in."

She could see that he already was familiar with Rodin and that the man beside him had told him who she was. Hopefully he only knew that she was Rodin's daughter, not that she was a cop. It was hardly something her father boasted about. On the contrary. And if the man had known and told velvet eyes, she would already be locked away or dead, so it was probably all right. It made her furious to stand here and hint that she or her father would ever buy invaluable antiques stolen from a country torn by war, but in this situation she had no choice. The dark-eyed man watched her searchingly, slightly amused. She appreciated the fact that he at least showed her respect enough not to try to pretend that he wasn't in charge here. She kept eye contact and hoped fervently that the white-hot anger and grief burning inside her didn't show.

"Give the number to Daniel." He gestured to a man who had been standing a few steps behind him and had probably listened to every word they'd said. "Have another glass of champagne, and I'll see that you get your answer shortly."

Stella nodded briefly, gave the office number to his assistant and walked toward the terrace. Again she gratefully accepted the heavy blanket one of the waiters offered her at the door, and wrapped it around her shoulders. Now her life might very well depend on if Nicholas realized what was happening and proved a convincing liar. It would be pointless to try to warn him. She had seen the assistant, Daniel, begin to dial as she turned away. Stella thought of Ali's body upstairs, then immediately forced herself to stop. If she wanted to grieve, she could do it later. First revenge. For Ali and the Maitreya and the rest of the war spoils inside. She spent the rest of her wait making new plans. There was still plenty of time before reinforcements would arrive. After a short while, the man called Daniel came to fetch her.

"Stella Rodin? Everything's in order; the auction will start in ten minutes."

Stella thanked him and locked herself in the rest room to prepare. She slipped her iPhone inside her bra to get the best possible sound reception. She carefully wiped Ali's cell with toilet paper, then tried to fix his gun against her thigh in a more comfortable position. She couldn't find one. Giving up, she set the cell phone between her breasts to record, then rejoined the throng outside. This time she carried Ali's phone in her purse. At the door to the auction room two forbidding but polite men were collecting cell phones from the audience. She had counted on that. They surely didn't want anyone to record this auction. She smiled a friendly smile, put Ali's phone on the table and put the number tag in her purse. The room, otherwise probably a large dining room, was furnished with numerous chairs turned to a podium, just as at Rodin's. Peter took the floor and spread his arms.

"Ladies and gentlemen. Welcome to this informal auction. I realize that you all want to be certain that the items we offer you are genuine." A slide presentation began on the wall behind him. Desert and caves. Close-ups of items being dug out of the ground with rough hatchets and shovels. "All objects for sale today have been discovered in Afghanistan. All of them have been found during the last year and are absolutely unique. In age, they vary from around one thousand BC to around five hundred AD. For reasons I'm sure you will understand, no documentation will be provided, so what I now tell you is the only guarantee you will have. However, we do have an expert on the relevant period present." He pointed to an elderly man who gave the audience a friendly nod. Stella recognized him; he sometimes helped Rodin's by authenticating objects. "Please make use of his expertise, and after the auction you are welcome to ask him anything you may want to know about the objects you have purchased. Now, let us begin." He spread his arms and stepped down from the podium. Another man stepped up in his place.

"The first post is this beautiful collection of silver dinars, minted during the fifth century AD."

The bidding became brisk. Stella bid on a couple of objects, but made sure not to win any of them. The atmosphere was so tense that you could cut it with a knife. Just as at a Rodin auction. Nobody

330

even glanced at anyone else; everyone stared as if mesmerized at the auctioneer and at the objects for sale. Everyone wanted to win. The room was simmering with passion, happiness, anger, frustration, but nothing could be heard or seen on the surface. When the magically beautiful bronze statue was finally displayed, Stella stubbornly bid until the Maitreya was hers. After all, it was just pretend money anyway—once the police arrived, everything would be impounded.

Once the auction was over and all arrangements about how and when money would be exchanged had been made, Stella retrieved Ali's cell. And finally held the Maitreya in her hand. She went back to the rest room to check on the recording made by the phone between her breasts. The important part was what the dark-eyed man had said. She hoped fervently that it would be evidence enough, but she knew how extremely difficult it was to get anyone convicted in cases of this kind. She mailed the sound file to Carl and added a text. Now only one thing remained. To find Ali's killer. It was eleven-thirty. She had forty-five minutes left. If she hadn't identified him when the police arrived, it was all over. She sat down by the bar again. Took out Ali's cell and sent a new text to the five last numbers on his log.

I know. The terrace at midnight.

That was all she wrote. She remained by the bar, watching the crowd. After a short wait she got two replies, which she immediately discounted. Obviously none of them had any idea of what she was talking about, nor were they at the auction. It was a quarter to midnight. She began to feel very stressed. At last she saw it. One of the guests discretely took out his cell, then put it back in his pocket and looked around. His forehead seemed damp and his hand shook almost imperceptibly. He hadn't been present at the auction. She slowly weaved through the throng to get closer to him. She was in luck. The expert on Afghan antiquity was standing almost directly next to the man she suspected of being the killer. She talked politely to him about the bronze she had just bought, meanwhile studying her suspect. All of his features were strangely colorless. She tried to come up with some way of taking his picture and sending it off to Carl, but realized that there was no way to do it without being seen.

The man had an expensive suit, but it fit him badly. When he turned to look at his watch she saw it. Three small, black, round stains on the cuff of his shirt. Blood. Good. She went out on the terrace. It was freezing cold, even with her blanket and the heaters set up. She liked the cold. It honed her brain. Waiting, she caressed the cool bronze of the Maitreya. Five minutes to go. At the stroke of midnight, the colorless man stepped out on the terrace. At the sight of him, Stella again set her cell to record. He looked around, realizing she was the only other person there. She gave him a warm smile and stepped closer, put her head on one side and lightly put her hand on his arm.

"Why? It's really all I want to know. After that, I'll leave you alone," Stella said.

He looked at her. Surprised. Uncertain how to react. She held her Maitreya in front of him. It was cold as ice. Stella spoke calmly, softly.

"We're all in the same boat here, so to speak. I don't want to know who you are. Just why you shot Ali. If I don't know why, I'll never be able to let go of it. I'll chase you forever just to learn why. So just tell me, here and now, and we'll go our separate ways."

Stella knew she had just fifteen minutes before Carl would arrive with his backup force. If she hadn't been able to make him talk before then, it was all over. But she hadn't dared risk that he would tell the dark-eyed man about her questions before more police arrived, so she had cut it as close to the raid as possible without risking the entire operation.

He looked uncertainly at her, gave a small, disdainful laugh and shook his head. Looked down at the ground. She stepped even closer.

"Why?" she whispered. "Why?"

"He asked too many questions. He wanted to take over. Tried to get close to Markus. I had to stop him. He—"

The silence of the black night was shattered by the sound of cars. Many cars. There was movement in the shadows. Steps crunched through snow. They had arrived. Stella glanced at her watch, realizing her mistake just a moment too late. The man had seen her gesture.

"Hell! You've called the fucking cops!" he yelled, pulling Stella to him with a sudden twist of his arm. Her head was thrown violently to one side. She felt a sting of searing pain. He held her neck locked hard in the crook of his arm. "Bitch," he spat in her ear. She felt her throat constrict. She couldn't breathe. Sparks lit up in front of her eyes. She felt panic rising within her. In a desperate attempt to break loose before fainting she grabbed the heavy, cold Maitreya in both hands, slamming the base of the statue up as hard as her fear and anger allowed. There was a crunching, thudding sound close to her ear. The man screamed and let go of her. She felt hot blood running down her cheek. She spun round and looked at him. His left eye was a mess of blood and flesh. She glimpsed the white bone of his eye socket. He fell screaming against the terrace railing, through it and into the snow below that immediately began turning red. Stella stared at him, frozen. Why in hell had the police come this early? She clawed her gun out from under her skirt. They weren't supposed to be here yet. A movement in the corner of her eye made her spin around. A man ran out on the terrace, the gun in his hand aimed at her. Before she could even react there was a loud bang behind her and the man fell headlong. Another man in a black uniform, helmet, and a bulletproof vest ran up to her. The police backup. With thick, black gloves he took hold of her arm, carefully but firmly pulling the gun from her hand. He looked searchingly at her through his protective glasses.

"Stella Rodin?"

She nodded limply and stared dully at the pink stain spreading through the snow around the man with the torn face. He had stopped screaming and lay silent. His warm blood had started to melt the snow under him. To her despair, she realized that all she felt was satisfaction at having had her revenge.

"Are you okay?" the policeman asked, much too distinctly. Stella shook herself to make the world around her return. She heard sounds of uproar, saw police officers in black uniforms and surprised, frightened and upset guests everywhere.

"Yes, I'm fine."

He nodded and ran off to help his colleagues. Stella stayed on the terrace, waiting while the first phase, that of pushing people

333

against walls and screaming at them, was going on. She saw paramedics lift the colorless man's body out of the snow. He was dead.
She had killed him. When the screaming began to abate she walked
back into the house, still with her blanket wrapped around her. A tall,
angular man came up to her.

"Did you find Ali's body?" she asked.

"Yes."

"Good. That one is the most important." She pointed at the
man with the dark eyes. "His name is Markus From. Then you should
talk to this guy, and those two." She walked through the room, pointing out those she knew had been involved. "Here's Ali's cell." She
handed it over. Saw that her hand shook. She felt that just seeing his
phone threatened to break all the floodgates and let out the grief and
shock she had kept locked away. "I'm off."

"But—"

"If there are more questions, I'll be in tomorrow morning.
You won't need me right now. Carl has everything I know and all the
evidence I could get."

"Okay."

She walked quickly to the cloakroom and got her coat. Walked
down the long, sanded path with short, careful steps. The torches
had gone out. The sky was turning the color of ashes. The damp cold
made her shiver. Her throat hurt. She crossed the road, down to the
pedestrian walk along the beach. Looked out at the smooth ice covering the bay. First she sent a short e-mail from her iPhone, then she
called Carl. He sounded tired and worried.

"Hi, Stella, I'm—"

"You have my resignation in your e-mail."

"But what the hell? You're overreacting."

"You lied to me about how dangerous this was. You forced
me to involve my family. And as if that wasn't enough, you didn't
trust me and it seems you can't even tell the time. It's your damned
fault I had to kill him."

"Now just calm down and stop being silly."

"I'm totally calm. Beginning today, I'm free of both you and the Swedish police department and your arrogance and damned incompetence. I've had it."

"And what do you intend to do instead? Run back home to daddy?" Carl was angry.

"It's none of your damned business."

Stella broke the connection, put her cell in her coat pocket and walked on along the beach. She saw no one, heard nothing in the sleeping suburb. The sky slowly shifted color from black to indigo to violet. Stella cried until her tears made little icicles in the fake fur lining of her coat. Cried until no tears were left. The ice-cold Maitreya rested in her pocket, both comforting her and accusing her.

Veronica von Schenck was born in 1971 and has been a computer gamer, a journalist, and editor in chief of a computer magazine as well as of a Stockholm event magazine. She is also a recruitment consultant and a mother of two, living in a Stockholm suburb with her family. She published her first crime novel, Änglalik (*a play on words, meaning both* Like an Angel *and* Corpse of an Angel), *in 2008 and her second,* Kretsen (The Group), *in 2009; the second was one of five nominated for the best novel of the year award by the Swedish Crime Fiction Academy. The two novels feature profiler Althea Molin, a heroine of half-Swedish, half-Korean extraction. A third Molin novel will be published. More recently, von Schenck also published three well-received juvenile crime novels based on historical events.*

TOO LATE SHALL
THE SINNER AWAKEN

Katarina Wennstam

Katarina Wennstam is a journalist, author, and lecturer. She was born and raised in Gothenburg, but now lives in Stockholm. For a number of years she was a crime reporter with the Swedish state TV network, but since 2007 she has been a full-time writer.

Wennstam is one of many Swedish crime writers whose fiction is based on her principled views on current social problems. Her novels and stories deal with violence against women, homophobia and intolerance. Her first crime novel was Smuts *(Dirt, 2007); her second,* Dödergök *(a made-up word borrowed from a children's song), in the opinion of this writer was the best published in Sweden in 2008. She has written three more novels and is currently one of the leading, and bestselling, crime authors in Sweden.*

This story marks the first appearance of one of Wennstam's recurring protagonists, Detective Captain Charlotta Lugn, who along with lawyer Shirin Sundin, plays the lead in a projected trilogy beginning with Svikaren *(The Quitter, 2012). It also reflects one of her basic themes. The story is set at Christmas, and non-Swedish readers should perhaps be familiar with two peculiarities of Swedish Christmas traditions. For one thing, Christmas is celebrated on December 24 in Sweden, which is the day Swedes eat their traditional Christmas ham and children expect Santa Claus to visit. And for another, virtually every year since 1960, Swedish state TV has shown a cartoon special called* From All of Us to All of You, *the 1958 Christmas special of the Walt Disney Presents series. The program runs for one hour, from 3 to 4 p.m., and is habitually watched by more than one-third of the Swedish population; it more or less defines a traditional Swedish Christmas celebration, and most people in the country know its recurring, classical Disney cartoons by heart: memorably, "Ferdinand the Bull," "Toy Tinkers," or "Santa's Workshop."*

Incidentally, until July 1, 2010, the statute of limitations in Sweden set a twenty-five-year limit on prosecutions for murder. The revised penal code since then contains no time limit regarding murder or attempted murder.

"WHO THE HELL PHONES IN THE MIDDLE OF DONALD DUCK"

Her phone is lying on the dining table and gives its urgent summons, an embarrassingly selected tune cheerfully calling to mind a pop song competition four years ago. Every time she hears it, Charlotta wonders why she never remembers to change it. Agneta glares at Charlotta's phone but immediately turns her eyes back to Cinderella, slips a piece of marzipan between her lips and sinks back against the couch pillows. The phone keeps playing its little tune.

"Why don't you answer it!"

"On Christmas Eve?"

"It's got to be your job."

"I suppose so."

Charlotta hurries to the phone, almost but not quite hoping that whoever is calling will give up. Hidden number. Charlotta takes a deep breath to confront whoever may be disturbing her in the peace of her home at twenty past three in the afternoon on December 24, of all days.

"Charlotta Lugn."

The phone is silent. She can hear that there is someone at the other end of the connection, but seconds pass. Nobody speaks.

339

"Hello? This is Charlotta Lugn. Who is it?"

"Hello . . . How are you? I'm sorry. I . . . I didn't mean to disturb you."

"No problem. What's it about?"

Charlotta looks at the couch, the lit candles, the Christmas tree and the TV showing dancing mice and small birds. Agneta on the couch, her legs comfortably beneath her. The bowl of Christmas candy beside her on the couch. She is sucking the bottom of a paper toffee mold to get the candy out, puts it in her mouth accompanied by Cinderella's singing. *Hurry, hurry, hurry, hurry, Gonna help our Cinderelly, Got no time to dilly-dally.*

Charlotta closes her eyes and knows already before she hears the voice on the phone that she will have to leave her Christmas peace behind.

Call it female intuition, call it twenty-six years of police experience, call it grim realism. Nobody making a work call on Christmas Eve does it just to wish a Merry Christmas.

"Oh, and Merry Christmas, by the way. I'm very sorry to disturb you like this. But it's important. I really had to phone you today."

"I'm sorry, but I still don't understand what this is about. Who are you?"

A small laugh at the other end of the connection. Indulgent, slightly embarrassed.

"No, of course not. You couldn't recognize my voice. It's been forever. I'm very sorry. Of course I should have . . . Well, you meet new people all the time, of course there's no way for you to remember . . . I just thought . . ."

The woman on the phone lets her sentences trickle out in endless silence. In some strange way she seems both stressed and very calm. As if she possessed some inner peace while at the same time being worked up, wanting to say too much in too short a time.

"Hnh. I understand. But couldn't you help me along a bit and tell me your name? That would make everything so much simpler."

"Oh, of course, how right you are. What would you say to doing it this way—do you remember Erik Granath? I'm his mother."

340

Hearing those words, Charlotta Lugn is absolutely certain that this Christmas Eve will resemble no other.

While still holding the phone to her ear she silently sneaks back to Agneta, kisses her forehead softly, soundlessly, and gives her an apologetic look. There's no need for more; Agneta understands.

Her expression is far from happy, but their agreement is old and they're both used to it. Charlotta's job doesn't end even when it's a holiday, or when it's night or someone's birthday or the flu is at its worst. How often she has rushed away from dinner parties, shopping rounds and quiet evenings at home.

But still, Christmas Eve . . . They had looked forward so eagerly to this evening. Their first Christmas in the new row house. Their first without any of their children. Their first without mothers, siblings or cousins. Just the two of them.

Charlotta caresses Agneta's cheek and her mouth soundlessly forms, "I'm sorry." And she walks out into the hallway. Puts her feet into her curling shoes without bothering with the heel zippers, pulls her heavy jacket across her shoulders.

"I'm on my way. How do I get there?"

Charlotta Lugn picks the downtown route. Takes a short cut across the Sahlgrenska hospital grounds, almost collides with a rattling streetcar at Wavrinsky Square. She can hardly see it, in the dark and heavy rain visibility is awful. Temperature is down to thirty-two and at any moment the rain can turn to sleet. The streetcar driver signals at the last moment. Those endless streetcars.

The streetcar snakes its lonely way up the incline towards Guldheden. Charlotta can see three people within, all of them dressed in black and seated far from each other, looking out the rain-whipped windows. Hopefully they're all on their way home to someone. She can hardly bear the thought of all those who are abandoned at Christmas. She wants everyone to be safe, warm, surrounded by their loved ones.

She knows better than most that it doesn't work that way. Least of all at Christmas.

As much as she loves Bing Crosby, shiny red wrapping paper, saffron buns and the smells of sealing-wax and mulled wine, she also intensely hates Christmas with all of its drunken and violent traditions. Regardless of how hard she tries to burrow down into her own and Agneta's married bliss, how hard she tries to glut herself with Christmas pottering and glittery garlands. Still the damned Christmas season remains the worst time of year to be a police officer.

All the other days of the year she loves her work, but at Christmas it stinks. She still remembers working her first Christmas night, when she had inaugurated her fairly new police boots by slipping in the blood of a woman beaten to death by her blind-drunk husband.

He had sat in a corner of the kitchen, mumbling. "She fell, the fucking cow. I swear, can't understand how she can be so fucking clumsy." The table was laid with their Christmas ham. Charlotta can still see the five slices cut from it on the plate. He had used the same knife on his wife's face.

Other Christmases she has cut down lonely souls hanging from telephone cords, their staring eyes still forlorn. She has cried secret tears into the soft hair of a little terror-stricken girl who had seen her mother beaten to a pulp by her raging, aquavit-stinking stepfather while "Ferdinand the Bull" was playing on the TV. Year after year she has been forced to face what everyone in fact knows but refuses to acknowledge while they're opening their gifts and watching their children's eyes glitter along with their Christmas tree lights.

No wonder Detective Captain Charlotta Lugn hates Christmas just as much as her private self loves it.

Charlotta arrives at St. Sigfrid's Square and turns in behind the Russian Embassy. The guard outside stands immobile with a face that gives no smallest hint either of the heavy rainfall or of the fact that the Soviet state disappeared long ago.

She drives on toward the luxury apartment buildings in Jakobsdal. Squeezes the car in between two others outside the last building on the cliff, where the view encompasses all of downtown Gothenburg. For a moment Charlotta stares at the play of light from the millions of small bulbs decorating the trees of the Liseberg amusement park at Christmastime, but the bitter wind wets her hair and bites her naked throat. Shivering, she enters the door code and steps into the building.

"Just walk straight in. I'll leave the door unlocked for you. I'm in the last drawing room and don't always hear the doorbell. You're very welcome."

Erik's mother, Lovisa Granath, has both given her careful directions and carefully explained why she specifically wants Captain Lugn to visit her this particular afternoon.

"I want to tell you what happened. I'd be very grateful if you could possibly listen to what I have to say."

Charlotta Lugn has waited twenty-six years for those words. But to be honest she never believed that she would really know. Somehow she has learned to live with the fact that her first major murder case is also the only one still unsolved.

What older colleagues have said about similar defeats in the end has made her understand that everyone's past includes cold cases. All of them at least once have had to accept that some mysteries remain unsolved. Have learned to live with the fact that not everything hidden in snow is revealed by thaw.

But what Lovisa Granath had said promised more.

"I know who killed Erik and I've kept silent much too long."

It feels strange, almost forbidden to open the door of a private home she has never visited and just walk straight in. Charlotta met the Granath family during the murder investigation more than twenty-five years ago. And even though they didn't live in this apartment back then, the feeling now is the same as it was then. Heavy furniture, objects of the kind you can call heirlooms, ugly paintings in colors so stifled that their subjects are difficult to distinguish.

With so much money you should be able to make things look a little brighter, but this home breathes of dull sorrow, uneasiness and restrained emotions. At the time, Charlotta had believed that it was all due to the sorrow and shock of having lost a child, but a quarter of a century later the feel of the Granath home is identical.

From the hallway she can see huge candelabras and lamps lit on side tables and writing desks, she feels cold and only very reluctantly hangs her rain-heavy jacket in the cloakroom.

"Hello," she calls towards the rest of the apartment, even though Lovisa Granath has asked her to just walk in without announcing herself. No reply.

From beyond the dining room and a farther room she feels certain is called the library, or possibly the smoking room, she hears a soft sound of music. The wallpaper is dark plaid, and giant leather armchairs are placed around a table with a cigar box and an ashtray. The walls are covered by full bookcases.

Charlotta Lugn walks through the rooms and finally enters the drawing room. Lovisa Granath sits by the window, watching the lit trees of Liseberg.

"Oh, there you are. I'm happy to see you. Please have a seat."

Lovisa Granath doesn't rise, doesn't shake hands, hardly even moves in the pale blue-striped armchair where she is sitting. The sitting room is a dramatic contrast to the rooms Charlotta has passed through. The wallpaper is light, the curtains hanging down to the floor are certainly heavy, but lime-blossom green and pulled open. The corner room is framed by four windows and in their deep recesses grow beautiful white cyclamen in the eight-edged pots designed by Prince Eugen.

Lovisa Granath holds one of her hands raised, immobile, palm up, fingers slightly bent. She is offering Charlotta Lugn a seat in a dainty couch.

"Please sit down. I took the liberty of making some tea before you arrived. I never have coffee this late in the afternoon. And I'm not at all fond of mulled wine . . . Would you like a cup of tea? Perhaps it would . . ."

Lovisa Granath again lets her sentences hang unfinished in the air. It seems to be a bad habit with her.

Charlotta Lugn shakes her head and sits down. Looks at the mother of Erik Granath, at how she looks twenty-five years later.

What is it they used to say, Charlotta thinks. Life hasn't treated her gently. The years have begun to tell. Consumed by sadness.

344

The expressions all fit the old woman. Charlotta remembers Lovisa Granath as genial, a woman who seemed out of place in the somber upper-class home. Today she fits in more naturally, as difficult to decipher as the dark paintings in the dining room and the library. On the verge of undernourishment, with sharp furrows around her lips and eyes. Ugly. From grief.

Lovisa Granath drinks her tea in small sips and meets the searching eyes of her guest. All at once the whole thing comes rushing back to Charlotta.

December 1981, the night of Lucia Day, Kungsport Avenue in central Gothenburg. Trouble and racket, kids in tinsel glitter and noisily drunk. Vomit at every street corner. For once snow, perhaps that's why there were so many people about, so much rowdiness.

Charlotta Lugn was a police assistant and, at least now, when glimpsed in the rearview mirror, as green as a newly sprung spring leaf.

Erik Granath was the high school kid found beaten to death on Geijer Street, a stone's throw from the revelers on the always crowded Kungsportsavenyn. People all around but no witnesses. Newly fallen snow, but no decent tracks of the murderer. A nineteen-year-old boy, already dead and gone.

Most indicated a drunken brawl gone too far, or a robbery. That Erik Granath was a victim of pointless street violence, something then a fairly new phrase as well as a new phenomenon. As if violence and murder weren't always pointless.

Drunkenness, many teenagers in the streets, no wallet and proximity to the entertainment area all supported the assumption, as did the absence of anyone who had seen anything of value. Not even back then, in the 1980s, did anyone care about two youths fighting in an alley.

But there was one thing both puzzling and pointing in another direction.

Erik Granath had worn a gold crucifix around his neck, a piece of jewelry he wore every day since his confirmation. It had been torn loose from its chain and was missing.

But it hadn't been stolen along with his wallet and money. During the autopsy, it had been discovered—forced deep down his throat. The throat which had shown dark lilac marks from the unknown killer who had strangled the young party-dressed man and left his body to be covered in silent snow.

Given that symbolic message from the murderer, the investigation spun off on a religious tangent, parallel to the robbery theory.

Additionally, the boy's family was deeply devout as well as active in a free church congregation. They were socially prominent, the boy's father a businessman linked not only to the free churches but also to Lions Clubs and Rotary International.

The question that had confounded the police at the time seemed simple but was impossible to answer: why had Erik Granath been killed? Was the motive related to his religion?

Many of Erik's friends were also Christians, friends from the youth seminars at his Pentecostal congregation as well as the children of his parents' friends from church. Charlotta Lugn particularly remembered how quickly they had discovered that the seemingly pious and devout teenagers drank and partied just like most others of the same age. But it had been almost more difficult to get them to talk about their drinking habits and sex life than to get them to share their suspicions about who might have wanted to see Erik Granath dead. The congregation had in many respects been a closed world, as difficult to penetrate and understand as the various criminal gangs she had encountered over the years.

Erik had had no girlfriend at the time of his death. No enemies, no known quarrels. An up-front guy, nice to the point of being dull. In spite of a large circle of acquaintances it seemed as if most of his friends hadn't known Erik Granath particularly well. Not deep down.

None of their leads turned out to get them anywhere. The feeling that there was some motive they were unable to see was inescapable, but in spite of that it remained possible that it was just a robbery that had turned bad. A perpetrator who had left a strange message entirely without meaning, done it in sheer panic and without any ulterior purpose. Such things had happened.

346

What tips they were given also petered out, and after eight months of futile investigations the case was shelved. Occasionally over the years it had been brought up from the archives, the tabloids had written about it, a new tip gave rise to a few news stories a couple of years ago.

But nothing new came to light and Erik's killer was still unknown, still at large.

And now. Christmas Eve. Twenty-five years had passed. So obvious. The statute of limitations had just ended. Charlotta Lugn smiles at Erik Granath's mother, but inside she is cursing the hag. All this time you've stayed silent. Who is it you've been protecting?

And how has she been able to keep quiet? After all, it's all about her own son. Her murdered son.

But Charlotta's lips display only a small smile. Her face neutral, she looks at Lovisa Granath with eyes concealing nothing. Tell me. Trust me. Charlotta knows how to conduct an interrogation. Nowadays.

"There was something you wanted to trust me with. I'm here now. I'm listening."

"I'd like to start by telling you why I phoned you personally. It suddenly felt so . . . Why I finally decided to reveal it all. But only to you."

Charlotta wrinkles her brow but tries not to let her feelings show.

Lovisa Granath bends toward the little side table to wrap her fingers around the wafer-thin teacup. Her little finger straight out, she carefully sips the hot brew. Smells the fragrance of the tea and seems to enjoy its taste. Charlotta Lugn is getting irritated with the woman's long-winded and slightly superior manner. She bites her tongue to keep from urging her on.

Lovisa Granath remains silent and Charlotta Lugn starts to look at the room around her. She notices a little porcelain statue on a side table. She truly doesn't appreciate that kind of knickknack, but there is something attractive about the fragile little girl in her bonnet and wide skirts. Without thinking she reaches out to take the figurine. It feels surprisingly cold in her hand.

"I would appreciate it if you didn't touch that."

"Oh, I'm sorry, I wasn't thinking. Is it valuable? It's exquisite."

"No, not particularly. But she is my favorite. I don't want her dirtied."

A strange choice of words. Charlotta Lugn doesn't like the undertone of what Lovisa Granath says. But she holds her tongue. She's good at that. She wants to hear what the woman called her here to tell her.

Lovisa Granath puts her teacup down.

"Actually I don't understand why you couldn't see what it was all about already back then. You were . . . I haven't forgotten you in all these years. Sometimes I've thought that if I'll ever tell someone, it must be you. Because if anyone would understand, it would be you. I really think that you did realize what it was all about. But you were too inexperienced. Not stupid, but afraid to trust you own intuition."

Charlotta Lugn suddenly realizes that she must look like an idiot. Her open look has been transformed to a dropped jaw. What is she talking about?

"I don't quite understand. You must know that I wasn't in charge of the investigation, I was just . . ."

"I know. But you were close to something nobody else even had a hint of. You put all the right questions, but never quite seemed to really listen to the answers you got. Do you remember when you came to our home, to the house we lived in then? The day after Erik died?"

Charlotta nods. And remembers. Erik's father, Lennart Granath, had greeted them at the door of their house in Örgryte, fully decorated for Christmas and cocooned in lovely snow. Icy cold inside as well as outside.

She remembers that he kept clearing his throat, particularly when Lovisa was talking. It was horribly irritating, but who will tell a father who's just lost his son to stop sniveling? She interpreted it to mean that Lennart Granath suffered from a severe case of macho ideals and would do anything to stop himself from bursting into revealing tears.

But it spoiled the whole interview. Both Charlotta Lugn and her much more experienced colleagues were repeatedly put off balance and lost their thread of thought by that wet hawking. It sounded as if Lennart Granath was trying to draw a huge wad of phlegm from his throat, and even now Charlotta shudders at the memory of the disgusting sound.

"Where is he, by the way?"

"He?"

"Your husband. Lennart."

"He's . . . He went to buy a newspaper. He'll be back soon."

It sounds silly, verging on the ridiculous on this particular day. As if the man at any moment might appear at the door dressed as Santa. It also doesn't sound very likely. Is Lovisa Granath lying to her?

Charlotta lets it rest. She wants to know more about the leads she should have seen twenty-five years ago.

"Please go on. What did you mean when you said that if anyone had understood, it should have been me?"

"What was the first question you asked?"

"Back then? I'm sorry, but I can't possibly remember that. It's more than twenty-five years ago."

"Try. The first question you yourself asked, not your colleagues. What did you ask?"

Charlotta Lugn closes her eyes for a second and suddenly that moment returns to her. How she leaned forward, almost interrupting her partner. Actually she had put two questions to them, or perhaps asked the same thing in two different ways. Was he at home the night before the day he was murdered? Do you know where he slept?

Neither Lovisa nor Lennart Granath had answered. Lennart coughed and hawked, and Lovisa sat staring down at her lap. Charlotta suddenly sees the scene in front of her, as if it all happened yesterday. Why didn't she react to the fact that they didn't reply?

And now she asks the same question again.

"Where did Erik sleep on the night before the day he was murdered?"

"I truly don't know. But we had our suspicions . . . Lennart said . . ."

She falls silent again. Sips her tea and draws a loud breath.

"I made my mind up almost a year ago. That's when I decided to tell you. Finally. When I read about you in the newspaper. I hadn't understood before that you were . . . well, that you were . . . well . . . I mean you were such a nice and pretty girl—how could I have even thought that you needed to be with other women?"

Charlotta knows all too well what Lovisa Granath is talking about. At the beginning of the year, the morning daily *Göteborgs-Posten* had published a major profile of her. With a provocative heading and an intrusive photo. "Lady, Law Enforcer, Lesbian."

When Charlotta Lugn assumed her new position, her sexual orientation suddenly became highly interesting. Despite her having been open about it for fifteen years. Despite her hardly being the only lesbian on the force. But she was the first lesbian detective captain. To her, it doesn't feel like some major thing, but on the other hand she didn't shy away from the attention it gave her. If she can help someone else to step out of the closet, or even just to feel a little less weird, she'll be happy to do so.

But she doesn't understand what Lovisa Granath is after. What does this have to do with the murder of Erik Granath?

"I don't understand. What . . . ?"

"You realized. You were asking about motive. You understood what it was all about. Really about. And I suppose you have to be . . . well . . . You were asking so insistently about Erik's girlfriends, if he'd had any romances that might have made him enemies, about where he'd slept the night before . . . It took someone like you to realize . . ."

Someone like you.

Charlotta turns a blind eye at the hidden insult, it doesn't stick to her. She's used to it, even if it always stings. Curiosity dominates and the pieces of the puzzle begin to come together. Homosexual. Someone like you.

It takes one to know one.

"Was Erik . . . ?"

"Are you asking me if my son was a faggot?"

She asks her return question in a hard voice and her small, tight mouth spits out the last word. Lovisa Granath holds her teacup in her hand and Charlotta can see that her hand trembles slightly.

"Was he a homosexual?"

"Of course he was. That you never realized that! The way you were snooping among his friends, the way you were digging and prying. Didn't it tell you something that you could never find any girlfriends, that a good-looking boy like him never . . . Didn't you understand? And you . . . who are also . . . and you were right there, poking around, getting so close with those questions. But Lennart . . ."

"Lennart?"

Lovisa Granath goes silent again. Her gaze drifts to the window and for a moment she doesn't just look tired, but entirely absent. Her eyes fixed on something far away. The Gothia Towers Hotel high-rise downtown, the rain whipping the windowpane, or perhaps some inner image reflected in the black glass.

She smacks her mouth loudly, and it feels uncouth and almost obscene coming from the finely dressed and strict woman. Her mouth seems dry; she sips her tea and finally meets Charlotta's eyes again. Is she drunk? Her gaze isn't as sharp as a moment ago. Her eyes are rimmed in red, but there are no tears.

It is obvious that this is hard on her, that her story is stuck deep inside her. That the words both want out and remain hidden in the dusk of secrecy.

"Would you be kind enough to put some more music on? The record seems to have ended. It feels a little easier to talk when the music . . ."

Lovisa Granath doesn't finish her sentence, just points to a stereo on a side table against the wall. The Christmas tunes greeting Charlotta on her arrival felt like such an ordinary backdrop that she didn't even notice the music stopping.

"Of course. Will the same record do?"

Her unaccustomed fingers grip the pickup. How strange that CD players have already made the gramophone feel like an ancient phenomenon. When her hand touches the black vinyl record she feels nostalgia for the pop records of long-gone days. Mahalia Jackson. "O Holy Night." Not a particularly timely choice for a Christmas record, but perhaps not unexpected in the Granath family.

First a scratching sound, then a second of silence, then the music begins. The organ roars and Mahalia's powerful voice fills the room with Adam's Christmas song.

"Tonight is Jesus' birthday. Tonight we must be grateful for the gift of God. For his coming to this world as a human being, as a naked child in the arms of a poor woman. Mary held him newborn and naked in her arms. We must be . . . Jesus is here with us tonight, as all other nights and days. All these nights I have . . . Oh, Jesus, what have I done? Forgive me, God. Forgive me, Erik."

Lovisa Granath sits back in her armchair, her eyes closed. She babbles incoherently. Charlotta Lugn remains standing by the gramophone, staring at the woman. Listening.

"I asked for it. I forced it. I settled on Lennart because he was . . . He was so clear in his faith, so strong and so uncompromising. I despised those other weaklings, all those who imagined that you could pick and choose among the words of the Bible and still call yourself a Christian. Those who thought that you could accept what fit and just . . . I wanted such a man. I wanted definite answers, I wanted a man to lean on, a firm ground to grow from . . . One who told me what to do. Who appreciated me as a woman and who was a real . . . Lennart was a real man. He truly was. Not a weakling. His father had raised him with equal parts love, rules and punishment. Spare the rod and spoil the child. And that's how he wanted to raise Erik as well, our weak, soft, damnably soft . . . Erik wasn't like other boys. Of course we knew that. Didn't want to be a part of our family, our community, our faith. He broke. . . ."

She falls silent again. Shuts her eyes hard and sips her tea again. The final drops. She makes a disgusted grimace.

Charlotta Lugn feels her heart beat wildly. She wants to hurry Lovisa Granath on, but she also wants to hear every uncomfortable detail. She knows better than to interrupt with questions or leading statements at this point. But the woman's slurred speech worries her. She seems to have had a stiffener or two too many, and . . .

Charlotta Lugn is suddenly conscious of the empty teacup in Lovisa Granath's hand. It sits loosely in her slack hand which now rests on her lap. Damn!

"Lovisa. Lovisa! Listen to me! Have you done something stupid? What is it you've been drinking?"

Charlotta Lugn crosses the floor to the woman and puts her hands on her shoulders. Her body feels slack and Lovisa Granath turns her face up to her. Smiles happily. She looks more at peace than Charlotta has ever seen her before.

"It's too late. You can't do anything now. I've been drinking this poison all day. And to tell you the truth, it tastes like hell."

Her hand goes automatically to her mouth, as if to stop the profanity before it crosses her lips. She smiles apologetically.

"It's up to you. Phone for an ambulance if you choose, but they won't make it in time. Or do you want to hear the end of . . . I really do want to tell you. I don't want . . . you must be my confessor. Even if I don't even believe in the penance of confession. Nothing can save a sinner like me, someone who has . . . Please sit down, won't you?"

Lovisa Granath's eyes briefly become hard. She wants to be obeyed.

"Are you out of your mind?"

Charlotta gets her phone out; she carries it in the back pocket of her jeans. The emergency service center is preprogrammed on a priority number. After four seconds she is talking to a colleague. Subconsciously she counts while speaking. Twelve seconds. A car will be on its way in . . . call it thirty seconds. At worst a minute, it's Christmas Eve. It's a fairly long drive from Eastern hospital. Is there any chance that they'll be in time?

Her last words to the emergency center: "You better fucking hurry!"

As if paralyzed, Charlotta Lugn sits down, as close to the old woman as possible. Unconsciously she holds her hands out to her and Lovisa Granath's thin fingers meet hers. She folds her warm hands around the cold and bony ones. Just sits there, looking hard at Lovisa.

"Lennart used to follow Erik on weekends and evenings. At first I thought it was just fine, a bit like those Dads on the Town

353

they've got nowadays. He was involved in what his son was doing, and wanted to . . . We didn't know who he met, you see, we noticed that sometimes Erik lied to us about where he had been. He didn't go straight home after his church meetings. But Lennart became obsessed. Sometimes he didn't even go to work just to keep track of Erik. He followed him, watched every step. It was . . . it was sick, it really was. Then of course I understood why."

Lovisa Granath clasps Charlotta's hand. She is surprisingly strong. Lovisa looks her straight in the eyes.

"You really must understand. I and my husband hate homosexuals. It's a sin. It's fornication. Against nature. God in his wrath will smite those who live in such sin . . . Who believes it can ever be the same as between a man and a woman. Who lies down with a man as a man lies down with a woman will suffer the wrath of God. And our son . . . our only son. An abomination. A degenerate. A . . . freak!"

The words make Charlotta shrink back. She tries to take her hand away, but Lovisa holds it firmly.

"I don't say these things to hurt you, my dear. I say them because I want you to understand. Understand why Lennart in the end could see no other solution. He knew that Erik would never . . . Erik was such a weak soul. And so easily led. He met the wrong people, they made him . . . God will forgive us in the same way he . . . God let his only son die on the cross to show his real . . . God will . . ."

Lovisa Granath is panting, as after a long run. She has talked so much and so fast and her strength seems to be fading. She licks her lips. They are very dry and Charlotta Lugn knows that it's only a matter of minutes. She glances at her watch. Almost three minutes since she phoned for an ambulance. It ought to be here by now.

She asks her heart if she's doing something wrong, if she ought to do more to try to stop this insane old woman from committing suicide. But what more can she do? Other than listen.

But there is one more thing.

"Lennart?"

"He has left. He knows you won't be able to . . . that you can't get . . . can't prosecute him. But I told him I would tell you the truth. That it was time. That God wanted to hear me speak true words, no more lies. He is already far away, abroad . . . He doesn't want . . . The shame. Everyone will . . . And I don't want to either . . . I want to be with Erik. It's the only thing I want."

"One more question."

"Uhnn . . . ?"

Lovisa goes ever deeper into her fog. She no longer looks at Charlotta, but she seems to hear her. And she can't refrain from asking.

"Why did he kill Erik? I mean . . . even if you hated his sexual bent. Did he really have to die for that?"

Part of her wants her to lean closer to Lovisa and slap her face. A good slap. You fucking nut. Kill your own son. Protect a murderer. Just because of God . . . She feels pure rage. Charlotta doesn't believe in all the drivel about abominations and words of God. It's just words. But obviously there were those who accepted the words as their law, as demands that had to be obeyed. Regardless of consequences.

"Do you see . . . Snow. It's snowing. The angels are no longer crying. Rain . . . it doesn't rain. Snow . . . Erik loved the snow. It's he who is . . ."

"But why kill him? Wasn't that going too far?"

"Uhnn . . . ?"

"Did anything special happen that night? That Lucia night?"

"Nothing special . . . or, I don't know . . . no, he . . . Lennart had been angry for so long . . . hateful . . . mad with rage. He thought Erik was fucking around. That's what he said . . . That Erik . . . Erik was a . . . He was out. Sinning. With some new boy. Lennart had followed them the night before. That's where he slept. And he supposed Erik was going there again . . . and, well . . ."

There is silence.

A minute passes. Lovisa's eyes are closed and Charlotta fears it is all over.

Where is the damned ambulance?

A quiet peace spreads over the woman's face, softens the hardened features and makes her look young.

"Lovisa?"

"Mhmm . . ."

"Is there anything more you want to tell me?"

"Mhmm . . . No. I . . . Thank you."

She whispers the last few words. The sirens can be heard outside, softly but getting closer. Charlotta envisions the car going up the hill at high speed, braking outside the bulding. But it's too late.

Charlotta Lugn feels Lovisa Granath's hold on her hand loosen, sees her thin fingers letting go. At the corner of her eye, she glimpses the white snowflakes.

Falling quietly outside.

Snow is falling from heaven.

Katarina Wennstam was born in 1973 and grew up in Gothenburg, but moved to Stockholm in 1994 and lives in the suburb Nacka with her two children. For many years, she was a crime reporter at the Swedish Television network, but in 2007 resigned in order to write and lecture full time. Her first two books were nonfiction: Flickan och skulden: en bok om samhällets syn på våldtäkt *(The Girl and the Guilt: A Book on How Society Views Rape, 2002), and a companion work,* En riktig våldtäktsman *(A Real Rapist, 2004), in which she interviewed sentenced rapists. For these books, as well as for her TV journalism, Wennstam was nominated for the August Award for best Swedish nonfiction book, and received the Vilhelm Moberg Stipend, the Journalism Award of the Swedish Lawyers' Society, and the Prix Egalia gender equality award. In 2007, she published her first novel,* Smuts *(Dirt). It was followed by* Dödergök *(untranslatable; a play on words from a Swedish children's rhyme), 2008, and* Alfahannen *(The Alpha Male); all three featured public prosecutor Madeleine Edwards, and involved one or more cases concerning relations between women and men. In 2012, she published* Svikaren *(The Betrayer), her first novel featuring Detective Captain Charlotta Lugn. As always in Katarina Wennstam's novels the theme is topical, concerning the intolerance for sexual minorities among athletes. Wennstam's latest novel, again featuring Lugn, is* Stenhjärtat *(The Stone Heart, 2013).*

ACKNOWLEDGMENTS

For their help, advice, and support during my work on this book, I owe thanks to a number of people. In particular, I would like to acknowledge:

- Otto Penzler and Morgan Entrekin, who believed in this project from the start, and particularly Otto, long-time friend, publisher, editor, and crime fiction expert extraordinaire, not to mention a great guy to go log-riding with;

- The authors with which I worked on many of these stories, and in particular Åke Edwardson, Eva Gabrielsson, Veronica von Schenck, Maj Sjöwall, and Dag Öhrlund. In this context, my thanks also to Jerker Eriksson and Håkan Axlander Sundquist, who but for unfortunate circumstances would have been in this book, and who were a joy to work with;

- Those others who helped above any call of duty, and in particular Astri von Arbin Ahlander, for translation assistance; Magdalena Hedlund, for her support and suggestions; Dag Hedman, whose

357

efforts, though as it sadly turned out were in vain, were greatly appreciated; Per Olaisen and Johan Wopenka for suggestions and for generously sharing their expertise.

- Finally, but as always most of all, my thanks to Evastina, first reader and critic, whose views, comments, suggestions, and encouragement remain vital.

John-Henri Holmberg
Viken, July 2013

PERMISSIONS

The individual stories in this book are copyrighted as follows: